Isaac W. Ambler, William P Freeman

Truth is Stranger than Fiction

The Life of Sergeant I.W. Ambler

Isaac W. Ambler, William P Freeman

Truth is Stranger than Fiction
The Life of Sergeant I.W. Ambler

ISBN/EAN: 9783337333478

Printed in Europe, USA, Canada, Australia, Japan

Cover: Foto ©Andreas Hilbeck / pixelio.de

More available books at **www.hansebooks.com**

THE LIFE

OF

SERGEANT I. W. AMBLER,

EMBRACING

HIS NATIVITY, POVERTY, AND TOIL WHEN BUT A CHILD IN THE COAL-MINES OF ENGLAND; HIS CONNECTION WITH THE BRITISH ARMY, SUFFERINGS AND DISSIPATION; HIS ESCAPE TO THE UNITED STATES, AND DISSIPATION CONTINUED; HIS CONVERSION IN NEWBURYPORT, MASS., UNDER THE LABORS OF REV. DANIEL PIKE; HIS LABORS IN THE CAUSE OF TEMPERANCE AND AS CITY MISSIONARY IN BIDDEFORD, ME.; AND EFFORTS, SACRIFICES, AND SUFFERINGS FOR HIS ADOPTED COUNTRY DURING THE LATE GREAT REBELLION.

THE WHOLE ILLUSTRATING THE FACT WITH WHICH WE START, THAT 'TRUTH IS STRANGER THAN FICTION,' AND MUCH MORE HEALTHY FOR THE MORALS OF THE PEOPLE.

Twelve Illustrations.

BOSTON:
LEE AND SHEPARD, PUBLISHERS.
NEW YORK:
LEE, SHEPARD & DILLINGHAM.
1886.

PREFACE.

Tnis book is dedicated to the public with two objects in view
one is, to lead hardened sinners, poor drunken men, to Christ;
the other is, to get bread for myself and family in my crippled
condition.

We think the above is all the preface that is necessary in giving
this book to the public, and we publish it in the fullest conviction
that while it may interest and help while away many a lonely hour,
at the same time it will not fail to improve the heart and mind of
its readers, making them better patriots and more practical Christians, and will shed a ray of light on the pathway of some now
hopeless wanderer, who will see that if there is hope for the
chiefest of sinners, like me, there is also salvation for him, if he
will only look to God for help.

1. W. Ambler.

ILLUSTRATIONS.

CONTENTS.

CHAPTER VI.

CHAPTER VII.

CHAPTER VIII.

CHAPTER IX.

CHAPTER X.

CHAPTER XI.

CHAPTER XII.

CONTENTS. ix

CHAPTER XIII.

CHAPTER XIV.

CHAPTER XV.

CHAPTER XVI.

CHAPTER XVII.

CHAPTER XVIII.

CHAPTER XIX.

CHAPTER XX.

CHAPTER XXI.

CHAPTER XXII.

CHAPTER XXIII.

CHAPTER XXIV.

CHAPTER XXV.

CHAPTER XXVI.

CHAPTER XXVII.

CHAPTER XXVIII.

CHAPTER XXIX.

CHAPTER XXX.

CHAPTER XXXI.

CHAPTER XXXII.

CHAPTER XXXIII.

CHAPTER XXXIV.

LIFE OF ISAAC W. AMBLER.

CHAPTER I.

I was born in Littlemore, Yorkshire County, England, in the year 1825 or 1826. The exact date of my birth I never knew.

My father was a smart, active, and industrious man, naturally quick-tempered, but soon reconciled. He was by trade a weaver. He was a kind father and an affectionate husband. My mother was a quiet, humble Christian, one who adorned the doctrines of our Lord and Saviour by a well-ordered life and conversation. I can remember when a child how she would place her hand upon my head and bless me. I was the only child. When three years old my father moved to a house near the New Dolphin. My grandparents lived near the Old Dolphin, with whom lived my uncle William. He had three sons and a daughter. Soon after my parents moved to the New Dolphin, my mother took me to see my grandparents. She carried me in her arms, and when returning home, in crossing a neighbor's field, she was frightened by a bull. My mother had on a red shawl, which caught his gaze, and, bellowing with rage, he gave chase; mother threw me into a thorn hedge, and started at a swift pace towards a stone-wall, which she reached just as the breath of the animal could have been heard behind her. In her haste to get over the wall she slipped and fell over, severely bruising her. She soon arose, and by a circuitous route came limping round where I was in the hedge, and took me in her arms, and with difficulty reached home. She never recovered from the effects of her bruises, but had to take her bed, from which she never arose. During her sickness, I was one night called to her bedside, and she put her hands upon my head and blessed me, gave me to God, and then breathed her last. Thus was I early deprived of a mother, whose gentle admonitions and humble prayers I shall never hear again. How thankful should I be that God, who is faithful to his people, has heard the prayers of my mother, though offered many years ago, and that in New England, far from my native home, he has sent his Holy Spirit to convince me of sin, of righteousness, and of judgment, and that through his help I have commenced a new life. How true are the words in the Scriptures, that 'the prayers of the righteous availeth much.'

My father belonged to a club, and it was the custom when one of their number, or family died, for all to attend the funeral services. On this occasion they had to go some three miles to the burial-ground; four men carried the corpse on their shoulders. When they came to Queen's Head, about one mile from home, they blew their trumpets,* and I remember of looking up to my father and saying, 'Father, mother is crying.' When we had gone about one mile from Queen's Head, I was crying so hard that my father told me to go to my grandparents, about one mile distant. I went a short distance, and sat down beside the road, when a stranger came along and took me into his carriage and carried me to my grandparents, and soon after I went home to my father's. A few weeks after my mother's death, my father took it so much to heart, as he worshipped my mother, and as his fireside seemed dreary, the chief attraction being gone, that he took to drink; and this led to gambling, and he passed much of his time in the ale-houses, neglecting his work, and running in debt. I remember one day of going to a neighbor's house, and he, knowing my father was a drinking man, abused me and told me to go home about my business. I went home crying, and told father, who was quite angry with

---

* A custom in country places at that time, when passing houses, to blow trumpets.

him and went immediately to see what he meant by abusing me; arriving there, he commenced to talk with the man, and they soon came to hard words, and then to fighting. Father was a very strong man, and he seized him and threw him over his head, nearly killing him. Father, as I have said before, was in debt, and the bailiffs came for his goods, and as the doors were fastened they went away, but soon returned with a sledge, and broke open the doors and entered. Father took me with him into an upper chamber and locked the door. The bailiffs took all the things below, excepting some straw which they left for us to sleep on, and carried them away. This was in the cold season, and I suffered much, not having enough to eat, and staying at home many nights alone. My father, having yet some feeling left, took me to my grandparents, and told them that he would pay one-half a crown per week for my support; they agreed to keep me, and he went away to Halifax, four miles distant, to work in the mills, weaving. He came to my grand-parents' to see me the two Saturday nights following, and the last night he came, called me up, as I was then in bed, and gave me three half-pence, and kissed me and left; and from that time I have never seen nor heard from him.

Now, truly, I was all alone,—my mother dead, my father the same as dead to me, without sister or brother, and dependent on charity. My grandfather was very poor, a shuttle-maker by trade. Both grandparents were pious, and members of the Wesleyan Methodist Church, and lived up to their profession. I was now about five years old. My grandparents sent me to school a short time, but money was scarce, and as they could not pay my tuition, they took me from school and set me to work winding bobbins for weaving. After working at this about two years, my grandparents taught me to weave, and be-ing too short to reach the looms, I was compelled to wear a pair of wooden clogs some two inches thick to reach the treadles. Business soon become dull, and we were left without work. My grandfather went to the overseers of the poor, to ascertain if they would assist in my support; but they would not assist any one away from the poor-house. Shortly after this, my grandmother asked me if I should like to go to Clayton, two miles distant; she said she would buy me some candy. I went, not expecting that she would take me to the poor-house; but poverty, to what straits will it not drive the most exemplary? When the pangs of hunger were driving them to desperation, she could not bear to tell me that she was going to take me to the poor-house. My grandmother, after she arrived at the poor-house, talked with a woman at the door a short time; then this woman took me under her arm, and while I kicked and screamed she carried me into the house. I ran out into a back yard where there was quite a garden spot that had a fence some ten feet high around it. I climbed up this fence, and got caught so that I could neither get up nor down. The woman came and took me down, and carried me into a room where there were a number of women and children, who stared rudely at me.

Here I was, a stranger. None knew me, and I knew none of them, and turning from their earnest gaze, I shrunk away into one corner of the room, and, covering my face with my hands, I wept bitterly. I cried until dinner was served up, which consisted of coarse porridge, and which I could not eat, as I could not subdue my tears nor stop the throbbing of my heart. In this way I remained until supper, when the mistress kindly brought me a piece of bread and molasses, a part of which I managed to eat; after that a big, brawny fellow took me to an upper chamber, where among quite a number of beds I was stowed away in one corner of the room upon a small cot. Thus left, I sunk into an uneasy slumber; thoughts of my early home and of my mother came upon me; I thought that I again stood by my mother's bed, and, with her hands upon my head, she blessed me as she did the night she died. These words, 'God bless and preserve the poor orphan,' seemed to ring in my ears, and bursting into tears, I awoke, and pulling the clothes over

Going to Almshouse.

my head, I again sobbed myself into a broken slumber. Again,
I dreamed of home and of my grandmother; I thought I knelt
by her side and repeated my evening prayer; again, my father
seemed to stand by my bedside, as on the night he left me; I
seemed to feel his burning kiss upon my cheek, and awoke to
find myself an inmate of the poor-house. I could not sleep,—
the hours passed slowly away,—every striking of the clock I
heard,—how glad I was when the first ray of morning light
found its way through the humble window. I hailed the bright
messenger and welcomed his first coming to break the long,
long darkness of the night. Ye, who sleep on beds of down;
ye, who pass the hours of night in pleasure and revelry, and
would stay the morning light, think of the poor orphan; and
may God, in his goodness and mercy, ever keep you from the
miseries of the poor-house.

2

CHAPTER II.

WITH the first dawn of light I fell asleep; how long I slept I knew not, but was awakened by the harsh tones of the mistress, who rudely shook me by the arm, and said:

'Come, sir, is this the way you want to spend your time?'

I hardly dared to gaze into her face, but answered that I had not slept until daylight.

'Well,' said she, 'we sleep here by night and work by day, and we allow no breaking of these rules. Now dress yourself and come down to breakfest.'

I dressed as quick possible, and hurried down. The room into which I went was a long one, and in the middle of it was a table reaching nearly the whole length, around which about fifty persons were seated. I seated myself beside a bright, pretty girl, about fourteen years of age, and while the others made some coarse remarks about me, this girl kindly moved my chair for me to sit by her side. As I sat down, the whole company stared at me, and as I thought how different from the little table that we seated ourselves around at my grandmother's, tears filled my eyes, which caught the gaze of my mistress, and she said, 'Come, we want no babies here, and you'll find we don't allow any baby whims. Now stop your crying, or go up-stairs.'

Stop my crying! As well she might have told the waves to stop their dashing upon the seashore, or stop the rays of the sunlight. I sprang from the table and ran up-stairs to my room.

The shades of night were drawing around, and as I looked from the window and heard the wind rustle through. the trees, how sad the sound to me; that which was music sweet to me at other times, now filled my soul with sorrow, and it seemed to

be the very echoing of my sad heart. But I gazed beyond, and
as I looked up to the bright heavens and saw the evening stars
twinkle, and the moon shedding forth her rays of light, and as
the darkness increased and the shadows of the trees appeared,
stretching forth their huge limbs along the dusty way, I was
startled by the cry of the blackbird. What shrill tones they
were! They thrilled in my ear like that sound which I never
shall forget, the trumpet tones that were blown at my mother's funeral. I thought when the trumpet was blown, of the
loss of my mother, and now this seemed to remind me of the
loss of my father. As I looked out I heard the rumbling of
wheels, and immediately a carriage came swiftly up to the door,
and a man alighted and took a child from the carriage. I heard
the treading of feet below, and the distant tones of my mistress's voice, and then the reply of a man. I saw the carriage
turn and hasten away. Another one, I thought, has come to
crowd the already over-filled poor-house. I leaned on the window-sill and wept. I then went and knelt down in one corner
of the room, and with upturned eyes I repeated my evening
prayer, and prayed that God would take me home to Him,
where my poor mother was. I then arose and went back to the
window, and leaned against the window-sill. Sleep came over
me. How long I slept I know not; but when I awoke the sunlight filled the chamber. I remembered of going to sleep at
the window, but I was now in my little cot, my clothes were off,
and I inwardly blessed the one who had cared for the poor orphan. While musing, a girl came to my side, the one I sat beside at the table. She said, 'Do you remember where you went
to sleep last night?' I told her it was by the window, I thought.
She said, 'My mistress came up with me last night, and seeing
you at the window, she said, "Dirty boy, let him stay there."
But after mistress was gone, I carried you to your cot.' I
thank you, I said, and could say no more. I felt happy to know
that there was one that felt and cared for the poor orphan. But
while talking with her I heard my mistress calling me to come
down. I got up and dressed myself, and went down and found

that the breakfast was cleared away, but the mistress gave me a cracker with a mug of water. The cracker I ate, but I felt weak, and I plead with her to send for my grandmother to come and take me home. But she paid no attention to my request, and I found it availed me nothing to plead with her. I felt the tears trickling down my cheeks, my head grew dizzy, and I fell senseless to the floor. When I came to myself, I was in my little cot, and watching at my side was the girl who had been so kind to me. I tried to rise, but fell back exhausted on the bed and closed my eyes to sleep. What dreams I had! In my imagination I was carried to a fairy land; it seemed as if thousands were gathered before me, and sweet music fell like the faint murmur of rippling brooks, and then in prolonged and swelling notes it seemed to break forth in such delightful strains that my soul was in ecstasy. I looked around on this vast assembly, and near me I beheld my mother. She looked at me, and an angelic smile seemed to light up her face, as she beckoned me to approach her. I hastened on; and as I neared her, stretched forth my hand to grasp hers. A few more steps and I should take her by the hand. But before me was a deep, dark chasm, into which I had almost plunged. I looked down this dark abyss, and could see no bottom. I raised my eyes, and the scene had changed; dark forests of trees were all around me; clouds seemed gathering over my head, and I turned and hurried from the place; but dark, black clouds were hastening after me; I turned to look behind, when a vivid flash of lightning, that blinded me for an instant, accompanied with a startling crash of thunder that rocked the trees, and seemed to rend the earth asunder, struck a huge tree at my side. A bright ball of fire struck the top, and scattering the limbs around, sunk deep in the earth at my feet. It awakened me; my lips were parched, my flesh hot; some water was at my side, I eagerly drank it down, and again I slept until morning dawned. When I awoke with what joy I learned that they had sent for my grandmother to come and take me home, thinking that unless they did, I should worry myself to death.

CHAPTER III.

How happy I felt, and how quickly I dressed myself and ran down to wait her coming to take me home. Looking out of the window to catch the first glimpse of my grandmother, how my heart beat as I saw her coming. I could not wait, but seizing my cap, I hurried from the room and ran down the road to meet her. When I reached her I threw myself into her arms and wept tears of joy. She was so overcome that she sat down beside the road and wept freely, and kissing me she said, 'If I have only one meal a day, thee shall have one-half of it, Isaac.' I felt so happy that I laughed and wept by turns, and I told her I would do anything for her if she would never send me to the poor-house again. She said she never would; and arising from the ground, we turned our backs upon the poor-house, and started for home. All my wardrobe I had was on my back, and as we went toward home how happy I felt, everything looked beautiful around me. The sun was shining brightly, and the earth was clothed in green; the fragrance of the blossoms was wafted on every breeze; my troubles were all forgotten; my poverty was at once changed into riches, for as I looked on the broad face of Nature, I thought, the sun is shining for me, the birds are singing for me, the sweet scent of roses was wafted on every breeze to me, and can I not enjoy the beauties of God's creation as highly as the person who can command his millions? For although his money is at his command, yet not the whole of it can stop the singing of the birds for me, or the rays of the sun shining for me, or blot out one of the thousands of stars that illuminate the heavens. Then am I not happy to be thus situated,—having wealth that cannot be counted,—riches that cannot be estimated conferred daily upon me? And as these thoughts rushed through my mind, how happy I felt. I would run some distance before my grandmother, until she would be just visible behind me, and then sit down beside the road to wait for her. When we arrived home I was set to weaving again: but business became dull, and we had very little to do, and I remember of hearing many prayers offered up to the Throne of Grace, that God would send them some work, that they might get some money to buy their daily bread, and often some little jobs would come, and thus we were kept along.

About this time a new kind of hand-loom, called the 'Jacquard' loom, was introduced for weaving. My grandfather took the job of boring the 'cumber-boards' (they were full of holes for the harness to pass through), and I used to tread the lathe to help bore them, which was very hard work for so small a boy, and I used to drip with sweat. My grandfather saved up some money by this job, but my grandmother was taken sick shortly after, and it took all the money he had saved to pay the expenses of her sickness, and thus we were left destitute again. But they trusted in God and prayed still, and in this condition we lived, getting just enough to keep us alive. One morning I overheard my grandfather say to my grandmother, that I should have to go to the poor-house again. On hearing this, I hardly knew what to do. The very thought made me sick. I thought of the coal-mines,—could I get work there? I was small, but boys worked in the mines as small as I was. I will try, I said to myself, and I ran out of the house and went to one of the coal-mines that was about a mile distant, and I hired out with a collier for six shillings and six pence per week. I then went back and told my grandparents what I had done; they consented for me to go to work the next morning. The coal-mines are the last resort to obtain a living, and no parents will let their children go into the mines if they can otherwise support them. Children, when very small, can get work in the mines when they could not at any other place. I went to work in the coal-pit.

In opening a coal-mine they first sink a shaft to the seam of coal, varying from one hundred to one hundred and fifty feet deep. Often, in sinking a shaft, the loose dirt will fall in, and, to prevent this, the upper part of the shaft is walled around, sometimes this is done nearly the whole depth. These shafts are from ten to fifteen feet in diameter. Another difficulty that arises is, that veins of water are struck, which immediately commence to fill up the shaft. This is excluded by lining the shaft with boards fastened to the sides, which is called tubbing. If the first shaft that is sunk proves successful, in most cases another is sunk about fifteen feet from it, and then at the bottom an opening is excavated to the other shaft; one of these is called the *down* cast and the other the *up* cast. The object is to get ventilation, the air descending the down cast and ascending the up cast.

In this mine I had to take coal in what is called a scoop or a small corve. This corve in which I drew my loads of coal was an oblong wagon, with small iron wheels, running on a railway. The distance to the mouth of the pit was two hundred yards. The passage was about two feet high. This corve was fastened to me by a chain, passing between my legs and hooking into a staple in a broad, leather belt around my waist. To haul a loaded corve, with the rigging attached, requires practice. At first it was exceedingly tiresome, and I have often fallen flat on my face from exhaustion, but by constant effort and practice it became less laborious. This corve I would haul by going on 'all fours,' or upon my hands and feet, while the weight of my body would be supported by the chain passing between my legs. In hauling my corve in this manner, I wore the skin off my hands so badly that my grandfather made me two wooden crutches to hold in my hands, and by them I was enabled to continue work without so much pain, as the crutches kept my hands from the earth and sharp pieces of iron ore that were in the bottom of the passage.

From the top of this pit to the bottom it was sixty feet.

This mine was worked on a cheap scale, no horses, no machinery of any kind, excepting a block and tackle to hoist the coal from the bottom of the pit. My corve I would haul to the mouth of the pit, where the 'banksman,' so called, as he stands at the top of the pit and hoists out the coal, would lower down a rope with an empty corve attached, which I would take off and then hook the rope to the loaded corve which the 'banksman' would hoist to the top of the shaft. Sometimes the 'banksman' would hoist so slowly that I would have to wait some time for him to lower down the empty corve, and my employer would throw large pieces of coal at me for being gone so long. Sometimes I have been struck so hard as to nearly knock me down. Then, again, I would hurry so fast with my corve to get back, that I have often struck my back against the ledge and bruised me so badly that the blood would trickle down at every step I took. The water in these mines was, in many places through which I hauled my load, six inches deep. Sometimes, striking the ledge, I have been thrown flat in the water, and I would pray that God would take me out of the world.

I worked in these mines two or three months, abused by all around me. I worked in the lower passage; above me was a passage or chamber, and one morning this chamber sprung aleak, and the water soon filled the passage that I worked in, so that I was obliged to leave off work. I went home and told my grandparents, and they set me to weaving, I worked a few weeks, but as I did not earn enough to keep me, my grandparents sent me to look up some work. I went about one mile from home, to another coal-mine, called 'hunting-pits,' old mines that had been worked many years before, and when left, the timber that supported the roof was knocked down, and the roof fell in, and considerable coal was in the passages. The work was to get the remainder of the coal. I hired here for eight shillings and sixpence per week. The colliers usually take their work by the job, and hire boys to work for them,

In the Mines.

and haul the coal out to the mouth of the pit, while they pick the coal out, which, of itself, requires practice and experience.

The colliers settled with the boys at the end of every week, and my money I used to take home to grandmother, she giving me a ninepence a week for spending money. The colliers were all hard drinkers, and very profane, especially the one I worked with. The keeper of the inn, where we used to settle, usually did a good business Saturday night; for much of the money that was paid to the boys would be spent before they went home; many times my employer, after settling with me Saturday night, would spend the balance of his money for drink, and then borrow of me. Since that time an act has been passed by Parliament, forbidding colliers paying off their help at taverns, under penalty of five to twenty pounds. The passing of this act has done a great amount of good to the poorer classes, and restrained drinking to some considerable extent.

One Saturday night the colliers had called for their help to go up to the tavern as usual, and settle. I, having worked hard that day and during the week, had pleased my employer so well, that he was bound to treat me; and by strong persuasions he induced me to drink with the rest of them, and by so doing I got intoxicated so that I had to stop at the tavern until late at night before I was able to go home. The scenes of that night are now before me, and I can easily trace much of the misery and sorrow which have followed me through a large part of my life, to the indulgences of that night. I started for home, and the first part of my journey my steps were irregular, but before I arrived home I was as sober as ever. My grandmother always sat up for me Saturday nights, and as I neared the house and saw the light burning in the window for me, my heart almost failed me; but, mustering courage, at length I opened the door and entered. My grandmother was up and anxiously waiting for me. She met me at the door, and said, ' Isaac, I am afraid that thee has been drinking with the colliers. I know that they all drink; have they not enticed thee to drink?" I could never tell my grandmother a falsehood, and I, therefore, told her the whole story. She talked long with me that night, and how earnestly she prayed that I might be saved from the temptations that beset me on every side, and that I might be kept from going down to a drunkard's grave.

How unhappy should I have felt if I had foreseen the evils that this act led me into. What great, and alas! what fatal results followed that first glass. When asked to drink I knew the evils of it. I knew the consequences, yet I had not the moral courage to say, No! Never taste or drink the first glass, and you will never be a drunkard; drink it, and the chances are against you. You may indeed say, as I did that night, 'It will do no hurt this once.' But if you drink the first time, you will be more liable to accept the second time it is offered you. Then, again, did you ever know a moderate drinker to say or even think that he would become a drunkard? They have not the least idea of such a thing. But who makes the drunkard, is it the sober, temperate man? No, it is the moderate drinker. Then, reader, beware, if you take your first glass because it is fashionable or manly, that you do not, by the use of strong drinks, bring your body to an early grave, and your soul unprepared to meet its God. That first glass that I took that night at the tavern, was the means of bringing misery and wretchedness upon me, and an appetite for strong drinks that well-nigh carried me to a drunkard's grave. But my readers must pardon my digression here, if such they term it. My excuse is, that it is demanded, and I should fail to discharge that duty which devolves upon me of portraying the evils that arise from the results of taking the *first glass*, if I lightly passed this over.

CHAPTER IV.

On Monday morning following, 1 arose early as I was accustomed to do, and took my scanty breakfast and started for my work. My way was through a narrow road called 'Stock's Lane.' This lane was about one-half a mile long, and one mile from this lane was the Sheffield Furnace Iron Foundry. The blaze that went up from the chimneys of that foundry would cast a light for miles around. One side of this lane that I traveled was shady, while the other was very light. By the side of this lane was Dolphin Chapel, with a burial-ground attached, where my mother was buried. I had often heard the old people tell of ghosts being seen here, and when passing this burial-place I used to keep on the dark side of the lane, so that no one could see me. Passing along early one Monday morning, on the dark side, I tripped my foot against something in my way, and fell headlong. I arose quickly, and hearing behind me a snorting and clanking of chains, I ran as fast as I could, my hair standing on end. I had gone but a short distance before I came in contact with some other kind of an animal, and again fell prostrate to the ground. Now fear seized me, and with sweat dripping from me, I started with all speed. Again I heard the clanking of chains, and thinking the 'Old Fellow' himself was at my heels, I ran into a shed and braced myself against the door. I remained in this situation until I heard the voices of the other boys going to the mines, when I went out and told them how I had been frightened. They laughed at me, and said that they had been frightened in the same manner, and told me what had frightened me was nothing more than two jackasses, owned by my uncle, that had lain down for the night, and had been suddenly startled by my running on to them, and being breechy they were clogged, a chain running from one foot to another. I joined the boys in a good laugh, and we went to the mines.

In these mines the water was some six inches deep. Working in this water my clothes would be soaked through; it being cold weather, when I went home my clothes would freeze stiff, and rub the skin off my legs, making it very painful for me to walk. These mines I would go into Monday morning, and would not see the sun again, only by glimpses up through the shaft, until the next Sunday morning, as I used to go in before it was light and leave the mines after sunset.

I was now about eleven years old, but much larger and stronger than boys usually are at that age.

About this time, a cousin, who lived under the same roof with me, came to work in the mines; whose mother always opposed strongly his going into the mines, but when she found that I stood the labor so well, and that I grew stronger and more robust, she at last gave her consent for her son to work in them.

He was very delicate, and after working in the mines a short time, in the water, he took cold, which brought on a cough, from which he never recovered. He was naturally timid, and as we passed through 'Stock's Lane,' I always used to go forward. About this time there were stories circulating of a wild man having been seen here, and he was more than usually timid. As we were going through this lane one morning, to the mines, early, before any colliers had arrived, we saw a bright light issuing from one of the cabins near the pit; and looking in we saw two men, one had a long beard reaching down to his breast. 'That's the wild man,' said I, and then running to the pit, I seized the rope that went down the pit, and slid down into the mines. My cousin followed; we were both scared, and ran and hid until the miners began to come; and then we came out and told them what we had seen. The men were probably travelers, who went into a turf cabin to rest for the night. My cousin had the skin worn off his hands so badly by sliding down the rope, that he was unable to work, and went home and never came back to the mines again. A short time after this, I was working in the mines one morning, when suddenly the roof broke down, and I was buried in the dirt; but one of the colliers near me, seized hold of my legs and pulled me out. I was bruised badly, and wished to go home, but my master would not let me. When I went home at night, I told my grandmother, and she kept me at home two days. While out those two days, as it was about the time to celebrate the 'gunpowder plot,' I got me a large iron cannon and some powder, and when I went into the mines I took the cannon and powder with me. I loaded it, jamming in stones and dirt; the colliers were most of them drunk, celebrating, and they dared me to fire it off. I took a candle, and while the men were staggering around me, I touched the powder. The cannon burst, and the pieces were blown in almost every direction, but none of us were struck by the pieces. For some time I worked in these mines, no serious accidents occurring, although hardly a day passed without some slight accidents happening. The following is taken from Tomlinson's Cyclopedia:

'The accidents in the coal-pits are very numerous. According to one return, for every one hundred men employed, seventy-two accidents occur annually, of which five are fatal. The accidents are almost entirely bruises and broken limbs, arising from the falling down of the coal and heavy materials from the mine. These accidents can only be obviated by a safer system of extracting the minerals, by a liberal supply of timber and lights, and by prudence and caution on the part of the workmen and overlookers. Such accidents are most numerous in mines where middle men, or butties, are allowed; they take the contract for a piece of work from the proprietor, and give it out to the men, and it is their interest to do the work as cheaply as possible, without any regard to the safety of the men.'

A few honorable exceptions are, however, mentioned in the Parliamentary Report. One of these is the case of a man named Mason, whose pit had, for a long period, been almost entirely free from accidents, and the reason assigned by the men was, that they met together to pray every day in the dinner hour. 'About one o'clock the drink goes down the pit, and if a man is not at the place of prayer in ten minutes after, he forfeits his drink. They sing and pray, and ask a blessing on what they are going to have, and then they sit down in the road and eat their dinner and drink their beer; and after dinner one reads out of the Scriptures and explains it, and tells the others what the preacher has said about it. Sometimes they get God's spirit among them very much, and sometimes less so.' Very few of these men could read, and it was stated that 'a man could not be allowed to join in singing and praying unless he was thought to be living as a man ought to do.' To work in these mines, the colliers have to exercise much caution, and an experienced workman can tell immediately, by sounding the roof, if the dirt is likely to fall in; and, if so, they support it with timber. While standing under the roof one day, one or two pebbles fell at my feet, and I had barely time to spring away from the spot before some two or three tons of dirt and coal fell with a crash, on the very spot where I had been standing. I went immediately to the mouth of the pit, and called for the 'banksman;' and just as I looked up, he dropped his 'tug,' as it is called, (a piece of iron used to haul in the loaded corves as they are hoisted up,) which struck me on my forehead, knocking me down instantly. In a short time one of the colliers came along and took me up. I recovered soon and went home, and my employer, finding that I should not be able to work for some time, hired another boy to take my place, which left me without work again. My grandfather soon after this went to a neighboring town to sell shuttles, and while partaking of a lunch at an inn, a gentleman asked him if he knew of any boy that he could hire to work in the mines. This man was a steward or surveyor of coal. My grandfather told him that he had a boy who would work with him, and he agreed to give me my board and clothes for my labor. When my grandfather returned home, he told me what he had done, and, as this was Saturday, my employer came for me the Monday morning following, and I went gladly with him, for I did not wish to be supported by charity. These mines that I commenced to work in were about 120 yards deep. My work was the same as in the other mines, only somewhat harder. In these mines was the choke-damp, so called by miners; it is a carbonic-acid gas, of suffocating nature. It issues from certain veins in the mines, and no person can long withstand its power. I have often, when descending these mines, been obliged to cry out for the banksman to hoist me back, having my candle go out, and being nearly suffocated by the vapor arising out of the pit. The surveyor sometimes would not believe me, and he would be lowered down only to be hoisted back again.

In these mines, in some places, the bottom of the passage would be entirely dry, while in other places the water would be from two to six inches deep. The boys used to work in the mines naked above their waist, and so begrimmed would they be by the coal-dust, that the only way we could distinguish one another was by the voice. There were besides the boys in these mines, seven girls that did the same labor, and were about the same ages of the boys. These girls were bright, intelligent, and very pretty; but when at work in the mines, a stranger would have taken them to be negro boys. One of these girls was the surveyor's (my employer's) daughter; she was a very pretty girl. She used to work along side of me, and oftentimes when my corve got off from the track, she would assist me in getting it on again. Soon after I came into the mines, she went away to work in the mills. I missed her much, but I thanked God that she had got out of the coal-mines. Employing girls in the coal-mines was tolerated in England only about sixteen years ago, and no slave girls upon a southern plantation are worked so hard as they were. When very small, they are put into the mines; usually, they are put in when younger than boys, for a singular notion of the parents that they are quick and more capable of making themselves useful. The following extract will show how they are worked in the coal-mines.

'The child has to descend a nine-ladder pit to the first rest, where a shaft is sunk to draw up the basket or tub of coal filled by the bearers; she then takes her creel or basket, a basket formed to the back, not unlike a cockle-shell, flattened towards the neck, so as to allow lumps of coal to rest on the back of the neck and shoulders, and pursues her journey to the wall-face, or room of work, as it is called. She then lays down the basket, into which the coal is rolled, and a man lifts the burden to her back. The tug or strap is placed over the forehead, and the body bent into a semi-circular form in order to stiffen the arch; large lumps of coal are then placed on her neck, and she commences her journey with her burden to the pit bottom, first hanging her lamp to the cloth crossing her head. One girl, noticed by the commissioner to examine coal mines, had first to travel about eighty-four feet from the wall-face to the first ladder, which is eighteen feet high; leaving the first ladder, she proceeded along the main passage (probably three and a half to four feet high) to the second ladder, till she reached the pit bottom, when she casts her load into the tub. This one journey is called a rake. The height ascended and the distance along the roads, added together, exceed the height of St. Paul's Cathedral, and it often happens that the tugs break, and the load falls upon those girls that are following.'

Many hearts were made happy when an act of Parliament prohibited females from working in the mines, also boys under ten years of age, with a heavy penalty attached to it, for those who violated the law. In this mine that I worked in now, they used a 'gin,' so called, for hoisting up the coal; this gin was worked with ponies. One night some evil-minded person went to the mine and nearly severed the rope used for hoisting and lowering the corves down into the pit; it was not noticed by the workmen in the morning, as the rope was carefully wound around the axle, so that the place where it was cut could not be perceived. The next morning two boys jumped into the car to be lowered down the pit; they had descended but a short distance, when the rope parted and they were precipitated some eighty-three yards to the first chamber, and crashing through this they went down with the car thirty-five yards to the bottom of the pit, and were instantly killed. They could not be recognized, as they were so crushed to pieces. I usually arrived at the pit as soon as any of the boys, but that morning I was late, and by being late I saved my life. A short time after this sad accident, a small boy that worked near me, about twelve years old, had loaded his corve too much behind; he stooped over to pull the coal forward, when a piece of iron ore, weighing some two hundred pounds, fell and struck him on the back of his head, instantly killing him. Some of the colliers carried him to the mouth of the pit, where he was hoisted to the top. I was a short distance from the spot at the time of the accident, and was ever reminded of it when passing the place where it happened. My employer got the consent of my grandfather to bind me to him until I was twenty-one years of age, and I willingly acquiesced in the arrangement, as I did not wish to be a burden to my grandparents; but my grandmother would not consent to the arrangement, and she came and took me home, and again I was without work. My grandfather could not keep me without work, as they could barely make a living while I was at work ; so in a few days I started in pursuit of work. I arose early one morning, and so earnest was I to obtain a situation, that I could not stop to eat my breakfast, but took a biscuit in my hand, and taking my hat, I was going out of the house, when my grandmother called me back and said, ‘Isaac, take my blessing before you go;’ and standing upon the doorstep, she put her thin hand upon my head, and said, ‘God preserve thee from danger, and may thee obtain some work, that we may be kept from starving;’ and, as she turned from me, I felt a tear drop upon my head. How that tear-drop thrilled me! It seemed to open a fountain of tears, and they burst

3

from my eyes; wiping them away with my jacket-sleeve, I darted from the house and ran until I was out of sight, and then I seated myself beside the road and wept freely. I had never seen my grandmother so agitated before, and I thought that poverty must be staring them in the face. I remained in thought a short time, but I knew that I must obtain work. I continued my journey about two miles, to some mines, where I obtained work. I hired out with a collier for eight shillings a week. This man was a hard master, and a hard drinker. In the pit where I worked, the water was continually dripping from the roof—the miners called it raining, so that in a short time after going into the mines, we would be soaking wet. The water in this pit varied from two inches to a foot in depth, and in some places it had stood so many years that it was cankery, or corroded, and working in it barefooted, it would eat the skin off between my toes, making it very painful. Working in this water, I took cold, and it settled in one of my knees, and it swelled so badly that my grandmother cut my pants open and bandaged it around, and in this condition I walked two miles to and from my work. This was in the cold season, and I froze my feet badly, so that I had to stay at home. The swelling on my knee grew worse, and my grandparents thought it would be a white swelling; but fortunately my knee soon got well.

CHAPTER V.

I **WAS** confined to the house some three weeks or more; but as soon as I could get about, I had to obtain work again. I did not want to go into the mines again, if I could obtain work at any other place. I spent some three days trying to get work, but was not successful. By some I would be greeted with a gruff reply, that they wanted no small boys; by others, no notice would be taken of my request, and I would leave without repeating the inquiry. But I must obtain work, I said to myself, and I must go to the mines again; so I went to 'shelve pit,' opposite an inn called the 'Shoulder of Mutton,' about one mile from home, where I got a job that kept me at work about a month, when the mines closed up, and I was left upon my grandparents again.

I went to L——, and hired out with a collier for nine shillings a week. This mine was worked on a different scale from the others. There was no shaft sunk into the ground; but a passage was made into the side of a high bluff, at an angle of forty-five degrees. Windlasses were used at the outside of the passages. There were two tracks, one for the corves to go down, and the other for the loaded corves to go up. In this mine twenty-five boys and fifteen colliers worked. The distance down the inclined plain was fifty yards; and from the bottom there was a level road about one mile long. The bed of coal, when I came into the mine, had run out, and they had come to a solid ledge of iron ore, through which we had to blast. To make a blast, they drill a hole about one yard deep, which is filled nearly full of powder, and in the top is jammed coal-dust, and then it is ready for blasting. We had gone some twenty feet into this ore, when one day, as we were making a blast, I took the canister of powder from my employer, and went some twenty yards to a passage that led to the left, where I should be safe from the explosion.

I was in such haste to get away from danger that I left my corve in the passage, which was only a trifle wider than the corve. The collier had lighted the fuse, and was hastening away from the blast, when he came to my corve, by which he managed to squeeze himself; but so enraged was he at my carelessness in leaving it in the way, that when he arrived where I was, he ordered me to go out and take it away. I was afraid to go, and I was still more afraid to stay; I turned to go, and had just got into the passage when the explosion took place, and one large piece of iron ore come with such force as to go through my corve, which was of iron, and I had just time to dodge back into the passage to the left, when it went past me with part of the corve. It was a terrible explosion. The roof shook over our heads, and for some time I thought it would come down and bury us forever in the passage. We all stood trembling there while it thundered back and forth in the passages. By the dim light of our candles I could see my employer's face, which was as pale as death. As the noise ceased, my employer said, 'This won't do—it is too risky—we shall have to give it up. If I am not mistaken, we shall find that much of the roof is thrown down.' We hastened toward where the blast was made, but we could not reach the place, as the roof had fallen in, and completely filled the passage so that we could not proceed. The 'boss' came to the conclusion that it would not pay to work the mine, and by doing it, run the risk of life ; he therefore took me with the rest of the boys, and carried us to another mine a short distance from this one.

From the new mine that I now worked in, there was a subterranean passage to the last one I worked, or the one we blasted, and I have often, with the other boys, gone through this passage to the mine. This passage was the means of saving my life, with that of my employer. One forenoon, a short time after I had commenced work in this mine, as there was no coal to hoist out, the banksman was away, and my employer and myself went into the mine alone, prospecting for coal. It was a muggy morning, the air damp and heavy, and we had been in the mine but a short time before the choke damp began to affect me some; my candle flickered and went out. I ran to the collier, who was but a short distance from me, and told him that my light had gone out, and that I could not stand the damp. He began to rave and curse the damp, but while talking, his own light went out, and we were left in almost total darkness, excepting the glimmering light that came down the shaft. The damp now began to affect my employer. 'What shall we do?' he asked. I took hold of the rope to ascend the shaft, but I was weak, my strength failed me. I was always expert in going up a rope, and had many times ascended the shaft in this manner, but my hope was now cut off here. We cried out for help, but none came! We were fast failing under the influence of this fell destroyer, when I thought of the subterranean passage! 'We are saved!' I said. 'What do you mean by saved?' said my employer. 'That our lives are saved. I know a passage that will carry us safely out, if I can find it in the darkness,' I said. 'Well, for God's sake,' he exclaimed, 'let us find it quick, for I can hardly stand.'

'Follow me,' I said, 'and we will try;' and upon our hands and knees (the passage would not admit of standing erect), we groped our way along. There was a trap-door that opened into the passage that I wanted to find. I hurried along as fast as I could (with a piece of rope tied to my waist, the end of which my employer had hold of, afraid that unless he did, I should get off, and leave him to perish) to find the trap-door. We groped in the darkness some distance. Once or twice I struck my head against the roof with such force that it stunned me, and I fell flat upon the bottom of the passage; but my employer coming up with me, would lift me up and push me forward. Before reaching the trap-door, I knew that we must take a passage to the left, and I began to think that I had taken the wrong passage, and was just on the point of turning back when I came to the one to the left. As I turned the corner, I knew that I was but a short distance from the door, and hope revived—but I felt the rope tighten around my waist! I turned and spoke to my employer, but received no answer. I hurried to where he lay senseless upon the bottom of the passage! I commenced to beat him with my fists, and to halloo in his ears: 'Courage!' I said, 'I have found the door, in a few moments we shall be safe. Follow me!' I hurried forward again, my employer following me, and soon came to the trap-door. I swung it open, and the fresh air rushing in, revived me, and I could not help falling upon my knees and thanking God for his care over me, and for our safe escape. I crept through the trap-door, and looked back for my employer, but he had fainted at the opening of the door. I pulled him through, and, shutting the door, ran to where some miners were at work (this passage was high enough to stand erect) and got some water, and dashing it in his face, soon had the pleasure of seeing him recover. We walked out to the mouth of the passage, and sat down on the ground until we had fully recovered. This was a narrow escape for us, but then the whole business is a risk, and in no part of it is a man safe, as may be seen by the daily reports.

Dr. Buckland, the celebrated geologist says of mining: 'Collieries are exposed to an infinite number of accidents, against which no caution can guard. The chances of explosion have, it is true, been a good deal lessened by the introduction of Sir Humphrey Davy's lamp; and some mines that are wrought, but for the invention of this admirable instrument, must have been entirely abandoned. But, besides explosions, which are still every now and then occurring from the carelessness of the workmen and other contingencies, mines are very liable to be destroyed by creeps, or by sinking of the roof and by drowning, or the eruption of water from old workings through fissures which cannot be seen, and, consequently, cannot be guarded against. So great, indeed, is the hazard attending this sort of property, that it has never been possible to effect an insurance on a coal-work against fire, water, or any other accident.'

My employer never went into the mines again, and as he did not want me any longer, he settled with me, and I went home to my grandparents. While at home, my grandfather was taken sick; this was his first and last sickness. He continued to fail for three weeks, and when near his end, my uncle Edward said to my grandmother, 'He will never speak again!' My grandmother went to the head of the bed and said, 'Jonas, how art thou?' 'I am happy! I am happy!' he said, and expired.

This incident made a deep impression upon me. I had stood beside those who had died—who had no hope in Christ; and when death came, they quailed before the grim messenger, and with bitter oaths and awful groans they left the earth. But how great the contrast between the death of the sinner and the Christian. Calmly and silently the Christian meets death, and feels happy to welcome him, knowing that to die and be with Christ is gain.

I felt sad at the death of my grandfather, for I had been with him so long, that I felt that he was the same as a father to me. Although my grandmother was spared, as she was poor, I thought my uncle Edward would have the control over me, and this made me feel bad, for I knew that he drank hard, and often came home drunk, and would then abuse his family, sometimes driving them out of the house. I heard my grandmother pray for him, that he might give up the intoxicating cup, and that he might be saved from the doom that awaits the drunkard. Oh! the power of prayer! Who of us can tell its mighty influence? When we shall stand at the judgment-seat of Christ, then will be unfolded to us the mysteries that we cannot now comprehend. Then shall we more fully understand than we now do, the power there is in prayer. The centurion, when he asked Christ to heal his servant, said, 'Lord, I am not worthy that thou shouldst come under my roof; but speak the word only, and my servant shall be healed.' Jesus said, 'Go thy way; and as thou hast believed, so be it done unto thee.' It was the faith of the centurion that saved his servant. Think of this, ye Christians, who may peruse these lines, and remember that your prayer for the poor drunkard shall not be in vain.

It was the custom then, at funerals, to have what is called a 'funeral cake,' and every one that goes into the house takes a piece of this cake as the remains of him that has passed away. I remember that my grandfather was carried to the Methodist church, where a sermon was preached; from thence he was carried to the grave, and there the minister made some remarks—spoke of my grandfather as being a consistent Christian, and of his adherence to the cause of Christ through difficulties and trials. The corpse was then lowered into the grave, and a hymn sung, and the company then went to the Dolphin Chapel Tavern, where they held a 'funeral burial drinking,' as it was termed. Each one that went paid one shilling, which money went to pay for the drink. They drank 'mulled beer,' and my uncle Edward drank so much that he got intoxicated, and had to be carried home. I drank with the rest of them.

My grandmother now broke up housekeeping, and my uncle William took all the things, excepting a loom that my grandmother kept to weave with. She tried to get along with weaving, so as to support herself and me; but we could not earn enough to support us, so my uncle William took me into his charge.

CHAPTER VI.

My uncle Edward drove a team to the coal-mines, and purchased coal, which he would haul to the village and sell. At the pit where he bought his coal, he got me work, and although I was unwilling to go to work in that mine, as I knew what a bad one it was,—passages very steep, so that the boys were in danger of being run over by their corves, and also bad water—yet he compelled me to go. The passage into the mines (it was an inclined plane) was just large enough to admit one corve with a little to spare. I could just squeeze by one. These corves had brakes fixed to the wheels to keep them from running over the boys when they went the down grade. The collier that I hired out with was a tyrannical fellow. Working one day, he thought I was gone too long with my corve, and when I came back, he began to curse and swear at me for having been gone so long. I told him that I went as quickly as I could, which enraged him, and he told me to come where he was, and help fill up the corve. The boys were not expected to shovel any coal, but sometimes when our corves were not full when we came back with the empty ones, we would help fill them. I went and took the shovel, and commenced to fill my corve, when my boss began to strike and kick me, saying, 'I'll learn you better than to contradict me.' I thought he would kill me! My grandmother told me that when any person abused me, to tell them I was an orphan boy; I therefore told him I was an orphan boy, and when I told him this, he ceased abusing me. I was not able to work the rest of the day, but he made me. When night came, I hurried home and told my grandmother how my employer had treated me; but all she could do was to pray for me, which she did earnestly, and I still kept to work in the mine.   A short time after my master had abused me so badly, I was going into the mine, when the brake slipped off my wheel, and as I could not hold my corve from going down the passage, I had to run as fast as I could before it, until at a turn in the passage, it struck against me, jamming my head severely.   I crawled up and got upon a loaded corve, as it was drawn up the passage, unknown to my employer, and jumped off, and hurried home.   When my uncle went to the mines after coal, my employer told him that I had run away.   My uncle then went to the house, with a whip in his hand, and ordered me to go back to the mine.   I showed him the bruises on my head, and told him how it was caused, and that I was not able to go back; he would pay no regard to my explanations, but ordered me back to the mine.   I ran behind my grandmother's loom, and my uncle came towards me with the whip.   My grandmother entreated him not to strike me, but he paid no attention to her entreaties, but struck me with the whip, and told me that unless I went back to the mines he would horsewhip me.   I started for the mines, and he followed, and when he came up to me, would cut me with the whip; thus was I compelled, although bruised badly, to go back and work in the mines.

I continued work in this mine about one month; I then went to work for nine shillings a week, four miles from home.   My uncle now had no control over me.   This mine was near 'Pickle Gate,' and near by was an old building that was reported to be haunted, and that many murders had been committed there. My uncle William was thrown out of employment, and came to work as brakeman on a coal-car, where I was; and wishing to get his family near him, he went to see if he could not get a tenement to live in.   He went to the owner of the old building, who told him that he might have the rent free if he would occupy it.   My uncle thought it was a generous offer, and immediately moved his family into the old building, and as it was some distance to my grandmother's, I went to board with him.

When we came home nights from work, the children would tell us that they had heard strange noises in the house, and they seemed to be frightened, and very loth to stay alone. In this manner it passed on several days, when one night, as my uncle and myself were returning from our work, my uncle said to me, 'I see a light in the cellar window.' 'I guess not,' I said, 'the girls don't go down cellar.' But he still persisted that he saw a light, and hastening toward the house, we went up the stairway, which was on the outside of the building, and opening the door, 'Have any of you been down stairs with a light?' my uncle asked. They replied they had not. The building was out of repair, and the only part that was tenantable was the second story. My uncle told us to wait for him, and, taking a lantern, started for the cellar; and passing noiselessly down the rotten stairs with his lantern shaded, he saw a light issuing from the key-hole of the cellar-door; and stooping down, he looked through, and saw, not more than ten feet from him, four men, one standing up, while the others were seated around on boxes, dressed like citizens, with the exception of a three-cornered cap which they had on. As my uncle was looking through, one spoke, and said to the person that was standing up, 'Captain, I'll tell you what it is, I'm not going to risk my life any longer; now there's them young ones up-stairs poking around; the first thing we know, we shall be caged.'

'Well, Jim,' said the captain, 'we must do something. You know I've sent a man here a dozen times to make a noise, and scare the children, and get them out of the house; but hang me if they don't stick like a leech. Jones, there is that lantern again; this is the second time you have let light strike the window; suppose some one was passing.'

'Don't be scared,' said Jones, 'the window is boarded up.'

'Well, the light might be seen by some one passing, if it is boarded up,' said the captain. 'But to go on. I'll tell you, Jim. That fellow up stairs is some kin to me, and I don't like to resort to harsh measures; but kin or no kin, if he don't leave soon, we will take some measure to remove him. But come, boys, we must be off, we have got a job, you know, to-night;' and upon this, they went to the farthest side of the cellar, and opening a door, passed out. My uncle was not naturally a timid man, but he felt rather uneasy as he overheard them talk so coolly of removing him out of the way; and then the captain said he was some kin to him,—he could not think of any person that was related to him that followed such a profession for a living. For some time he was lost in meditation, but arousing, he thought of his children who needed his care. He turned and hastened up stairs, where we were anxiously awaiting his coming. We eagerly asked him what he had seen; but he told us that he would relate the circumstances to us in the morning. After supper, he told us to go to bed, while he kept watch over us. The next day at the breakfast table he told us the whole story, and that day he moved his family back to the old house.

The fire-damp was in the mines that I now worked in, carbureted hydrogen gas that issues from veins in the mines. Tomlinson's Cyclopedia says:

'The great and terrible scourge that distinguishes coal mines, and especially those of the great northern coal-field, is the escape of large quantities of fire-damp, which, mingling with the air of the mine in certain proportions, forms a mixture that explodes on contact with flame. This gas is much lighter than common air, and mingles readily with it, and when poured out into the workings, moves along with the ventilating current in the direction of the upcast shaft. The quantity of gas thus poured out is considerable, but subject to great variations, some seams being more fiery or full of gas than others; and in working these fiery seams, it is not uncommon for a jet of inflammable gas to issue from every hole made for the gunpowder used in blasting. The gas issues from these cavities with considerable noise, and forms what is termed blowers. These blowers are sometimes so constant in their action that the gas is collected and conveyed by a tube into the upcast shaft, continuing for months or years to pour out hundreds or thousands of hogsheads of fire-damp per minute. When thus provided for, the blowers are not necessarily a source of danger; but when one of these reservoirs, containing the pent-up gas of centuries, and consequently under an enormous pressure, is suddenly broken open, the gas is set free in torrents, and, mingling with the air of the mine, forms an explosive mixture which the first spark or naked flame may ignite, and thus cause a fearful destruction, both of life and property. Nor is the explosion itself always the thing to be dreaded most; for the ignition of the fire-damp kindles the coal-dust which always exists in great quantities in the passages, and, in a moment, causes the mine to glow like a furnace. This conflagration is succeeded by vast columns of carbonic acid gas, or choke-damp, as it is emphatically called, from its suffocating nature, and this destroys those whom the explosion had spared.'

Near the mine where I worked was a small stream of water, that I have often dammed so as to stop the flow of the water, and when it had run off below the dam, touch the bottom with a lighted candle, and instantly the whole bed of the stream would be in a flame. One morning there were two men going down the shaft with a lighted rope's end, when the blaze touched a vein of fire-damp, and it caused a terrible explosion, blowing the landing boards to the top of the shaft, and the two men some fifty feet into the air, killing them instantly.

This sad accident made me somewhat afraid of the coal-mines, and I made up my mind not to work in them any more. I went home to my grandmother and told her of the awful accident that took place at the mine, and the conclusion I had come to, of not working in the mines again on any condition whatever. My uncle set me to weaving on a 'Jacquard' loom. I was now about 13 years old. I worked with my uncle a few months, but as I could not make enough to support me, I left and went to Bradford, about four miles distant, to work with a man named Ackroid, weaving. I soon left this man and went to work for his brother, who agreed to give me my board and clothes for my labor. He was a great drinking man. I had heard of him before I went to Bradford, and if I could have done better elsewhere, I would not have worked with him. He used to bring liquor to his house, where he would sometimes treat me to a drink; but as he was very snug I was not treated often, but he and his wife would both get drunk together. I used to work hard for this man, and earned him fifteen shillings a week, and all I received was my board; and as for my clothes that he was to furnish me; all I got were second-hand articles that had seen their best days.

I went home every Saturday night to see my grandmother, and one Saturday night I found her sick; but Monday morning I had to leave her, and with tears in her eyes she bade me farewell, and told me to remember the counsel she had given me, and be sure and not go into the army (this she had many times before entreated me not to do), saying that she should never see me again, she bade me farewell, as she supposed, and which afterwards proved forever. I had to leave, although I thought that I should never see her again alive. I went back sorrowful, and stayed until the next Saturday night, then I hurried home to my grandmother's. I found my grandmother dead; she died on the same day of the month that my grandfather did. She was buried Sunday, and I stopped to the funeral and followed her to the grave. I saw her in the coffin, but I did not weep. I had passed through so many scenes that my heart was hardened. Her remains were carried to Dolphin Chapel, and a funeral sermon preached, where, just one year before, I listened to my grandfather's funeral sermon. Her remains were then carried to the grave, and as they lowered her down into the ground, the tears began to flow, and I thought, now I have the wide world before me—all my kindred that loved me are gone, and all I love,—now my home is wherever I may roam. No kind friends will weep at my departure; no friendly tear be shed; but henceforth I am a wanderer. But I thought of what my grandmother often told me, that God was a father to the orphan, and that if I loved Him, he would never forsake me. When I went back to the mill I often thought of those words, and prayed that God would take care of me, and oftentimes, when drinking with a friend, the pale face of my grandmother would seem to come up to reprove me.

About one month after my grandmother's death, I was playing with some boys in the mill-yard, and was thrown down and broke my wrist. I wrapped it around with my apron, and went to my employer's house. I was afraid to go in, and I therefore sat down on the door-step. My employer's wife saw me there, but did not take any notice of me, although I was crying; but one of the boarders, named Daniel Sharp (may God bless him for his kindness to me at that time), asked me what I was crying about. I told him that I had broken my wrist, and did not know what to do, and burst into tears.

'Don't cry, lad,' he said, 'we will get it fixed up; come with me;' and taking me by the hand, started off to find a surgeon to set my wrist; we went a short distance, and Sharp led me into a physician's office. ' Ah!' said the surgeon, ' whom have we here?'

'A poor boy, who has broken his wrist, and wishes it attended to,' said Sharp.

'You must seek some other place,' said the surgeon, 'as I have a call to make immediately; good day,' he said, and advancing towards us, he fairly compelled us to go out the door, and deliberately shut it in our faces.

'Blast his pictur,' said Sharp, 'I had a good mind to have knocked the contemptible puppy down—the old snipe is as rich as mud, and snug as an oyster; he knew at a glance that it wasn't a paying job, and he took that method to get rid of us; but cheer up, we will try again.'

Sharp led me rapidly by shops and streets until we stopped by a stairway. 'There,' he said, 'we will try here, and see what we can do;' and leading me up the steps, he opened a door, and walked into a room where there was a pleasant-looking man, who bowed, and arose at our entrance. I felt cheered by his pleasant look, and thought my journey was over. 'Dr. Jameson, I believe,' said Sharp.

'That is my name,' said the occupant; 'can I do anything for you to-day?'

'Can you set this youngster's wrist?'

'Yes, I ——' but here he stopped, for a girl came hastily in, and handed him a note, over which the doctor hurriedly looked, and said, 'Must I go immediately?'

'That was my mistress' request,' said the girl.

'Well, I suppose I must go;' and turning to Sharp, said, 'Sorry that I cannot attend to the boy, but you see this is one of my patients, and I must attend to the case immediately.'

Sharp said not a word, but pulling me along, hurried out of the office and down the stairs.

'Well, my lad,' he said to me, 'are you tired?'

'I am not tired of walking,' I said, 'but my arm pains me.'

'Well, we will try again;' and hurrying me across the street, he entered a druggist's store, and addressing the clerk who stood behind the counter, he asked, 'Is the surgeon within?'

'You will find him in the rear of the store,' he said, pointing to the back part of the shop.

We passed through into an office, in which was a man with the most forbidding countenance I ever beheld. Not giving us a chance to speak, he said, 'I am very busy, you see, just now—had to turn three patients away,' and looking sharply at me, said, 'Poor, I see, t'wont do. I can't afford to lose my time. Here, John,' he said, opening the office door, 'just fix that compound.' Then turning to us, he continued: 'You see how it is, I am dreadfully drove compounding at present.' He stood with his sleeves rolled up, with a spatula in one hand, scales in front, on a table, while various colored powders were heaped around.

'A new discovery,—entirely new; cures bronchitis immedi-

ately, upon two applications; one application effectually re-
moves warts, and four destroys the bites or stings of the most
venomous animal. How many boxes will you have?' he said,
addressing Sharp.

'I don't want a single box; I want this boy's wrist set,' said
Sharp.

The compounder did not pay any attention to what Sharp
said, but seemed to be absorbed in mixing the different powders.

'There, it is finished,' he continued, and taking a small wood-
en box, he filled it up, and handing it to Sharp, said, 'there,
friend, you need not be afraid of corns.'

'Well, I am not afraid of corns, not by a d——d sight,' said
Sharp.

'Hold on,' said the surgeon, 'let me explain; as I said before,
you need not be afraid of corns with that box in your pocket
it is a sure cure if applied immediately.'

'Hang your corn powders; I want this boy's wrist set,' said
Sharp.

At this point of the conversation, I noticed the clerk beckon-
ing us to come out, and I pulled Sharp out into the shop.

'He is out of his head, poor fellow; he runs all on compounding; good joke, aint it?' said the clerk.

We thought it was a *poor* joke, and went out; by this we
were delayed half an hour.

'Now, lad,' Sharp said, 'I will go with you until we get some
one to attend to your wrist.'

We went a short distance to another surgeon's office, where
there was an elderly man, with spectacles on. 'Hurt?' he said.

'Yes, a broken wrist,' said Sharp. 'Can you attend to it?

'Have you anything to pay for attending to it?' said the surgeon, seeing we were dressed poorly.

'This is a poor boy, whom I found in the road crying. I suppose he has nothing to pay with. I am sure I have not,' said
Sharp.

4

'You must take him to the Infirmary; they will attend to him there, though you will want a certificate. Let me see,' and taking off my apron he examined my wrist, somewhat to my discomforture, after which he wrote a line on a piece of paper. 'There,' he said, 'you will want two more names. Let me see, I will give you the address of two of the nearest surgeons.' And writing them down on the back of the small slip of paper, he handed it to Sharp.

We thanked him, and then went out to find the two surgeons to get their names, which we accomplished without much difficulty. We went to the Infirmary, and I had my wrist set, and then I went to my employer's house. I remained out of the mill three weeks, and then I went to work again with one hand in a sling.

CHAPTER VII.

ONE Saturday night, after my wrist had got well, I went to see my uncle William and stopped until Monday morning, when I arose early and started for my work. I had gone but a short distance below Dolphin Chapel, when I saw something black blow across the road. I went and picked it up and found it to be a muff. I took it along with me to the tavern at foot of Stony Lane, that I have referred to before, and went in .Two men were playing cards in the bar-room, and one said, 'What have you got there?' as I held the muff up. I told him that it was a muff I had found but a short distance from the tavern. He examined it, after which he asked me how much I would take for it. I replied that I did not know how much it was worth, and that I did not know as I had any right to sell it, as it was not mine to sell. The man laughed, and told me as I had found it, it was mine, and that he would give me a half a crown for it. I told him he might have it, as I did not know the worth of it, which I afterwards learned was twenty-five dollars, or five pounds. But as fifty cents was more money than I ever had of my own at any one time, I quickly took up with the offer that he made me, and then went to my work.

The next day there came out a notice in the papers of a highway robbery having been committed at such a place, and a reward offered for the recovery of a muff, etc. The same day, two constables came into the mill where I was at work, and carried me to Bradford jail, and put me in a small, damp, dark cell, and kept me in that miserable place three days and nights (and long ones they were to me, being unused to stopping in such places), to answer to the charge of highway robbery. Not quite 14 years of age, what a precocious youth I must have been to stop a carriage with a gentleman and lady, and demand their money! How sad I felt to be confined in a jail, and for nothing that I had done to deserve it. But I was cheered by the thought, that as I was innocent of the crime, and that they could not sustain the charge, that I should necessarily be freed. But how mistaken I was. I have learned by bitter experience since, that the innocent often suffer in this world, while the guilty go free. On the forenoon of the fourth day I was brought before the magistrate, to answer to the charge against me of highway robbery. The gentleman and lady appeared against me, but could not swear that I was the robber; yet, circumstantial evidence, the finding of the muff at the tavern, my selling it for half a crown, was so strong against me, that the charge was sustained, and I was ordered to be confined in jail three weeks, until the session of court. My heart sank within me when I heard the decision, and I seemed to feel that every one was against me. The next morning an officer came and handcuffed me, and took me from my cell. I was glad to get out of it, supposing that I could not get into a worse one, but I was mistaken. I was carried eighteen miles to Wakefield jail, the worst prison in England, and was there shown into a large room, where I was told to strip. They then brought me a shirt, a pair of pants, with yellow, black, and green stripes,—one leg of which was some inches shorter than the other; then a vest, the original color of which could not be determined, and to finish, a pair of clogs, which were so large that I could step into them; and after being rigged up in this style, I was told to look in the glass. I was somewhat startled at the change effected in my appearance, in so short a time. I was generally called decent-looking, but I had undergone such a transmogrification, that I do not think crows would have ever troubled a corn-field with such a figure as I was stuck up in the center of it. After having my head shaved, I was taken to a miserable cell, with a small cot in it, where I was told to make myself at home, and the officer went out and locked the door after him.

I looked around the room to see what I could do to pass away the time. The cell was about seven by nine, and my cot occupied one corner, while in another was a jug of water; these were all there were in the cell. Through a small grated window, the light came in, and by pulling my cot along underneath it, I could look out and see the boys and girls playing on the common. It was in the spring of the year, and all was beautiful, and never before did the earth, the sky, the flowers, and the trees look so fair as they did to me, as I gazed out of that grated window!

Everything seemed to be at liberty but me, and I was confined in prison, and for what? I tried to think what I was there for, but I could give no other reason than that of finding a muff, and selling it for half a crown. As I would ponder the matter over in my mind, it would cause my blood to boil with indignation, and my evil passions would be aroused, and a spirit of revenge would be enkindled within me! When I was liberated, I would seek out the man who appeared against me, and kill him. And then again, I would think of the words that my grandmother used to read to me out of the old Bible: 'Do good to them that despitefully use you,'—'Love your enemies;' and when these thoughts would come over me, how it would still my troubled mind, and quiet my angry passions. Then I would gaze from my window, and as the gentle breeze bore to my ear the merry laughter of the boys and girls on the common, the tears would course down my cheeks, and I would wish that I was dead. 'Why is it,' I said to myself, 'that every person seems to be against me, and that I am spared to be thus persecuted, while other boys have all the privileges and enjoyments of life? I have as much right to them as they.' It seemed as if I was indeed battling against the world—all against me. How unequal a warfare it is indeed, I thought. Thus I thought as I walked the floor, and, rushing to my cot, I tried to drown my thoughts in slumber. I sunk into a drowse, but my mind was as active as ever. It seemed as if I was upon a high precipice, beside the ocean, and was opposing a foe that I could not perceive, whose folds seemed to entwine around me, which I sought in every way to elude, but found myself completely in his control. With superhuman efforts, I endeavored to break from his grasp, but after a vain struggle, I sank exhausted to the earth. My strength returning, I arose to renew the contest, but it seemed as if my strength was nothing, compared with the monster; but by a lucky blow, I laid the monster prostrate at my feet, it seemed; but as I turned to hasten from the spot, a strong, irresistible power detained me, and turn which way I would, it seemed to meet me. The ocean was behind; I turned toward this—some power detained me! Death, I thought, is better than battling with an unseen foe; and springing from the bluff, I went through the air at a frightful speed—down! down! I went, until I plunged deep into the surging billows! I sprang from my cot, shivering! Thank God, it is all a dream! But what a frightful one! It was a singular dream to me. Should I heed it? I thought before the dream, that there was one way for me to make my escape, and that was to take my life; but I had not the courage to think of it now. My dream had broken the foolish train of thoughts. It seemed to be the voice of a superior being that spoke to me through this singular and timely dream. It was dark when I laid down upon my cot, but now the morning light came into the window. 'Thank God,' I said to myself, 'that my grandmother is not alive, and that I have no friends to lament my condition; but that I alone must bear it!' In this state I continued through the day. The next day was rainy, and it did not seem to be so dreary within, as it was disagreeable without; but toward night, the clouds parted, and the sun shone out in all its splendor, and the dew-drops on the trees glistened like diamonds.

I felt sad now, and miserable, to be thus deprived of the common blessings of life! Never do we know how to prize them until we are deprived of them. The liberty to rove over the earth, under the broad canopy of heaven, with the whole face of nature before us,—to enjoy all its beauties,—to feel the invigorating breeze, and to experience that enjoyment and pleasure that he alone can feel who is at liberty! Why had I not died years ago, rather than to be left here with none to care for me, and none to love me? Would that I were buried beside my mother in the grave, and covered over with the cold sods of earth, for how much better would it be than to live, if I am freed at last, suspected and shunned by all around me! How shall I go into the world again, although innocent as I am will the world believe it? I shall be pronounced guilty, and be ashamed to look the people in the face as I pass them on the street, for wherever I may go, this deed which I have not done, but for which I am pronounced guilty, will meet me, and I shall be pointed at with the finger of scorn. Oh, how often I prayed that God would take me from the world!

In this manner I passed three long weeks. One morning I was taken from the prison, and in company with twenty-one others, carried to Pomfret, all of us chained together as criminals. I was the smallest of the company. We were carried in a horse-car, huddled together like cattle, and when we arrived at Pomfret, we were put into a large cell, or room under ground, and straw thrown down for us to sleep upon. The next morning they commenced to take out the prisoners to be tried for the crimes declared against them, each one in his order. Every one that went out before me was sentenced from four to twenty-one years to Van Dieman's Land. What a dreadful scene it was to witness the agony of the poor fellows, and some of them, I have no doubt, were as innocent of the crimes charged upon them as I was! A blacksmith welded an iron ring around the ankle of those that were to be transported, as soon as they came back. As I saw the poor fellows return, I thought that my time would come soon, and I expected to get transported with the rest. I remained in this miserable hole three days before my turn came, and then I was called out. I was handcuffed and taken to the court-house,—my handcuffs taken off, my crime read against me for committing highway robbery at such a time and place, and after this was read to me, I was asked, 'Guilty or not guilty? I did not know the meaning of guilty, and while I stood looking at the people around, a gentleman told me to say, 'Not guilty,' which I did; but if he had told me to say 'Guilty,' I should have said it as quickly. I was then asked if I had any counselor, or any friends to speak for me. A very righteous inquiry,—confined three weeks in jail, and seeing no one in all that time to speak to, but the man who brought me my food. I was asked if I had anything to say for myself. I told them that I did not do the deed that was charged against me,—that I was going to my work when I saw the muff blow across the road, and that I picked it up and carried it to the tavern, and there I sold it for half a crown to a man in the bar-room, as I was ignorant of its value,—that I had no friends, neither father nor mother, sister nor brother, grandmother nor grandfather, and that I was alone in the world. This I told with tears in my eyes, which created much feeling for me. Witnesses were called, but the gentleman did not appear against me to sustain the charge, and I have no doubt he felt ashamed of the part he had taken in the matter, and therefore dropped it where it was. I never believed that they had a muff stolen from them, but to raise an excitement, he advertised the muff in the manner he did, having no idea that it would be carried so far. As no one appeared against me, I was taken to the room under ground, and kept there that day, but as no one appeared, I was liberated the next morning.

How happy I felt when I got into the world again! I went into a large public square, and there I told a man that I had just got out of prison, and had no money, nor friends to apply to for help, and that I was some thirty-six miles from the place where I worked. He told me to go back to the court-house, and tell them my condition. I went back as he told me, and stated my case, and was given eighteen pence, or one halfpenny a mile, to carry me back to my employers. The first thing I

Prisoners going to Pomfret.

did after I received the money was to go into a shop where they sold pies and cakes, and get something to eat; I spent about one-half my money—filled my pockets and hands full of cakes, and started on my journey. It was a beautiful morning, and the road was a fine one, and for some distance trees were upon both sides, which completely shaded it. Before I had gone two miles, I had eaten all my cakes, but I soon came to a small village, and I here invested the balance of my money in eatables, and these I ate up before I had gone much further. Feeling tired, I sat down beside the road until I saw a man coming in a wagon. I asked him if he would let me ride a short distance with him; he gave his consent, and stopped his horse, and I clambered into the back part of the wagon.

CHAPTER VIII.

WE jogged along about seven miles to his house, though I could have walked the same distance in about the same time, when I thanked him, and got out of the wagon, and continued on my journey. It was getting towards noon, and I began to feel hungry. I had no money nor friends to apply to, and I therefore came to the conclusion to beg. I saw a small neat-looking house but a short distance before me, and thought I would try and get something to eat; I went up to the house, and knocked at the door. It was opened by a pleasant-looking woman, and I asked her if she would give me something to eat.

'Where you from, my boy?' she asked.

What should I do? I hesitated before speaking, but at length I told her that I had just got out of prison, where I had been wrongfully kept by a false charge made against me,— thinking it was best to tell the truth.

'Come in,' she said; 'you shall have enough to eat. I am glad you told me the whole story, and I believe it, because a boy would not be likely to tell anything like that, unless it was true, and I believe you are innocent.'

She took me into a room, and asked me to be seated while she went to get me something to eat. I sat down, and she soon returned with a bountiful supply of provisions, and set them before me. After I had eaten my fill, I thanked her for her kindness, and was going out of the door, when she said these words: 'Always tell the truth, under whatever circumstances you may be placed, my lad; and remember that God can always bring you safely out, no matter how dark and discouraging it may look.'

I was somewhat astonished at these words! She probably had divined my thoughts, while I was hesitating what to say, when I stood upon the doorstep. This was a lesson that I did not soon forget, and it made a good and lasting impression upon me. I hurried on my way, strengthened and encouraged by the pleasant words, as well as the food that the woman ha1 been kind enough to give me. I passed some small villages on my way, and toward night I came to quite a large place, and as I was tired, I thought I had better try and get some place to stop all night. I went up to a house and asked a man there if he would put me up that night; he said he did not want strange boys in his house, as he did not know who they were,—they might set his house on fire in the night. I asked him if he would let me stop in his barn.

'No, I will not let any one sleep there; I would not risk my stock, hay, and carriages; why, I might have them all burned up!'

I turned away from his door to find some person more hospitable. I had not gone far when I came to a fine house that sat in back from the street, and I thought to myself, I will go in and see what I can do; I therefore opened the gate to enter, when I heard a gruff voice from the grounds, in front of the house, which arrested my progress. 'We do not allow strange boys to come in here, so you may go out.'

I found that I had got into the wrong place, and hurried out. On the opposite side of the road, was rather a poor-looking house; I will try here, I thought, and see if I can make out any better; and entering the gate, I went up to the house, and rapped at the door. A little girl came, and kindly asked me to come in. I told her that I was hungry, and asked her if she would give me something to eat, and let me stop there that night. She asked me to come into the house, and she would speak to her mother, who was at work in the garden. I went in and sat down, while the girl went out to call her mother, who soon came in; and while she stopped to wash in the entry, I heard her remark, 'Poor boy! he looks hungry and tired! Come, my daughter, set something on the table for him, and always remember to "Do unto others as ye would that others should do unto you."' Those words, how often had I heard them said before,—strange, I thought, this woman should repeat them. The girl hastily complied with her mother's request, and placed before me good healthy food, to which I did ample justice.

After eating, I asked the woman if she would let me stay all night in the house, telling her that I would sleep on the floor.

'I will let you stay,' she said, 'but you may sleep on a bed.'

'But, madam, I am a stranger to you, and I have been turned away from two places; and in one place, I asked the man to let me sleep in his barn, but he would not.'

'I know how to pity the unfortunate, and I always remember in mercy those that have no shelter at night—no pillow to lay their heads upon. My husband,' she continued, 'is a soldier, and I am a soldier's wife; and no one that seeks shelter of me shall be turned from the door as long as I have a shelter to cover me.'

'God bless you, madam,' I ejaculated, before I was aware of it.

'But I suppose that you are tired, and if you will follow me, I will show you where you can sleep;' and leading the way into the attic, she pointed me to a neat bed, and bidding me good-night, left me. I slept sweetly that night, and when I awoke, the sun was just rising. I arose and dressed myself, and went down stairs, and found the good woman was up, and the little girl was setting the table. I noticed three plates on the table, and I could not help wondering who the third plate was for, as I saw but two persons in the house; I took my cap, and telling the woman that I would hurry along, I thanked her, and was going out of the door, when she called me back, and said:

'You must have some breakfast; what we have, you are entirely welcome to.'

I took off my cap and sat down to the table, and ate my breakfast with them. I then knew for whom the third plate was put on the table—it was for me. I finished my breakfast, and thanking the woman for her kindness, I took my leave, and continued my journey. I had some fourteen miles to travel to reach Bradford, and I thought I would try and go that distance without asking for anything to eat on the way; but when I had gone half the distance, I felt faint and tired, and I sat down beside the road to recover myself. I rested about half an hour, and then resumed my journey, but I felt hungry. I had been kept so poorly while I was confined in the jail, that I could now hardly restrain my appetite. I found that I must beg something to eat, and as the nearest house was a large brick one, I felt rather backward about asking for anything there, but my appetite was clamoring loudly, and I hastened up to the house, and rang a bell; the door was opened by a portly gentleman.

'Will you give me something to eat?' I said, timidly. He stared at me for some time, and then remarked:

'We do not encourage beggars here,' and shut the door in my face.

I might have known better than to call there, I said to myself, it is not the large houses where the people have large hearts, but the small ones. So intent was I with my thoughts, that I did not see a boy at my side, until he said, 'I overheard the talk you had with that man; come with me to my mother's, and you shall have as much as you want.' Taking me by the hand, he fairly ran with me along the road, until he came to a small, neat-looking house, with a yard in front, filled with flowers. 'Here is where my mother lives,' he said.

'Have you no father?' I asked.

'No,' he replied, 'my father has been dead a number of years. I have a sister and a kind mother.

We had now reached the house.

'Mother,' he said, running up to her, while I stood by the door, ' here is a poor boy that wants something to eat.'

' Well, my son,' she said, ' he shall have something;' and then addressing me, said, ' Come in and sit up to the table, and I will give you something to eat.'

I sat down to the table, and eagerly ate what she sat before me, as I was very hungry. I answered the many questions she asked, and having finished my meal, thanked her for her kindness, and went on my way.

It was but a short distance from Bradford, as the woman had told me; I therefore hurried on as fast as I could, and soon arrived there. I felt somewhat afraid to go to my old employer, and therefore went to a woman that I knew, who kindly gave me something to eat, and I stopped there that night. I arose early, and went to another mill and got work. I had worked here but a short time, before my old employer came for me, and I went to work with him again.

A short time after, there was a riot, occasioned by reducing the wages of the help employed in the mills. Some of the men plugged the boilers, letting the steam off, so that the mills stopped. A great crowd collected near the counting-house, and began to throw brickbats through the windows. A company of the 17th Lancers was called out, and a man standing near me threw a brickbat which struck one of the horse-soldiers, who immediately wheeled his horse, and dashed out of the ranks, and chased the man into the river, over which he swam, and saved his life.

The riot act was read, and they were then commanded to disperse immediately; but not obeying, the Lancers made an attack, riding down many; and the people, finding that they would be killed, unless they dispersed, went to their homes. I was with one William Ackroid at that time, and we went to our boarding-house. He worked in the same mill that I did, and we were in the habit of going down into the firing-room, where the boilers **were,** and talking with the men. One day I asked Ackroid to go with me into the firing-room. As we were going into the firing-room, the fireman spoke to some men that were in there, and said that he was afraid that the boiler would burst, and advised them to come out, but they only laughed at him. The words had hardly escaped his lips, before the boiler burst. Ackroid and myself, upon hearing the fireman, stopped outside the firing-room. There were in the room three men and a boy, besides two masons who were repairing the furnace. One of the men escaped by a trap-door, the others, inhaling the hot steam, immediately ran into the street, and dropped down, and were taken by some men and carried to the Infirmary. The two masons that were repairing the furnace had to walk through water boiling hot, that was a foot in depth, to get out of the room. These two men were carried also to the Infirmary. I had gone to the Infirmary, and was in the room when they brought them in; it was a sad scene. They could live but a short time; two of them were young men, in the prime of life. One was about to be married, and his betrothed fainted when she came into the room. The friends of the others were gathered around them, to take a final leave. I have witnessed many sad and solemn scenes, but none is impressed so indelibly upon my mind as this one. How merciful was God to me, and how had he spared my life, while others perished around me! Why was 1 spared through all these accidents ?

CHAPTER IX.

THE next morning after the sad accident, by which five lives were lost, I said to Ackroid, 'Let us go and enlist.' He said that he would, and we decided to start the next. morning; but he was afraid that I would tell his parents, and ran away before the time, and enlisted in the 17th company of Lancers. He came and told me what he had done, and I started for the rendezvous, and enlisted in the 61st Regiment. The next morning I went to one place, while he went to another, and I had enlisted for twenty-one years. I had to go to Leeds to pass through the surgeon's hands for examination. I passed, but when measured I fell short three-fourths of an inch of the required height. Thus my fond hope of being a soldier was cut short.

I had given up all hopes of ever seeing Ackroid again, and felt extremely sorry, as we had been boon companions for some time. When I got back to Bradford, I went and told his mother that her son had enlisted in the army, and upon hearing it, she fainted away, but throwing some water in her face, she recovered.

The next day, while walking the street, I saw Ackroid across the way, and hastening over, shook him by the hand, and asked him why he was not with the army. He replied that he was rejected by the surgeon. I felt glad that he was, and we both went to work in the mill again, weaving.

One evening, there was a celebration of some kind, and fireworks on the common. Besides Ackroid and myself, there were two more young men with us, named Charles Green and Joseph

RUNAWAYS SELLING CAP.

Riggs, and we all agreed that night that we would run away
the next morning, and we set a time and place to meet. The
next morning we were all there, faithful to our promises, and
started for Liverpool, about seventy-two miles distant. I had
some clothes at my uncle William's, whose house was on the
road that we were to travel, and when we arrived there, I told
my companions to wait for me, while I went in and got my
clothes. The folks were all gone away, excepting one of my
cousins, and I told her that I wanted to get my clothes, and
went up-stairs, and put them on over my other clothes, and then
came down. My cousin asked me, as I came down, if I was going to Halifax. I told her I was not, but was going another
way, and perhaps she might never see me again. Tears filled
her eyes, and I turned and hurried from the house, ashamed to
let her see the tears that were trickling down my face. We
then continued our way to Liverpool. We had gone about
eight miles from Bradford, when we began to feel hungry, and
as none of us had any money, I pawned a cap (as I had two
with me) for half a crown, and with this money I bought some
bread for us to eat. We then journeyed until night when we
arrived at Rochester, tired and foot sore. We managed to get
a bed which we all four had to occupy, which was rather snug
quarters. We were awakened in the morning by hearing the
wooden clogs, worn by the girls, clattering upon the sidewalk, as
they went into the mill. We arose, and went down stairs, and
having paid for our lodgings, which took all my money, we
started on our way again. We traveled five or six miles, when
we began to feel hungry. I went up to a house, and asked the
woman if she would give me something to eat, but she told me
to go home and get something to eat, if I wanted anything. I
then asked her for a drink of water, which she gave me, and we
all drank, and started on our way, and soon arrived at Man-
chester. We passed through a few streets in the city, when we
came to a broker's office; I there pawned a vest and handkerchief, and with the money we satisfied the pangs of hunger,

5

which had troubled us exceedingly the last four miles. The money lasted us until we arrived at Liverpool, when we went down to the dock, and hired out on board a man-of-war, for seven years. We then started up town to see the city. Passing through one of the streets, we were invited into a recruiting rendezvous, where we were treated by the sergeant to beer; he then measured us (as he said) in sport, to see how tall we were; one of us, he said, could'nt get into the army. He then gave three of us that were tall enough, beer sufficient to get us intoxicated, and then conducted us to a bed up-stairs. The next morning we were somewhat surprised to find ourselves in the place we did. We arose and went down stairs, and met the recruiting sergeant, who told us that we had enlisted in the army. We told him that we had not. He then spoke to the keeper of the house, and asked him if he did not see us take the enlistment money. (When a person enlists, he is paid one shilling, and when sworn in a half crown more.)

'Yes,' said the keeper, 'I saw them take the money, and put it in their pockets. Come, young men,' he continued, 'just feel in your pockets, and I guess that you all can produce the shilling.'

Feeling confident that the money was not in our pockets, we each one unhesitatingly put our hands into them, and as a matter of course, produced a shilling piece. 'There,' said the sergeant, 'what's the use of trying to lie out of it? You must go with me to the magistrate and be sworn.' We were somewhat surprised to find the shilling pieces in our pockets, but I came to the conclusion that they were put there while we were intoxicated. To get out of the scrape we should have to pay twenty-one shillings, which is called 'smart-money.' We were in for it now, and as I thought of the mean tricks that were practiced, of which this played upon us was a specimen, to get young men into the army, my opinion of it diminished exceedingly, but not so much as it has since. Near ten years in the English army were long enough to convince me that the officers, many of them, were never soldiers or privates, but purchased their commissions by paying a certain sum of money, and were therefore more tyrannical, and their discipline and the mean living that the young recruits had, would not be very strong inducements for young men to enlist.

We went before a magistrate and were sworn, and then received half a crown apiece. We were now fully launched out into life, and thought that we would soon be on our way to the field of glory and fame, to reap honor and win laurels that none but a soldier can win. So we thought at that time, but we found afterwards that winning laurels and wearing them were two different things,—the soldiers win laurels, and the officers wear them. We were taken from Liverpool to London, and were then billeted out. Ackroid and myself were sent together about two miles to an inn. We arrived there, but the keeper having no room for us, gave us half a crown to pay our lodgings at some other place. Being unacquainted with the city, we did not find any place, and we therefore started for the recruiting sergeant's quarters, and as Ackroid and myself could not agree as to which street to take to carry us back, he took one way, and I another. I was more lucky than Ackroid, and arrived at the sergeant's quarters, and stopped that night. The next morning Ackroid was missing, and the sergeant directed the police to look him up, but they were not successful. We were detained by this two days. The second day, in the forenoon, I went down into a square where the Queen's Guards were parading. There were thousands witnessing the scene, and I saw Ackroid in the distance. I knew him in a moment by his white head, and made my way through the crowd where he was. He was glad to see me; the old difficulty that separated us was forgotten, and we went to the sergeant's quarters. We might have run away easily, but the sergeant had told us that we should go together, and praised us up exceedingly, by telling us we were cut out for soldiers. He took us with the other recruits aboard the cars, and went to Portsmouth. Here we stopped one night, and were placed in the guard-room, and sentries placed over us. We slept on nothing but boards for a bed. The next morning we continued our journey, and took the steamboat for the Isle of Wight, and arriving there, we traveled four miles to our barracks. Here we thought we could take our ease and live like gentlemen, but how soon we found our mistake; instead of ease and comfort, we found it a life of bondage, and to drown our sorrows, we had recourse to the ale-house. The first night in the barracks we spent in the 'dry-room,' where they put prisoners. Some straw was put upon an iron bedstead, upon which I slept. I well remember that night, for I rolled out of my cot (it was only two feet wide) upon the floor, which made the rats, which infested the place, scamper to their holes. The next morning, the barber came and shaved our heads closely. I told him that the recruiting sergeant said that we might wear our hair long, but the barber told us he had his duty to perform, and that we might as well dry up. After this was done, we were passed over to the surgeon's hands, and then we went back to our barracks, and put on our regimental clothes. My old clothes I sold for two quarts of beer, and my companion did the same with his. The first thing we had to learn was our drill. Before breakfast we had to drill one hour, then again from eleven to twelve, and from three to four o'clock in the afternoon; making three hours a day, and the remainder we most always had work of some kind to do. The soldiers had two meals a day; the first at eight o'clock in the morning, and the other at one P. M. Our morning rations consisted of one pound of brown bread and a bowl of coffee ; this brown bread was sometimes so soft, that when thrown against the wall, it would stick there. At dinner, we had a pound of meat, and two-and-half-pence allowed each man, to buy sugar, tea, etc. In the barracks where I was quartered, there were in each room seventeen, where they lived, slept, ate, and worked. At our meals, two officers served out the rations, consisting of meat soup, to each soldier. I could not say they showed partiality,

but it looked like it.   They would proportionate the meat soup
out, and then one would stand with his face to the wall, while
the other officer would hold up a plate, and ask, 'Who is this
for?'   The officer whose face was towards the wall, would say,
for B and so on; and in this way, they would pass through with
the whole.   I was the youngest in the room, and somehow or
other, if there was a large bone without much meat upon it, I
was sure to get it.   I stood this as long as I could, and at last
I told the color sergeant how I fared, and he changed me into
another room, but here I did not fare much better.

CHAPTER X.

ACKROID and myself used to drill together, and often talk of home, and wish we were out of the service, as we had seen enough of it. One day there was a young man confined for losing some of his clothes, or disposing of them. This man was put into the guard-room, and tried by a regimental court-martial, and sentenced to receive one hundred and fifty lashes with the cat-o'-nine-tails, a whip with nine lashes. At the close of the court-martial, the bugler sounded for orders. The orders that day were, that on the next day there should be a parade of all those who were off duty and out of hospital, and a court-martial read on parade. The next day at ten o'clock the bugle sounded for the soldiers to dress; and in half an hour, the bugle sounded for them to fall into rank and file. After we had formed our lines for marching, the word was given, 'Quick march.' We were then marched into the 'riding school,' as they call it, where the flogging was done. Here the young recruits were marched up alongside where the person was to be flogged, that they might by this become hardened, and kept in fear. I remember that Ackroid at this time was beside me. In this riding school, where they did the flogging, the minister held up a crucified Saviour, and the culprit was tied to the pulpit in which he stood. Many have I seen sacrificed upon the altar, but it was not acceptable sacrifice. The buglers of each company, and the drum-major of the depot of soldiers, are stationed beside the victim. The drummers do the flogging; a number being selected out, and each one gives twenty-five lashes, and if there are not drummers enough to make out the one hundred and fifty, the first one gives twenty-five more, and so goes round again, until the full complement is given. The drummer, rolling up his sleeve, grasps the 'cat' firmly in his hand, and raising it slowly over his head, brings it down with his whole strength upon the bare back of the poor victim, making the blood fly, and counting every blow given, until he has given twenty-five, and then resigns the whip to his successor. Every person unacquainted would naturally suppose, that when a person is whipped, and the one who inflicts the blows has no enmity against the prisoner, that the blows would be light, but it is not so; each one takes pride in striking a heavy blow, and the one that can strike the hardest is considered the best fellow. Thus the prisoner always gets a dreadful whipping.

When the prisoner had received his one hundred and fifty lashes, a white cloth, saturated with salt and water, was then thrown over his back, and thus *pickled*, he was sent to the hospital, where he stayed until his back was well. Sometimes when a soldier is whipped, he has a lead bullet put into his mouth, to chew, that he may be kept from biting his tongue, and I have seen it taken out after they were whipped, ground in pieces. In my regiment, there was a full corporal, a man that was despised by all the soldiers that were under him. He would confine the soldiers when they had been drinking, and endeavor to get them court-martialed, that they might receive a whipping. The soldiers were determined, in some way or other, to get this man whipped.

One day this corporal, with some soldiers, went to Newport to a tavern, when the soldiers and the corporal drank; the corporal got intoxicated, and the soldiers left him at a house of bad repute, where he stopped three days. The officers, supposing he had deserted, sent out detachments of soldiers, and scoured the country around, to endeavor to find him. The third day he was found at the house referred to, and some of his clothing was gone. He was brought before a garrison court-martial, and was sentenced to receive one hundred and fifty lashes. This pleased the soldiers exceedingly. It used to be a favorite expression with him, when a soldier was whipped, and he cried out, or even groaned, 'That he was a coward,—a baby.' One of the drummers, who was to wield the 'cat,' belonging to the regiment of which the prisoner was corporal, was six feet two inches in height, a very robust and powerfully built man, and said in my hearing, the morning of the punishment, 'I will make him cry out, or my arm shall come off;' and as he said the words, he stretched forth his muscular arm, and no one doubted but what he would be as good as his word. I was on sentry at the time of the flogging, and every blow struck, caused the flesh and blood to fly about me. The flesh was whipped off from one of his shoulder blades, so that the bone was bare. But I will not dwell upon this disgraceful scene, which was too degrading for human beings to be engaged in. Thank God! the whipping in the army has been abolished! The poor victim was taken to the hospital, and remained about a month before he was able to be upon duty again; his badges were taken off, and he was made a private. This, in itself, is considered a great disgrace to an officer. There was flogging about once in three weeks; sometimes oftener. I came near getting one hundred and fifty lashes, soon after I came into the army. One night I was upon sentry, box number six, and near by was an apple orchard, the trees being loaded with fruit. I left my station, and went to the orchard and filled my hat with apples. I made as much haste as possible, that I might get back to my box before the half-hour call came round again. I was returning when I heard the cry from number one, 'All's well!' and thus it continued through the numbers, until it came to number six, my station, and no cry was heard. I had not reached it, and the sentry in station seven cried out, 'All's not well!' And thus it went through all the numbers. Number one cried out, 'All's not well!' which brought out the sergeant with a file of soldiers, and they immediately went to number twelve. The sentry there said, 'All's not well!' number eleven; and thus it was followed back, until they came to number seven, and there the sentry told the sergeant that no cry was heard

WHIPPING A SOLDIER.

from number six.   In the meanwhile I had got back to my box, leaving my apples outside; and the sergeant asked me why I did not cry out 'All's well!' I knew that I must tell the best story for myself that I could, and I told him that I was thinking of home, and forgot to give the signal. The sergeant was friendly to me, and gave me some advice in regard to the matter, and told me that if some other sergeant had been in the guard-room at the time, I should not have escaped a flogging. He then left me, and I never heard of the matter again, but felt under great obligations to him for pardoning me at that time for such neglect of duty.

One night I was on sentry at the hospital, when a man named Stinson was carried by me, on a table, by four men, to the hospital.   He was a man of fine education and of superior abilities, and had left his regiment in the East Indies, on account of his health, and come to the Isle of Wight. He was a great drunkard, and a wicked and profane man, and he always boasted, as he was an infidel, that when he died, he would go out of the world like a roaring bull. When he was carried by me, he was roaring like a bull; he was in a state of delirium tremens, for three days and nights, and made this noise continually. The fourth night after he was carried to the hospital, between the hours of eleven and twelve o'clock, he was carried by two men to the dead-house, on a sheet. His hair was torn from his head, and he was so mangled that he could not be recognized.   I was put the next night sentry over the dead-house, and my orders were to kick on the door of the dead-house every ten minutes, to keep the rats away from the dead that were in there.   I did not like the situation.   I seemed to see Stinson before me all the time, and made an exchange with another soldier, and took his place, and he took mine.

I remained at the Isle of Wight about nine months, when an order was received from the Horse Guards, for a draft of the 97th Regiment and the Rifle Brigade, to fill vacancies at Corfu, and I felt joyful to leave this place. Our accoutrements were examined, and we were given firelocks said to be ours, with locks off, and many of them with the breech broken, and we were charged so much for repairs, and then good ones were given us, and the old ones kept, probably to pass off on the next draft that was made. In a few days we were in readiness to go to Corfu; the bugle sounded for us to fall into rank and file. There were one hundred in the whole, and we were ordered to march forthwith to Dedford. We were marched down the barracks, while the band played 'The girl I left behind me;' and many of the soldiers, having married without the consent of the commanding officer, were obliged to leave their wives and children behind them. All around me, the soldiers were shaking hands, and kissing their wives, and bidding them adieu, probably for the last time. There was no one to bid me farewell, or to shake the friendly hand; no one to shed a parting tear for me; and, as I looked upon the scene, I thought, oh! that I had a friend to bid farewell, it would seem to relieve me; for my heart was full, as I saw the tears trickle down the sunburnt cheeks of the rough soldiers, and the mothers holding up their young babes that they might kiss them before they left.

But there is an end to parting. The word was given, 'Quick march,' and we hastened on. We had to march four miles to Cowes, where we were to take the steamboat, and as I never marched with a knapsack on before, I thought that I should sink beneath my heavy burden. We took the steamboat for Portsmouth, and then the cars for London. From London we marched to Dedford, and there we were billeted out for the night. Another young man and myself were billeted together. We were sent by twos and threes, and I wished to be sent with Ackroid, but they sent us as was most convenient to them. In the morning, we had to meet in the dock-yard; the bugler sounded for us to fall in.

We went aboard the ship, and went below, and took off our knapsacks, and then had to go to work upon deck. We were three days and nights going down the channel, and the third day we arrived at Cove-of-Cork. There we stopped three days, and took in the 34th Regiment, and then sailed for the Mediterranean. While we were on our way, a young soldier picked up a 'chin-strap' (a strap that goes under the chin to keep on the military cap). This young man inquired for the owner, but not finding him, he used the strap for himself. The owner in a short time noticed it, and knowing that it was his, made a complaint to the commanding officer, and the young man was made a prisoner, tried for stealing before a regimental court-martial, was found guilty, sentenced to be tied to the main-mast, and receive fifty lashes. This young soldier slept in the hammock beneath me, and when they took him to be flogged, he plead his innocence, but was carried upon the deck, and received his number of lashes. He received a severe flogging; the flesh was left in ridges, and the blood ran down upon the deck. After his flogging he was covered over with a white cloth, soaked in salt and water, and then put in his hammock. He was said to have been a fine young man, and one that would have made himself conspicuous, but the whipping crushed his spirits. He had been full of life and activity, but from that time he was sullen and morose, and would not hold conversation with any one. One day we were sailing along, about thirteen knots an hour; the breeze increasing, the studding-sail tore out of the bolt-ropes, and a number of us were called upon deck, and told to go aloft, and assist in taking in sail; and as the soldiers were inexperienced, one of our number fell overboard, and was lost. The gale increased, and at night it was my watch on deck. It blew now almost a hurricane, all sail was taken in, and we were scudding along under bare poles. I went by one of the port-holes, and laid down, and while there, a wave dashed over the side, unshipping the gun, and I was carried along by the wave, but caught the halliards, and thus saved myself from being swept over the ship's side. The crew were called up, and the soldiers spiked down beneath the deck. At times, the waves made a complete breach over her, and she leaned so that her spars at times touched the water. At the dawn of day, the gale abated somewhat, and we found that a number had been washed overboard. I looked around for Ackroid, but could not find him above or below deck, and thought that he must have been washed overboard. As he had been very sea-sick, I expected that he was gone, and that I never should see him again. While searching, I thought of a place under the long-boat, where a man could just get in, and going there, found Ackroid. He was wet through, and had laid his head down upon some tar, which held him fast. Before he could be removed, I found it necessary to get a knife, and cut away a portion of his hair; and having procured some water, I washed him, and he revived. I then went up where the hogs were kept, and stole their breakfast,—black biscuit; and I believe I never felt so cheap as I did when I stole the bread from the hogs; but I felt that the necessity of the case demanded it, and asserting 'border rights,' I boldly entered the pen (the very last place where I should have thought of picking up a living), and by dextrous management, succeeded in obtaining something to satisfy the cravings of my appetite. Those biscuits tasted quite as sweet to me as the nicest bread I have ever eaten since.

CHAPTER XI.

WE reached Gibraltar, and there we took in some water, and continued our way to Corfu. We had sailed some two days, when we had a dead calm that lasted three days. We forgot about the gale we had experienced, and the fiddle and the flute sounded merrily upon the deck, whilst the sailors and the soldiers danced to the music; and for three days nothing but songs and merriment were heard. The soldiers were allowed a glass of rum a day, but as Ackroid was sick, I took his share, and I then had more than my allowance of rum, and have for many years since. The fourth day, a fine breeze set in, which soon carried us to the shores of Italy, where I could plainly see the burning lava upon the sides of Mt. Vesuvius, that cast a beautiful mellow light, in the evening, upon the hills around. After a somewhat long voyage, we dropped anchor in Corfu, in Greece, and went ashore. This place seemed cursed with the worst kind of people. The grossest corruption pervaded all classes; justice was openly bought and sold. One writer says, 'When they were placed under the rule of England they were lazy, ignorant, cowardly, superstitious, and blood-thirsty.' Sandys, one of the best English travelers who ever visited the Levant, writes thus in 1610: 'They will threaten to kill a merchant that will not buy their commodities, and make more conscience to break a fast than commit a murder; he is weary of his life that hath a difference with any of them, and will walk abroad after daylight. The laborers do go into the fields with swords and partisans, as if in an enemy's country, bringing home their oils and wines in hog-skins, the inside turned out.'

Dr. Holland, who visited this place in 1812, says, 'that the number of assassinations in Zante has been more than one for each day in the year, though the population was only 40,000.' Corfu, from its proximity to the snowy mountains and also the black mountains of the interior, is subject to very sudden changes of temperature, and, in the hot seasons, is terribly unhealthy, a consequence in part from the vapors arising from the marshes of the shallow seas to the north-east. Booths were built for the guards to stand under in the hot season, and I have stood under my shelter, when on guard, when it was so hot that a piece of beef could be tossed from where I stood on to the rocks, and be tolerably cooked in ten minutes, and facing, at the same time, the mountains that were in plain sight, whose summits were capped with snow. It was no wonder so many English soldiers died here like rotten sheep. There were six hundred men that came from the Isle of Wight to Corfu, many of whom died. One regiment, by a fatal malady, lost every man but one. The 34th Regiment went to 'Bell Barracks,' and those of us that belonged to the Rifle Brigade and the 97th Regiment went to the citadel or fortress. Our draft was put in the marine guard-room, and then the soldiers hurried down to see us, hoping to find some one they knew. I saw one young man that came from the same place that Ackroid and I did, and we were very glad to meet one another so many miles from home. This young man went immediately and got a quart of wine and some refreshments to treat us with, and we felt so happy with the rest of the soldiers, and made so much noise, that one of the officers told the captain, and he came and spoke to us, and said these word: 'Young men, you have got into a place where there are no back doors, through which you can run home to your mothers.'

The next day we were ordered to wash and dress ourselves, and were then paraded before the commanding officer. Our place of parade was on the esplanade, and when we arrived there, the officers were waiting to take us to the different companies, there being sixteen in the whole. I was picked out for the Light Infantry, and Ackroid was chosen for the second company, and thus we were about to be separated. The thought of this began to make me feel bad, and I could not restrain myself, and the tears began to flow down my face. One of the adjutants seeing that I was crying, said, 'What are you weeping for?' I told him that the young man with a white head had always been with me, and that we had enlisted together, and that as we were about to be separated, it made me sad. He went immediately to the commanding officer, and got Ackroid into the company with me. We had then our arms and accoutrements served out to us. The first thing we now had to do, was to learn our drill, which was somewhat different from that we had learned at the Isle of Wight. Some of the soldiers were sent to the reserve battalion, in West Indies, and the others were in the first battalion, in the Ionian Islands. There was a poor simple fellow that came with us, who could not learn his drill, and he was sent to Zante, and there they could not make anything of him. The doctor said that he was making it, and that he could bring him out, so he was sent to the hospital. The doctor one day heated an iron poker, and with this he burned the young man so badly that he died. The same doctor, a short time after, died a very sudden death, which pleased all the soldiers, and he was brought to Corfu to be buried. A volley was fired over his grave, and I thought at the time that I would much rather have fired a bullet at him, than a blank cartridge over him. We soon had to mount guard, and the first time I was on, the heat of the sun so overpowered me, that I fell down senseless, and was taken up and carried to the hospital. I recovered soon, and came out of the hospital, although hardly able to stand. I was next put on guard upon Mt. Tabor, over the Greek prisoners. My watch was two hours, and no place that I was ever on sentry was so desolate and solemn as that. I could hear the rattling of the chains of the prisoners; also the wild boars on the sides of the mountain.

During the night, the corporal brought a pail full of wine, which was drank by the soldiers on duty. I was sentry over the old senate, so called, and there was one prisoner in there that had been confined *thirty years* in one cell, and had not seen the light, only through the gratings of the window; he seemed to be happy, for I heard him singing Greek songs. In the next cell there was a young man, and when I was on sentry, two young Greek girls came to see this prisoner. They entreated me to let them carry some luxuries to him, and I could not withstand their earnest pleading, but let them go into the cell. If I had been caught in this act, I should have been confined, and probably got severely punished.

The sergeant, one evening, went out of town, and got some wine, and while he was away, some of the other officers brought wine to the soldiers, and before he returned the guard were intoxicated, and the next day when we were relieved, one of the guardsmen was confined for getting drunk, and the following day received one hundred and fifty lashes. There were sixteen flogged that day for getting drunk, when upon garrison duty. When I saw these poor fellows flogged, I thought to myself, that I never would get drunk when on duty. In a few days after, I was warned for garrison picket, and a corporal asked me to go out of town with him. We went to a wine shop, and there drank some two quarts of wine, and became partially intoxicated, and when I arrived at the barracks, was confined for getting drunk. I had been in the guard-room a short time, when one of the men said that I should get a flogging, and this sobered me in a minute, and I spoke to the sergeant of the guard, and told him I was not drunk. 'But,' said he, 'you are confined for getting drunk.' All the soldiers said I was not drunk. That night I did not sleep much, expecting that the next day I should be more intimately acquainted with the cat-o-nine-tails, with whose satanic majesty I desired no intimacy. The following day I was carried before the commander, and he told me that I was reported as having been drunk when on duty. I told the sergeant that I was not drunk, and that I could prove it by the soldiers. 'But,' said he, 'the sergeant said that you was drunk. Young man,' he continued, 'you are commencing too soon to lead a bad life, but I think we will punish you.' I begged that he would not, as I had always tried to obey the discipline. The commander said, 'As you are a youngster, I will forgive you this time, but never be brought before me again; if you do, you will have to suffer the penalty for transgressing the rules.' I escaped the 'cat' again, and I made up my mind that I never would run the risk of a whipping, by getting intoxicated when upon duty.

There was a rich Jew that kept a shop in the fortress, where he sold wines and other things to the soldiers. He was as snug and exacting a person as could be met with. He used to sell what they called 'black puddings,' to the soldiers, who said that they were made out of rats; but the soldiers, when they went in there, would get liquor to drink, and then they would eat anything. The soldiers used to say, that if a person would rob him, it would be a good deed. One night, as I was on sentry, I thought to myself, I will rob that Jew, and as he has stolen money away from the soldiers, when they were drunk, it will be no worse for me to steal from him; and with this thought, I put my gun down, and went to his door, and tried to open it, but it was fast. I then put my shoulder against it, and pushed it open, and went in, and opened the money drawer. I put my hand in, and found some farthings; and in another drawer, I found a sovereign piece, and some small silver pieces, but I left the small pieces, as the sovereign was enough for me, and went out and shut the door. I went away a short distance, and buried the sovereign piece in the ground. I then went back to my post, and had just arrived there, when a sentry came to relieve me. When I arrived at the guard-room, I laid down upon the bed, but felt somewhat uneasy about the deed, as I remembered what the orders were; and if a soldier when on duty left his post, to go away for plunder, that the penalty was a severe one. The

6

next day, when the Jew came to his shop, he found it had been broken open and robbed, and he went and told the sergeant. The sergeant said that he could not believe it; but the Jew took him along with him to his shop, and showed that it had been broken open. The sergeant went to the soldiers that had been on sentry near there that night, and questioned them in regard to the affair. We all said we knew nothing about it. That night, I went, after I was off duty, down to the place where I buried my sovereign, and taking it to the money changers, got it changed into shilling pieces. I then went and found Ackroid, and we went out to the shops, and spent half a crown for wine and eatables. I left Ackroid, and went down to where the old batteries were, a short distance, and hid my money in an old rotten timber there, and then went back to barracks. The next day, I went to the old battery to get some money, but was somewhat surprised to find that it was all gone. Where it had gone was more than I could imagine, and I was pretty confident that no one followed me to the place; but one thing was certain, my money was gone, and I felt then that the proverb, that 'riches certainly make themselves wings,' was a pretty true one. I came to the conclusion, as I went back to the barracks, never again to take anything that did not belong to me. They never knew, I believe, who committed the robbery, and they did not exert themselves much to find out. The soldiers were glad of it, and the officers were not sorry. Perhaps one reason why the officers did not endeavor to find out who committed the deed was, that they did not believe the old Jew's story. They thought he had made it up to excite sympathy; and then again, the officers said it was not likely that a soldier would have broken into the store, and then left silver scattered around; and, upon the whole, they neither knew, nor cared much about it, and it therefore dropped.

A few days after this, a barrack was to be built within the fortress, and I was chosen, with some other soldiers, to work on this one month. Our task was to wheel one thousand bricks a day, some four hundred yards from the sea-shore, up to the barracks, which was a very hard job, as part of the distance was very steep, and I have sometimes slipped, and my bricks would come down on me, and my barrow would roll down over the hill. We had a corporal for a task-master over us. He sported white kid gloves and a cane, and was quite a gentleman. In Ireland, where he came from, he was a turf-digger, and worked in the mud. I worked on the barracks about a month, and saw many flogged for drinking while at work there, and the task-master would swear that they were drunk, if they had taken any at all.

CHAPTER XII.

The batteries were situated upon a bluff, some two hundred and fifty feet high, near the sea. It was a level plot, upon which some two thousand could be accommodated. Above the batteries, on the top of this bluff, was the hospital and dead-house. A short time after I came here, there was one man in the hospital that was pronounced dead, or so near it, that it would be safe enough, as they thought, to put him in the dead-house, and he was therefore carried and put in there, and while there, the rats began to lay claim to him, which was the means of arousing him, and he got up and crept around as best he could. The sentry, hearing a noise in the dead-house, called the sergeant, and the soldiers turned out of the guard-room, but not one of them had courage enough to enter. At last they got a lantern, and, opening the door, they called out, 'Who's there?' They received no answer, but heard a noise, as if some person had fallen down. After some time they went in, and found the poor fellow, who was now dead. He was actually frightened to death.

An incident happened when I was in Corfu, although not connected with me, which I cannot refrain from stating. A man named Rogers, that belonged to the Rifle Brigade, and had been a school-mate of the sergeant of the same company, got angry with him, as the sergeant, from some cause or other, took every opportunity that he could to confine him, and determined to have his life. One night, Rogers took another man's fire-lock, and went to the sergeant's bed, and putting the muzzle of his gun to the sergeant's head, fired. The ball passed through his head, killing him, and down into another room, into one of the soldier's cots. The alarm was given, and the firelocks examined, to see which one had been loaded recently, and the owner of the gun was arrested; but while being carried off, Rogers sprang from his cot, and said that he was the man that did the deed. The other soldier was released, and Rogers was taken and put into the dead-cell, and there confined to await his trial. He was tried by a general court-martial, and was sentenced to be hung. On the morning of the execution, the prisoner appeared as lively as ever. At ten o'clock, the bugle sounded for the soldiers to dress, and in half an hour, for them to fall in. All were marched up to witness the execution; and when upon the scaffold, the prisoner made one of the most affecting speeches that had been heard for many a day. He exposed the petty officers, how they tyrannized over the soldiers, and concluded his remarks with such feeling, that the tears ran down the faces of the rough soldiers, and some of them, it was said, even fell in the ranks. At that time, his speech was heralded throughout the land as a remarkable one. Thus perished a scholar and a soldier; one that had every requisite qualification to make a man respected and honored by his countrymen.

A short time after the execution, a soldier, belonging to the same regiment with myself, wanted to go into town, and as sentries were stationed all around, he dressed himself as Rogers was dressed when carried to the place of execution. As he approached the sentries, they fled before him, as they thought he was Rogers' ghost; and he succeeded in getting to town and back safe. Having made such a successful trip, he thought that he could go the next night, but an old soldier was on sentry, an Irishman, called Tim. He was as bold as a lion, and nothing could frighten him; and as Galgree (the name of the soldier) was passing him, he cried out, 'Who comes there?'

No answer came, and he cried again, 'Who comes there?'

But he received no answer, and again cried out,

'The divil take ye, by St. Pathrick, av ye doant be after givin the signal, its meself that will make daylight shine through ye. Who comes there?'

No answer came, and Tim snapped, but his firelock flashed in the pan, or poor Galgree would have made his last night's excursion. Tim now charged bayonet, and Galgree took to his heels, with Tim after him. He soon brought him to a stand between two high bluffs, when Galgree said, 'Tim, don't you know me?'

'By me soul, its meself that's not ackuanted with the likes av ye,' said Tim.

'But don't you know Galgree?'

'Well, Galgree or no Galgree, av ye doant be after marching to the guard-room, I'll jist tickle ye with the pint of my bayonet; and faith an ye'll find that's meself that's too ould a soldier to be scared by the ghosteses.'

Galgree marched toward the guard-room, with Tim following close at his heels, with the bayonet at his back, and, arriving at another sentry-box, the sentry, seeing the ghost of Rogers, as he supposed, with a screech, took to his heels. Tim still kept marching him along until he came to the guard-room, and then ordered Galgree to open the door. The sergeant was making out his guard report when the door opened, and the ghost of Rogers stared him in the face. He was so frightened that he overturned the table, and the noise awakened the soldiers who were in the room; and seeing Rogers' ghost in the door, some cursed and swore, while others shrunk into the back part of the room. Tim now began to get mad at the cowardice of the soldiers, and bellowed out, 'The divil and sure Rogers has come back, and what a boald lot av soldiers ye are; its meself that would not be afeerd to face a regemint like ye, an is it the likes av ye that are put on guard, thats afeerd of a shader? this is nothing more than Galgree who is playing the ghosteses on us.'

The words of Tim restored the soldiers to order again, and they began to come out and show themselves. Poor Galgree was taken up into a chamber and fastened in, and the next day he was brought before the commanding officer, who, when he was brought in, imitated the rest of the soldiers, and holding up his hands and starting back, to make fun of the frightened officers, he said, 'I thought we hung you the other day, but we will see if we can give you some more punishment;' and he gave orders for him to be tried by a court-martial, and he was sentenced to break stones fifty days where Rogers was hung.

My companion Ackroid about this time was taken sick, and was carried to the hospital. What little money I obtained, I would spend in buying him luxuries. I was not allowed to carry wine to him, but sometimes smuggled it in a small flask, concealed in my stockings. I went to see him one day, and whilst there the drum-major came in with a letter sealed with black; it was written by his sister, and contained the unwelcome news of the death of his mother. She had written to him many times, urging him to get his discharge from the army, which he could have done by paying twenty-one pounds, and she offered him the money to pay it; but I would talk him out of the notion, and tell him that we should soon go to a station nearer home. But the most prevailing argument I had, was that we had been companions so long that I could not get along without him, as they were all strangers to me here, and by this I persuaded him to remain. Ackroid read the letter and passed it to me, but I could not read, but knew that something was written there that caused my companion to weep, and he told me that his mother was dead. While the tears coursed down his cheeks, he said these words to me: 'Isaac, there is something in sickness that breaks down the pride of manhood, and softens the heart, and brings it back to its infancy!' Who that has languished upon a sick-bed, in neglect and loneliness in a foreign land, that has not thought of the mother who in his childhood smoothed his pillow, and administered to his helplessness? There is something in a mother's love for a son, which transcends all other affections of the heart. It is neither to be stifled by ingratitude, nor daunted in danger; for she will surrender everything for his enjoyment, and sacrifice everything for his pleasure. If prosperity should overtake him, she will exult in his success; and if adversity, she will lament over his misfortune,—though all the world cast him off, she will be all the world to him! I never expected Ackroid to get out again, but he soon after began to mend, and left the hospital.

I remained in Corfu some three years, and then an order came from the Horse Guards, for the 97th Regiment to go to Malta. We sailed in the man-of-war Vengeance, and every heart was glad to leave, expecting to go to a better place, but we were taken to a worse one. While we were sailing up to Malta, they practiced shooting with a seventy-four gun. The first lieutenant had one eye, and if there was a tyrant in the British service, it was that man. I have seen him, when the gunner was elevating his piece, strike him with a rope's end, if the position of the gun did not suit him, and lay him prostrate on the deck.

We landed at Malta, and were marched to our barracks. The regimental guard was the first place where I was upon duty. The Maltese gave the soldiers wine, and got them intoxicated, and there were so many of them confined for drunkenness, that the guard-room was nearly full. When we went into the streets we were often attacked, and many were the escapes we made from the Maltese while we stopped in that place. One evening, one of my companions, a drinking fellow, went out upon the street, and got into a fight; several Maltese were against him, but he fought his way through, and arrived at the barracks, covered with blood, and wounded badly. The mosquitoes and sand-flies troubled us exceedingly, so that it was difficult for us to sleep in the guard-room, and we used to tie our pants around the bottom, to keep them from biting our legs; and although we used every means to keep them off, we could not get rid of them. By these troubles, we could not sleep much in the guard-room, and when we went upon sentry we were very sleepy, and at one time, I remember it distinctly, I sat down when upon my post, and fell asleep. The sergeant, making his regular visit to the sentries, and finding me asleep, seized my firelock to take it from me, but I was awake in a moment, and my bayonet at his breast. He told me that I should have to be confined; but I informed him that the mosquitoes and sand-flies troubled us so in the guard-room that we could not sleep, and that I fell asleep at my post before I was aware of it. This sergeant had always been friendly to me, and he did not report me to the commanding officer, or I should have stood a chance of getting fifty lashes.

The soldiers having had a falling out with the Maltese, could not go into the streets without running the risk of their lives. Our regiment, about the time of this trouble, had to furnish the main guard; there were twenty-seven others besides myself upon that guard. One evening, the band was playing in front of the guard-room, in a large public square (the band was formed in a circle), and there were three soldiers and a corporal that walked around the circle, to keep the crowd back; but one man that had been drinking, broke in, and the corporal arrested and carried him to the guard-room, and confined him. As soon as the man was arrested, the crowd rushed toward the band, breaking their circle, and overturning some of them by the rapidity of their movements. The guard was called out under arms, and I was standing beside a soldier named Vass, when a large rock was thrown, grazing his face. This and similar demonstrations aroused the soldiers, and in the confusion the prisoner escaped from the guard-room, and ran down the street, with the corporal after him. We presented bayonets, and kept the crowd back. My bayonet was at the breast of a priest, and the Maltese men looked exceedingly fierce at me, while the priest was continually crossing himself. The corporal caught up with the prisoner, and seized him by the collar, but quite a number of the Maltese gathered around to rescue him, when the corporal saw Tim (the Irishman before referred to), walking along near by; he cried out for him to assist, and Tim, seizing a large cane from a bystander, came to the corporal, and as the crowd were just endeavoring to rescue the prisoner, he laid a number of them prostrate, and took the prisoner, and marched him to the guard-room. The Maltese, seeing a number of their men struck down by Tim, would not be satisfied or suspend hostilities, until he was arrested and confined, which was accordingly done. He was kept in prison forty days, and was then honorably acquitted; and when he walked the streets of Malta, the citizens treated him with more respect than any other soldier, on account of his bravery.

CHAPTER XIII.

I WAS on the new Senate Guard while in Malta, and there were many Turks there, and I was attracted every morning by seeing them bow down and worship the sun. While upon this guard I was taken sick, but I thought I would much rather die in the barracks than in the hospital. But growing weaker every day, at last I could just get around; and as the corporal came around to the barracks and inquired if any were sick, I gave in my name, and was carried to the hospital. The doctor came to see me, and asked, 'How long have you been sick?' I told him that it had been nearly a week.

'You are a dead man, then. Why did you not report yourself before?' he said, with an oath.

One day the general doctor came to visit me; I had been then three months in the hospital, and was almost a skeleton, and he said that I could live but a short time. I felt frightened by his words, knowing that I was not prepared to die, and I pledged myself, that if God would raise me up, that I would serve him the remainder of my days. That night my feet grew cold, and I was told my time had come. These words nearly frightened me to death; when one of the soldiers that was intoxicated, seized a pan, and filling it full of hot water, put my feet into it, scalding me severely. I closed my eyes in death, as I thought then, and lay speechless, when the person who had charge of me took from my pocket a Spanish dollar, and exchanged his old boots for a pair of new ones that I had. I opened my eyes, and the man finding I was not dead yet, returned the dollar and replaced the boots. That night I was able to speak, and continued to recover slowly. I was soon enabled to walk, and obtained liberty to go out of hospital, down upon the sea-shore, and at first, I had the Maltese assist me back to the hospital a number of times, being too weak to return. After I had recovered so as to go upon duty again, the Light Infantry received orders to go upon the opposite side of Malta, to take charge of a fort. While at the fort, a soldier belonging to Number Two Company had been drinking hard, and he took his firelock and loaded it, and going into a bowling alley that was near, tied a string to the trigger of the gun, and, placing the muzzle under his chin, was about to pull the string, when the sergeant went in, and knocking the man down, caught the gun as it dropped; it went off and drove the ball into the ceiling. The soldier was taken up and carried to the hospital.

We stopped in Malta about sixteen months, when an order was received for the 97th Regiment to go forthwith to Halifax, in the ship Java. We left in the fall of eighteen hundred and forty-eight, and arrived at Halifax in some fifty days; and as we had thin clothing on, we suffered extremely from the cold. We went ashore and pitched our tents on the common, where we stopped three days and nights, part of the time it rained and hailed, and we had to dig small drains in our tents to carry off the water. The bottom of our tents was covered with straw, upon which we slept, until the regiment whom we were sent to relieve, went away,—then we went into the barracks.

Some of the soldiers and officers were so vexed by the treatment which they received that they ran away from the army. We had at that time the finest grenadier company that there was in the British army; but many of these deserted. There were three full-sergeants and two color-sergeants that deserted. The three sergeants went away at one time, and a police-sergeant that belonged to the 38th Regiment, volunteered to go after them. The sergeants, as we learned, were in a Scotch settlement, some distance from the army; and the police-sergeant, taking some other soldiers with him, went to this settlement, and found the house where they stopped. Leaving his men upon the outside, he went into the house, and whilst in the lower part, one of the sergeants came down stairs. As soon as the police-sergeant saw him, he drew his pistol, and told him to stand, and that he was his prisoner in the Queen's name. But the other two sergeants came down, and one of them knocked the police-sergeant over, and took the brace of pistols away from him, and then they fought their way through the soldiers at the door, and escaped to the States. The sergeant got such a severe whipping that he was laid by for some time.

Soon after our regiment arrived at Halifax, I was appointed corporal in the Light Infantry; this was a great misfortune to me, for it gave me greater liberty inside of the barracks, and plenty of drink outside; and I forgot the promise I had made God when I was sick, and plunged deeper into dissipation. I was ordered to mount the 'ordnance guard,' with some old soldiers, and having been recently appointed, I was expected to stand treat for all hands. I told them I should not, for I had seen enough of the results of drinking when upon duty; but one of the soldiers said that all corporals treated when appointed. I would not consent, but one of them brought a bottle of brandy, and soon another was brought, until some half a dozen bottles had been drank by the soldiers, and they got partially intoxicated. What to do, I could not tell! If the commanding officer should see them in such a condition, they would be confined, and myself with them. I therefore went and brought a couple of pails of water, and threw this on them, but it did not sober them, and I then turned to, and gave them a pretty good thrashing, which sobered them in a great measure. When we went off from duty, the commanding officer inspected the guard, and they passed all right.

I had charge of fifteen men, and one of these got a pass from the commanding officer to go out of the barracks and stop all night. His name was Thomas Wilkinson, and he and myself were boon companions, and used to have our times, generally, together. He was a hard drinker, and something of a fighting character. Wilkinson asked me to come out after tattoo, and I told him I would, if possible. After the roll was called, and when all the men were asleep in the barrack-room, I arose and dressed myself, and went down near the 'Canteen,' and climbed over the fence, and went up where Wilkinson was, and there got something to drink. I stopped here a short time, and then went to a saloon, and while I was there drinking, a police-sergeant (the same fellow that did not take the sergeants that deserted) came into the shop and asked me if I had a pass. I told him that it was none of his business, as he had nothing to do with the regiment that I belonged to.

'If you do not tell me, I will call in my men at the door,' said the sergeant.

'Well, call them in,' I said, and being in drink, I was not afraid to face them.

The sergeant called in two men at the door, and they dragged me out of the shop into the street. As they arrived opposite where I left Wilkinson, I called out for him to come out, but he was too far gone to pay any attention to me. I had made up my mind not to be carried to barracks, and intended to get Wilkinson, and both of us I knew could have flogged the sergeant and two men that he had with him, easily; but as he was not with me, I determined to do it alone.

The sergeant was in the rear, and a man on each side of me, and I took an opportunity, when their attention was attracted in another direction, and gave the sergeant a blow under the chin that laid him flat upon his back. Then turning quickly, I knocked down one of the men at my side, and ran as fast as I could with the third one after me with a cane; and, overtaking me, he knocked me down. I was up in a trice and off again, and escaped the fellow, and passed the sentry and got safe into barracks. I went to my room, and there I undressed and feigned sleep, for I supposed that I should have callers soon. The police-sergeant went to the barracks and reported to the major-sergeant that I was out of barracks, and they both went to the color-sergeant of the regiment that I belonged to, and, in company with him, came to my room. The major-sergeant, coming to my cot, shook me and managed to awake me. I got up, and wiping my eyes, asked what the trouble was.

'Oh, the rascal,' said the police-sergeant, and he swore that I had been out of barracks, and that he could bring proof of it. I awakened my men, and they all said that I went to bed when they did, but the police-sergeant being so positive, and still maintaining it, the sergeant-major said, 'Corporal Ambler, you may consider yourself under arrest,' and then the three left my room. If they had examined my clothes they would have found evidence enough against me, for they were covered with mud; but in the excitement they forgot it.

The next forenoon I was brought before the commanding officer, and the charge read against me of breaking out of barracks and assaulting an officer. I had borrowed a pair of pants and a coat, so that I appeared before the officer in pretty good shape.

The sergeant-major had been up, before I was brought before the officer, to the place where I had been the night before, and there learned that I had been out of barracks. I was aware that he had been out, and I made up my mind to tell the whole story. I therefore told the commanding officer that I had been out and up to town, and perhaps took a drop, and while I was in a shop, the police-sergeant came in and asked me to show my pass. I told him that it was none of his business, which made him angry, and he told me that unless I showed my pass he would call in two men that he had at the door, and take me to the barracks. I consented to the arrangement, and he brought his two men in and they took me a prisoner, but that they did not carry me a prisoner to the barracks; I went there alone, and went to bed and got asleep, and so sound that the sergeant-major could hardly wake me. At this point the sergeant-major and color-sergeant were laughing, and the police-sergeant, seeing that he was not likely to make much out of it, was going out, when the commanding officer said:

'When you attempt to bring prisoners to the barracks, remember after this to bring them all the way.'

This was a severe cut on the police-sergeant, as the incidents connected with the three sergeants that deserted, and that he did not bring back, were fresh in the memory of all present. He left the room, while those present smiled at the remark. The commander then turned and told me to go about my business, and not to be brought before him on any such charge again, for if I was I should certainly be punished. I faced to the right-about and went out of the room, finding at the door all my company waiting for me, expecting that I should get confused. As I came out I said, 'It's all right, boys,' upon which they gave a shout, and taking me upon their shoulders, carried me to my room.

CHAPTER XIV.

THE soldiers used to have some good times when upon duty, and I remember that one night when I was placed with three men under me, upon the Magazine Guard (this was the furthest guard from barracks), one of the men asked me if we should have some rum; but as I had seen the effects of it too often, I told him that I would not allow any to be brought. When soldiers set their minds on having rum, they will most always manage to get some, and one of the men said that if I would allow them to get some, that he would get a goose, and another said he would get some potatoes, and upon this I gave my consent. They went off and soon returned with their provisions, and we kindled a fire and baked our goose, and cooked our potatoes and drank our liquor, and had, in our opinion, a fine time.

A soldier's life, although it is hard and dark, yet has some bright spots, which are like the oases in a desert. They serve to lighten the cares of a soldier's life, and cheer him in his laborious and irksome duties. We would look back upon the little sprees and good times that we had with pleasure, as we sat in the barrack-room, and laid out our plans for the future.

As I succeeded well as corporal, and kept my men in good condition without being confined, the color-sergeant of the company asked me how I managed to get along so well; and, in the course of our conversation, he said, 'There is one room with ten men in it, and some of them are confined about every night, and I want you to take charge of the room, and to commence to-day.'

I went to my new quarters and told them that I was appoint-

7

ed to take charge of the room, and that upon the commencement intended to have order. The first night I stood at the door of the barrack, and the first man that came in drunk I knocked down; the second was served the same; I thought that it could be stopped in this way, but I found that I was mistaken. The next night, in carrying my plans out, I got into a regular fight, and one of the men threw a piece of iron at me which just grazed my cheek and struck the wall, leaving its mark. After we got quieted down, I tried to reason with them, and met with good success. I told them that I was the youngest of any of them, and that I had had before good success in taking care and keeping order in my room, and that now I was placed over them, as I had been so successful. I still further told them that my reputation and my honor were compromised (for I had told the color-sergeant that I could keep order), and that I now appealed to them, as men of honor, to assist me. One old soldier, that had been in the army many years, said, 'I will give my word and honor that I will not get drunk again while you have charge of the room, and I will not speak to the soldier that does.' This encouraged me, and I thanked him, and from that day it was the best and most orderly room in the barracks.

I have ever since that time thought much of moral suasion and have found that man has a heart, and that it is never so hardened but that it is capable of receiving good impressions, and being touched by words of kindness. God has given rational beings the power of reasoning, which is the greatest and most potent instrument that can be applied to man to bring him from vice and evil.

A short time after this, I was chosen to go after a deserter to Pictou, some 120 miles distant, and two men were selected to go with me as an escort. Before we left, my orders were given me, and quarters were provided on the way. We started off with our knapsacks on our backs, and our arms with us. But passing a detachment of the 97th Regiment, we left our knapsacks, as they were so heavy and impeded our progress considerably, and then continued our way. The first day we marched about twenty miles and arrived at our billeting quarters, where we got something to eat and stopped that night. We only had two meals a day, one in the morning before we commenced our march for the day, and the other at night where we stopped. The next morning we continued our march, and went about the same distance that we did the day before, and arrived at our quarters. The third day it rained hard, but we had to travel twenty miles to our stopping-place; here we all stood before a large fire, and dried ourselves the best we could. In conversation with the landlord, I told him our next stopping-place.

'You must be careful there,' he said, 'the landlord of that place is a villain; but a short time ago a pedlar was murdered there, and if you carry any money with you, you had better keep an eye on it.'

I told him that I thought that we should not meet with any difficulty, but thanked him for his words of caution, and then we retired for the night. The next day we arrived at the tavern that the last keeper had cautioned me about, and met the landlord at the door. I was immediately struck with his pleasant appearance. As we went into the house, we saw his two daughters, and I thought to myself, surely this man can be no murderer. When night came I was shown to a room below stairs, while my two men were carried up-stairs; this I thought looked suspicious, but I kept all the firelocks in my room, and told the men that if they heard an alarm to hurry down as soon as possible to my assistance. When I laid down for the night I put a firelock at my side; but I could not sleep, my thoughts were running upon what the tavern-keeper had told me in regard to the man whose roof I was under. As I lay there, I heard some one approaching my room who seemed to stop at my door. I seized my firelock, and as I was accustomed to challenge when upon sentry, I cried out, 'who comes there?' I received no answer, and as I heard no more noise I laid down again upon my bed, but as I was still listening, I heard voices. I arose and went to the door and listened; it was the voice of the landlord in prayer; and as he concluded, the daughters followed, and they concluded by singing a hymn. I felt more secure after hearing those prayers than I did with my guns by my side, and I threw aside my firelocks, and laid down and slept sweetly. The next morning we tried to get some rum of the landlord, but we were not successful (we had got it every morning before), and we had to leave without it.

We had traveled some five or six miles when I began to feel faint and hungry, and I told my men to keep on whilst I went into a cabin by the side of the road, and got something to eat. I had been so used to my rum that I could not get along without it. I went into the cabin where there was an elderly lady and her sick daughter that was near death, and I asked her if she would get me something to eat. She brought me a cup of coffee and a buckwheat cake, which tasted good to me; after eating I offered the woman some money, but she would not take it, and thanking her, I left the cabin to overtake my men, but they were some distance before me. As I was hurrying through a piece of woods to overtake them, a man jumped out from the bushes before me with a bayonet in his hand, and approached me in a threatening manner. I presented my bayonet and made a rush toward him, upon which he turned and took to his heels, and jumping over a ditch by the side of the road, he dropped the bayonet out of his hand. I crossed the ditch and picked it up, and continued on my way, and soon came up with my men, and showed them my bayonet that I had captured in my attack upon the man who had assaulted me.

We continued on our way, and arrived at our place for refreshment and there I showed the bayonet, and the keeper said that he had had two horses stolen from him, and that a number of the families around had lost some articles. We immediately gathered some of the neighbors, and started off in pursuit of the robber. The next day we came to a village about twenty miles from my place of destination, and found my quarters and had something to eat, and then I went with my men into the bar-room. Whilst there a number of young men came in, and we had a pretty merry time. One young man, of about my size, wished me to exchange my military clothes for his, and then for me to go with him to his father's house, which was about three miles from the tavern.

I was ready for any kind of sport, and therefore willingly complied with the request, and we went into an adjoining room and exchanged clothes, and, going out, we got into a carriage which the young man had there, and started for his house. We had both taken too much liquor to navigate a horse well, and at the first start had some narrow escapes. We had gone about a mile, when we came into a clearing, where the road was not easily discernible. We were going about twelve knots an hour when the chaise all at once sunk into a ditch, and stopping suddenly, I was thrown forward on to the horse's back. The horse breaking away, and jumping at the same time, somewhat disturbed my equilibrium, and I fell into the mud, while he went off at full speed. In a short time I came to myself, when hearing a noise near me, I thought I was on sentry, and cried out, 'Who comes there?'

'Why, don't you know me?' said my companion.

'I don't think that you would know *me*,' I said, 'for I am in the mud, and my, or I would say your clothes are pretty well daubed. But where are you?'

'Well, I am in the mud too, and I believe that I have broken my wrist.'

'Well, I profess to be something of a doctor, if you will just come and pull me out, I will see to your wrist.' I was beginning to get pretty sober, as the cold mud and water had a wonderful influence on me.

'I am out,' said my companion, and coming to where I lay, he took hold of my hand and pulled me out.

One glance at my military clothes showed me that they were

none the better for this night's excursion, and I saw a number of places torn, but I consoled myself with the thought that there were none here to inspect them. After brushing off the mud, we started for our horse, but not finding him, we continued on our way. We soon arrived at the young man's house, and found that the horse had arrived all right. My companion went up to the door and knocked. The door was opened by his father, when he said, 'Can you accommodate two poor soldiers here to-night?' The old gentleman said that he did not think that he could, and was just pushing the door to, when the young man said, 'I have no place to sleep to-night, and it is rainy, and I should like to sleep on the floor,' upon which the old man opened the door wide, and we went into a room where the young man's mother was, who eyed us rather narrowly, and then turned to her son who had on my clothes, and exclaimed, 'My son,' and fainted. She soon came to, and I was treated finely by the old people, and then started to go back, the young man showing me the way.

The next morning we resumed our march and soon arrived at Pictou, and went to the jail and found the prisoner there. As it was night, and I had an order on a tavern for refreshments and lodgings, I left the jail with my men, and put up.

CHAPTER XV.

THE next morning we went to the jail and saw the sergeant, who gave the prisoner into my hands, saying, 'Here is a deserter from the army; by orders that I have received, I give him over into your hands.' I took the prisoner and put on the handcuffs, and started for Halifax. After going about a mile, I told the prisoner that if he would give me his word not to attempt to escape, I would take the handcuffs off. He replied that he would not give me any trouble,' and I took them off.

That day we stopped at the place that we had been billeted to, and I was troubled how to take care of my prisoner. I felt that I had something at stake, and thought that it was of as much importance as if I had a thousand to look after. After much reflection upon the subject, I thought of a plan; I therefore slept with the prisoner, and had my left hand handcuffed to his right one, feeling pretty confident that my prisoner could not get away without my knowing something about it.

I think that this way of securing a prisoner was original, but I would not recommend it, especially if a person wishes to sleep much. Every time the prisoner turned, it would cut my wrist, and every time I turned, it would cause the prisoner to cry out, and *vice versa.* To say that I felt as tired in the morning as I did the night before, would convey no idea of my condition. If I had been three days and nights upon a forced march, without closing my eyes to sleep, I could not have felt worse, and I thought that the next time I took a prisoner, I would let him go before I would torture myself as I did that night.

The next morning we resumed our march and arrived without any adventures to our quarters, where we stopped for the night. The next day was the Sabbath, and I made up my mind to stop at this place during the day. I therefore had my prisoner lodged in jail, telling the keeper at the same time that I should look to him for his safe keeping, and then went to church. After meeting I went to the jail, as I felt somewhat anxious, as some prisoners had made their escape from the jail where I had put my man. I found all right, but the man wished to come out and walk around some, he said, so I told the jailer to let him out, and I presented bayonet, and the prisoner marched before. We had gone some fifty yards, and had got out of the main streets, when the prisoner turned around rather fierce at me, and started to run. I cocked my firelock, and sung out for him to stop, or he was a dead man, which he quickly did, and coming up with him, I told him to 'right about face,' and marched for the jail. After giving him into the hands of the jailer, I went to the tavern, and found that my two men were drinking in the bar-room with two deserters that were there, and they agreed among themselves to rob and kill me, and then to leave with the money, as I had some little with me. One of my men that was with me was an old soldier that had been in the army fourteen years, and he thought to himself, that in seven years more he would receive a pension for life, and he therefore determined to have nothing to do in the affair, and came and told me the whole story. One of these deserters was the same man that took care of me when I was sick in the hospital, and took my Spanish dollar and exchanged boots with me, and I can assure you that I had no very friendly feelings toward him at that time. I told my escort, or the one that informed me of the plot, that he had better appear the same as if nothing had been said about it, and when they came to my room I would be ready for them. This conversation was in the bar-room, and seeing one of the deserters coming in, my escort stepped out of the way. As he came in, a thought struck me, and I spoke to him and said, 'Did you not see two escorts who are in the village in search of you and your companion? now, take my advice, and leave as quick as possible, or you will be taken.' He turned pale as I was telling him about the escort, and left immediately, and I have never seen either of them since.

The next morning I commenced my march, and reached Halifax after being absent sixteen days, fourteen of which, if I am not mistaken, it rained. I lodged my prisoner in jail, and he was kept there six months, and was then sent to England, where he was confined in prison about three months, and was then liberated, and went to America.

The next guard that I mounted was over the prisoners. The sergeant-major picked me out for this guard, as he said, because it was an easy one, I having just returned from a hard march. I had to go on guard at four o'clock in the afternoon, and stop till eight o'clock, and all this time I was not allowed to speak aloud or laugh. I had to sit on a seat erected on one side of the room, and on this seat I could look over all the prisoners. On the opposite side was the provost-sergeant, who had charge of the prisoners. When I went into the room where the prisoners were, all in rows, I noticed many that I knew, and had been with many times on a spree; and as the prisoners were not allowed to speak, those that knew me began to make signs. I went up and took my seat, but it seemed a strange place for me. All the prisoners were facing me, and one, a drummer, a comic and mimicking fellow, looked very sober at me all the while. Those around him began to smile, and I began now to comprehend his meaning. The fellow was pretending that I was a preacher. I burst out into a loud laugh, in which all the prisoners joined, which astonished the provost-sergeant, and he said that he would report me to the commanding officer. One of the prisoners now spoke and said that the provost-sergeant had no right to speak, and general confusion ensued. This guard was the hardest one I ever had.

The next guard I went upon was the citadel guard. Previous to my mounting this, an officer belonging to the Scotch highlanders brought in thirty-six deserters, who were transported, and put in the dry-room, a place where criminals were

· kept. The building was of granite, and the windows were secured by strong iron bars, to prevent the prisoners escaping. A sergeant went every two hours through the room where the prisoners were, and with a piece of iron would let it strike against the bars as he passed, to see if any of them had been sawed into. One of the prisoners, during the intervals of the sergeant's visits, sawed a bar of iron off, and made a passage large enough to admit a person, and through this quite a number escaped. One large man in endeavoring to get through, got wedged in, so that he could not get back, and the other prisoners finding they could not get him out, informed the sentry, who gave the alarm, and soon the whole guard turned out, and opening the door of the dry-room, saw the man fast in the window. We pulled him back, but I certainly thought it would kill him, and then started in pursuit of those that had escaped. We were not successful, and although detachments were sent throughout the surrounding country, we never heard from them. How they escaped out of the fortress we never knew, for after getting out of the window, they had to drop some ten feet to the ground, and then they were inside of a granite wall some ten feet high; this they managed to scale, and thus effected their escape.

There was a place called 'Waterloo Tavern,' kept by a man named Murphy; it was a low, miserable place, and one night a man belonging to the sappers and miners went to this place, and having considerable money about him, was murdered and thrown into a well. A short time after, his body was found there, and so enraged were the sappers and miners that they determined to have their revenge. They commenced to lay a train of powder a number of yards distant, and extended it to the tavern. They were some time in accomplishing the undertaking, and one dark night they ignited the powder, and instantly an explosion took place, and the building was at once enveloped in flames. The bugler gave the alarm of fire, and the engines were hurried out, and great exertions were pretended to be made to subdue the flames, but it was burnt down, together with some persons in the building.

CHAPTER XVI.

In our company there was a sergeant named Pullinger. He was a smart, shrewd man, and had a good education. He was the color sergeant, and was intrusted with a considerable amount of money, being considered a very honest man. He and a man named Smith were determined to leave the army. Before leaving, the sergeant bought himself a splendid suit of clothes, and a footman's suit for Smith; and watching an opportunity, made their escape, the sergeant taking considerable money that was intrusted to him. They passed off on the road as gentleman and servant, and a number of detachments of soldiers who were in pursuit of them, passed them on the road, but as the sergeant was dressed finely, they did not dare to say anything to him, although they saw that he was about the same height as one of the deserters.

They came one day to a guard, and Smith, the footman, was ahead; the guard stopped him and began to inspect him, when he told them that his master was a few steps behind, and that he would settle with them for stopping his servant; and upon this they let him go. The sergeant soon came along and they stopped him, but he told them that he would report their proceedings to the commander for stopping a gentleman on the road, and I wished to know if they intended to insult him so much as to stop him upon the pretense that he was a deserter. He would have them to know that he was a gentleman, and that he would make them smart for their behavior. And feeling somewhat ashamed, the soldiers let him off, and with his footman he escaped to the States; and now lives in the State of New York.

There was a sergeant in the 7th Regiment, a very strong and courageous man, named E———. I well remember receiving some pretty severe threshings from his hands, although not so large a man as I was. He was a great drinker, and sometimes would come up into our mess and get so drunk, that we would have to carry him to his quarters. In the Russian war, the sergeant was on the field of battle, and fell, pierced with nine balls, and left on the field for dead. He came to, and getting up, took a firelock that was near, and, loading it, walked up to the enemy's position where there was a sentry on guard over three prisoners; he fired and shot the sentry, and the prisoners escaped. They went toward their quarters, and while going, a field-piece was fired at them; the ball grazed the sergeant's foot, taking the sole of his boot completely off. When he arrived at his quarters the balls were extracted, and he was soon after sent to England with a pension.

The Queen and her maids of honor received him, her Majesty making some remarks, and, speaking of his brave conduct, offered him a home in England, or he might go to Halifax where his wife was, and make his home there. The sergeant, thinking that there was no place like 'sweet home,' went to Halifax, and as he left, one of the maids of honor walked arm in arm with him to the place of embarkation, where the Queen presented him with a white silk handkerchief, saying, 'that it was hemmed with her own hands,' and was given to him as a mark of her esteem for his bravery.

We remained in Halifax about twelve months, and then were ordered to St. John, New Brunswick. We immediately went and took our respective quarters. Soon after we came to St. John I was appointed sergeant; this was another bad thing for me, it gave me still greater liberties. I went in company with the sergeants, who were all drinking fellows, and I had the privilege of drinking to the greatest excess. I had been here but a short time, when one evening as I was walking down one of the streets, I saw in a window on the opposite side, three

First Meeting with Wife.

young ladies, who, upon seeing me, looked up, and one of them said, 'Look at that nigger soldier.'

On hearing this remark, I felt vexed. It did not surprise me, however, for I had burnt my face so badly whilst in the warm climate, that I was almost black. I thought to myself that I would marry the one that made the remark about me.

The young woman who had spoken thus, was the daughter of a lady that lived in great style and moved in the first circles, and how to get acquainted with her was now the question. I knew a soldier in the guard-room that could write, and I told him that I wanted him to write me a letter, which he accordingly did, and I sent it. I received an answer the next day that checked my ardor a little. It read thus, 'How dare you, sir, have the presumption to address me a note?' Short and sweet, yet I determined to persevere in my suit, and get acquainted with her.

Passing her house one day, I saw her in the garden, and went around to the back side of the house, and walked softly up behind her as she was picking off a rose. She heard my step, and, turning around, was upon the point of hurrying off to the house, when I said, 'Madam, you will excuse my presumption, (I never heard the word before I heard it read in the letter that the young lady sent me, but I thought that I must bring out every thing that I could, in my opening speech; I had got it all by heart to deliver some time before I met her in the garden,) in entering your garden so unceremoniously, but the beauty of your flowers attracted my attention, and I hope you will excuse my boldness.' She pardoned me, and showed me around the garden, and soon after I left, feeling well pleased with my success.

While at St. John, I was appointed caterer of the sergeant's mess, and to sell rum to the soldiers. This berth gave me a pretty good opportunity to drink as much as I pleased. I drank up all my pay, and all my profits on the liquor, and was very dissipated whilst I held that berth. We used to play cards when not on duty, and one night one of the officer's servants came in to play, and we all drank very hard. The servant made a mis-play, and I told him of it, which made him angry, and he reached across the table and struck me in the face. I had drank so much liquor that I was under its influence considerably, and this enraged me. I jumped up and put the light out, and cleared the room of all excepting the servant; and now I was determined to give him a threshing. He grabbed me by the hair with one hand, and with the other he had me by the throat. In endeavoring to free myself from his grasp, I left a large portion of my hair in his hand. Then I was at liberty, and springing toward him, I seized him, and hurrying to the door which was open, I was just upon the point of pitching him headlong over the verandah, down some twelve feet to the pavement below, when I was arrested by one of the company. When I got sobered down a little, I felt extremely glad that I was stopped from doing an act whereby I have no doubt I should have taken human life, or been the means of it.

The next morning I was awakened in my cot by a tap on the shoulder. I knew what it meant well; when a soldier has been insulted, and wishes satisfaction, he goes early in the morning and taps the person on the shoulder who has insulted him as a signal to get up and go fight it out. The instant I felt the touch, I was awake and knew what was wanted; he was the one that I shoved out of the room the night before. I tapped my chum, Tim Wilkinson, upon the shoulder, and asked him to go with me, and he arose, and we went out. 'How much is this for?' said I. 'For a quart,' replied the sergeant. (The first one that received a clip in the face, would have to pay for a quart of rum.) I gave him the first clip, and thus wounded honor was appeased, and the satisfaction deemed complete, and he paid the liquor and all was settled; and to tell the truth I felt well pleased to get off so well, for he was a powerful man, and a superior boxer, and would have been likely to have laid me on the ground, if he had struck me.

Such scenes as these were very common with us whilst I was caterer for the mess; and many were the skirmishes we had.

I was once sent with a company to take charge of the magazine at Fort Howe, Portland, St. Johns.

We had a room up-stairs where we used to play cards, and many of the citizens used to come and play with the soldiers, bringing liquor with them, and they would sometimes get drunk, and quarrel with one another. One fellow who came there had lost both legs above the knees, and he used to get drunk every time he came. One night I went with him to his home, as he was so intoxicated that he could not go alone, and, in returning to my quarters, the police stepped up to arrest me (thinking that I was a drunken soldier, as they had just arrested some), but I turned and made fight, knocking down the one that had seized me, and escaped to my barracks.

One of my soldiers, soon after my escape from the police, told me that he saw a soldier of Number Two Company in a rum-shop in citizen's dress, and that he intended to desert, and if I did not arrest and confine him, he would report me to the commanding officer. I went down to the shop where the soldier was, and went in and seized him, and told him that he was my prisoner in the Queen's name, and with some considerable difficulty dragged him into a back room, and then called upon the keeper to watch him whilst I went after some of my men. I soon got them, and then carried him to the main guard, where he was confined. About this time the Orangemen in the province were making great demonstrations, and there was a good deal of ill-feeling between them and the Irish Catholics. The Irish citizens had a large banner flying in town, at the foot of the hill on which Fort Howe was located. The Orangemen formed in line, and the leader—representing King William— dashed along on his high-mettled charger, and, drawing his sword, cleft down the flag. The Irish Catholics immediately commenced firing upon them, wounding and killing a number. The Orangemen retreated to their head-quarters, and, arming themselves, returned and fired upon them indiscriminately, some of them pitching headlong into the streets from the windows where they stood watching the advancing column. The havoc was fearful on both sides. The infantry and artillery were called out, and charged upon both parties and drove them off.

The Orangemen determined to burn the Catholic church; and the priest getting wind of it, came to me and told me the night they had fixed upon for destroying his church, and begged me to prevent it. I told him if the church was fired it would blow up my magazine, and I would lose every man before it should be done. He seized me by the hand and said he could trust me. I immediately placed a sentry at the church, and notified my men what would be attempted after I had received grand rounds, and the guard had turned in. And here it may interest some to explain what is meant by 'grand rounds.'

A field-officer comes. The sentry challenges. The officer answers, Grand rounds. Sentry replies, Stand grand rounds, and calls guard, turn out. The sergeant falls in the guard, then takes two men as escort and marches up in front of grand rounds, ports arms, and says, Who comes there? Officer answers, *Rounds.* Sergeant says, What rounds? Officer answers, *Grand* rounds. Sergeant says, Stand grand rounds—advance one, and give the countersign. The sergeant receives the countersign at the point of the bayonet, in a low tone. Sergeant answers, All right, and orders the guard to present arms. Officer asks, 'Is guard all right?' Answer, 'All right, sir.' The officer then says, Turn guard in. The sergeant then orders, Guard, shoulder arms, right face; longe arms—a term used for dismissed. Soon after having received grand rounds, as explained, there was seen a crowd of men slowly winding their way along a narrow defile at the foot of the hill. My sentry challenged, 'Who comes there?' No answer. We were on the watch for them. Sentry said, 'All's not right.' I took two men, advanced and challenged, and no answer. I did so three times. I called

my men,—Face to the right about, double march to the rear.
I then ordered them to fall in with the front section, and gave
the word, Forward men by your right—prepare to *charge—
charge bayonets*, and my men, on the double quick, drove the
poor fellows pell-mell down the hill like frightened sheep.

This act, which saved the church from being burned, secured
for me the good-will of the priest, which was turned to a good
account afterward, as will appear in my escape from the British
army. I was ordered to stop at this magazine one month, and
as the time had now expired, I returned to the barracks.

8

CHAPTER XVII.

THERE was in the company to which I belonged, a sergeant named Smith, who one night broke out of barracks, and on the same night, unknown to him, a private broke out. They met in a rum-shop, and getting into difficulty, came to hard words. The sergeant left the shop, and the private followed, and overtaking him, they got to fighting, and as this was near the main guard, the sentry gave the alarm, and as I was on guard at the time, I ran to the place, and seizing the sergeant, separated them. The private, taking a bottle from his pocket, was in the act of striking me, when I gave him a blow which knocked him down. This sergeant had always favored me when I got into any scrapes, and he told me to bear in mind how he had always befriended me. I told him that I would get him out all right, and delivered the private into his hands, and told him to keep him, and I would get some men and take him to the guard-room. I soon brought a file of men, and took the private, and carried him to the guard-room. The next day he was brought before the commanding officer. He said that the sergeant had also broken out of barracks. 'We are not here to try sergeant Smith, but to try you,' said the commanding officer; and he was ordered to be put into the cells for seven days.

Soon after this affair, the same sergeant, who was a good friend to me, was on guard, and I wished to go out of barracks, and he gave me a permit; but on returning in the morning, as I was climbing over the fence, to get into barracks, the sentry saw me, and as he was the same soldier that was out with the sergeant, and whom I had taken prisoner, he gave the alarm;

but before the guard came out, I was in my room. Two sergeants came into my room, and finding me there, said that the sentry had reported me out of barracks. The next day I was brought before the commanding officer, and as the sentry brought no proof against me, he failed to make out his case. I ordered him to be confined for telling a falsehood, and he got seven days more in the cells.

I was taken sick about this time, and was confined to the hospital about three weeks, before I was able to be upon duty again. This sickness was owing in a great measure to the dissolute life I led.

One night I wanted to go out of barracks, and the sergeant agreed not to inform against me, and I went out, but had not been gone long, before he reported that I had broken out of barracks. An escort was sent after me, and I was taken back a prisoner, and the next day brought before the commanding officer, who ordered that one of my badges be taken from my coat. I felt this more than I should if I had been cowhided, and I got a soldier to write to my 'intended,' and inform her of the circumstances. She wrote me an encouraging answer, but I could not bear to be thus disgraced, and I determined to take advantage of the first opportunity to make my escape. I got the young soldier to write to my 'intended,' informing her of my intention to escape from the army. The young soldier was one that I could trust—we were firm friends. I received an answer, advising me not to make the venture, as she would soon, if I wished it, purchase my discharge; but I would not think of such a thing. I had seen enough of the army, and when sober, how to escape was always uppermost in my thoughts.

I was encouraged by an incident that happened about this time; three men who deserted and went into the woods were surrounded, or rather every place where the deserters wished to come out was guarded. After remaining there some six days, being nearly exhausted with hunger, they came out and gave themselves up to a kidnapper, as the soldiers termed him, (one who caught deserters and returned them to barracks). He gave them something to eat, and then secured them that night. The next morning he tied their hands together, and taking them into a wagon, started for the barracks. One of the prisoners got his hands loose as they were riding along, and untied the prisoners near him, and then knocked the kidnapper off his seat into the road, while another prisoner seized the reins. The kidnapper drew his pistols, but before he could use them, he was seized by two of the deserters and bound. They tied him to a tree, and gave him two dozen lashes with the whip, and then getting into the wagon, rode into the States. They then got out of the wagon, and started the horse toward his home.

Some person liberated the kidnapper, and I was upon sentry when he came into the barracks and told his story, but he did not receive much consolation from the soldiers, who only laughed at his misfortunes, and wished that he might get another whipping.

Monday, the regiment was ordered to Halifax. At twelve o'clock M., I came off guard and went to dinner, and then I told Tim Wilkinson, my chum, that I intended to escape, and gave him the key to my chest and all my things, and told him to keep silent about it. In a short time the orderly came to inspect the dinner, and I knew that now was my best time, as all the men were at dinner, so I went out of my room into the yard. There was a high fence with iron spikes in the top (the fence was eight feet high), and springing up, I got hold with my hands and drew myself up and jumped over. Here I had to get over a wooden picket fence, which I did somewhat in a hurry, and hastened to see my 'intended.' I arrived at the house, and told her that I had left the barracks for good. The mother of the young lady (her father being dead) seemed much pleased with my endeavoring to make my escape, and I have no doubt wished that I would get off so far that I would never trouble her daughter again, and made me up a bundle of clothes, and gave me a sovereign, and wished me good luck. I told her that I was afraid to go through the streets with a bundle in my hand, and asked her if she would not let her daughter go to Portland, about one and a half miles distant, and carry my bundle for me. After some time, I prevailed on her to let her daughter carry it, and we started off, her daughter going some ten yards before me. We had gone but a short distance before she turned toward me, and said, 'There's a picket of soldiers coming this way, and they are after you.' They had been to Portland, St. John, but not finding me there, were returning. I looked up, and saw them on the top of a little hill, not more than fifty yards distant. 'What will you do?' said my intended, 'you will have to give yourself up.'

'No,' I said, 'I will show them a trick.'

There were two streets at my left, that ran nearly parallel, and led down to the sea-side, which were about one hundred feet apart. I started to run down the one that was nearest to me, and the picket of soldiers started down the other; seeing them go down the other street, I turned back, and came up with my 'intended,' and kept on for Portland. As I passed the street, I could not help laughing to see them run down the street in pursuit of me.

I arrived at Portland without any trouble, and went to see a man that I knew would help me. I found him, and he told me that he would assist me in every way he could.

CHAPTER XVIII.

Before I left Portland, I wanted to get married, and I had tried to get a license at the Register's office, but could not without the consent of my commanding officer. I went out, and fell in with two Irishmen, and asked them to go to the Register's office and get a license in my name. They succeeded in getting it, and I hurried back to where I left my 'intended,' and with her I went to a Methodist clergyman and was married, and giving my marriage certificate to my newly made wife, I bade her adieu, and left for the man with whom I had stopped. I exchanged clothes and gave him my military suit, and when it was dark, started off.

In the mean time the regiment had started for Halifax, but had left a number of men, who, with the police, were searching the country around for me.

Before going into the woods I went to a Scotchman's house and asked for something to eat, but was refused, and I went on until I came to a house where an Irishman lived, who gave me two potatoes and a piece of fish. I told him that I had just come from the house below. 'Well, that fellow will inform against you,' he said, knowing that I had escaped from the army; and, taking out a gun, 'Here,' said he, 'take this to defend yourself, and I will run the risk of your returning it.' I took the gun, promising to return it if I lived, and, thanking him, left the house and went into the forest.

It was about 12 o'clock at night when I entered the woods, and although darkness covered the earth, it seemed all bright to me. I was now my own man, and felt like singing, but I had to keep silence here, knowing soldiers were stationed all around the forest. Having found a place to lie down, I slept well, and when I awoke the sun was high in the heavens. In my haste to make my escape, I never once thought of taking any provisions with me, but it was in the fall of the year, when berries were ripe, or else I must have perished or given myself up. I found berries enough, and managed the first day to get a good living, and made up my mind to stay in the woods as long as I could.

The second night I slept on the watch, knowing that not a man of the company would come near to take me in the day-time, but fearing they might see and watch me until night came on, and after I was asleep, seize me. I did not get much sleep; every noise I heard aroused me, and I would jump up and present my gun at what I imagined was a man.

The second day I picked some more berries, but found that they did not satisfy my cravings. I had been used to liquor every day, and to be deprived of it now was as bad to me as taking away my bread, and I hardly know which I missed the most. I wandered around all the first part of the day, and as the sun began to sink in the heavens, I thought I would try my luck and see if I could not get out safely. I had taken partic-ular notice of the woods and the lay of the land, so that I could find my way out, and, taking my course, started to go back. I walked quite briskly for about half an hour, and began to think that it was time for me to get out of the forest; but I kept on some time. I had no idea that I had gone so far into the woods, but after walking some distance further, I could see the open fields.

I went along now cautiously, looking upon all sides to see if any one was near; but not seeing any person, I went out into a field. Finding myself not far from the place where I entered the woods, I crossed the field to the road, and as I got near it I saw two men coming. I thought if I went back across the field they would surely see me, so I laid down beside the fence, and as they came along I heard one say, 'He will be shrewd enough not to fall into their hands, I'll warrant you.' 'But,' says the other, 'how can he get out? the places are all guarded, and he cannot help being taken'——and here I could not understand what was said.

Well, I thought to myself, my chance is a hard one, and getting up, I looked about me and saw a wagon coming. I must keep still at present, or I shall be taken. What a fool, I said to myself, am I for coming out here in open day. I might have known better, if I had stopped to consider, than to leave the woods. I waited until the wagon had passed, and then thought I would make for the forest, but I saw another wagon coming, and I was kept there until night, when I returned to the forest, feeling thankful that it once more afforded me a secure retreat.

I managed to get some berries, which partially satisfied my craving for food, and having selected a place to rest, I broke off some twigs, and spreading them around, I laid down to sleep.

I staid in this wood just one week, when I made up my mind to get out and go down where my wife lived and get something to eat, and run the risk of being taken, as I was almost starved.

I went to the edge of the wood, and when it was dark took a back route, and went down to what was called 'Lower Cove,' and as I was going through the streets I met two of the sergeants. They knew me the moment they saw me, and I started on a run, into my wife's uncle's house, the sergeants after me. I ran out of the back door, down to where my wife lived, and went into the house and got something to eat and a cup of tea, and bidding my wife good-by, I hurried out of the house, telling her that I would see her again before long. I went down the street (it being dark and the soldiers after me) upon all-fours, like a dog, until I came to the sea-side, and keeping near the water's edge, walked along until I came to a high cliff. I swam around the several cliffs, near a mile, until I came to Marsh Bridge, and dragged myself upon dry land,

Escape from Indians.

chilled and exhausted; and here I was a little bewildered, and crossed the bridge, taking my right-hand road instead of the the left, as I should have done, before I went over. I trudged on in the dark until I was suddenly seized by some Indians and taken prisoner by them to their encampment.

The English were at this time paying the Indians five pounds per man for every deserter they could bring in. Of course the red-skins were *fast friends* to us lonely wanderers, and were ready *to take us in.* I was made to lie down between two strong fellows, for the night, to sleep if I could. One thing was sure, if I did not sleep, I played sleep to the best of my ability. The Indians had been out on a hunt during the day, and being pretty tired, were not long in getting to noddle's island; of which I was notified by their loud snoring. Generally speaking, snoring was very offensive to me; but I must confess, under the *peculiar* state of things, no music was so sweet as that made by the snouts of these red men. And I said inwardly, blow your nasal organs louder and longer, and keep doing so until distance lends enchantment.

I arose, first on one knee, and then on the other; and, looking round, I saw a stick of wood against the door, with which I thought I would brain the rascals; but wisely decided their blood should not be on my head if I could get off without it. I finally succeeded in getting outside the wigwam without waking my captives, and escaped, by the way I came, down to Marsh bridge; and crossing, got upon the right road, and under cover of night, made my way rapidly up the river, into the woods to the house of two Catholics, who had been made my true friends by my charge on the Orangemen and saving their church.

These two men promised to help me escape down the St. John river, in a small boat, to the steamer 'Maid of Erin;' lying at St. John, and bound for the States. A hiding-place was prepared for me in the woods, where I had to remain several days, coming out occasionally to get something to eat. One morning, about three o'clock, these faithful fellows came and took me down to the steamer, where I was stowed down in the coal-hole. The priest who came to me at Fort Howe to save his chapel, had enjoined upon these men to save me from being retaken, under the penalty of being anathematized by the church, if they were not faithful to their trust. On reaching the steamer, they told the man who knew of my coming on board, if he informed against me it would not be safe for him to appear in St. John again. I knew that before the steamer sailed officers would be on board to search for deserters, so I dug down into the coal, covering myself entirely with it, until the officers had made their search and left.

After the steamer had got under way, I showed myself on deck, and the ticket master coming along, wanted my fare, which was two dollars. Having but one dollar, I got the helmsman to lend me another, and told him that my wife would pay him.

I intended to get out at Eastport, but as there was a severe storm, the boat could not land, and I went to Portland, Maine. When the boat touched the wharf I jumped out, and asked the captain if I was on 'Yankee land?' 'Yes,' says the captain, staring at me, as I jumped up and gave three cheers, 'but are you Sergeant Ambler?' 'That's my name,' I said. The captain turned and went below.

Now I felt that I was free, and, turning around, hardly knew what to do, I felt so happy; it had been so long since I had enjoyed freedom, that I was like a bird let out of a cage. I felt that I was in a new world; the great country that I had heard of from my youth up, and for which I had sighed when in the lonely hours of night I kept my sentry watch, or when beneath a scorching sun I marched many a weary mile, was now before me. This free country (of which so many songs were heard around the tap-room bar, as we would quaff the ale, and jovially pass the time away) I had now reached.

As I stood upon the wharf, what prospects seemed to be before me! Everything looked beautiful, and I thought that at last I had reached a land where I could enjoy life. No more court-martials to be tried before, no more shall I be brought before commanding officers, to answer to charges brought against me. And above all these, I thought, no more liquor to take away my reason, and make me incapable of performing the duties incumbent upon me. No more restraints upon my actions, I can now live as I choose, and go where I wish. Had I been permitted to look into the future, I should have shuddered at the gloomy wretched prospect before me, and should have turned with disgust from the country that looked so beautiful, and returned to the army. How thankful should we be that the future, with its weal or woe, cannot be revealed to us.

I thought that I stood in the same position that the Pilgrim fathers did. They left their native land for this country, to free themselves from tyranny and oppression. But I thought again, that no friends welcomed them, and the bustle that greeted me they did not witness. They landed indeed in a strange land; the wild animal was lord there, and forest trees covered these shores. How great the change! Friends were here to welcome me, who had escaped from the army.

And as these thoughts came upon me, I could not but uncover my head and pay a tribute of respect to the noble land that sheltered and defended me and so many of my countrymen. Only those who have passed through the scenes that I have can realize the emotions that were stirred within me as I stepped upon the land of freedom.

CHAPTER XIX.

I WENT up into the city, and as I came near the sugar-house I met a woman that knew me, and she said, 'There is Sergeant Ambler coming.' Her husband belonged to the artillery, and had, a short time before, made his escape from St. John.

She asked me into her house and gave me something to eat. With what eagerness I seized the food and devoured it, for I had been without so long, that I was nearly starved. When I went on board the steamboat I had a small piece of bread, which I ate, and that was all I had eaten for three days, I now felt very hungry and weak.

I informed her that I had got away from the army at last, and that I supposed it was 'easier for her to get along here than it was in the other country, when she stood behind the tap-room bar—she used to sell liquor in St. John. 'What do you mean?' she asked.

'Why, that they do not sell rum here in this place.'

She laughed, and said, 'I guess that you'll find as much liquor as you will want here.'

'Why,' I said, 'I thought there was a law here that forbids liquor selling. I have heard the people in St. John speak of it.'

'You wait here a short time and you can judge for yourself,' she said.

I remained a short time there, and soon her husband came, who appeared very glad to see me, and after lighting our pipes, I told over my adventures that I had passed through in making my escape. He also related to me what success he had met

with in the 'Yankee land,' as we designated the United States.
I informed him of my marriage, and that my wife was in St. John,
and that if I obtained work here I intended to send for her.

'Well, come Ambler,' he said, 'let me show you around a
little,' and he took me out into a back room and pulled out a
keg from under the bed, and drew off some liquor, and filling
up a glass, presented it to me, which I drank. It had been so
long since I had drank, that it created an intolerable thirst for
more, and before I was fully aware of it, I was intoxicated.

I stopped in that back room that night, and the next morning went to find work, and was successful in getting a chance
on the railroad, shoveling gravel. I received one dollar per
day, which I thought was great pay, and that I could live and
drink like a hero, not taking into consideration that things
were more than twice as high here as they were in England.
I worked here, with nothing on my feet but a pair of slippers,
in the water sometimes knee-deep, but my 'boss,' taking pity
upon me, gave me a nice pair of thick boots. I worked here
about three weeks before I settled, and found that a good part
of what money I received, would have to go to pay for the
liquor that I drank, as I took it regularly, night and morning,
and I found that it was sold some higher here per glass.

While I was at work here, I sent for my wife, telling her that
I had obtained work, and that I should like for her to come on.

My wife's father had lived at D——, and owned a fine farm
there. He was a ship-builder and transacted considerable business, but he died in the midst of it, and thus left many unset-
tled accounts, and as there was no one to look out for the
property, it was soon reduced, and the fine farm had to be sold.

The family then moved to St. John, and as they went in the
first society and lived in good style, they had to keep up ap-
pearances, which they did, by selling piece after piece of their
furniture, as it could be spared. When I first became acquainted with my wife, they were somewhat reduced in circumstances.

My wife was not aware that I was such a drinking man as I

was; if she had been she would never have come to Portland to live with me. I had always kept pretty sober when I was going to see her; and if, when under the influence of liquor, I met her upon the street, I would keep as distant as possible, and take the first opportunity to absent myself; and although she was told by others, she could not believe that I was as bad as they represented me. I soon received a letter from her, telling me that she would come in the boat such a day. I was at the wharf on the arrival of the boat, and met her, and we went to the place that I had stopped and remained there that night; but as they could not accommodate us, and as my wife had brought some furniture with her, we took a rent in an attic. It was a miserable place. We could see out through the roof, and were never long in finding out when it rained.

I did not like my situation on the railroad, and went to the gas-works, and obtained a situation in the purifying house, where I received the same pay. Soon after, I moved into a tenement in the house of my employer, named Barker, who took quite an interest in me, and did many favors for me, which I never shall forget.

In a short time, I moved into the upper part of the city, into an old house, and while there my wife was taken sick. During her sickness I still had to work, leaving her alone until I returned from my labor. She was very sick, and while thus she made me promise that I would leave off drinking. In a short time, she began to recover, but when she got about I forgot my promise, and drank the same as ever. The house we lived in was so cold that we could not keep ourselves comfortable, and I therefore got a tenement down by the sugar-house; and soon after I moved, my wife's mother came to visit us.

It was now near the spring election, and in the shop where I obtained my liquor all of the talk was upon that subject; and we were told that if such a man was elected, that we should get no liquor, and that if we were suspected of keeping any at our houses, that we were liable to have our homes searched. I wished, from the bottom of my heart (as all poor drunkards do), that all strong drinks were out of the way; but then the rum-seller told us that assembled there, that our rights were assailed; and as I was a great stickler for rights, of course my indignation was aroused, and with the rest I loudly asserted that I would never submit to have my home searched. This was a constant theme for some time before the election, and although I was not a voter, I felt as much interest in the result as any one. The day of the election came, and I was treated, as about all were, to plenty of rum; and we were told that at night they —that is, the rummies, were going to give Neal Dow* a serenade. I was in for it, with the rest of them, as I was intoxicated, and at night I was amongst the gang of ruffians (as I look upon them now) and went with them to his residence. There we commenced our unearthly strains, and made the air resound with our noise, and the night hideous. No notice was taken of our demoniac exhibitions, and at last we left disgusted, or I was, with the evening's entertainment.

I drank so hard that my wife's mother could not put up with it, and she got me to go with her to New York, where she had a son. When I arrived there, her son showed me around the city and the suburbs; but as they lived in good style, and as I was not used to it, I did not feel at home; so the next morning, before they were up, I started off, and went to an island near, where there was a regiment of soldiers, and saw many there that I knew. They wanted me to go with them to California, as that was the place they were ordered to; but I would not go, and I soon left the island. I since learned that every man of the regiment was lost on their passage. I took the steamboat for Boston, and, arriving there, I went into the fort, and with some other soldiers got intoxicated, and hardly knew myself where I did pass the time; but I stopped there three days, and then took the boat for Portland, and when I arrived there, I had not a cent in my pocket. The 4th of July, 1852, I

* I have had, since that time, the pleasure of asking the gentleman's pardon.

was living in Portland, and the morning after, having nothing in the house to eat, I started out, and in going up the street I found twenty-five cents, and a short distance further on I picked up twenty-five cents more. With this money, I went into a provision store, and bought me some beef, and carried it home. I obtained a chance to work in the foundry, and while there, I used to drink hard, and neglect home. About this time an incident happened that came near depriving me of my liberty that I prized so dear. I was going to the depot one day, when a soldier met me that had escaped from the same regiment that I did, and he said, 'Sergeant Ambler, your old captain has just gone aboard the Admiral.'

'Well,' I said, 'I will go down and see him.'

'If you do, you will be taken,' said the deserter, 'for he is after ——, and a number of others that have escaped.'

'I will risk his taking me, and I am going down to see him,' I said, and starting off, I went down to the wharf, and went on board the steamer; but not seeing the captain on deck, I went into the cabin, and saw him. The moment he saw me, he said, 'Ah! Sergeant Ambler, how do you do?'

I took off my hat, as I was accustomed to do in the army, and saluted him, and said that I was pretty well; and looking toward him at the same time, I noticed his wife in the stateroom, and being acquainted with her, I went in and spoke to her; and as I turned to come out, I found the door fast. I put my shoulder against it and broke it open, and as I stepped out into the cabin, the captain said, 'You are my prisoner.' Paying no attention to his words, I hurried out of the cabin and jumped upon the wharf, and then I turned to my former captain that had followed me, and said, 'Good by, captain, I will meet you again,' and then turned to go home. The excitement had taken my strength almost away. Arriving home, I found my wife almost crazy, as some one had told her that I was taken a prisoner, and was carried off in the Admiral; but my presence put an end to her grief, and I felt pleased in getting away so easily.

CHAPTER XX.

I did not feel quite at home in Portland after my adventure with the captain, and one day I was going toward the depot, when I saw a loom. I was somewhat surprised, as I had not seen one since I left England, and inquired of a man where it was going. He informed me that it was going to the mills in Saco, Me. I went home to my wife with an idea in my head, and telling her that I meant to follow that loom, I found her perfectly willing.

The next day I settled in the foundry, and took the cars for Saco, and on arriving there, went down to the mills, but they would not let me go in; so I went over to Biddeford, on the other side of the river, and went into the Pepperell counting-room and got a permit. I went into the weave-room, and met a fellow-countryman, and asked him for work. 'What can thee do, lad?' he asked in the Yorkshire tone. I replied in the same tone, that I wanted to learn to weave, and that I used to weave when in England. He said that he would take me, and the next morning I went in and commenced work. I was placed in charge of a man to learn me to weave, but when I had worked two hours, he went to the overseer and asked him what he meant in fooling him, for the fellow, he said, can weave as well as I can. The overseer then came and put me upon two looms, and the next day I commenced to work upon four and earned one dollar a day.

I worked about three weeks and then I went after my wife. I moved my furniture to Biddeford, and, not getting a tenement, we boarded on Alfred street. I went back into the mill, and soon run eight looms a day, having a small girl to shuttle 'cops' for me.

I took my wife into the room where I worked and learned her to weave, and we both used to make about sixty dollars a month. I paid thirteen dollars and fifty cents per month for my board, and of the balance of my money, I am sorry to say, the most of it went for liquor. I did not get drunk, but I coul l take quite a number of glasses a day, which, at the end of the month, would make quite a bill. I had drunk much liquor in my life, but the 'Yankee liquor' did not agree with me as well as that which I got in the British dominions, and I was taken sick, and went up into the country, out of the way of liquor, and soon recovered. When I returned I went into the mill again, and kept pretty steady. and in a month we had saved up fifty dollars. I felt pretty well pleased, and began to think about going to house-keeping; so I moved to Sullivan street, and as soon as I had got settled, my wife's mother came from New York to visit us. I felt the importance of making every thing tell, and invested a part of my funds in a couple of pigs, and, fixing up a place for them, I put them into their new quarters. I felt well pleased with my pigs, as they were the first animals I ever owned, and took real comfort in looking at them

All went smoothly for about a week, when a small boy came into the mill and reported to me that my pigs had broken out of barracks, and that my wife's mother, with an escort of boys, were after the deserters, but had not succeeded in arresting them. I went to the overseer and asked him to let me go out and find my pigs, but he would not. I remained in the mill as long as I could; I seemed to see my pigs running before me as I went about my work, and feeling that necessity demanded it I went out to find them. I went to my house, but my pigs were not there. I then started and went back upon the heights and met my wife's mother, with her escort, returning in triumph with the prisoners in a bushel basket. I carried my pigs home and secured them in the pen, and then returned to the mill, informing the workmen that I had been successful; but they made fun of my pigs, and my wife laughed at me.

Those two pigs were the instruments in bringing considerable trouble upon me. My overseer proposed that I should stand treat, as I had found my pigs, and I could not well refuse. We went out and I treated him, but as soon as I had the first glass I wanted another, and thus I went on until I got intoxicated. I stopped out of the mill a week and spent all the money I had, and then my glasses that I ran in debt for were chalked down upon the door. The man's name, that kept the shop, was Swindle (a name very appropriate to his business), and he had chalked down to me, besides what I had spent, three dollars, and to get his pay, he wanted me to sell my pigs. I took my pigs one morning, after I had got partially over my spree, one under each arm, and started off to find a customer. I found one on Alfred Street, and disposed of both of them, and meeting some persons that I knew, I invited them into Swindle's, and before I left we had drank my pigs all up. I got quite intoxicated while in the shop, and had some light skirmishing. One young man I thought had insulted me, and I watched an opportunity to chastise him, but did not get a chance when in the shop. When he went out I followed, and, overtaking him upon Adams Street, I commenced to box him, when, escaping from me, he seized a large stone and threw it at me, but fortunately it did not strike me. He then started on a run, and I followed, but not making much progress in running he escaped.

I went back to the shop, and after getting a few more glasses, I started for home. I succeeded in getting as far as Alfred street, but even in that short distance a number of persons ran against me, and once I got against the broadside of a building, and it seemed to whirl around so that it was with the utmost difficulty I made my way along; and the last I remember for the night I was by the side of the road trying to find my hat in the gutter. Early in the morning I came to myself, and found that I was in the mud. I crawled out, looking rather sheepish, and made my way toward home. I soon became sobered, and felt very bad that I had spent my money, and thus made a beast of myself; and I went back to work with the determination to keep steady, that is, only to take my regular dram. I thought that I could not get along without that, as I had, a great portion of my life, been accustomed to it.

At this point I had another trouble. My wife's mother had been living with us, and this drunk quite upset her, and she determined not to stay longer with such a degraded son-in-law, and asked me to get a team and take her to the depot with her trunks. So I went on to the street and met Isaac Clifford, and asked him if he could tell me where to get a team to take her to the depot. He said yes, you can get Skillings'. He has got a horse that wont let you ride in the dust after anybody, for he is a regular black hawk; can go in 2:40; can beat the engine; and the old man is a No. 1 horse-jockey, and can just drive him too. So I went and found the old fellow, and told him to call at my house, on Sullivan street, next day, at 10 o'clock, to take me and mother with her trunk to the station. He says, 'Where is your house?' I told him, it was the next house to Judge Berry's. 'All right,' says Skillings, 'I'll be on hand.'

Next day at the time named I heard a knock at my door, and went to the door to see who was there, and as I opened the door I saw Skillings with his beautiful steed hitched into a regular go-cart. 'Good morning,' said he. 'Good morning,' says I. 'And is that your team?' 'Yes,' said he, 'I guess it is no other one's.' Well, the horse looked to me like the old pewter-cased watch that John Gould once sold to me, for all the watch-makers in Biddeford could not wind it up into going order. I said, 'Skillings, is that the horse that Clifford says can beat a flash of lightning his whole length on trotting a mile?' 'It is true, as I am a misbegotten son of poverty,' said the old man. Didn't I laugh. He looked to me as if he was a number of degrees below any horse flesh I had yet seen; such a poor jackass-looking skeleton of a horse I never saw before. He looked as if he had just been marched from the camp of starvation, and had been fed on water gruel after being all night in a barrel of molasses and water. His hair was looking a thousand ways for Sunday,—long-necked, cat-hammed, heavy-headed, flat-eared, crooked-shanked, narrow-chested, swelled-hocked, and as solemn as if he had been contemplating his latter end for the last twenty years. And his tail,—oh what a tail! It looked as if it had been cut off and drove in, being pretty well battered and bushed up in the operation; or, as Mark Twain says, ' he had set down on it too hard.' Well, it is no use, I won't attempt any further delineation of that wonderful horse, and the cart was altogether indescribable, especially the jolting part of it; but on our way to the depot I could say, without exaggeration, that it was better felt than expressed.

> What a jolting, and creaking, and splashing, and din;
> The whip how it cracks, and the wheels how they spin;
> How the mud right and left o'er the hedges is hurled,
> Old Skillings at length makes a noise in the world.

And in this way I, poor man, had to accompany my poor mother to the train, which was to bear her away; and all this for selling my pigs and getting drunk on the proceeds. I could say, 'O Poverty, where are thy charms that sages have seen in thy face?'

I had been at work pretty steadily for three moifths, when my overseer asked me one day if I should not like to go out and take a drop. As I could never resist an invitation, I went out with him and his brother into a liquor shop, where the overseer treated us, and I followed. We drank quite a number of glasses, and, going over into Saco, we drank more there; and, to finish our day's recreation, the overseer proposed that we should go up by the railroad bridge, and have a swing. We went up by the side of the river, and while there, the overseer laid down upon the bank, and fell asleep. His brother proposed, as he had only treated once, to rob him, and to treat ourselves, to which I readily assented. We searched his pockets, but found no money there; but I knew that he had money about him, and I was not disheartened yet, and pulling off his boots, I found in his stockings forty-one dollars. When his brother saw it, he said, 'Now we will have a spree, let us go over to Saco again.' 'I am ready,' I said, and, starting off, we went over, leaving the overseer asleep on the ground.

When we arrived at Saco we went into a shop, and called for some liquor and drank it, and I paid for it with my own money, as I had some left. My companion wanted me to break into the money, but as I had some left of my own, I would not. We soon went over to Biddeford, and I gave the money to my wife, telling her at the same time where I obtained it. The next morning, when I went into the mill, the overseer, the moment he saw me, became very much excited, and with harsh language asked me where his money was. 'I have not your money,' I replied. He soon left me, but my wife came in soon, and, going over where he was, gave him the money, and told him the circumstances about it. He felt so well pleased that he went out and brought in a bottle of brandy and treated us, unknown to my wife.

I was in the habit of going with a scout into the woods every Sunday to learn them the military drill, and to go through the sword exercise, and thus pass God's day. We often ended in a regular drunken skirmish, and returned home carrying the marks of war upon us.

CHAPTER XXI.

As I went to and from my work, I noticed a pretty polite little fellow that kept a saloon in Dudley's block. When I met him he would most of the time have a covered basket, and many were the conjectures that were made in regard to what he carried in that basket. I thought one day that I would go into his shop and see if he kept anything to drink. I therefore went in and asked him for a glass of ale, which he gave me, and I thought that it tasted much better than that which I obtained at other places. I followed getting my beer regularly here for some time, and was treated so politely by the keeper of the shop that I could not help thinking how foolish I had been in getting my liquor at the low holes, as I thought they were, that I had been accustomed to. In a room in the back part of the shop was a domino-table, around which quite a number of young men would be seated every night. I used to be called quite a skillful player when I was in the army, and the table attracted my attention, and I soon commenced to play there, and used to win tickets which I would spend for beer. One evening, while playing there, I noticed a teamster coming into the shop, and he made some motions, upon which the keeper reached under the counter (I had my eye upon him), and taking a cover from a butter-firkin, pulled out a decanter, out of which he turned a glass of liquor and handed to the teamster, who drank it down in a hurry. I soon finished the game and arose and asked the keeper for a glass of that article that he kept under the counter.

'Won't you say anything about it?' he asked.

'Of course not,' I replied.

The keeper then turned out a stiff glass, and telling me to drink quick, I eagerly seized it, and drank it instantly. I never drank such liquor before; I thought that it would truly burn me up, and in my eagerness to get some water, I kicked over the domino-table and made considerable confusion before I succeeded.

'What kind of liquor do you call that?' I asked.

'Why, that is the fourth-proof brandy, and the very best that can be obtained,' he replied.

'We never have such liquor as that in the old country,' I said.

'Ah! you get cheated there; they don't care what they sell to a man, and they probably water it considerably before selling, but we don't treat our customers so.'

I felt quite satisfied with the reasons that he had given me, and thought that I had found a place where I could get good liquor.

There was one young man who visited that place, a free-hearted and pleasant fellow, that did not spend his tickets for liquor (that he won by playing dominos), but for custards. The keeper of the saloon, when settlement was near in the ship-yard, would bake up some two or three dozens of custards expressly for this young man, who always came in as soon as settlement, and commence at one end of the custard board and 'sweep all before him.' And it was a common saying among the frequenters of the saloon, when near settlement, to say that it was about 'custard time.' I continued to get my liquor at this place on 'tick,' which I would square up every settlement, paying from five to ten dollars for liquor per month.

One night, while in this saloon, I took quite a number of glasses, and when he closed his shop I heard the sound of a fiddle behind it in a small house. Having some pork and beans and herring for my Sunday dinner, as this was Saturday night, I buried them in the snow, and then went up to the house and went in. I was acquainted with a number, and joined in the dance with them. After having danced a short time, a woman asked me if I was not going to treat, upon which I ordered a quart, which was brought and drank ; and after drinking I said something that enraged some of them, and they seized me to put me out of the house. I knocked down quite a number, but they overpowered me and put me out, minus my hat and part of my coat. I felt that I was an injured man, and I started upon a run for the watchman at the covered bridge, but as I went running toward him bare-headed, without my hat, he took to his heels and ran with all his might, and finding that I could get no help, I determined to venture into the house again. I went in and found that they had broken the fiddle and were abusing the fiddler. I took his part, but being the weaker party, we were roughly handled, and put out of the house into the street. I went and found my provisions that I had secreted in the snow, and, having found my hat, I started toward home with my companion, who made a grab at my herrings, taking a number of them. I told him that if he was not peaceable that I should box him ; but he paid no attention to it, but made another levy upon my herrings. This somewhat aroused me, when I began to box him, giving him a pretty severe whipping, but lost some of my provisions. I went home in a somewhat dilapidated condition, and I have found ever since, that 'those that dance must pay the fiddler.' One night I was in the 'Yankee Saloon,' as the English termed it; and as he did not have much liquor, I went into an Irish house, and there I met an Englishman, and we drank together, and in the course of the evening we got to quarrelling and he challenged me to fight him. At that time I was ready for a challenge, and we went out in the street; the snow was some two feet deep, and we fought some two hours. We both found ourselves in a sorry plight at the close of our long-contested conflict. I remember going home feeling rather ashamed. I tried to keep steady again, and succeeded in doing so about one month, and saved up a little money, and with it I bought me a watch, the first one I ever owned. Soon after I bought my watch, I thought I would show myself in the saloon kept by the polite fellow in Dudley's block. I had not been in there for some time before, and when I entered the keeper remarked, 'What a stranger you are!' 'Yes, I am somewhat a stranger,' I replied. 'Come and take a glass, will you?' he asked. 'I never refuse,' I replied, going up to the counter and drinking the liquor that he set before me.

I drank quite a number of glasses that evening, and traded watches a number of times, and made something in trading. I followed up trading watches, and made some forty dollars, which I soon spent on a spree, and sold the watch that I had left for five dollars, which I spent for drink. After I recovered from my spree, I again said that I would keep steady, and I kept so for some six weeks, and then one morning I was told that I was a father; and as it was the custom in the old country to take a drop, and as I felt happy, I went to the saloon, and obtained a glass, and then another, and became quite intoxicated, and remained so for some three weeks. When I came to myself, I told my wife that it would not answer for me to stop in Biddeford, and asked her one night to make me up a bundle of clothes, and I would leave Biddeford, and try and find some place where I could work without getting drunk. My wife picked up my things, and one morning, bidding her good-by, I started off. I went up on the heights, and then turned around and looked back to the house. I felt bad to leave my wife, and thought to myself that if liquor was out of the way, how happy I could live, and what comfort I could take in life. I thought some of returning, 'but it's no use,' I said to myself, 'if I stop here, I shall die;' and, turning my back toward my home, I walked away. I continued my way until I came opposite the rum-shop kept by Swindle, and I thought that as I was about leaving town I would go in and bid my friend good-by. I entered his shop and told him where I was going.

'Well, take a glass before you go,' he said, taking down a decanter. 'I don't care if I do,' I replied; and drinking it down, I was upon the point of leaving, when an acquaintance of mine proffered me another glass, which I drank. I did not intend to get intoxicated, but was bent upon getting out of Biddeford. I therefore bade the keeper good day, and went up to the depot, and went into the ticket office, and producing a two dollar bill, I asked the man to give me a ticket to carry me as far as they could for the money. 'Do you wish to go down?' he asked. No, sir,' I replied, 'I have been going down for some time, and I want to go up now.' He gave me a ticket, with some change for Newburyport. I waited some time for the cars, and when they came I went aboard, and got out at Newburyport. I was in rather a poor condition; I looked as if I had been dropped from the bag that is generally carried on behind a tin-man's cart.

I went down to the mills, and succeeded in getting a situation in the Ocean Mills, and my employer obtained a boarding-place for me. I went to work the next morning, and kept pretty steady for about a month. At the end of the month I wrote to my wife (I had learned to write, so that with some labor she could decipher it), and sent her the balance of the money that I had left after paying my board. I owed a small grocery bill in Biddeford, and as my wife was about to move, the furniture was attached; but my wife's mother paid the bill, and she moved to Newburyport, where I was. I met her at the depot, and as I had a tenement ready to move into, we soon got settled in our new quarters, and my wife felt well pleased with the change. I told her that I had not drank since I left Biddeford. I kept steady for a short time after my wife and her mother came; but one evening, as I was in the store where I obtained my provisions, I saw the keeper hand the man a small flask, and immediately my old appetite was aroused, and I went home and procured a small bottle, and, returning to the store, I had it filled with brandy, and put down in my store-book as groceries. I had gone but a short distance before I drank the whole of it.

I went to the house and went to bed, without my wife's knowing that I had been drinking. The bottle I would get filled regularly every other night; but my wife soon began to mistrust me, and when the month was out, and she saw the bill that we owed for groceries, she was astonished. But I told her that grocery bills would tell up fast, and that I expected our bill would be somewhere about that amount. But she was not satisfied, and said that if I would leave off trading at that place, she would go into the mill to work. I left that place, and found another, and my wife went to work, leaving the child to the care of her mother. I am surprised, as I look back upon my past career, to see what a life I led; but I know that the bad, as well as the good, must go together in making up these pages, and that I should fail to give my life, unless I told the scenes that I have passed through, although I often blush to think of them.

CHAPTER XXII.

At the place where I now obtained my groceries, I found that there was more liquor sold than at the old place, and in a short time I drank as hard as ever. I made the acquaintance of some Englishmen who were great drinkers, and we used to have some merry times together, and as I was a pretty good singer, these fellows would get me to go out evenings and sing, and then treat me. We used to frequent a certain rum-shop, and play cards until morning, and then I would go home and get a little sleep, and then go to my work at the usual time; this I followed up for some weeks. The Sabbath day I would join a scout of fellows who went off to play cards. I would not play, put would keep watch while the others did.

One Sunday I went down to a liquor shop, and the keeper told me that there was a smart fencer in the place, and that he had challenged me to fight with the sticks, saying that the one who received the first blow should pay for a pint of gin. I accepted the challenge, and the man was brought in, and I was introduced to him. We went into a large cellar, and finding a couple of broom handles, we commenced in good earnest. I soon found that I had a hard one to deal with, and I brought out all the skill that I was master of; and, at last, by a dexterous movement, I struck his arm, knocking the stick instantly from his hand. The keeper of this shop was out of liquor, but he said that he could get some at the shop that supplied him; and, taking a jug, he started off, and soon returned with some gin, as he said, and tasting of it pronounced it good liquor. Turning out three glasses, he mixed them up, and then passed them to us, and we all three drank. I thought that the first glass that I drank at the 'Yankee Saloon' at Biddeford was strong, but it was nothing compared with this. It was something like taking down live coals, and I fairly yelled with pain, while the other two rolled upon the floor. I said to the keeper that it was the hottest stuff that I ever took into my throat. I hardly knew what to do; the keeper took to his bed, and as I could not rest, I went out of the shop toward home. As I was going along on the street, I thought I should burn up. I told my wife that I had drank some gin down to Fowles', and that I thought he had made a mistake, and given me fluid. I could not rest at home, and I therefore went down to the rum-shop again, and found him in as bad, if not in a worse condition than I was. We sent to the place where the gin came from, and found out that the man had made a mistake, and sent us fluid. I took an oath that if I got out of this scrape, I would never drink again. I went to work, and kept steady for a short time, and at settlement, when I went to pay my bill at the grocery store, the keeper wanted to know what the trouble was, that my bill was so small. I told him that I was going to be a temperate man. The next day I went after some groceries, and as he had just taken in a fresh supply of liquor, the keeper said, 'Now, Ambler, we have got some of the best of English cogniac, and I want you to come in and take a glass.' He knew that if he could get me to take one glass, that I should want another. I looked at the door where he used to chalk the glasses down against me, the last time that I was in there; the two panels of the door were covered with chalk-marks, but now they were all rubbed out; they were all settled. I was pondering what to do, when the voice of the keeper aroused me. 'Come,' he said, 'I'm bound to treat you at my expense.' I drank the liquor, and soon the chalk-marks began to make their appearance upon the door again. I went that night with my old associates, and we had a drinking party.

The next day I staid out of the mill, and, in company with

six others, went on a 'spree.' At night we went into an Eng-lishman's house, and drank and sung, and at last got to fight-ing and broke the furniture and did some other damage before we left. I started to go home, and it was raining very hard, and as I went past a saloon I heard a cry for help. I rushed in and saw a colored man with a wound on his head, occasioned by a drunken sailor's throwing an oyster-plate at him. When I entered, the colored man was in the act of seizing the sailor, but quite a number of his companions interposed. I always joined the weakest party, and I therefore immediately seized the sailor and sung out for the police, who soon came in; and I helped him carry the drunken sailor to the watch-house. His companions started after me, being angry, as soon as the police left, and I ran down into a lumber-yard, near the water. They searched some time for me, and one man took hold of the stick of lumber that I was behind, but as it was quite dark, he did not see me. They soon left, and I came out of my hiding-place, feeling very uncomfortable, as I was wet through. As I went toward home, I passed by the house where my grocery man lived, and, as I was wet through, I thought I would get a glass of gin, and, going up the steps before the door, I stepped upon a verandah, and, as I could hardly see, I walked off and fell some twelve feet and struck upon my head upon the ground. I was senseless for some time, and when I came to myself the rain was beating in my face. I got up, but I felt dreadfully. I was wounded badly, I knew, for I could hardly walk. I did not know where I was, but going up to a house, I asked where Russia street was. I was told that it was the next street above. I went to the next street, and entering it, I came to a house that looked like the one that I lived in, and went up and knocked. My wife came to the door, but as the wind blew, she shaded the lamp so that I could not see her face, and I asked, 'Does Mr. Ambler live here?' She was frightened, thinking that I was indeed out of my head, and when I went in she almost fainted, as my face was bruised badly. She thought at first that it was done in a drunken row, but I told her that I had had a fall that occasioned it. In a few days I had recovered so that I was enabled to go to work.

I told my wife, soon after, that I wanted to move, as I never had any luck in the house. I found my wife liked the proposal, and I immediately went before breakfast and obtained a tenement, and, borrowing a wheelbarrow, I moved all our things to my new quarters upon it, as the tenement was but a short distance off. I went to work again in the mill, and kept pretty steady at my work, only taking my glass regularly every morning; and strange to say, these regular glasses did not make me have an appetite for more, as it did if I took a glass at other times. My grocery bill was so large at the end of the month that we could make just money enough to pay it.

One afternoon, as I was out of the mill, I went into the store and got some liquor. It made my head dizzy, and I went home and laid down upon the bed. My wife, knowing what the trouble was, and thinking it was high time to stop my drinking, went down to the grocery store and told the keeper that if he sold me another glass of liquor she would inform against him. She returned to the house, and soon after I arose, feeling rather disagreeably, and took a small flask and went down to the store and asked the keeper to fill it.

'I can't sell you any more liquor,' he said, 'for your wife has been here and forbidden it.'

I was enraged upon hearing this, and swore that I was under no woman's thumb, and that I would learn her better than to meddle with my business. 'I'll tell you what I can do,' said the keeper; 'she forbade my selling you a glass of liquor; I will sell you a pint, and can charge it upon the store-book as pork, and your wife need not know anything about it.' As pork was ninepence per pound, my pint of brandy would be equal to two pounds of pork. I thought it was an excellent way to get over the difficulty; but I am sure I should never have thought of this way if the rumseller had not proposed it.

It probably was not a new method to him. I obtained the brandy, and upon my book it was put down, 'two pounds of pork, at twelve and a half cents per pound, twenty-five cents.' I went home, feeling somewhat displeased with my wife; but as I had a pint of liquor with me, I came to the conclusion not to say as much as I intended to in the outset. I said, ' Well, wife, things have come to a pretty pass, that I am not allowed to take a glass of liquor.'

'I have stood your drinking as long as I intend to; you have made our home unhappy long enough, and now I intend to see if I can't stop it,' she said. We had quite a talk, and I thought as soon as I drank the pint of liquor that I had in my pocket, I would not drink any more. I soon left the room and went into the cellar and drank my liquor; and then, hiding the bottle, I went up-stairs, and told my wife that I should not go out that evening. My wife felt well-pleased with my determination, and I felt well repaid in staying at home. It was the first evening that I had spent at home for some time; and, although I felt happy, yet I missed my companions, and I have no doubt but that I was missed in the den where I was accustomed to spend my leisure time. I had no idea that my habits had such a hold upon me, and it was indeed not without a struggle that I stopped at home that evening. Oh! how I wished that I could break the chain that bound me, for I felt that I was in bondage; but I could not subdue the appetite that was leading me, step by step, down to a drunkard's grave. ' Where will this end?' I asked myself, as I looked back upon the downward road that I had traveled. I did not ask the help of God. I did not come to Him who is able to save the poor drunkard, and ask for that grace that He alone can give; but I made resolutions in my own strength, and endeavored, without Divine assistance, to break off my evil habits.

I kept pretty steady at my work a short time; but, as it was coming cold weather, the evenings grew longer, and as I did not like to spend long evenings at home, I sought my old com-

10

panions in the rum-shops. I had only got *pork* twice at my grocer's; but my bill was so large that I could not pay it at the end of the month, and as it was now settlement, the keeper of the store said he wanted me to square up, as he intended to close up business. I told him that I did not have money enough to settle my rum and grocery bill, but that I would pay for my groceries, and that he might take a dining-set that I had to his store, and sell it and take his pay. Soon after I left my crockery ware at the shop he failed, and, meeting me one day on the street, he said:

'Ambler, you owe me five dollars, and I want it.'

'But,' said I, 'the set of ware will more than pay your bill.'

'I did not realize enough out of it to pay my bill by five dollars,' he said.

I knew that the rumseller was hard upon me, as my ware was worth five dollars more than his bill, but I told him that I would pay him as soon as I obtained some money.

As the store where I obtained my groceries was closed up, I asked my overseer to direct me to one where no liquor was kept. He directed me to a respectable place, where I could not obtain liquor. I was invited one evening down to F——'s, who kept a liquor hole, and as I neared the place I heard the sound of a fiddle, and I thought that the company were having quite a merry time. I went in and the keeper treated me to a drink, and I soon had taken quite a number of glasses, and felt pretty well. There was a large, stout-built man there, bragging of his exploits; we did not agree very well, and we soon got to fighting, and made such a disturbance that the others there called for the police, and I had to take my leave, or get into the watch-house. I chose the former, and in going down the stairs I was seized, but breaking away, I started on a run for home, which I soon reached. I fastened my door, expecting that some one would be after me, as I knew that my opponent had got a pretty severe whipping; but no one came, and I went to bed. I used to have many drunken sprees with F——, and many were the quarrels that I have had in his rum-shop; but I will forbear relating many incidents of my life, that happened about this time, as I am well aware that the pages of this work will be extended to a greater length than will be profitable or edifying to the reader.

After working in the Ocean Mill a number of months, I left and got work in another mill, and also moved about the same time into a room that I obtained about one mile from my work. Soon after I moved, I went on a 'spree' with a number of other men; one of them, I remember, was as good and as free-hearted a fellow as I ever saw, and would always help me when I got into difficulty; and although he led a miserable life, he gave me good advice, which, if I had followed, would have saved me from many troubles and difficulties that I have undergone. We all agreed to leave the place, and go to Biddeford.

When I went home, I told my wife that I intended to leave; and the next morning I did so, leaving in the house only a peck of potatoes for my wife to live on. When I got to Biddeford, I went into the weave-room upon the Pepperell Corporation, and obtained a situation. I worked in the mill two or three days, when two of the men that agreed to come to Biddeford came into the mill where I was working, one of them so exhausted, having been without food for some time, and walked from Newburyport, that he fainted in the room, and had to be carried out. I got work for the two men. As soon as I received some money, I sent it to my wife, who immediately came to Biddeford, leaving her little furniture behind. I drank so hard now, while in Biddeford, that my wife could not put up with it, and she told me that she was determined to leave; and as I could not persuade her to stay, I left my work, and went to Portland with her, and to the wharf where she took the steamboat for St. John.

I stood again upon the same wharf that I had stood upon about four years before, but under what different circumstances! I thought that I had escaped to a land of freedom, but I found that I had only got myself into a worse condition than I was in when in the army; for there I was under a discipline that restrained me to a considerable extent, but here I did as I wished, and I thought how fast I had gone down hill the past four years. But the boat was about leaving, and, bidding my wife good-by and kissing my child, I jumped upon the wharf. Oh! that it should come to this, that my wife should have to leave me, because I was such a brute that she could not live with me. I never had abused her, never struck her; I felt glad that I could say that much, but again I thought that there was much that I could not say. I had not provided for her as I should, and my conduct had brought misery and degradation upon her. These thoughts came upon me as I watched the boat fast disappearing from my view; and, wiping away the tears, I went up into the city, and, as I had no money, I sold some clothes off my back, to get money enough to carry me to Biddeford again.

When I arrived at Biddeford, I felt ashamed to go into the weave-room, and I went over into Saco, and got a situation upon the York Corporation, but meeting some boon companions, I went on a 'spree,' and lost my chance. When I got sober, I determined to leave Biddeford, and selling some extra clothes that I had, obtained money enough to carry me to Newburyport. When I got to Newburyport, I went to the place where my furniture was, and found it all safe, and then I tried to get a chance to work in the mill, but was not successful. I now began to lead a worse life than ever, and shortly after I came back, got into drunken row in the house of an Englishman, and had to run for my life. As I had no boarding-house, I walked the streets two nights and three days without sleep or food of any kind. The next night I went to the friend that I have referred to before, who had helped me out of difficulties many times before, and he gave me half a dollar, which I spent for something to eat and a lodging for the night. The next day I tried again to get work in the mill, and was successful.

I was now boarding with a man named T——, who kept a

man and his wife beside myself. The man that boarded with me was a great drinker, and would often come home intoxicated. He came home one evening intoxicated; he was jealous of his wife, and had often threatened her life, and she was always afraid of him when he was in drink. She followed him to his bed-room, and she there heard him handling his razor and strop, and talking about taking life. She hurried down stairs to the keeper of the house, who was an old man, and informed him that she was suspicious that her husband meant to take her life. The boarding master came and told me that I must take care of the fellow. I took the tongs, and stationed myself beside the door that he would pass through as he came down stairs. I soon heard him coming down, and as he reached the door, he saw me prepared to meet him, upon which he halted. I saw the razor in his hand, and I said :

'Bill, what are you going to do? If you do not instantly put aside that razor I will knock you down.' Seeing that I was determined to be as good as my word, he put the razor down upon the table, saying, 'We have always got along well, and I don't wish to have any quarrel with you.'

'Well then,' I said, 'if you do not wish to have a quarrel with me, you must go up to your bed-room and stay there.'

He went up to his room, and did not show himself until morning, when he left the place, without taking his wife.

I soon commenced drinking again as bad as ever, and one Sunday a number of us assembled in a drinking-house, and I fell in with a fighting character, and as I was known to box a little, I was matched against him for a pint of brandy. The one that got the first clip would have to pay for the drinks. We stood up, and commenced to strike and parry, and I soon gave him a light blow in the face. I let my hands fall down by my side as soon as I gave the blow, and my opponent, taking advantage of my exposed condition, struck me a pretty severe blow, knocking me down in the corner of the room. I was upon my feet in an instant, and before the company could arrest me, I gave him a blow that threw him against the wall. Here the company separated us, and the fellow apologized, and paid for the liquor.

After we drank I started to go home, the people were just coming from church, and I felt rather ashamed to be seen in the condition that I was in, and I ran down upon a wharf that was near, and as this was in the winter, jumped upon the ice. It was in small cakes, and I sank into the water. I arose, but could not get out, as I was entirely surrounded by small cakes of ice that would not support me. I cried out for help, and F——, that kept the rum-shop, with another man, came to my rescue. They pulled me out with some difficulty, and after recovering some, they invited me to go and have a drink, but I would not, and went home, looking, as the saying is, 'like a drowned rat.'

A short time after, a few of us met in F——'s rum-shop, and for sport, one said that he could tell our fortunes by the bumps on our heads, and putting his hands upon the young man's head, said, 'You will live many years, if you do not make way with yourself.'

The young fellow said, 'I intend to live long enough to pay my debts, and then I shall take my life.'

This answer, that seemed to be made in good earnest, sent a chill over the company, and we soon separated, but I did not forget the answer that was made. It seemed to me just as if the young man meant what he said, and I thought that if I lived, I would see to what an end the man came.

I had written to my wife a number of times, and had sent money for her to come up with, and as I thought she would be up soon, I secured a tenement, and had my furniture moved to my new quarters, and thought that I would keep bachelor's hall until she came. Not long after this, my poor, long-suffering wife joined me once more, and did what she could to keep me out of the rum-shops.

CHAPTER XXIII.

I HAVE now reached the period in my history, the most important. Hitherto I relied upon my own strength, but I now called upon one who was able and willing to save to the uttermost, all that put their trust in him. The inebriate's friend, the sinner's Saviour, the only one that is able to sustain us when the hour of trial comes, and place our feet upon a sure foundation.

About this time, a vestry, where the children of God held stated prayer-meetings, was moved to a spot near where I lived, and one evening I told my wife that I was going in to see how they performed. I had never attended one since I was a boy; I therefore took my boy with me and went into the meeting. As I entered, a female was engaged in prayer. How strangely it thrilled me! It seemed to bring back my early days, when I knelt beside my little bed, with my grandmother at my side, and repeated my evening prayer. The prayer seemed to touch my heart, and it was with considerable effort that I restrained the tears from flowing. I would have given anything to have been out of the place, but I could not stir from the spot. When the meeting closed, I went home, and my wife asked me how I liked the meeting. I told her I did not think much of it, but I felt at the same time that I was telling a falsehood. I went out of the house and down to a shop where I drank a glass of liquor, to drive away the feeling that existed within me, but it was of no avail. I could not stop my thoughts, and I felt as bad as ever.

In a day or two after, some one came into the mill and told me that a woman that worked for me, and that I had missed

from work, wished to see me, as she was near death. I went
to see her, hardly believing the sad news, as I saw the woman
the day before in perfect health, but I found her speechless and
near death, and I soon went back to my work in the mills, but
I was restless, and I went out of the mills to the house where
she was sick, and found her dead, and friends weeping over
her. Although I had passed through many trying scenes, yet
I shed tears at that time.

As I went back to my work, what thoughts rushed through
my mind! Are you prepared to die? I could not answer this
question as I wished I could, I was not prepared. I thought
of the promise I made God when I was sick in the hospital.
Oh, that I had kept it. I thought that this was a warning to
me, 'Be ye also ready.' It seemed as if God had spoken to me
by his providence numerous times.

That night there was a prayer-meeting again in the vestry,
and I went with my little boy. As I entered I was interested
by the hymn that was sung, which they had just commenced as
I entered; the first words were these, 'Jesus died on Calvary's
mountain.' How sweet they sounded to me, and I thought,
Did Jesus die on Calvary's mountain for me? Did Jesus do
this for poor sinners?—all this, and I have rebelled against him
all my life. And as they sung another hymn with the beautiful
words, '*Children, come home,*' I thought those words cannot
apply to me, it is to those alone that love him, and have been
faithful to him. I felt that I was not a child of God, that I was
living far from him, therefore those sweet words could not be
addressed to me. I trembled in my seat. The sweat dropped
from my brow, and I felt that I should sink to the floor. After
the hymn was sung, the minister prayed, and others followed,
and all their prayers seemed to be directed to me. I could not sit
upon my seat, I must do something; and with considerable difficulty, I pulled myself up by the seat before me, and told them
that I wished to become a member of their society (as I had
never been to a prayer-meeting since a boy, I was not acquaint-

ed with their rules and customs, and was altogether ignorant). As I sat down, the people smiled all around me, and some even laughed aloud, whilst others seemed to be angry, thinking that I was making fun of them, as I had led such a dissipated life. Soon after the meeting closed, the minister came along and shook me by the hand, and said: 'God bless you.' This was something new to me, to have a respectable man shake me by the hand, as though I were a brother, and say, 'God bless you.' I could have withstood the curses of a companion, and could have replied to him, but the voice of love, of sympathy, and kindness was something new, and I could not withstand it; I could not say a word, but burst into tears. I left the place, and went home. My wife asked me how I liked the meeting. I replied that I liked it much. 'But wife,' I continued, 'I want you to pray for me, I am no scholar, and I do not know how.' But my wife made no reply to my request, and I thought, I will pray myself. But then, I said to myself, how can I pray, sinner that I am, will it be acceptable? But whilst these thoughts rushed through my mind, I remembered the hymn that was sung at the prayer-meeting:

> 'Just as I am, without one plea,
> But that thy blood was shed for me,
> And that thou bidst me come to thee,
> O Lamb of God, I come!'

I fell upon my knees and confessed my sins to God and asked his pardon. My wife could not subdue her tears, but falling down beside me upon her knees, we both prayed earnestly and humbly to God, and He came down and blessed us there.

I always thought, before that, that prayer was a senseless, cold, heartless ceremony; but what a mistake I made, for I felt my heart softened, and that Jesus that died upon Calvary's hill was near me. I felt the peace of God that passeth understanding whilst I was upon my knees; and, although ignorant as I was of spiritual things, the great mystery of salvation and the atonement came like a ray of light from heaven, and illuminated my benighted soul, and we both arose justified, I believe, in the sight of God. As I arose upon my feet I felt that I was a new being. I was loaded with guilt and sin when I bowed before the Throne of Grace, but now it was gone, and I felt that I could say amen to the passage in the Scripture, 'For my yoke is easy, and my burden is light.' I felt like a child, and, as I looked back upon my past life, I thought, 'Oh that I could live my life over again, and that what I know now I had experienced in the morning of life! Oh that I had found Christ years ago; what a progress I might have made in life, and what comfort and happiness might I have enjoyed!'

I think of my grandmother now,
   And of the warm tears that she shed,
And how at night-fall she did bow
   By the side of my lowly bed.

And with her hands uplifted there,
   Methinks that her form I can see,
Now kneeling beside the arm-chair,
   As she offered her prayer for me.

Earnest and long she plead for me,
   And her spirit seemed crushed within,
That I from the tempter might flee,
   And be kept from the ways of sin.

Those prayers still ring in my ears,
   Though offered long, long years ago;
As I think of them now, the hot tears
   Down my cheeks unbiddingly flow.

The prayers that my grandmother prayed
   Have found favor with God on high,
And though long in the earth she's laid,
   Her spirit seems now ever nigh.

The next day I went to my work; and, as I entered the mill, some laughed at me, as they had been told that I spoke in the prayer-meeting; but I paid no attention to the sneers or remarks that were made, as I felt happy for the first time. I went with my wife to the next prayer-meeting, and in the course of the evening I arose and said that I was a great sinner, and that I desired their prayers for me. Some laughed, whilst a few said amen. The meeting closed, and the minister came and shook me by the hand; and, as this was Saturday, asked me to attend church next day. I made no reply, as I felt ashamed to tell him that I had no clothes to wear. Whilst I was going home, the words that were spoken by some one at the meeting, 'Give up all for Christ,' seemed to ring in my ears, and I thought, 'What can I give? I have no clothes, money, or anything;' and then again, I thought of the words in the hymn,—

> 'In my hand no price I bring,
> Simply to thy cross I cling.'

On the Sabbath I remained at home, and tried to read the Bible; but I did not succeed very well, and I laid it aside. Sabbath evening I attended the meeting, and told them that I had peace and joy in calling upon the Lord, and that I felt that He had heard my prayers. No one laughed at me now, as they found out that I was in earnest.

I attended the prayer-meeting regularly, and soon obtained suitable clothes and went to church, and listened to the preaching of the gospel, and felt strengthened in the Lord. My appetite for liquor continued for some time, but with the help of God I was enabled to overcome it.

CHAPTER XXIV.

As soon as my eyes were opened and I saw the goodness of God, my heart went out for others, and I succeeded in getting some of my old companions into the prayer-meeting. My low songs that I before had sung in the bar-room, were now changed into hymns; and I purchased me a hymn-book, and my wife read the hymns to me until I could repeat them, and I soon began to sing, which I found profitable to me, for it kept my mind active, and made me forget the old habits which somewhat clung to me.

Oh! if poor drunkards could come to Him who is mighty to save, and who alone can lead them safely through this world, then would they know in whom to put their trust, and they would find Him a high tower to which they could flee in time of danger. The poor man who resolves to leave off in his own strength, how often he falls by the way! Not so those who put their trust in the Lord, for they are *strong* in Him, and all the powers of darkness cannot prevail against them; and whenever trials come, they will find his grace sufficient for them.

I continued to walk in the way the Lord directed, and to grow in grace; and I was asked by a number of the brethren to unite with the church, and after some thought upon the subject, my wife and myself were baptized, and united with the Christian Church, under the care of Rev. Daniel Pike, May 7, 1857.

The minister, when he received us into the church, held up the Bible, and told us to take it for our guide; it was a blank book to me, for I could not read its pages, but I felt that I would try and explore it, and find the hidden treasures there. I studied some three months upon the Bible, and learned so that I could read it tolerably well. How proud I felt! I went to the meeting and I told them that I could read the Bible. That evening I heard them pray for a revival, and although I had heard the word before, I did not know its meaning, and I went home and asked my wife, who explained the meaning of the word to me.

On Christmas evening (I never shall forget it), there was a prayer-meeting, and although there were but few there, yet God was with them, and the few Christians there prayed earnestly for God to revive his work. From that time there was manifested quite an interest, and soon the candle of the Lord shone in our midst, and our little vestry, that we were wont to assemble in, was filled with inquiring sinners.

We commenced a protracted meeting, which was held every evening for some time. There was one young man that attended those meetings regularly, and seemed to be interested, but yet was not converted; one evening, I remember, the minister's mother spoke of the goodness of God to her; she spoke with a broken voice, and it touched the young man's heart, and he arose for prayers. I heard this young man say, after the meeting, that he thanked God that he ever heard her speak. It was the voice of a female engaged in prayer that arrested my attention. The tones of a female in prayer seemed to carry me back to my childhood days, when my mother blest and gave me to God. No doubt the thoughts of the young man were carried back to his childhood days, when he heard the woman's voice. Perhaps he thought of the time when a kind mother blessed him and taught him to say his evening prayers.

There were near three hundred that went forward for prayers during those meetings. The revival first commenced in the little vestry, but it soon spread over the whole city.

No Christian that passed through those glorious scenes, when

God made his people to sit together in heavenly places in Christ Jesus, can ever forget them, but they will be ever fresh in his memory, and when the church of Christ is low and in darkness, the memory of those scenes will serve to lighten the Christian's heart, and cause his faith in Christ to be as strong as the prophet of old, who said: 'Although the fig-tree shall not blossom, neither shall fruit be in the vine; the labor of the olive shall fail, and the field shall yield no meat; the flocks shall be cut off from the fold, and there shall be no herd in the stall; yet I will rejoice in the Lord, I will joy in the God of my salvation.'

Many came from the country near the city to our meetings, and found him of whom Moses and the prophets did write. Many of the churches of Christ were refreshed by the presence of the Lord, and were strengthened in faith and numbers. One beautiful and marked feature of the great revival was the union of different denominations, and the harmony and oneness that existed at that time, no former period ever witnessed. The world had heretofore charged the churches with coldness to one another, but this barrier being broken down, the world could only look on in wonder, and exclaim: 'This is the Lord's doings, and is marvellous in our eyes.'

I continued to attend the public services in the house of God, and to be prompt at the social prayer-meetings.

Soon after I joined the church, Mr. Stone was Sunday-school teacher, and he gave for a lesson for us, Exodus 2:11, 12, to give our opinion upon; wife read the story to me. I thought Moses was a good man, and would do no wrong, or it would not have been in the Bible. Wife was at work with me in the mill at this time. The overseer seemed jealous of me, because I would get thirty and forty cuts per week, of cloth, from eighty-six looms, more than anybody else. Wife had sixteen cents per cut for weaving, and the overseer would complain that some of her cuts were not wove well, and he would cut her down ten cents a cut. One day I examined her cuts before they went to the trimming-room, and found they were all perfect. When they were taken to the trimming-room, as usual, the overseer sent back two of her tickets, cutting off twenty cents again of my poor wife's earnings. She then went to the overseer and asked why it was done, and asked to see the cloth. I was watching the old scamp, and I could tell by the motions of his mouth that he was abusing her, and he called her a hussy. I thought then, is it right for me, an Englishman, who had married an American woman whose grandmother used to feed the soldiers of the Revolution, to stand by and see her abused. I had professed religion and wanted to do right. The overseer belonged to the same church with me. Our Sabbath-school lesson came up, and as everybody said Moses was a prophet and a good man, and wife had read to me Exodus 2:11, 12, 'And it came to pass, when Moses was grown, that he went unto his brethren and looked on their burdens; and he espied an Egyptian smiting a Hebrew, one of his brethren. And he looked *this* way and *that* way; and when he saw there was no man, he *slew* the Egyptian, and hid him in the sand,' and quick as a flash I said, here goes for this Egyptian. I made a rush for him, and told him to take care of himself, I was going to thrash him or he should me. I hit him under the ear and knocked him end over end, bringing the blood from his ears and nose. When he got up he ran for his life, and I after him. Wife got hold of me to stop me, and pulled my shirt right up out of my trowsers behind, and the girls ran to help her, and I caught one of them up and tossed her right slap astride of a loom that was running; but she was too thick for filling and the loom stopped, and I rushed on after the overseer, and he went running and tumbling down through the machine-shop and into the office, and told the agent Ambler was crazy, and he fled for dear life and hid. Well, I thought if this Egyptian had hid himself it would save me the trouble of killing and hiding him myself. You see I was determined to be a Christian after the pattern of Moses, and so I felt justified. It is true, I fell a little short, but my intentions were fully up to the pattern.

Well, I was called before the church on a charge of misdemeanor. What a jaw-breaking word that was! What could it mean? They told me it meant striking one of my brethren of the church. So I got up and told them all about it, and also about brother Stone's Sabbath-school lesson, and how wife had read the whole story to me, and I would show myself as much of a man as Moses was. He pitched into the Egyptian for abusing one of the brethren, and was not my wife as near to me as Moses' kinsman, and would I show myself a man if I did not whip the rascal for abusing a poor hard-working wife? The church was of two minds about it. The most of them favored the Hebrew, and so I came off with flying colors, with a slight admonition which I suppose meant something like this, viz., that I should look this way and that to see if anybody was looking, the next time I gave any lessons in Hebrew.

But, seriously, I tried to behave myself as a Christian, so as to merit the approbation of my conscience and good men, and the chastisement given the overseer was considered no unchristian thing, as the following testimony of the agent of the mill where it occurred will show:

Dear Sir,—The bearer, Mr. I. W. Ambler, was formerly an employee in the Ocean Steam Mills, and is now devoting his time to the work of a city missionary in Biddeford, Me., and is desirous of obtaining an education that he may be the better qualified for the work in which he is engaged. I hope he will meet with that encouragement he deserves, and that he may have the sympathy of all those who delight in doing good.

Respectfully yours,

E. S. Lesley, *Agent Ocean Steam Mills,*

Newburyport, Mass.

About this time I heard that Ackroid, who had been my companion through a portion of my life, had been killed at Sebastopol. I felt thankful to God that I had escaped from the army, and that He had shown me the error of my ways, and brought me, as I trusted, into his fold. I felt a strong desire to see men come into the kingdom of God, and this desire so pervaded my mind, that when at my work this was the thought that was ever uppermost; and so much did it engage my attention, that I told my wife that I could not work, and that I thought of going to Biddeford and inviting my old companions there to come to Christ. I left the mills in the spring of 1859, and took the cars for that place.

I remained in Biddeford some three weeks, and was invited by the different evangelical churches to act as missionary in that place, and after going back to Newburyport and packing my furniture, I returned again with my family, and commenced my labors, and here let me thank the members of the different churches of Biddeford, who have assisted me in my work by their earnest prayers and generous contributions.

And here let me say that there seemed to be a fitness observed by these good Christians in myself, in a business point of view, viz., that 'it takes a rogue to catch one;' for had I not been through the mill from Alpha to Omega, and if I did not know the ropes I must have been a dull scholar, for what path of vice had I not trod? If any live man knew how to pity the poor, the ignorant, the despised, and drunken, and knew who 'had woe, who had sorrow, who had wounds and bruises without number,' that man was I. W. Ambler. And who knew better how to sympathize with destitute fatherless and motherless children than myself, and for the salvation and comfort of such my heart yearned.

There was light in my soul I knew, and feeling enough in my heart, but oh how I sorrowed to think I had not an educational vent to the fullness and richness of God's love that dwelt within me, so that by just hoisting the gates, rivers of truth might burst forth and overwhelm all around me with such a sense of God's love as to make them cry out, 'I yield, I yield, by dying love compelled.' Well, here I was, nothing but poor,

11

ignorant Sergeant Ambler; what was to be done. Well, I had read in the Bible that God could thresh mountains with worms, and I said that coat fits me; I guess the mountains will feel cheap when a worm like me knocks them to pieces and wheels them into line for the kingdom of God. I had read, too, that Jesus, when he wanted to catch men, called some fishermen to help him, and they left their nets without stopping to get an education, and he made them fishers of men; and I said, a soldier is as good material to start with as an old fisherman, and my blessed captain, Jesus, has never lost a battle, and has called me to charge on the ranks of sin and capture as many as I can and compel them to come into the camp of the Lord,— and so I will go out into the highways and hedges and get some recruits for the army of the Lord.

The first work, then, was to get quarters where I could enlist, instruct, and drill all who would come into the army of Captain Jesus. With some help, I got a hall into which to gather the children and others. One of the first obstacles to be overcome was the bare-legged, bare-footed, and bare-headed condition of the poor children, rendering them unfit for promiscuously assembling; and it was astonishing, too, how little the sleek, fat, easy church-going people knew of the terribly squallid condition of the poor children in the city. I went to work begging old clothes, hats, caps, and shoes, and new cloth when I could get it, to make up for them. We formed a circle of ladies for charity sewing, which met at my house every week. My wife, being a milliner and dressmaker, used to cut the garments, and the good ladies made them up, and in a short time we got them clothed so neatly that they were not ashamed to go to meeting, and our hall filled up so that we had not room enough for all.

In the morning I preached temperance to them, not in great jaw-breaking words to make their eyes stick out and wonder, and for two reasons: first, I could not wear Goliath's big coat if I wanted to. I remember Deacon Cole came in to see how I got on with my big family, as I was making a speech to the children. I told the deacon that David once tried it, and it was no go; but when he got to the brook, he took a stone and put in his sling and hit old Goliath plump in the forehead and brought him down, and in that scrape Goliath got something *new in his head.* And the second and chief reason was, that I don't believe in any such way of reaching men's hearts. Paul says, 'I had rather speak five words with my understanding that I may teach others also, than ten thousand words in an unknown tongue.' So I told them my experience, how I used to get drunk and disgraced myself and wife, and went hungry and cold, and was despised, and how I wanted to leave off, and how rumsellers and old chums would get me to take one drink with them, and then down, DOWN, DOWN I went into the gutter; and then how God helped me at last when I prayed to Him, and had kept me by His grace out of the clutches of rumsellers. Now I was happy, my wife was happy, and my child was happy, and we had enough to eat, good clothes, and got into good Christian company, and was respected. Drinking men would sit and listen, and begin to cry, and come to me when I was done, and tell me they were tired of living so, and wanted to leave off; and sometimes I would cry with them and for them, I could not help it; and then they would get hold of my hand and ask me to pray for them; and they would sign the pledge, get steady work, good clothes for their families, and get out to church with them and get converted, and they would begin to catch men by telling them their experience. So the good work went on. Reader, this is the way to catch men. When a man forgets all about how much or how little he knows, and begins to tell others how he was saved just as well as he can with a warm heart, the leaven begins to work, and his experience, told in this simple way, becomes the wisdom of God and the power of God unto the salvation of his hearers. Persecutors are thrown off their guard in this way, and the gospel-hook gets such hold that you can pull them right in.

In going through the city I saw many sad sights. I remember of finding in a place called Dudley's block four children locked in a room with a little bed of straw in the corner, without chairs or other furniture aside from an old broken stove, and a few odds and ends of crockery. I talked with them through the window; they were hungry and nearly as naked as when they came into the world, and they told me their mother was at work in the mill and would be out at noon, at which time I went again and saw the mother, and found the children were fatherless, and the poor mother with poor health was dragging herself back and forth to the mill, when she was hardly able to be off her bed, to get bread to put into the mouths of her little ones. I went with a friend whom I called to witness the scene of wretchedness, and got some chairs, clothing, and food, and took to this poor family. The mother and children followed me to the door, blessing me until I got out of hearing.

Truly this is real gospel; and will it not be said at last, 'Inasmuch as ye have done it unto one of these little ones, ye have done it unto me.' It seemed as though devils that others could not cast out would be brought to me. One gentleman who ran a shoe-shop said he had a good workman who was an awful drunkard, and if I would make a sober man of him, he would believe. Mr. N. pointed him out to me from the other workmen, and I went into the workroom and introduced myself to him, and told him some of my history, how *hard* it was for me to leave off drinking, but I had got the victory. It seemed to wake him up; but he said it was no use for him to try to do anything; his wife had left him, etc., and he was too far gone. I told him if he would sign the pledge I could get his wife back; that he *could* leave it off; God would help, and his wife would help him. Well, he says, if you will get my wife to come back I will sign the pledge. I told him to sign first and I would take it to her and show her what he had done; she was then boarding in the city. He signed the pledge and passed it to me. I told him to put on his coat and come along. We went to the place where she stopped and took a seat in the waiting-room, and a servant went for her. When she came into the room she seemed much surprised. I arose and said, Mrs. ———, shall I introduce you to Mr. ———, who has signed the pledge.

She sat right down, hardly able to speak a word, and began to feel of her apron, taking hold of it with both her hands, fingering the hem and nervously passing it through from one side to the other. I told her how God would help them both, and how happy they would get along, and I was sure her husband would keep the pledge, and soon she began to melt, and they began their cooing like young doves. I seized my hat and ran away, and left them in this happy state. This was a genuine reform, and he has kept the pledge from that day to this. My friend, Mr. N., now believes. Well, go on Mr. N., many believe and have not seen.

CHAPTER XXV.

One more item connected with my missionary work here I will relate. A Mr. Higginbottom, whom we got to sign the pledge, and was true for some time, was induced by two brothers, who kept a rum-shop near a church in the city, to go in. They at last got him to take one glass, and then all his old appetite revived and he drank until he got intoxicated, and then they kicked him out into the street, and he was taken by the police to the station, where, during the night, when he began to come to himself and see what he had done, he was so filled with remorse that he took his knife and cut his throat. The keepers got the knife from him until he sobered off, and the terrible gash was sewed up. I was notified and went to the station, and the poor fellow gave the knife to me all covered with blood (which I now keep), and told me all about it. The next evening I attended the church near by, and the brethren prayed this rum-shop might be removed, and, feeling inspired to do so, I jumped up, and told them the rum-shop never would be removed until they put their shoulder to the wheel and helped to remove it. I think it was the next day when I left my house I prayed and said, 'O God, help me this once to put my shoulder to the wheel and stop this rum-shop.' These brothers that kept this rum-hole were both professional fighters, and the people seemed afraid to meddle with them. On I went to the place, the spirit of the Lord with me strengthening me, and I entered. One of the brothers stood behind the counter, and the other was out. I went up to him and told him not to stir out of his tracks, if he did I would shake him out of his boots. I went behind the counter and smashed the decanters and one or two jugs of liquor, and kicked over the counter and found a very large jug under the counter full of whisky, which I seized and took under my arm, and walked out amidst a crowd that had gathered, and pulling out the stopper let it spill along the street until it was emptied, the people cheering me as I went along. The poor rumseller remaining like·one spell-bound in his den. I then returned and asked him how much damage I must pay. He said *nothing*. I am glad you have done it. On returning home I fell in with a friend who passed along up Alfred street with me, and who should we meet but the other brother, who asked me what I meant by spilling his liquor, and said he would knock as much out of me. I said you can't do that, as I have had none inside of me for three years. He struck me in the face and knocked me round, and before I recovered struck me again upon the other cheek. My friend told me I must spunk up, or he would get the better of me. I told my friend that the good book said, 'When thou art smitten upon one cheek turn the other also;' but it did not say what I must do after that, so here goes. He came upon me again, and I knocked him down, hoping that brief argument would convince him of his mistake; but he up and made for me again. I gave him a second knock-down argument, and as he lay across the side-walk with his head hanging over it, he being a very large strong man, I concluded a few inferences drawn from these strong points already made, and well laid over his head, would bring on a strong conviction of his errors, and change him for the better; so I jumped upon him with one knee on his breast and one hand hold of his throat, and gave him a few 'arousements' over his head and ears, until he sued for mercy. I told him I would let him up when he promised me solemnly he would leave off rum-selling. This he finally concluded to do, and took the pledge before God and me and my friend never to sell liquor again.

This was the first and last time that I ever hammered tem-

perance into a rumseller; and it made me think of Rev. Peter
Cartwright, that muscular old Methodist saint.　A blacksmith
of great physical strength attacked him one Sunday when on
his way to his appointment, and said he would hammer him to
death if he did not stop his d——l proselyting work.　The good
old man knocked him down, and cuffed him until he promised
to become a Christian, and the minister said over the Lord's
prayer, and made the blacksmith repeat it after him, until he
could say it all.　In brief, he converted the blacksmith, and he
joined the Methodist church, and used to laugh afterward about
Elder Cartwright's pounding the gospel into him.　This rumseller did leave the business and became my fast friend, and I
afterward got him a good place in Portland where he could
work and earn an honest living.

I don't advise people to this way of reforming men, but there
was once a time when the loving Jesus made a scourge of small
cords and went at the money-changers and drove them out of
the Temple.

The good work went on, and my labors were sometimes very
perplexing, especially when I came to the money matters.　I
found a lot of Mr. Wishwells and Mrs. Hopewells, but the family of Dowells were not so numerous.　It is said, 'Money makes
the mare go,' and a truer saying never was uttered than that,
of missions.　It took a good deal of cash to carry my mission
along, and I had a good chance to learn human nature on this
matter.　Some lessons I will give, and if I should hit anybody,
I hope it will hurt as well as hit, and the poor stingy souls will
never get over it until a gospel blister is drawn deep enough to
let off some of their covetousness.　Really it seems to me if
such professors could see just how they look as others see them,
they would go into hysterics, like the girl that saw herself the
first time she ever saw a looking-glass.　Her parents were poor,
and in addition to their poverty had religious objections to look-
ing-glasses.　They moved into a village, and sent the little girl,
who was ragged, dirty, and hair uncombed, to a neighbors, and

as she entered the house she came in contact with a mirror, and beholding her own face, she screamed and ran home, declaring to her parents that she had seen the devil, and when she described him they at once saw the point. If I should hold up a glass and any one should say, after they look into it, they had seen the devil, I should say at once, no, no, it was only a reflection.

Here is one funny little thing which was the result of a misapprehension, and was apologized for immediately on finding out the mistake. I had been out begging old clothes, and had a large bundle on my back given me by good souls around the town, and I entered the front yard of a gentleman of large influence and means to get more clothing, and I met the proprietor on the front steps, who immediately challenged me before I had time to tell him my errand, and with a terrible growl ordered me to go about my business, supposing me to be a pack-peddler, which class of persons he always held in abhorrence.

His wife told him that he treated the city missionary rather rough. He was all taken aback when he learned *that*, and sent for me and made a very gentlemanly apology, and had a good laugh at it, so I did not kill him for driving me off.

One time, when collecting clothing for the children, I called at a clothing-store which was run by two very pious men, and told them what others had given, and asked them to help a little; they got some small hats that were out of style, and a few yards of cloth and gave me. This they afterwards charged to me, and also six dollars which they handed to a friend afterwards for the support of what was called the Evening Free School, because I was so unfortunate as to be in his company at the time. They afterwards sued me for these things and the six dollars given to another man, and I was brought before the court and judgment found against me. Here I was in a fix without a dollar, and the only witness I had to disprove a part at least was in the army. I had no great desire to go to jail, but then good old Paul had been in prison, and I concluded I could stand it. God opened the way for me out of this. The friends who felt ashamed for them subscribed the cash on the spot, even the judge opened his purse and helped. It was a foul blot. I will not name the mean men, but I will here introduce the affidavit of the man who received the six dollars instead of myself.

Boston Harbor, Mass., Galloup's Island,
Nov. 29th, 1864.

In the winter of 1859, I received six dollars from Mr. Daniel Stimpson, in the city of Biddeford, Maine, as a charity gift for a mission school, called the 'Evening Free School,' Mr. I. W. Ambler standing at my side at the time. Mr. Ambler did *not borrow the money of the aforesaid D. Stimpson.* In proof of which I hereby affix my name, George H. Blake.

Subscribed and sworn to before me, at Galloup's Island, B. H., this 29th day of November, 1864. D. T. Corbin, Capt. 13th Regt. Vet. Res. Corps, *Judge Advocate.*

I would not of course call any names, but I dare not mutilate the affidavit, and if anybody should suspect the name of the firm from anything contained in that, it would be a most unfortunate thing.

During my work in Biddeford I found, at what is called Smith's Corner, in a wretched old house, a family consisting of a grandmother and two motherless children in a sad condition of poverty. The children about six and eight years old, a boy and girl. When the mother died, she gave them to the grandmother, who had maintained them by going out at washing until the poor woman's health had given way. The children had no other bed than a pile of old rags in one corner of the room. They were nearly naked. The poor old lady told me the sad tale of their suffering and poverty. With her consent, I took the two children into the street, concluding their nakedness and emaciated forms would constitute a living epistle so eloquent that my lips would hardly need to be opened in their behalf. I met several Christian men, and asked for something for them and the aged and sick grandmother. I was turned off at first with the request to go to one L. B. and state my case, or rather theirs. This man was noted for his note-shaving and money-loving nature, and I suppose these good men thought these little living sermons would be vain with him; at any rate it seemed to me that they thought this would be a test case. I went to my friend L. B. and stated the facts, and with a tear in his eye he said, 'Ambler, I believe you,' and drew his wallet and gave me five dollars and told me to call on him for more if it was needed; and here let me say, I never went to him in vain, while many who mouth the heavens with their prayers gave me the cold shoulder.

The first ones after my success with L. B. helped like good men, and I soon had them nicely clothed and led them back to the good old grandmother, who hardly knew them, their good clothes and clean faces so changed them. She cried for joy, and blessed me again and again. The poor old lady was not forgotten, and was made comfortable. This poor little girl had often tried to get work in the mill, but had been repulsed with the remark, 'you are too small.' Oh, how it brought back to me my own struggles when a child. Her condition was so like mine, mother dead and her father a drunkard, and the poor child often crying for bread. Here is a bit of poetry that tells the loneliness and sorrow of such better than I can describe it:

> Out in the gloomy night, sadly I roam,
> I have no mother dear, no pleasaut home;
> Nobody cares for me, no one would cry
> Even if poor little Bessie should die.
> Barefoot and tired, I've wandered all day
> Asking for work, but I'm too small they say;
> On the damp ground I must now lay my head,—
> 'Father's a drunkard, and mother is dead.'

Chorus—Mother, oh! why did you leave me alone,
          With no one to love me, no friends and no home;
          Dark is the night, and the storm rages wild,
          God pity Bessie, the drunkard's lone child.

          We were so happy till father drank rum,
          Then all our sorrow and trouble begun;
          Mother grew paler, and wept every day,
          Baby and I were too hungry to play.
          Slowly they faded, and one summer's night
          Found their dear faces all silent and white;
          Then with big tears slowly dropping I said:
          'Father's a drunkard, and mother is dead.'
                                        Chorus—

          Oh, if the temperance men only could find
          Poor, wretched father, and talk very kind,—
          If they could stop him from drinking,—why, then
          I should be so very happy again;
          Is it too late? 'men of temperance' please try,
          Or poor little Bessie may soon starve and die.
          All the day long I've been begging for bread,
          'Father's a drunkard, and mother is dead.'
                                        Chorus—

Many cases of the kind might be named, but space will not permit. But I must not, I will not leave out one other case. Soon after the case above named, one night, after I had gone to bed, there came a knock on my door. I called to know what was wanted. Was told that a woman who was very sick and who lived on Emery's lane wanted to see me. I dressed and went down, and found in the front room a bar where liquor was kept for sale. I was shown into the kitchen, where lay the sick woman. She asked me to pray with her. I told her I could not pray with that liquor in the house. She said, I shall loose my soul if it is not taken away. I asked her if I should destroy it. She said, yes. I rolled the cask out into the back-yard, and, taking an axe, knocked in the head and let it run. An old covy came along, caught up a dish and dipped up what he could in the yard and drank it. I then went in and prayed with the woman, and she found some peace. The next day Mr. K. gave me a team, and I took the woman and moved her to Mrs. ———, who took care of her until she got better. I then went and told the Rev. Mr. Tenney of her case. He called and prayed with her, and she soon came fully into the kingdom, and finally joined his church and became a shining light. She moved to Lawrence, and soon sent to him some money to be used as he thought best. Rev. Mr. T. called on friend H. and asked what had better be done with it, and he suggested putting it into a corner-stone of a new church as a memorial of a convert's first offering to the Redeemer's cause, which was done. Brother Tenney, God bless him, never failed to go to the call of the poor when I made known any case of the kind to him. God blessed me in my work, and a goodly number found the pearl of great price. Our Sunday school was a joy to us all. We had some of the sweetest little singers I ever heard among them, and, during my labors, we gave some interesting exhibitions, and I must say I never felt so big in my life as I did when marching at the head of a company of 200 children to our Sabbath-school exhibition, who had been picked up and clothed and trained in the way of righteousness.

During my work in Biddeford I felt the need of education, and I wanted funds to help me to books and schooling, and as my life and former history had been made known to some of my friends, they suggested the idea of my publishing my biography, it being such a checkered one I might realize a sum from that which would secure the funds I needed. I followed their advice and found a very good sale for my book, and was getting together funds for that purpose, when the terrible rebellion broke out; this was nearly a year after I began my missionary efforts in Biddeford.

CHAPTER XXVI.

I was in Boston, selling my book, on that memorable 13th of April, 1861, when the rebels fired on Fort Sumter.

Rev. A. L. Stone and the editor of the *Boston Journal* suggested to me, that having been a drill-sergeant in the English army, it was my duty to leave all book and missionary work, and enter at once on the work of instructing our men in military tactics, to prepare them for the battle of freedom and union. I abandoned my book sale, putting it in charge of my wife, and on the 15th of April, I formed the Young Men's Christian Association of Boston into a drill club, and gave them their first lesson.

I believe it was right to teach the disciples how to use the sword, although as a means of reform it might not be justified; but there were times in the Saviour's day, after the disciples had showed their faith and meekness by turning the other cheek when smitten on the one, and taking no purse nor scrip; when they should take their purse if they had one, and arm themselves too. Luke 22: 35, 36,—'And he said unto them, when I sent you without purse and scrip and shoes, lacked ye anything? and they said, nothing. Then said he unto them, but now he that hath a purse let him take it and likewise his scrip; and he that hath no sword, let him sell his garment and buy one.' It was a waste to have a sword and not know how to use it, and it shows that there are times that a disciple is better off without a coat than he would be without a sword. And this time of rebellion seemed to me to be the time for Christian men to buckle on the armor and fight for God and humanity.

When I went to Boston to sell my book, I took some letters along, so that the good people had something besides my face in which to see my character, which papers secured for me the ears of the Governor of Massachusetts and others, when I opened on them for halls, etc., for training recruits. I will only give one or two of them.

BIDDEFORD, Dec. 8, 1859.

This may certify, that Mr. Isaac W. Ambler has been employed during nearly a year, by the Evangelical churches in this city as a city missionary, and has sustained an excellent character. He has the entire confidence of this Christian community. He is very anxious to educate himself for the ministry, and for this purpose is now engaged in selling his own biography. This book, I have no doubt, is an authentic account of a life full of incident and adventure. I commend Mr. Ambler to the kind sympathies of all the friends of Christ.

Signed,   CHAS. PACKARD,
Pastor of the 2d Cong. Church.

I most sincerely concur in all the statements of the above certificate, and cheerfully commend Brother Ambler to the favorable notice of all.   H. B. ABBOTT,

Pastor of the M. E. Church, Biddeford.

I hereby concur in the above.

P. JAQUES,
Pastor of the M. E. Church, Saco.

BIDDEFORD, Dec. 8th, 1859.

Mr. Isaac W. Ambler, for a year past, has devoted his time and energies to missionary labor among the poor of this place, and especially to soften the hardships of the poor children, collecting for them with untiring diligence, and dispensing with good judgment clothing, so as to bring them in classes into the

Sunday school, and to enable them to go to the public schools decently clad. Mr. Ambler is a conscientious, good man, I verily believe, self-sacrificing and charitable in the best sense of the word. His life has been somewhat adventurous, so that in order to help himself to a home he has caused a book of narrative of his life to be published, which I hope will afford him some profit. AUGUSTINE HAINES,

Agent of the Laconia Mills.

Being a stranger in Boston, or nearly so, such letters at once gave me a hearing, and also secured for me the confidence of the people.

F. B. Wentworth (God bless his big heart!) bought me a full military suit and gave it to me, so I could put on military airs at once. It was of great use in stirring up young America, and old America too; as I found the old boys paying as much deference to my epaulettes as the younger ones. Thus accoutred, I went upon the street. Our flags were flying from every part of the city, and upon State street there was great excitement, and everybody was out talking over the state of things. Notice was given out that Fletcher Webster, the son of the great Daniel Webster, was going to speak from the balcony of the old State-house. This was on Sunday, and the crowd surged in that direction. Some of the boys that I had been drilling when they saw me in my soldier rig, made a rush for me, and took me right up and carried me on their shoulders to the State-house, and walked up the steps with me on their shoulders on to the balcony, amid the shouts and cheers of the multitudes.

This was pretty good for Ambler, I thought, for who was poor me to be lionized in such a way, ignorant as I was, never having been to school a day in my life. It almost knocked the wind out of my sails to think of it, of speaking to such a crowd. When Webster got through, they sung out for Sergeant Ambler. Of one thing I was sure, viz., that if I did not understand how to speak grammatically, I did understand military matters

SPEECH FROM OLD STATE-HOUSE.

as well as the best of them, and this put me at ease, and at the same time I felt that God would help me. I took for my subject *Christian Heroism*, and the duties of the hour. I told them, although I was an Englishman by birth, I was then an American by adoption. That I had suffered oppression in my fatherland by those invested with a little power, who exercised it to the very letter. In this land of freedom, your forefathers fought for that independence of which you and I now boast. The Duke of Wellington was my commander-in-chief in 1842, when I joined the English army. The iron duke was the hero of a hundred battles. Napoleon Bonaparte was the king of warriors in the European world; but these two illustrious generals dwindle into insignificance when compared with your illustrious Washington. They fought for despotism, he for liberty and equality for all men. I then pointed to the flag above us, and told them I had fought for the union-jack, but now I would fight for the stars and stripes so long as God would give strength to my good right arm. Your country is my country, where you go I will go, as you are ready to pour out your life-blood for this union, undivided, now and forever, so am I ready to pour out my blood to keep that good old flag from trailing in the dust; and to preserve this glorious union, this best form of government the world ever saw, where every man is a king, and a king is but a man. At this point I did not know but they would all run wild. They shouted and cheered, and threw their hats into the air as if they never cared whether they ever had another hat or not. There was something in the *very air* on the occasion, in everything about us, that would almost make a dumb man eloquent. I will not say that I was eloquent, and I am sure I would not say I was not, for I have some religious objections to lying; but one thing is sure, the steam was up; the old American war-horse snuffed the battle, and not very far off.

But enough as to my speech. It pained some of my friends to hear of my speaking to a crowd upon the perils and duties

12

of the hour on the *Sabbath,* and Major Sturgis wrote me a letter expressing his regret at this step; he also thought I had better not get outsiders into the drill-room with the Young Men's Christian Association, it was mixing things up too much. Well, I was sorry to offend such a good man. I told him it would not do. We had a big job on our hands, and we must have *all the boys we could reach inside and out* to finish it up. He afterwards saw and acknowledged I was right, and was an unflinching, faithful friend, and often felt for me clear down into his breeches pocket.

At this time the numbers multiplied so who wanted to learn the drill, that I had not room for them at the Young Men's Christian rooms, and I went to see the governor for accommodations. He told me to go to the postmaster, and tell him to let me have the hall over the post-office, which I secured; and in the mean time, several other gentlemen got another hall on Washington street, and Deacon Hobert furnished another, so the ball was rolling good.

In these rooms I worked from five A. M. until ten P. M., drilling the different squads of men. Some of the rooms were for officers, and some for privates. I was so much on my feet, drilling men in the broad-sword and bayonet exercise and marching, that my feet became swollen so I could not put on my boots, and often worked in my stocking-feet.

At this time, Mr. Dwight came to me, and wanted me to aid his son (who was then stationed at Staten Island) to raise three hundred men to fill up his regiment. I went to work with all the energy I possessed to raise the men. I thought I would try a little of the old style to rope in the old country boys; so I got an Irishman and put a military suit on him, and put ribbons on his hat, and furnished him with a fifer and drummer, and the trio went down to Haymarket square, and through among the shipping offices, and the boats where they would be likely to find the boys, and in this way we soon got up a regular military fever, and in less than a week I got the three hundred men to fill up Colonel Dwight's regiment. Dwight was lieutenant-colonel at the time, and on the receipt of this addition, making a full compliment of men for his regiment, he was made colonel. Captain Bugbee, in this regiment, whom I had aided in filling his company, expressed his gratitude for my services in the following letter.

Co. H., 1st Regt.,
CAMP SCOTT, June 29th, 1861.

BROTHER AMBLER:

Dear sir,—I take a spare moment to thank you for your kindness and the services you rendered me. We are here and at home. Well received and kindly treated. Colonel Dwight is a fine man, a good officer, and well beloved by all, and we are all happy we are here; my company musters ninety-two men, and I expect to have one hundred inside of the next twenty-four hours.

Edlesson, who was sergeant but now second lieutenant, wishes you to have those instructions in the sword written off for him.

With friendship,

Capt. W. H. BUGBEE.

The captain had good reason to feel obliged, for I had drilled him and also his company, either in person or by proxy. Perhaps I ought to explain what I mean. I had so many men and officers under instruction, that I would give a sergeant a lesson and send him to the company to give the same lesson. This is what I mean by drilling by proxy.

I furnished my own swords and other drill articles with the exception of muskets, and those I obtained by such letters as the following:

BOSTON, May 2, 1861.

To ADJUTANT-GENERAL SCHOULER:

Dear Sir,—I have known Mr. I. W. Ambler for some time, and have all confidence in his integrity. Any arms the department may commit to his care, I have no doubt will be both properly cared for and accounted for.

Very truly,

HENRY HOYT,
WILLIAM R. STACY,
CHAS. H. PARKER,
CHAS. W. BABCOCK.

I got up a company of Englishmen who afterwards went to the front, and made many a rebel bite the dust. These fellows were true as steel and were well drilled, and no Yankee was more earnest and true. Some of the old British formality still clung to them, as the reader may see by the note which they usually sent me on drill nights, which I here insert.

BOSTON, June 11, 1861.

I. W. AMBLER, ESQ.

Sir,—The members of the Boston British Drill Club are to meet to-night in Revere Hall, Bowdoin square, at eight o'clock precisely. Your attendance is earnestly requested, therefore please fail not.   By order,

Clerk pro tem.

P. S. Any friends you may know interested in the cause invite them to meet with us and enroll their names, as we shall be happy to have an augmentation to our numbers.

These men were converts to the good cause made by my big speech from the balcony of the State-house on that memorable Sunday. I might as well call it a big one, for it was about a big thing, if the rhetorical flourishes were lacking, and it bore fruit that the rebs found rather hard to take.

I drilled Colonel Webster and some of his officers of the 4th Mass. Vol., who soon left for the seat of war.

For several months I toiled in the old Granite State, giving myself hardly time for food and sleep. The papers had considerable to say about my work at this time. Here is a little sample from the *Boston Journal* of June 5, 1861:

BOSTON AND VICINITY, June 5, 1861.

SERGEANT AMBLER AND HIS LABORS.— In justice to true merit we feel called upon to say that no one in our city has done, or is doing, more to inculcate a military sentiment among our people than our patriotic fellow citizen, Mr. Ambler. Leaving the pulpit for the drill-room, *he has given his whole time, without remuneration,* to the instruction of recruits; laboring incessantly for their benefit and for the cause, regardless alike of fatigue and personal comfort.

Mr. Ambler is an accomplished military tactician, having seen long service, and is equally at home with the musket, bayonet, or broadsword; and to him is due not a little of the skill of some of the officers of the Massachusetts Volunteer Militia in the use of the sword. To thorough experience in all branches of the military, he unites gentlemanly deportment and a felicitous manner of conveying his knowledge to others. His positions are classic and faultless, which, with his agility, gives him a wide range of personal defense.

He now has a large class receiving daily instructions in the broadsword exercise, and although no one scholar has taken more than six lessons, yet a remarkable progress has been made, and the proficiency manifested fully attests the ability of Mr. Ambler.

The highest terms of praise are bestowed by his pupils, who would take great pleasure in seeing him at the head of a military school upon a much larger scale, under the patronage of the State, which is due not less to the personal sacrifices he has made for the cause than to the acknowledged ability which he brings to the business.

On reading such squibs, the people in Maine began to feel as though they had some claims that a 'white man was bound to respect,' as I was a resident of that State, and letters came pouring in upon me, to go down and help them whet up things and show them 'how fields were won.'

CHAPTER XXVII.

The Sixth Maine were in camp at Camp Preble, and the following officers sent me an invitation to come and drill them in the broadsword and bayonet exercise, and the word of command: Col. Hiram Burnham, Capt. M. W. Brown, Capt. James Snowman, Capt. Benjamin F. Harris, Maj. Frank Pierce, Capt. Charles Day, Lieut. B. J. Buck, Lieut. W. Buck, Capt. W. H. Stanchfield, Adj. John D. McFarland, Lieut. Otis W. Kent, Lieut. George P. French, Lieut. H. B. Strout, Lieut. John M. Lincoln, Lieut. George Roberts, Lieut. W. P. Wardwell, Lieut. G. C. Poor.

On the 9th of July, I went to Camp Preble, and commenced my labors drilling the whole regiment. The officers insisted upon my going to the front with them, assuring me that I should receive the same pay and fare that they received from government. I decided to go with the regiment and instruct them, and share with them the fortunes of war. I intended to have enlisted and be mustered in with the rest of them. I got a pass from the colonel to spend a couple of days with my family at Biddeford, and, while at home, orders came from Washington to march at once, and the regiment was mustered in before I reached the camp, which accounts for my name not appearing on the muster-roll as an enlisted soldier, which afterwards proved most unfortunate for me, as will appear hereafter. On getting news that orders had come to go to the front, I hastened back to camp, accompanied by my good wife and little boy. As the regiment had no drum-major, I assumed the position, and we broke camp, and came into Portland, my wife and boy trudging along by my side.

When coming over Bramhall hill we met an old man, who gave me the first meal of victuals after my escape from the English army into the States. The poor old fellow threw up his hands and cried right out, and said, 'Sergeant Ambler, you are gone, you are gone, you'll never come back,' and this set wife and boy to crying, and I confess to a rising in my throat that made me a little uneasy; but I hushed them as well as I could, and told them God would take care of me wherever I went; but it was pretty hard. Civilians often have witnessed these partings; but they cannot know anything of the emotions that heave the heart of the husband and father, when he is leaving wife and children for the field of carnage. I had seen such parting scenes in the old world; but when I sailed away from old England for the Mediterranean, I was a poor orphan, caring for nobody and nobody cared for me, and I could not realize anything of the anguish that wrings the husband and father's heart until now. I was trying to comfort wife, but I needed ten men to keep the lumps down in my throat. It is said, misery loves company; but I don't believe it, for there were hundreds of friends following their dear ones to the depot, and it only made me feel worse to see so many crying around us. Little did we know who the angel of death was fluttering over, and who were shaking hands for the last time, to meet no more until Gabriel's trumpet calls us to judgment. The command came, 'All aboard,' and the Sixth Maine Volunteers rolled out of the depot for the seat of war, while the women and children were throwing kisses after us, and waving good-by with their handkerchiefs. Nothing of interest occurred until we arrived in New York, where we halted without leaving the steamer. A brief speech was made, and a beautiful silk banner was presented by the sons of Maine. Colonel Knowles responded. We then proceeded to Philadelphia, where a splendid collation awaited us, of which the boys partook, with many a hearty 'God bless the Quaker city.'

We took the cars at Philadelphia, and proceeded by the way

of Havre-de-grace, where we were delayed several hours. At
this place, a baker attempted to poison us by putting ground
glass in the cakes and pies which he sold us. None of the men
died from its effects, although some of them were severely injured. I had swallowed several mouth-fulls before I detected
it by crunching it with my teeth. I spit it into my hand, and
rubbed it in my fingers, and cut them with the fine particles of
glass, and could see them in my hand. I showed it to Captain
Snowman, who ran out and gave the alarm. One of the boys,
in attempting to get past the guard, to get at the baker, caught
his coat-sleeve on the cock of the gun, and the piece went off
and shot him just below the left nipple. I took him into a
house and got him into a bed. He told me what he wanted
said to his friends, and how he died. I said to him, you are
not going to die. You are not in half so much danger now as
we are, who have been eating glass; but I was mistaken. We
stripped him and found the ball had passed through him, and
he died in a few minutes. The boys were desperate. They
found the bake-shop and the machine that he ground the glass
with. They captured the rebel scamp and he got away, and
while pursued, one of the regulars shot him through the back
and killed him on the spot. The whole regiment loaded up to
be ready for any event. We soon were rolling on for Baltimore.
We marched through that rebel city in full expectation that
blood would run before we got through. The colonel ordered
me to the center of the regiment, to help protect the flag as it
was borne aloft. The plug-uglies were on the sides of the
street with bowie-knives, some of them drawn; but the rascals
saw by the white of our eyes that we meant business, and no
violence was offered. We reached Washington late at night,
July 19th, and no preparations had been made to 'fodder the
flock,' and our haversacks were troubled with the contribution-
box disease, viz., a terrible *emptiness.* We were quartered in
an old hall where we laid down our weary limbs on the soft
side of a hard floor, where we spent a sleepless night with

e.npty stomachs. The next morning, after a lunch of bread and coffee, we took up our line of march for Chain bridge. For some reason, some of our baggage-wagons did not arrive, so that when we got there, about half of our men had to sleep on the ground or under the bushes, anywhere they could get.

In the morning, we were awakened by the roar of cannon in the direction of Mannasas Junction and Bull Run. All through the day, heavy cannonading was going on. At night a courier arrived with dispatches, telling us that our troops had been routed, and the rebels were in full pursuit in the direction of our camp. This made the boys' eyes stick out, for it looked like business. Immediately company H. were hurried across the Potomac to go on picket-duty. The next morning the straggling hosts began to arrive. In no part of the world did I ever see such a sight. Some of them were black as negroes, smutty, and stained with blackberries upon which the poor fellows had fed coming through the woods. Some with every bit of their shirts above their breeches entirely torn off, or hanging in shreds about them. Some old soldiers that had fought at Sevastopol, were crying with rage and sorrow like little children, and I cried myself on meeting them in this terrible plight, and could not help it. Oh, it was a sad day for the Union army, and the country. I picked up two Zouaves, and helped them into camp, who had been wounded. One had a terrible wound in the thigh from a bayonet, and the other with a ball in the leg. I saw our surgeon extract the ball, and also a piece of his pants that had been carried into the flesh with it. Others were retreating towards Washington. The roads were blockaded with baggage-wagons, ambulances, artillery, and all the paraphernalia of war. One very tall man from the same place that I came from, run his poor horse until he came to the blockade, and leaped off, and with every particular hair standing on end, rushed over broken carts, dying horses, and every incumbrance, and reached the capital long before his horse could arrive, as I was told. The scene of that disaster beggars all description, and

God grant my eyes may never witness another such. The vanity of some of our shoulder-strapped gentry met a terrible rebuff, and, in truth, I must say that the attempt of some of them to lay that Bull Run defeat on the men, showed an unfairness not warranted by facts. For some of these raw officers showed about as much fitness to command armies as a toad does for the duties of a plenipotentiary. Another, and painful illustration of the need of such instruction as I had been so long endeavoring to impart without remuneration, with the single hope of rendering some aid to my adopted country in her time of need.

The Sixth Maine was the only regiment at this time at Chain bridge, and our duty was to hold it and prevent the victorious rebels from entering Washington in this direction. We had a whole company thrown across the Potomac, several miles out on picket, to give notice of the approach of the enemy. Captain Mott's battery was stationed on the bluff, commanding the bridge, so as to rake the enemy on their approach. I suggested to Captain Mott that a cavalry, dashing at full speed, might effect a crossing, and we had better take up every other plank on the bridge, and this would not hinder our troops from using it, and we could mow down all the rebs they could crowd on to it on foot, with our grape and canister. Colonel Burnham and Captain Mott ordered every other plank taken up and thrown into the Potomac, which was done by our men in double-quick. That relieved us from any fear from the enemy's cavalry. There was a large brick building at the end of the bridge, on the Virginia side, that might serve as a cover for the rebels on their approach, to which we paid our compliments. The battery, with solid shot and shell, plowed through the walls, tearing away the brick and stone, until it came down with a crash. We remained in possession of the bridge for some three weeks before we crossed in force into Virginia. About every night the alarm was sounded, and these shrill blasts of the bugle, ringing out on the night-air, would bring us to our feet in a trice; but the enemy did not appear in force. The alarms were occasioned by the firing of some rebel scouts at some of our pickets. This business was much harder for me than if we had been in battle. Our officers and men were feverish with anxiety to get on in their drill, and I made long days drilling them in the broadsword and bayonet exercise, which every military man understands is the hardest work done. Part of the time on picket in addition to this, and then sleeping on the ground after such exercise through the day, stiffened me up, and brought me a good deal under the weather. We were hard up for grub, and suffered a good deal from the diarrhœa, brought on by eating such green stuff as we could pick up in the fields, small fruits, crab apples, etc. One Sunday our good chaplain preached us a very touching sermon, telling us that the Sixth Maine were the greatest cursers, the greatest swearers, and the greatest thieves on God's footstool. During the following week I went to him and told him I was starving hungry, and I must have some bread if I had to steal it; and I told him I would get some bread, if he would get some meat, and we would have one good meal. He said he would do it. I went to an old Dutch woman's, and told her I wanted bread; she said she had none. I told her I didn't believe it, and if she would not give it to me I would take it; and she gave me two Johnny cakes, and I trotted back to camp, and found the chaplain had got five or six pounds of beef. I asked him how he got it, and he said it was none of my business where he got it. I told him that if God spared my life to get back to the State of Maine, I would tell them how the reverend gentleman stole beef down in Virginia.

He said, 'Ambler, if you do I will horsewhip you.' You had better believe, dear reader, that meat and bread tasted good, if the minister did steal it. About eight years after this, I met the parson in Portland, and sung out to him, 'there goes the chaplain that stole the beef in Virginia,' and he jumped right out of his wagon and horse-whipped me up Exchange street, and that squared our accounts. We have both kept our word like good honest men that we are.

I hope nobody will think either of us the worse for this, for we did it on the same principle that the disciples did when they 'began to pluck the ears of corn and to eat.' When the Pharisees saw it, they said 'Behold thy disciples do that which is not lawful to do on the Sabbath day.' The Master said unto them, 'Have ye not read what David did when he was a hungered, and they that were with him. How he entered into the house of God, and did eat the shew-bread which was not lawful for him to eat, neither for those which were with him? Or have ye not read in the law, how that on the Sabbath days the priests in the temple profane the Sabbath and are blameless?' There, brother T——, have I not been pretty good to you, after my horse-whipping, to make such a strong apology for your hooking the beef?

But to return to the thread of our discourse, as the preachers say; notwithstanding my hard work, I was on the look-out for everything that looked suspicious, and in reconnoitering down the river one day, I discovered some works thrown up by the rebels preparatory for mounting a battery during the night, about one mile below Chain bridge, on the Virginia side on a high bluff. I immediately notified Colonel Burnham, who sent a squad of men over the bridge to look after them. The rebels fled on the approach of our men. One Sunday Lieutenant Furlong and myself started for Arlington, on the Virginia side, to see them operate the balloons, while reconnoitering with them. As we were trudging along through a piece of woods, I stopped to light my pipe, and the lieutenant got on a little distance ahead, when a small squad of rebels rushed upon him, and would have captured him if it had not been for his wonderful presence of mind. He sung out at the top of his voice, 'Come on, boys, here they are,' and they took to their heels for dear life. I ran to see what was to pay, and they were just disappearing over the hill. That was what I called a good Yankee trick. In a day or two after this, General McLellan came up to reconnoiter, and gave his horse into my charge, and went over Chain bridge on foot to take a view of things, and when he came back, he called for three hundred men to go into Virginia on a scout. I asked the general if I could go with them. He said, '*certainly*,' and I gave the horse again into his charge to go on the scout. He made us a neat speech at the bridge, and, giving him three rousing cheers, we started. We had been perhaps a half an hour in Virginia, when the boys commenced firing; but what the brave fellows saw to shoot I never knew, for I did not see a reb. Nothing resulted from this tramp, and we returned to camp.

A few days after this, our pickets found the rebels throwing up some works near a place called Langly, about five miles from Chain bridge. Lieutenant Fitzgerald, accompanied by Captain Mott's battery, marched at once upon them, and a brisk skirmish commenced. Captain Mott opened upon them with some of his heavy guns. The rebels returned the fire from some of their pieces which they had got in position; but our fire was too hot for them, and they commenced their retreat, leaving several of their dead on the field. Some of our men were wounded, but none of them killed. As soon as we had routed them effectually, and sent them skedaddling up the Lewinsville road, orders were given to limber up and return to the other side of the Potomac. I felt considerable interest in the success of Mott's battery, as I had something to do with drilling a portion of them, and one of the gunners (named Charlie Lynch) was an Englishman who had been in my company in the English army, and so I asked the lieutentant how Charlie behaved under fire. 'Oh,' said he, 'he fought like a tiger.'

Very soon after this, General McLellan sent orders not to fire a gun, as preparations were going on for the whole army to move into Virginia, and when everything was in readiness for the Union army to march, the firing of a cannon was to be the signal.

CHAPTER XXVII.

AT this point, while the reader is waiting for our regiment 'to move on the enemy's works,' I will give some of the religious history of the Sixth Maine Volunteers while at Chain bridge. As a Christian, I felt as though we ought to find enough among us, who meant to serve the Lord, to make up a goodly number for a prayer-meeting, and so about the fourth day after we arrived at Chain bridge, I proposed to hold a prayer-meeting in the evening, to begin at early candle-lighting; and went through the streets of the camp and notified them that I would hold a prayer-meeting under a big elm tree within the lines. When the evening came, I took my Bible and went out to the old tree, and out of about eleven hundred men, five or six only came to the prayer-meeting. I told brother Strout, one of the privates present, that we had enough to claim the blessing. I stuck a bayonet into an old limb which was broken off the side of the tree, and put a candle in the socket, by the light of which I read a portion of God's word, and then called on good brother S—— to pray, and I tried to pray also. God blessed us both, and I tried to talk to them. No others took any part this first night. I gave notice that we would have a meeting at the same place the next night, and soon as I got through with the drill I would go throughout the camp and give notice of it. So as soon as I dismissed the men from the drill the next afternoon, I went all round and notified them, and to make sure of a congregation, I told them if they did not come to the prayer-meeting I would not drill them. I think I had over four hundred the next night. We used the old bayonet again for a candlestick, and I read God's word, and the Holy Ghost fell on us, and it was one of the best prayer-meetings I ever was in. Some backsliders confessed, and a number got up and asked for prayers. One backslider told us he had praying parents down on the old Penobscot river; that he had gone against them and hurt their feelings often; that he had once known the way and wickedly backslidden, and wanted us to pray for him. He said, 'we are now facing the rebels and can almost see them eye to eye, and if he was shot down, he wanted to be prepared to meet his God.' And he came out happy; he said he never was so happy in his life. He was a great help to the meetings, and proved faithful during my stay with the regiment. Oh, it was a glorious meeting; they cried and shouted for joy. Yes, you dear, easy, old Christian, in your carpeted church, with your great organ, and splendid choir, and big sermon, you never had a better meeting, with all your rich surroundings, than we did with the green earth for our floor, and the starry canopy of heaven over our heads for a roof, and the dim old candle shedding its faint glimmer around. There was an awfulness, a grandeur, a wonderful glory that fell on us in melting power, producing such a nearness to God as many had never before known. These were the first prayer-meetings held in the army, and I had rather have the honor of instituting such a work than all the honors of wealth and ease. The next night I gave the same notice after drill, and our numbers increased, and the power of God was with us. On the fourth evening, our chaplain came in with us, or rather up to the tree with us, and God spoke to us under the bush, if not out of it, and the chaplain got up and said, 'the Spirit of God is with you;' and I said, 'amen,' and brother Strout shouted 'hallelujah' at the top of his voice, and our chaplain poured out the truth among us with greater power than I ever heard him before. It was easy to speak. The waters were troubled and hearts were in the mood to hear, and so hungry for this manna from heaven that they seemed to eat every word, as though they felt it was God's bread fresh from heaven. And now, so much of the Holy Ghost was with us, that our good chaplain could discount considerable from the statements he made about us the first Sunday here.

He began to see there was amongst us some wheat as well as chaff, and that we were not all 'the greatest curses and thieves on God's footstool,' and of those who were a little off the track then, there was hope if the good work went on. Our meetings continued to increase in numbers and interest, until a large part of the regiment that was not on picket duty would be present, and quite a number were converted, and a good number of backsliders were reclaimed. I was gloriously rewarded for the extra efforts I had made. I often drilled eight companies in the bayonet and skirmish exercise in a day, besides twenty officers, giving them each separate lessons in the broadsword exercises, and then, after attending prayer-meetings, sometimes would go out on picket with the boys to spend the night; so you will see, my reader, that I eat no idle bread.

There was one little incident that occurred while here that touched me. One poor fellow was drowned in the canal, and was brought up and laid close to my tent, all covered with mud, and the flies were eating out his eyes and in his ears. I told the nurse (a good lady from Boston) that I knew he was a poor foreigner, and I was afraid, if I should die or be killed, that that was the way I might be left in the filth, with the flies and maggots eating my poor body. She said, 'no, drill-master, I will see to it myself,' and she went and washed the poor fellow all up clean, and then put our new silk flag over him. I looked on him after this good Samaritan had laid him out, with the flag lying on his manly breast, and I said, 'it is enough, I am content.'

Coming back now to the movements of the regiment into Virginia, I will begin with the visit of President Lincoln to our camp, accompanied by Secretary Chase and Charles Sumner. I was drilling some of the officers in the broadsword exercise when the president arrived, who seemed to take great interest in it, and clapped me on the shoulder, and laughed and said,

'that is very well done, very well done.' After the president
had gone to see Captain Mott's battery, Lieutenant Furlong
stepped up to me and said, 'that compliment from the president
is a feather in your cap, drill-master.'

On the arrival of the president and suite to the battery, Captain Mott fired a salute. The good president, after examining
our position, etc., talked with the soldiers, taking many of them
by the hand and speaking to them and encouraging them to be
true to the flag, and seemed like a father amongst his children.
The president left amidst the cheers of the whole camp. The
firing of the salute was taken as a signal along the lines for
moving into Virginia, on account of the previous orders not to
fire, and it made considerable confusion; but things were soon
explained to the satisfaction of the general, and Captain Mott
was excused for this little blunder. A day or two after this, a
negro who was employed to cook for some of the boys belonging to Mott's battery on the Virginia side of the Potomac, saw
a man near the cook's tent that he knew, and sung out to him,
'How are you, Massa?' The man scowled upon him and said,
'Cuffee, you don't know me.' 'Yes, Massa, I knows you, de
Lor' bless you, Massa; you spees I din know you, when dis
here chile help you build de battery at Manassas Junction?
golly, Massa, dis chile spec's you done gone to de wrong place.'
The boys began to smell a rat, and seized him and took him to
General Smith's head-quarters. I met him when the boys were
bringing him over Chain bridge and said to him, 'Well, old
boy, we've got you.' I never saw a man look so savage as he
did at me, and he swore like an old pirate. I told him the old
darkey was too sharp for him to come prowling round our camp.
On stripping him they found a complete plan of all our works
sewed up in one side of his vest, and the poor old rebel was
afterwards hung as a spy, I suppose. On the picket line a good
many rebel prisoners were taken by our boys and brought in;
sometimes as many as twenty or thirty in a day.

My labors were intense about this time, and the weather was

very hot. One day I had drilled several companies, going through it practically, and then with the colonel crossed the Potomac and went on to the picket line, and had a long tramp reconnoitering, and then came back to camp in the hottest part of the day. I found, on my return, that some of the officers of the Vermont regiment had called for me for a drill in the bayonet exercise. I went out to drill them with a Zouave cap on my head, and gave them instructions, explaining and then going through the exercise; and while at it I was sun-struck, and fell to the ground. I knew nothing for some time, and when I came to myself there was a crowd around me who thought I was dead. I felt strangely, and put my hand to my head and took hold of my cap to pull it off, and all the hair came off the top of my head with my cap. When Colonel Burnham found me in this condition, he sent me to Washington, to the care of Hon. D. E. Somes, our representative from Maine, where I was kindly treated until I was able to return to the field.

When I was on my way to Mr. Somes' I met a fellow townsman (James Andrews) whose services in going for a doctor and medicine will ever be gratefully remembered. In a short time, I returned to the regiment, and continued my labors among the officers and men, whose improvement in the arts of war was very marked. In consulting the officers of the regiment and others, it was decided that I could accomplish ten times as much for the country in returning to the East, and giving instruction to new regiments then forming, of officers and men, as it was possible for me to do as a private carrying the musket, especially since my being sun-struck; and as my name was not on the muster-rolls,—the reason for which I have before given, —there would be nothing in the way of my doing so. I had got my trunk packed, and intended to bid good-by to the boys in a day or two, when orders came for the army to march into Virginia. I resolved to go with them into this fight. After crossing the Potomac, we deployed to the right and left, and threw up what was afterwards called Fort Ethan Allen.

SUNSTRUCK AT CHAIN BRIDGE.

There was a long piece of woods at the left of the turnpike where the rebels went to cover, and from which they picked off a good many of our men. These woods were a little below Chain bridge, and extended several miles.

Orders were given to cut down this forest, and thousands of men from the different regiments were detailed for the work. The boys worked with a will, and in an incredibly short time we had the fire sweeping over thousands of acres. The smoke had hardly cleared away when a courier arrived with dispatches, saying that the enemy were upon us in force, and our pickets were coming in. I wanted to see how our boys would behave under fire, and I resolved to go with them and share with them victory or defeat.

Pretty soon our pickets began to come in, shouting as they arrived on the double quick, 'The rebels are upon us!' The long roll was beat, calling our men to arms. Some of our men were down on the banks of the Potomac, getting out the dead bodies of our boys, who had been shot by the rebs and thrown into the river.

Colonel Burnham ordered me to go over to the river and rally the boys there, and he would fall in the regiment and be ready to march on my return. I ran as fast as my legs would carry me, and shouted to them as soon as I got in hearing, 'The rebs are upon us, and our pickets are driven in. Now is your time to strike for your country, and show what kind of stuff you are made of.' We struck a bee-line for the regiment. Passing a sentry, I seized his musket, telling him to get another, and sung out to the boys, 'Now men, I have showed you the theory of war, I will now show you the practical part.' They cheered and sung out, 'Bully for Ambler.' The regiment had fallen in and were on the march as we came up. I rushed up to the picket line, and Captain Mott's battery came tearing along with twelve horses dragging one of his big guns, the others following, and I got so earnest for the fray, that I fell right in with the battery and rushed with them, until we found

ourselves face to face with the enemy, when we halted and unlimbered for action, and poured in our fire upon the rebel troops
and some of his cavalry, our big gun cutting awful gaps in
their ranks. For two hours there was fighting all along our
lines, until we routed them. How many were killed and wound
ed we never knew.

We lost some men, and some were taken prisoners. We then
returned to camp pretty well exhausted, and pretty well satisfied with our day's work. Men never behaved better under fire
than the Sixth Maine Volunteers. The day had been intensely
hot. At night, it came on to rain, and the whole regiment had
to sleep on the ground in the mud and water. Perhaps, reader,
you may think Ambler puts himself pretty prominently into
this picture. Well, if you think I am egotistical, you shall
see what an eye witness had to say about it, and you must remember, too, that I am writing about myself. Here is what
was published in the *Boston Journal* at that time, referring to
this event:

Sergeant Ambler.—The following extract from an army
letter, contains some intelligence of a gentleman who will be
remembered by many in this city as an accomplished drill-master. He has been connected with the Sixth Maine Regiment
as an instructor, and was with them in the recent reconnoisance
on Lewinsville. He writes thus: 'Accompanying the Sixth
Maine Regiment was an Englishman, a teacher of the sword exercise, well-known in Boston as a teacher of fencing and bayonet exercise (I. W. Ambler), who stands at the head of his profession, and has won the esteem of the whole regiment by his
active and energetic disposition, and kind and generous nature;
and he showed himself to be a soldier, not only in theory but
in reality. Although he had packed his trunk and made all due
preparations for leaving for home, his term of engagement having expired, when the cannon began to boom, he took a musket
from a sentry, and marched at the head of the regiment, saying,

'Come on boys, now is the time to show whether you can fight,' and led the way up to the pickets amid the cheers of the regiment, and cries of 'bully for Ambler.' The pervading spirit of the troops seems to be an eagerness for action, prevailing so powerfully, that even the sick will smuggle themselves into the ranks against the orders of the physician. With such a spirit pervading our army, what may we not expect as the result of the war, and what have we to fear?'

No better fighting was done during the war, and there were instances of personal valor that would shed a lustre on the old Spartan days. As I was looking out for stragglers and others who had got separated from the main body next day, I met Captain Wm. E. Strong, of the First Wisconsin Regiment, coming in covered with blood, with a hole shot in his cheek. He looked every inch a hero; a strong, manly form, only twenty-two years old, who had rushed from College to the battlefield. He tells his own story better than I can, and I give it here as he gave it.

'As I was passing through a thicket I was surrounded by six rebel soldiers, four infantry and two cavalry; seeing I was caught, I thought it best to surrender at once, so I said, 'Gentlemen, you have me.' I was asked various questions as to who I was, where I was going, to what regiment I belonged, etc. all of which I refused to answer. One of the footmen said, 'Let us hang the d——d Yankee scoundrel,' and pointed to a convenient limb. Another said, 'No, let us take him to camp and hang him there.' One of the cavalry, who seemed to be the leader said, 'We'll take him to camp.' They then marched me through an open place; two footmen in front, and two in rear, and a cavalry man each side of me. I was armed with two revolvers and a sword. After going some twenty rods, the sergeant, who was on my right, noticing my pistols, commanded me to halt and give them up, together with my sword. I said, 'certainly, gentlemen,' and immediately halted. As I stopped they all filed past me, and of course were in front.

'We were at this time in an open part of the woods, but about sixty yards to the rear was a thicket of undergrowth. Thus everything was in my favor. I was quick of foot, and a passable shot. Yet the design of escape was not formed until I brought my pistol pouches to the front part of my body, and my hand touched the stocks. The grasping my pistols suggested my cocking them as I drew them out. This I did, and the moment I got command of them I shot down the two footmen nearest me, about six feet, one with each hand, and ran for the thicket. The confusion of my captors was so great that I had nearly reached cover when they fired. One ball passed through my left cheek and out of my mouth. Another musket ball went through my canteen. The two cavalry separated, one to my right, the other to my left, to cut off my retreat. The remaining two footmen charging directly down on me. I turned and fired three or four shots, but the balls flew wild and on I ran, when I got over a small hillock and had nearly regained one of our pickets, I was headed off by both the mounted men.

'The sergeant called on me to surrender. I gave no reply, but fired at him, and ran in the opposite direction. He overtook me, and just as his horse's head was nearly abreast of me, I turned and took good aim and pulled the trigger, but the cap snapped. At this time his carbine was unslung, and holding it with both hands on the left side of his horse, he fired at my breast without raising the piece to his shoulder; and the shot passed through the side of my coat and shirt just grazing the skin. The piece was so near as to burn the cloth about the size of one's hand. I then fired at him and brought him to the ground, hanging by his foot in the left stirrup, his horse galloping toward his camp. I saw no more of the other horseman on my left, nor of the footmen; but, running on, soon came to our pickets, much exhausted from my exertions and loss of blood.'

Sure enough, with such a spirit as that we had a right to expect a victory, and I think such daring should be written in letters of gold, and I say '*Hurrah for Captain Strong.*'

One more touching incident, of which I was an eye-witness, and with which I had something to do, I will describe before I leave the front. It was about this time that William Scott, a private of a Vermont regiment, while on sentry went to sleep; and in this condition was found, and taken before a court-martial, tried, found guilty, and was sentenced to be shot. I visited the poor fellow in the guard tent, and said, 'William, I hope God has prepared you for the awful trial.' He was deeply moved. Tears ran down his sun-burnt cheeks. He looked at me a moment, and then looked up to heaven and said, 'If it is God's will that I must be shot, O God, thy will be done! Drill-master pray for me, and pray for me in your meeting to-night under the old elm tree.' I talked to him as well as I knew how, and got down on my knees by his side and prayed God to strengthen him; but my heart was too full for utterance, and my feelings for my poor comrade found vent in tears much better than in words. We had his case mentioned under the tree in our prayer-meeting, and there were many groans and tears and prayers for poor Scott that night. We knew he was a good soldier, and never would have slept on his post if he had not been exhausted from heavy marching and overwork. When the day came for him to be shot, orders were given for twelve muskets to be placed in position, six of them to be loaded with balls, the others with blanks, and all capped; and twelve men were detailed for the painful duty, each to select his gun, so that neither could know who had shed his comrade's blood. The men filed out, six on each side in a line, and William Scott in the centre. I took my place beside him, and orders were given,—'Attention, forward march.' As I walked by his side I told him to keep up good heart, and die like a soldier and a Christian. He held the Testament in both hands, looking down on it, and kept turning one thumb over the other. I wanted to see if Americans could stand up to be shot as boldly as some Europeans had done. I had seen English soldiers kneel on their coffins, and open their bosoms with their own hands, until six bullets pierced them, and fall headlong in their coffins. I was anxious that William should stand as firm.

When we reached the spot where my comrade was to die, all the regiments, some ten thousand men, had fallen in and formed round in the form of a triangle, its open point looking off into Virginia, opposite which William stood. I stood beside him when his crime was read and the sentence of the court-martial to be shot, encouraging him to put his trust in God, and meet death like a man. I then stepped aside, as the twelve men were getting into position to fire. He looked toward the open space, off into Virginia, and then looked at me and dropped his head. At this moment word ran along the lines that a horseman was seen approaching, waving his sword in the air. He dashed up to the lines, his horse covered with foam, and waving his sword again, handed a dispatch to an orderly, who passed it to the officer in charge. He opened it with a trembling hand, and with a more tremulous voice read the pardon sent by President Lincoln, while cheer after cheer rent the air as the president followed rapidly in his coach. When the word *pardon* fell on Scott's ear he ran to me and fell on my neck with both arms around me, exclaiming, 'I am saved.' I cried like a baby, and could not help it; and the eyes of the soldiers filled with tears as they cheered the good president for this just act of clemency, and full well did William Scott merit it. Most, if not all of my readers, have read of William's heroic conduct afterwards, until he met his death on the field of battle, gallantly fighting for the Union.

THE SLEEPING SENTINEL.

'T was in the sultry summer time, as war's red records show,
When patriot armies rose to meet a fratricidal foe,
When from the North, and East, and West, like the upheaving sea,
Swept forth Columbia's sons to make our country truly free.

Within a prison's gloomy walls where shadows veiled decay,
In fetters on a heap of straw a youthful soldier lay,
Heart-broken, hopeless, and forlorn, with short and feverish breath,
He waited but the appointed hour to die a culprit's death.

Yet, but a few brief weeks before, untroubled with a care,
He roamed at will and freely drew his native mountain air,
Where sparkling streams leap mossy rocks, from many a woodland
        fount,
And waving elms and grassy slopes give beauty to Vermont.

Without a murmur he endured a service new and hard;
But wearied with a toilsome march, it chanced one night on guard
He sank exhausted at his post, and the gray morning found
His prostrate form, a sentinel asleep upon the ground.

So in the silence of the night, all weary on the sod
Sank the disciples, watching near the suffering Son of God;
Yet Jesus, with compassion moved, beheld their heavy eyes,
And though betrayed to ruthless foes, forgiving, bade them rise.

But God is love!   Finite minds can faintly comprehend
But gently mercy in his rule may with stern justice blend.
And this poor soldier, seized and bound, found none to justify,
While war's inexorable law decreed that he must die.

'Twas morning.   On a tented field and through the heated haze
Flashed back from lines of burnished steel the sun's effulgent blaze;
While from a sombre prison-house, seen slowly to emerge,
A sad procession o'er the sward moved to a muffled dirge.

And in the midst with faltering step, and pale and anxious face,
In manacles between two guards a soldier had his place.
A youth led out to die!   And yet it was not death, but shame
That smote his gallant heart with dread, and shook his manly frame.

Still on before the martialed ranks the train pursued its way,
Up to the designated spot whereon a coffin lay.
His coffin!   And with reeling brain, despairing, desolate,
He took his station by its side, abandoned to his fate.

There came across his wavering sight strange pictures in the air.
He saw his distant mountain home. He saw his mother dear.
He saw his father, bowed with grief through fast declining years.
He saw a nameless grave, and then the vision closed in tears.

Yet once again, in double file advancing, there he saw
Twelve comrades, sternly set apart to execute the law;
But saw no more. His senses swam, deep darkness settled round,
And, shuddering, he waited now the fatal volley's sound!

Then suddenly was heard the noise of steeds and wheels approach,
And rolling through a cloud of dust appeared a stately coach.
On past the guards and through the field its rapid course was bent,
Till halting 'mid the lines, was seen the nation's president!

He came to save that stricken soul, now waking from despair,
And from a thousand voices rose a shout which rent the air.
The pardoned soldier understood the tones of jubilee,
And, bounding from his fetters, blessed the hand that made him free.

'Twas spring. Within a verdant vale, where Warwick's crystal tide
Reflected o'er its peaceful breast fair fields on either side;
Where birds and flowers combined to cheer a sylvan solitude,
Two threatening armies, face to face, in fierce defiance stood.

A sudden shock, which shook the earth 'mid vapors dense and dim,
Proclaimed along the echoing hills the conflict had begun.
While shot and shell athwart the stream with fiendish fury sped,
To strew among the living lines the dying and the dead.

Then louder than the raging storm pealed forth the clear command,
Charge, soldiers, charge! And at the word, with shouts, a fearless
    band,
Two hundred heroes from Vermont rushed onward through the flood,
And upward, o'er the rising ground, they marked their way in blood.

The smitten foe before them fled in terror from his post,
While, unsustained, two hundred stand to battle with a host!
Then turning, as the rallying ranks with murderous fire replied,
They bore the fallen o'er the field and through the purple tide.

The fallen! And the first who fell, in that unequal strife,
Was he whom mercy sped to save when justice claimed his life.
The pardoned soldier! And while yet the conflict raged around,
While yet his life-blood ebbed away through every gaping wound,

While yet his voice grew tremulous, and death bedimmed his eye,
He called his comrades to attest he had not feared to die.
And, with his last expiring breath, a prayer to Heaven was sent,
That God, with his assisting grace, would bless our president.

It must not be forgotten how his pardon was obtained. His sister, hearing of his sentence, came on to Washington, and on her knees pleaded with the president for her brother, telling him that her brother left home against the wishes of his father and mother, all glowing with patriotism, determined to fight for the flag; that his father was a minister, and that shooting William would carry her father and mother broken-hearted to the grave; and, with upturned and streaming eyes, saying, 'Dear president, spare, oh spare my poor brother.'

CHAPTER XXVIII.

And here I leave the boys for the East, to help blow up the
the Union fire there, and show the new regiments how to use
the implements of war. Poor fellows, how I pitied them, lying
in the corn-fields, with no tents, covering themselves with corn-
stalks, anything to keep the dews and night winds off; often
waking up to find it raining and themselves in puddles of water; many sick with diarrhœa. It was the hardest time of the
war. Arrangements had not been perfected for the comfort and
health of the men, everything having been done in haste. Regiments had been hurried to the front to protect the capital, without the necessary conveniences with them to make their condition even tolerable; but such are the fortunes of war. But I
must leave. The work of drilling the new regiments demanded
my attention, and my motto had been, 'Help the country anywhere and anyhow.' I had now been toiling some seven
months without pay, and when I left the boys I had no money
to get home with, or to buy rations on the way. When I got
to Georgetown, I sold my watch and ring to get something to
eat.

When I got to Washington, I called on General Scott, to see
if I could get a pass to Maine. His orderly took me in to
see him. As I entered his room, I gave him the military salute.
Well,' said General Scott, in his peculiar military short-hand,
'what do you want, my man?' I said, 'I want a pass to go to
Maine.' Then the general said, 'What are you doing, sir, at
the front?' I told him I had been drilling the officers and men
of the Sixth Maine Volunteers and some others. Said he,

' Where did you learn your drill?' I told him, 'In the English army, which I joined in 1842.' 'Who was your commander-in-chief?' asked Scott. I told him 'the Duke of Wellington.' 'Who,' said he, 'the Iron Duke, my bosom friend? What tactics are you drilling in?' I told him, 'Scott's heavy infantry, and sometimes in light infantry; but I had been drilling mostly in the bayonet and broadsword exercise, and the skirmish exercise.'

'Well,' said the general, 'suppose you have a company standing at "attention" with their fire-arms, explain the shoulder of arms to me in common time.' I said, 'at the word "shoulder" is only a caution; at the word "arms," the fire-lock must be thrown, in one motion, and with as little appearance of effort as possible, into its proper position on the left shoulder, the hand crossing the body in so doing. Stand steady, men. Wait for the word "two." At the word "two," drop the right hand as quick as possible to the right side. Stand steady, men, not a move.' 'That will do, that will do,' said the old general, 'here Mr. ——, go with this soldier to Thomas A. Scott, the Secretary of War, and tell him to give this man a pass to Maine and back. There was a little advantage in going to the old general, for an order from him was immediately attended to, although there were about the office of the secretary several hundred applicants; I got my passes without a question or delay. It is a little funny that I was recognized by the war department for service and passes, but not for pay. Here is one of the passes from the Secretary of War:

WAR DEPARTMENT,
WASHINGTON, Sept. 10, 1861.

AGENT N. H. & N. L. AND STONINGTON RAILROAD Co., Boston.

Please furnish Sergeant Ambler, Sixth Regiment Maine Volunteers, with passage free of charge to him from Boston to New York, on government account.

Relieved from duty upon certificate of Thomas A. Scott
Cause,—returning from recruiting.

By order of the Secretary of War,

THOMAS A. SCOTT.
General Manager of Government Railways and Telegraphs
Received Ticket, ——— ———, 1861.

Note.—Please file this order and return it to the department,
with account stated to the first of each month, properly certified for payment.

My passes from Washington to Maine were given up of
course, and placed on file in the war department at Washington, according to the note appended to the pass I have inserted.
Not returning to Washington, this one was not used, therefore
it remains in my hands. The reason of my not returning to
the seat of war, was not because my whole soul was not heartily in the cause, neither was it because I did not get any pay
for my service, for I have ever felt confident, that when the
facts of my relation to the army, sufferings and service were
fully understood, a just government would not allow a poor
fellow like me to go entirely unrewarded.

My condition was such that I *could not* go back, as the following communication in the *Portland Advertiser* will show,
better than I can describe it. It is headed:

SERGEANT AMBLER. *Mr. Advertiser,*—A case of great
hardship has just come to my knowledge, and I must beg your
help.

Sergeant Ambler, so well known as a soldier of the Cross,
after giving his whole time and all his earnings for the last
twelvemonth to the service of his adopted country, is now suffering—he and his family—both from sickness and want.

After giving,—literally *giving* instructions to the officers and
men of the Massachusetts and Maine Volunteers, month after

month; after training the Sixth Maine Regiment in Virginia, and the Fifteenth Maine Regiment in Augusta, he had his right wrist dislocated by the stroke of a sabre,—took a severe cold there in camp, which was followed by a rheumatic fever of three months; and then came to Portland intending to teach the bayonet and broadsword exercise, with most encouraging prospects, hoping to secure something for his family before he returned to the South; but while giving the second lesson here in the bayonet exercise, he ruptured a blood vessel, and might have bled to death, but for the patient kindness and providential care of strangers. At this time, having nearly lost the use of his left hand, partly on account of an old sabre stroke, and partly from the waste of blood, he is now helpless, and almost hopeless, though upheld by a Christian faith.

Nothing worthy of note occurred on my way home. I felt somewhat jaded out with my hard work at the front, and my long ride day and night to reach the old Pine Tree State; but it was good to sit down again with my family, and a few days of rest, with the good nursing and care of a faithful wife, put me on my 'taps' again as good as new. My services as drill-master, at home and at the front, had given me some notoriety, and the papers dragged me into notice again. I was immediately beset from all quarters from new regiments then forming, for instruction in the various drill exercises, and I could not stay at home if I would, and I am sure I would not stay at home if I could, when my glorious adopted country was in peril, and the boys needed instruction in the arts of self-defense.

I got up a company of over a hundred men in Biddeford, whose names I now have on my list, and drilled them. I did not expect to deviate from the usual course of instruction in this company; but after teaching the officers the broadsword exercise, and all of them the bayonet exercise, and the various maneuvring, marching, and word of command, the privates insisted in being taught the broadsword exercise as well as the officers. It being in my own city, and the boys my own neighbors and friends, I gave the whole company instruction in each exercise, so that the privates were not a whit behind the officers in the use of the broadsword. This pleased them, and, on the whole, gratified me, for I felt some pride in having the city where I lived well represented on the field. Every man was prepared, if an officer fell, to take his place.

They made such progress, that I concluded to give a public exhibition, for three reasons. The first was to get up a military fever among the citizens, and so fill up the regiments. The second was to show what skill the boys had attained. And the final reason was to get a little cash; for there was a very solemn sound in my larder about this time, calling on me to recruit a little in that direction, if I would escape a merited curtain lecture. So I selected sixteen men of the company, and gave an exhibition in the city hall, of which the *Journal* gave the following report:

Sergeant Ambler's Military Exhibition. Another Tremendous Battle.—Amid the tumult and wonderful revelations of war, it is not surprising that the fiery waves of battle should break over the quiet city of Biddeford, for places no less prosperous and happy have been quite as seriously visited.

But the premonitions of the conflict of which we are writing had been so freely scattered among us as to arouse and prepare the people, in some degree at least, for the opening of the warlike drama. Nor had the announcement that a West Pointer, a pupil of the idolized McLellan would appear, served to diminish the already excited anticipations of the people.

The hall door was besieged by no noiseless throng long before they were opened, and after they were, a continual crowd poured in until every nook and corner of the spacious room was alive with human forms. Never before was this hall so densely packed, and we believe it never will be again, unless

Drilling Infantry — Bayonet Exercise.

Sergeant Ambler should repeat his performance, which he has already been requested to do.

The immense audience, all restive and anxious, grew impatient.

Finally the exhibition opened, and the audience were enlightened in the use of the bayonet and sword, giving them some idea of the skill which a soldier must acquire in order to do good service in battle.

The exercises with the sword and bayonet elicited universal admiration, and as the movements, which no unfamiliar person could comprehend, were explained by the sergeant, his magic words fanned the burning excitement into one long, wild shout of applause, as the gale fans the kindling flame into a terrific conflagration.

The grand performance of the evening was the cavalry charge. Taking the masked battery. Sergeant Ambler commanding the centre, rode in upon his splendid charger, purchased expressly for the occasion, with Haley and Horton upon the right and left wings. The conflict was long and severe; and as Ambler clung to his horse with obstinate tenacity, his praises were borne upward from every part of pit and gallery.

The fight grew hotter; and as the keen and perceptive sergeant saw that the courage of his troops was changing to dismay, and fearing another Bull Run stampede might occur, unless his own brave deeds could rally them, he dismounted, and leaving his unterrified charger loose, despite the vociferous admonitions of the audience, 'hitch him,' 'tie him,' etc., etc., walked up to the very face of the masked battery, which was all the time pouring out shot and shell from its savage Columbiad, followed by his defiant troops, who now seemed bent on victory or death. The rebels under Beauregard resisted with unwonted obstinacy, and were only overpowered after a long and cruel fight, such as the people of this city have seldom been called upon to behold.

Strange to relate, none were killed in this engagement, but

14

among the wounded were the following, who are all injured more or less severely:

Sergeant Ambler, Co. A, First Infantry—side and leg, caused by a severe collision of his body with a sightless weapon in the hands of a rebel.

Dr. Haley suffered a facial disfigurement.

Stephen Andrews, contusion on the cranium.

Henry Hutchins, injured arm.

William Hoppin, abrasure of the skin on the shoulder.

Mr. Horton, West Pointer, wounded in the back and elbow by a sword thrust.

William Annis, wounded in the back.

Many of the best features of the performance would improve by repetition, and we hope to hear from our worthy citizen soldier again.

Notwithstanding admitting my Company, and the Sabbath-school I had formed in the city free, besides some other dead-heads, with an admission fee of only ten cents, I realized over seventy dollars, which I handed over to Mrs. Ambler with my compliments, and for which she smiled like a May morning, and of course the promised curtain lecture was indefinitely postponed. I then went to Augusta to drill some of the First Maine Cavalry in the use of the sabre. The Fifteenth Maine Volunteers were in camp here at this time, and also the Thirteenth. General Dow, of Portland, was then colonel of the Thirteenth Maine Volunteers, the officers of which I drilled in the various exercises, and whose mark was made on many a battle-field. See General Dow's letter.

I know Sergeant Ambler well, and have done so for many years. Without pay or position, he rendered me important aid in drilling company officers, mostly new and green, in my command, as they came into camp from their various localities.

NEAL DOW, *late Brigadier-general, U. S. Vols.*

While drilling the Fifteenth Maine Volunteers, I met with an accident which put me back some in my work here. When drilling Captain Prescott my right wrist was dislocated, and then set by Dr. Kimball. This, in connection with lying in a cold camp, for it was winter, brought on a rheumatic fever which laid me by for some time; but with good nursing after getting home, by the best wife in the world, I got about again, and went to Portland to drill the officers of the camps in the vicinity. Mayor McLellan gave me the use of the city hall for this purpose. My wrist had not got very strong, but the needs of the officers were so great for instruction to prepare them for the field, that I ventured to do the best I could. I could get on very well with the sword exercise with great care. While drilling a lieutenant in the bayonet exercise at self-defense, I gave word for him to longe out in prime. I parried in prime. The socket of his bayonet and the muzzle of his firelock struck against the center of my firelock with force, bringing my left wrist back and badly breaking it. This would not have happened had not my right wrist been weakened by the recent dislocation at Augusta, which prevented my parrying in prime with sufficient strength to withstand the longe in prime of a heavy man. While endeavoring to recover my balance, so as to save myself from falling, I ruptured a blood-vessel, and the blood flowed freely from my stomach. I asked the boys to take me to Rev. Mr. Tuckerman's, who aided with others in stanching the blood. Any continued violent effort to this day sets me to bleeding, and from which I never expect to fully recover. I was taken home to Biddeford, and doctors Greene and Hill set my wrist and put on splints, and as I had become considerably exhausted from loss of blood and pain from my broken arm, they proposed to me to take a little brandy. I told them no, I would die before I would touch another drop of liquor. It had well-nigh made me over, soul and body, to the devil, and once fully out of his clutches, I preferred death to returning to the old fellow's camp and rations.

As soon as I was able to go out, with my left arm in splints,

I went to Augusta; as the cry was still coming from the regiments there for help in the drill, and with my broken arm slung behind me, I drilled the Sixteenth Maine Volunteers. I was obliged to be very cautious, on account of the old rupture of the blood-vessel alluded to before; I got on very well, but drilling is a very dangerous work at the best. One day, while drilling back of the State-house, a large number of spectators being present, among whom was the mayor of our city and Mr. Chas. Hardy, I met with another mishap. I was giving a lesson in the sword exercise to one of the officers, who made a false thrust and stuck the point of his small sword through my right-hand, between the thumb and index finger, which came very near giving me the lockjaw. Here I was, a double and twisted cripple. My left wrist broken, my right hand terribly cut, and inwardly ruptured, so that nobody would have bid three cents for me if I had been put up at auction, except my wife, who insisted upon it that she wouldn't abate a cent from my value on that account. What strange creatures these women are! The more a fellow is used up, the more they set by them. Well, that was my case. When I got home, my wife not only had to earn my bread for me, but to put it into my mouth, and then laugh at me because I had the blues over it. In this condition the boys of the Sixteenth made me the first donation that I had received since I entered the service.

But time, that old doctor that has done so much since Adam to heal us all, had done well for me, my right hand got well and I went again to Augusta, and drilled the Twenty-first Regiment, of which Colonel Johnson was in command. I had to do the work with one hand, the other slung behind me. The editor of the *Kennebec Journal* at this time, writes: 'Colonel Johnson, of the Twenty-first, requests us to say, that he feels greatly obliged to him (Sergeant Ambler) for the instruction he himself has received, and that imparted to the officers and men of his command by Mr. Ambler. Few men during the war have done more, with less reward pecuniarily, than he. If thanks could make a man rich, Sergeant Ambler would be wealthy indeed, but unfortunately it takes something more substantial to support life. We hope his case will not be forgotten by the Legislature.'

At this time volunteering began to slack up, and it was hard filling up these regiments. I went to Bath and made a speech to raise men, and soon got over a hundred men for the Twenty-first, with the promise that I would drill them. I found 'lip exercise' as important as anything at this period, and having seen long service in the English army and some at home, I could get men, when the 'go-boys' speech-makers often failed. I went to Biddeford and spoke, and to Boston where I first opened fire, and spoke there again and again, and got hundreds of my countrymen to enter the service. Here, I was requested to go to Long Island and Galloup's Island, to drill General Deven's command. This was a rendezvous where men were carried as fast as recruited, to be drilled and sent to the front. I spent a good deal of time here, from the last part of 1863, to April, 1865, instructing both officers and men, as my passes will show. I here give the general pass, with its date, and the date of the last indorsement on the back of it, by Captain Rand, captain of the guard.

HEAD-QUARTERS, DEPARTMENT DRAFTED MEN,
LONG ISLAND, BOSTON HARBOR, Oct. 8, 1863.

Pass Sergeant Ambler to Long Island and return, by boat. Good until further orders.

By order of Brigadier-general Devens,

W. A. HILL, *Lieut. A. A. A. G.*

This shows my first service here, and the last. On the back of this general pass is the following from Captain Rand.

April 4, 1865.

Corporal of the guard will consider this good until further orders.

(Signed) RAND.

Thus the reader will see, from the time the first gun was fired on Fort Sumpter up to the surrender of General Lee, I worked for my adopted country in every way in my power. Can any man upon the muster-rolls show a prompter, a more patient and unwearied service for the Union, from the beginning to the end of the war, though he were native born?

'Tis true, I could not say of my wounds, broken bones, and disabilities, that they were received while gallantly leading in the charge, and so excite the admiration of all by such daring; but they were received as truly in the country's service, in more humble and less exciting scenes; but often requiring more self-denial and patience in duty, than when inspired by the presence of the enemy, the shrill notes of the bugle's call, the thundering of cannon, and the rattling musketry, and the echoing commands of the plumed officers dashing along the lines on their foaming chargers. These things have an inspiration to make men valliant, when a mightier will and a higher patriotism only can hold a man up to the work amidst less exciting scenes at home.

When the war had ended, and the dust and din of battle had ceased, and the good old flag floated in triumph once more over our undivided country, in looking over the whole matter, I could not regret the steps I had taken. I felt inwardly that I had played the part of a man, and could I have multiplied myself into a thousand drill-masters, all should have been laid on the altar of Liberty and Union. But here were now some shadows that would not down at my bidding. Painful realities stared me in the face that I must now grapple with as best I could. My health shattered, a cripple for life, and a family looking to me for bread, with the little means I had saved up to educate myself with all gone, poverty—dire, cruel, pittiless—staring me and mine in the face. Oh, it is easier to face armies with a man's heart and hopes, than to stand crippled and helpless, with grim want shaking its pittiless finger in your face. I was obliged, from my crippled state and with my proud heart, to say,

'To dig, I cannot; to beg, I am ashamed.' Without an education, and one hand useless at my side, and the constant danger from a ruptured blood-vessel, it was not much unlike human nature to have a set-to with the blues, with a family on my hands, and no prospect of ever being a sound man. See the surgeon's letter.

Saco, Me., March 13, 1871.

This may certify, that I have known Sergeant I. W. Ambler for a long series of years, both before and since the 'War of the Rebellion,' and on the breaking out of the war he threw all aside, and entered heart and hand into the service of the United States; while thus engaged, he received an injury causing the rupture of a blood vessel, from the effects of which he has never fully recovered; as over exercise ever since, and at the present time, produces a repetition of the trouble. He also received a dislocation of the right wrist and a fracture of the left, and since these injuries has been unable, and, in my opinion, ever will be, to attend to business of any description to advantage.

J. E. L. Kimball, M. D.,
Late Surg. 27th Reg. Me. Vols.

CHAPTER XXIX.

When I began to work for the Union cause, I had some funds which I had saved from the sale of my book, for the purpose of educating myself to preach the gospel as I felt it my duty to do, all of which I used up to support my family, and to pay my bills while drilling our officers and men at home and in the field. My wife's mother gave me eighteen hundred dollars during the war, for the purpose of securing a little home that I could call my own. A part of this also, together with some over two hundred dollars given me by the Sixteenth Maine Volunteers, to which I have already alluded, and the boys on Galloup's Island, and several other gentlemen, I paid out in the service. With the balance I purchased some property for a home, paying $1000 down, and gave my note and mortgage for a balance of $500. So the reader will see my prospects were not very flattering. I had tried to be prudent, but I spent a good deal in trying to regain my health, and to recover the use of my arm; but it availed nothing. I still felt anxious to get on with my studies, and perhaps more so now than before, because my health was gone, and, being a cripple too, I was sure that now, more than ever, I must be dependent on my wits for my bread. My friends who had been cognizant of my labors for the Union cause said, 'Sergeant, why don't you apply to the general government for a pension, and pay for your services during the war? It is your duty to do so.' Such advice from prominent men, whose wisdom and kindness I could not doubt, seemed to me ought not to be disregarded; and especially, when it so completely coincided with my own opinion of the

Drilling Cavalry.

case, and I concluded to do so, not as a beggar, for I did feel (and I don't admit that it is ostentation to put it in that light) that I had a just claim on the government for some remuneration for my services during the whole war, and to be *reimbursed* for what I had expended of my own funds while drilling the boys for service. If I am wrong in my views of the matter, lest any one should feel that I am stubborn about it, I wish them to distinctly understand that I am willing to be forgiven.

Here I must not omit to state, that having done all in my power to aid those around me, for I could not see a brother soldier hungry, and not divide my loaf with him. I had, fortunately, or unfortunately, got a little notoriety in that line, and if anybody was sick or suffering, I was pretty sure to be sought out. Good friends, while I was city missionary, often filled my hands with good things for the needy, and I have no doubt I often got credit for benefits that others bestowed through me; but after I entered the service for the Union, these sources were generally dried up, and what I could do now, I must do out of my own penury. To a soldier's call I never could turn away. The country had said, 'go to the bloody field and save us, and you shall have laurels placed upon your brow, and your graves shall be strewn with flowers, and your little children and widows shall be taken care of, not as paupers, but as the children and widows of heroes, whose name and fame we delight to honor, and for whose families we can never do enough, not as a charity, but as a debt the country will delight to pay, as a slight token of her appreciation of the noble deeds of her fallen heroes.' Well, that was flattering, and many a noble heart by such words was charmed away from wife and children, in the hour of his country's need. And many, too, have been cared for since their return; but alas! how many have been left through some informality, in some way, to pine away and die in poverty and want.

Private Wm. Kelly, who belonged to the Sixth Maine Vols., who had served more than four years, and who was honorably discharged at the close of the war, June 28, 1865, was one of these cases, whose condition and death, with its sad surroundings, I will describe. He had fought in the battles of Lee's Mills, Williamsburg, Golden Farm, White Oak Swamp, Antietam, and Fredericksburg, was several times wounded, the last of which was by a ball that pierced his breast, passing nearly through him, and was finally extracted by Dr. Warren, taking it out from under the shoulder blade, leaving him very much reduced, so that he never was well afterwards. I had not seen him since I drilled him with the rest of the regiment at the front. One night, an old gray-headed lady very poorly clad called on me, and asked me if I knew William Kelly of the Sixth Maine, and said he was very sick and wanted to see me. I told her I thought I did, and would visit him immediately. It was his mother, who, on her return, told her son that his old drill-master, Ambler, was coming to see him. He arose to dress, and fainted. His wife ran to meet me, and I hastened to the miserable dwelling, up one or two rickety flights of stairs in a back way, into a wretched open room with no furniture save a few broken chairs, and an old stove and a miserable bed upon which lay poor William, who reached out his withered hand while the tears ran down his cheeks and said, 'O drill-master, I am so glad you have come,' and sobbed and cried like a child. On looking round I found them suffering for food to eat, they had nothing, actually nothing that could be called eatable in the house! I said, 'William, how is it that you are in such a condition as this?' He turned his head toward his wife and said, 'ask Mary, she will tell you.' Here is her story:

'We lived in Portland, and William was not able to do much. I took in washing to get something to eat. One of our little girls was taken sick, and I had to attend to her; but the child grew worse till I closed its eyes in death. I bargained with the undertaker to wash for him to pay for the coffin, and poor William was unable to pay for a hearse, and the corpse was carried on a dray to the burying-ground, and William dug the grave himself. Then the other girl was taken sick and died. William went to the undertaker's and got a coffin, and carried it home on his shoulders, as he was not able to hire it done. And we put the last little girl in the tomb. We were in debt and could not get the money to pay with, and work was hard for me, and we were both discouraged. I concluded to come to Biddeford to get work in the mill, and that is why we are here. When I go in the mill I have to lock the room so they wont disturb William until I get back. O sir, it is hard times with us.' This was Mary's explanation. I looked round, there was no medicine, no, nothing to make a poor sick man comfortable. I went and got some provision and a few groceries out of my own funds for my sick comrade. Poor William got up in his bed and sat up, and prayed such a prayer as I never heard, and then said, 'O drill-master, Mary did not tell you half our sorrows. I tried and tried to get a pension, but there was always some reason for delay; some officer could not be found whose signature was necessary; but, drill-master, I shall soon have my final discharge, and shall not need a pension in that land where I am going. I want you when I am dead to bury me beside my poor darlings,' and turning over on one elbow, he drew from under his pillow his discharge, and handed it to me. 'Here,' said he, 'is my discharge. I want you to get my pension if you can, and pay yourself first for your trouble, and then my funeral expenses. Mary, will you listen to my last request, and see that I want drill-master Ambler to be paid for all his trouble, and for all he pays out for my sickness and funeral expenses, and the balance to you,' to which she assented.

I went to Portland, and asked Mr. Drummond to endeavor to get William's pension, carrying his papers with me; but the same delay and putting off that William complained of continued, although I urged his present condition and needs; and so again and again, while he lived, I tried, but certain officers were wanted to sign certain papers and they could not be found, until, vexed and disappointed, I took the discharge papers home with me. I had no less than three doctors to see William, who did all in their power to save him, and they made him as comfortable as they could while he lived. Among them was Doctor Warren, who immediately recognized William as the man from whom he extracted the ball that passed through him. The doctor was very attentive to him while he lived, and neither of the physicans would take a cent' for their care. I continued to care for him until one night, about midnight, the wife and his mother came for me, and said William was dying. I hastened with them to his house. The poor man had battled terribly against grim death, to try to live until I came, but in vain. And oh, such a sight! He had torn his bed in his dying agony, and, as I opened the door, he lay dead, with his head hanging off the bed, his mouth open and tongue out. The wife and mother screamed and ran from the house at the sight. I laid him tenderly down upon the floor, and went for some help., Meeting one of the police, I asked him in; but the sight was too terrible, and he would not stop. I laid him out, but could not close his mouth. I got a pillow and put it under his head, and while doing it both his eyes opened. I was startled and said, ' William, what is the matter?' and felt his pulse and found all was still. I closed his eyes and laid some coppers on them, and went in search of the trembling, frightened women, and when they came, such wails I seldom ever heard. I called in some of the rich to see how *patriots* were sometimes left to die in poverty and want.

I buried William at my own expense, paying out fifty-nine dollars for funeral expenses alone, besides my time and traveling expenses. As William and the family were Catholics, I had him buried from the Catholic church, and mass said for him as usual with them. The soldier's organization, called the Grand Army, of Portland, when I reported to them, paid me fifteen dollars toward the expenses, and no doubt would have done more, but for the many calls which are made on them for help. Some seven dollars more was afterwards handed me by friends.

After William had been buried some time, Mr. Drummond succeeded in getting a pension for the widow, who quietly took it, but failed to remember William's last request, viz., that the expenses of his sickness and burial should first be paid from it. Query—when William was alive and I had his papers to present, how was it nothing could be done to relieve his wants by the way of a pension; when very soon after he was buried a pension could be got for his widow without his discharge papers?

Well, thank God, I did my duty, and feel satisfied to know that I helped to light my poor comrade down the dark way, through which we all must pass before we reach our final rest and reward.

But to return. After the suggestions of my friends to ask government for pay, I concluded, on the whole, to petition Congress for pay for my services, or a pension, and to be reimbursed for the money I had paid out to support myself and family while at work for the country. The question now to be settled was, how to get the money to pay the bills. To hunt up the men whose signatures I wanted on my petition, and to go to Washington and present it personally, would cost me considerable. I was bothered a good deal to raise money for the purpose. I thought of that old story of the rats, who held a conference one time to consider what was best to be done about the old tabby-cat who had intruded upon their haunts. After various suggestions from some of the most venerable of these gentlemen long-tails, one smart young rat made a speech, advocating the putting of a bell on the cat, as that would give them due notice of her coming, so they could have abundance of time to scamper off to their holes. This brought down the house, especially the younger members of the house; when a long-tailed, gray old fogy squeaked out his approbation of the main plan, stating, at the same time, that one little objection arose in his mind, and the longer he thought of it the more serious it became, and he would state it in the form of a question;

and with a twinkle of his old eye, he asked, 'Who will put the bell on?' and the meeting broke up in a row. I decided that I must have some money; that was young America; but the provoking question how to get it well-nigh broke up everything. I tried a long time, but folks did not like a second mortgage. At last, by paying extra interest, I got a loan of $400 by giving another mortgage on my little homestead.

It took me near six months to get the names I wanted to indorse my petition, for I did not mean to go off half-bent. My wife worked making bonnets and at dressmaking while I was working up my petition, and in this way we got our bread. I guess I ought to mention a little business matter here, to show how the devil takes the advantage of poor fellows like me when in a strait place. A runner came into our little dressmaking-shop and wanted wife to buy some lace collars. She refused to buy, telling him I was going to Washington and wanted every cent we could raise. 'Oh,' said he, 'I don't want pay till he gets back; you can take your own time.' And she bought them and a few other matters, some forty dollars' worth in all; and as soon as I was off, he sued and took over $100 worth at whole-sale price from our little stock, and the stuff was sold at auction for about twenty-five dollars for the whole, leaving poor wife seventy-five dollars out.

Before I started for Washington, I used a considerable part of the money I had hired, and as I had now got my petition ready and was short, I hired sixty dollars more, for which I had to pay two dollars per month, or forty per cent, hoping my petition, which I here introduce, would be a success, and then I could pay my debts. I think it was the strongest paper ever presented to the Military Committee.

PETITION—SERGEANT I. W. AMBLER, ASKING COMPENSATION FOR SERVICES RENDERED IN DRILLING TROOPS DURING THE WAR.

To the Hon. Senate and House of Representatives, etc.:

The undersigned, Sergeant Isaac W. Ambler, respectfully

represents, that, having had long experience as a soldier and drill-master, he dedicated himself at the beginning of the late rebellion, to the instruction of soldiers and officers for the service of the United States, entering upon this work in Massachusetts the 15th of April, 1861 (the second day after the attack upon Fort Sumter), and continued to be so engaged in Massachusetts, Maine, and Virginia, until the 4th of April, 1865, without any compensation therefor, either from municipal, State, or national authorities.

During this time, Sergeant Ambler assisted largely in recruiting and drilling a very large number of men and officers in all branches of military tactics, which service he respectfully submits, was of far greater value to the government than any he could have rendered as a company officer merely. Sergeant Ambler was crippled in his left arm by a bayonet wound, received while engaged in drilling, by which wound he has ever since been disabled, wherefore he prays, that your honorable bodies may pass a special act for his relief, authorizing his muster into the United States service for the period above named, in the grade of First Sergeant, with pay and other allowance of that grade, and pension, or such other relief as may be deemed just and proper.

Not having contemplated making any claim for the services at the time they were rendered, Sergeant Ambler presents such evidence only as is herein inclosed.

1st. To establish the equity of his claim, the document signed by Hon. John Neal, Governors Chamberlain, Washburn, jr., Claflin, Stearns, Padelford, Goodwin, and Generals Hooker, Burnside, Fessenden, McClellan, Devens, Shepley, and others.

2d. To establish dates as stated, the papers marked passes, letters, and newspaper extracts.

3d. For proof of disability, etc., the certificate of Dr. Kimball, and citizens of Biddeford.

All of which is respectfully submitted,

I. W. AMBLER.

January 24, 1872.

Referred to the Committee on Military Affairs.　　Lynch.

CERTIFICATES.

Portland, Me., March 15, 1871.

This may certify that I have personally known Sergeant I. W. Ambler ever since 1859, that I have always found him trustworthy, earnest, and laborious, a capital swordsman and drill-master, and gifted with uncommon natural eloquence, though uneducated, whereby he has been enabled to accomplish great results as a lecturer on temperance, and as a lay preacher. His services and sufferings in the late rebellion would entitle him to great consideration if they were known to our rulers, though technically he may have little to claim on the government, his services being not only voluntary, but almost wholly gratuitous, and the injuries he has sustained, whereby he has lost many years of his life, suffered greatly, and been put to heavy charges, not having befallen him while in actual service. Nevertheless, as we are so largely indebted to him for instruction and example in the several regiments mentioned in his papers, it would seem that he has claims, which, if not legal and technical, are at least equitable, and ought not to be overlooked in this our day of reckoning and generous acknowledgment of such services as he has rendered our country.

Entertaining these views, I do most heartily recommend him to the consideration of our national lawgivers, and to the President of the United States, and the Secretary of War. All which is respectfully submitted.

John Neal.

We, the undersigned, concur in the above representations, and hereby join in the recommendation.

Joshua L. Chamberlain, *late Maj. Gen. U. S. Vols.*

James D. Fessenden, *late Brig. Gen. U. S. Vols.*

Israel Washburn, Jr., *Ex-Gov. of Maine.*

G. F. Shepley, *U. S. Judge, late Brig. Gen. U.S. Vols.*

Seth Padelford, *Governor of Rhode Island.*
William Claflin, *Governor of Massachusetts.*

It is with much pleasure as well as with a deep sense of duty that I write this commendation of Sergeant I. W. Ambler, drill-master, and fully concur with the accompanying recommendations. I personally and intimately knew Sergeant Ambler in the Army of the Potomac in the autumn of 1861; how hard and successfully he labored to drill the raw officers in sword, and soldiers in musket and skirmish exercises, particularly in my Regiment, the Sixth Maine, and I remember instances in which his courageous example and soldierly bearing was of great service to our troops which had not been under fire, as for instance, the affair of Lewinsville, Va., under General Smith. Sergeant Ambler was the man selected to bear the colors of the Sixth Maine through Baltimore, when the regiment was on its way to Washington, and when an attack by the mob was expected;—received great injury by poisoned food in Havre de Grace, etc., etc. I remember, also, that for his hard and valuable services in 1861 he received no compensation; that he was subsequently broken and crippled in body for life in his efforts to aid the Union cause, as his many scars to-day will testify, etc. I will only say more, that as I know what I above stated is true, I most earnestly hope a just and grateful country will acknowledge and reward his services.

Z. Thompson, *Chaplain 6th Maine Reg't*, 1861–62.

I know Sergeant Ambler well, and have done so for many years. Without pay or position, he rendered me important aid in drilling company officers, mostly new and green, in my command, as they came into camp from their various localities.

Neal Dow, *late Brig. Gen. U. S. Vols.*

I know Sergeant Ambler. He drilled many officers under my command. I concur fully in the recommendations above.

Chas. Devens, Jr., *late Brev. Maj. Gen. U. S. Vols.*

15

I am not personally acquainted with Sergeant Ambler, but from my knowledge of the persons whose names are above subscribed, I think him entitled to consideration.

ONSLOW STEARNS, *Gov. of N. H.*

I am glad to concur in the above recommendations favorable to Sergeant Ambler.

A. E. BURNSIDE, *Maj. Gen. U. S. A.*

I concur in the above recommendations.

J. HOOKER, *Maj. Gen. U. S. A.*

Having long and favorably known Sergeant Ambler, I fully concur in the foregoing recommendations.

ICHABOD GOODWIN, *Ex-Gov. of N. H.*

From the above indorsements I feel certain that Sergeant Ambler is entitled to great consideration, and if any irregularity exists in regard to his muster in, it would seem to be the duty of our lawgivers to fully reimburse him, and pay for his services.

WM. COGSWELL, *late Brig. Gen. U. S. A.*

I know Sergeant Ambler as an instructor of troops and a teacher of the sword, and am happy to concur in the above recommendations.

FRANCIS FESSENDEN, *Brig. Gen. U. S. Army.*

I have read the papers in this case, and although I have no personal knowledge of the matter, I am satisfied that Sergeant Ambler is fairly entitled to the generous consideration of the authorities for valuable services rendered during the war, and that it is a case wherein technical objections, if such exist, ought not to stand in the way of ample recompense being awarded him.

GEO. B. McCLELLAN, *late Maj. Gen. U. S. A.*

I concur in the recommendations of Generals McClellan, Hooker, Burnside, and others.

C. C. MEADE, *Maj. Gen. U. S. A.*

January 22, 1872.

I have known Sergeant Ambler personally and by reputation for many years, and I have no doubt that he is eminently deserving the aid and relief he seeks. His services and his sufferings alike, entitle him to this recognition.

J. G. BLAINE, *Speaker of the House of Representatives.*

WASHINGTON, D. C., Jan. 23, 1872.

I have been acquainted with Mr. I. W. Ambler for many years, as city missionary in Biddeford, Maine, and while in the service of the United States, as drill-sergeant, during the late war. Mr. Ambler came to my rooms, in this city, some time in August, 1861, disabled from sunstroke, and remained with me until he was able to return to the field. Learning that he is about to apply to Congress for compensation for his services in defense of the Union, I deem it a duty, as well as a pleasure, to earnestly commend him to that honorable body as a gentleman worthy of confidence, and, in my judgment, entitled to relief. D. E. SOMES.

PORTLAND, ME., 14th August, 1871.

I, J. Pierrepont Neal, Justice of the Peace and Quorum of the County of Cumberland, Maine, residing in the city of Portland, do hereby certify that the foregoing are true and correct copies of letters and testimonials in the possession of I. W. Ambler, which he has shown to and which have been carefully examined and compared by me with the foregoing.

J. PIERREPONT NEAL, *J. P. & Q.*

BIDDEFORD, MAINE.

Sergeant I. W. Ambler proposes to leave us for a season; and we the undersigned cannot permit him to go without bearing willing testimony to his Christian character and fidelity, as a good missionary among the poor of this place. He has been abundant in labors for their good; ministered to their wants, reclaimed many inebriates, kindly expostulated with sellers of liquors, and persuaded them to give up their traffic; visited the sick, consoled the dying, gathered at one time about one hundred and seventy little ones into a most interesting mission school, and the good people of Biddeford clothed the most of them. He has preached the glad tidings frequently, and to many in season and out of season.

Mr. Ambler is an accomplished military tactician, having seen long service in foreign lands, and when the news came in 1861 that his adopted flag had been insulted, and that it no longer waved from Sumter, he immediately left the pulpit for the drill-room, giving his whole time, without remuneration, to the instructions of officers and men, laboring in Maine, Massachusetts, and Virginia; giving his whole time and energies to aid the cause of freedom, regardless alike of fatigue and personal comfort; and by so doing has been made a cripple for life, thus depriving himself and family of those comforts which otherwise they might have enjoyed.

Mr. Ambler is a reformed man; he has gone through all this war and touched not, handled not, tasted not, any intoxicating liquors. 'He that ruleth his spirit is better than he that taketh a city.'

> LEONARD ANDREWS.
> CHARLES HARDY.
> Rev. JOHN STEVENS, *Freewill Baptist Minister.*
> JAMES M. PALMER, *Pastor 2d Cong. Church.*
> CHAS. TENNEY, *Pastor Pavilion Church.*
> E. H. BANKS, *Merchant.*
> J. HUBBARD, Jr., *Pastor Baptist Church.*
> CHARLES A. SHAW, *Mayor.*
> ALVAN BACON, *M. D.*
> DRYDEN SMITH, *M. D.*
> WM. YEOMAN, *Pastor Free Baptist Church.*
> WM. BERRY, *Police Judge.*
> ABEL H. JELLESON, *Judge Municipal Court.*

G. N. WEYMOUTH, *Attorney at Law.*
WM. P. HAINES, *Treasurer of Pepperell Mills.*
R. M. CHAPMAN, *Cashier Biddeford, Me., Bank.*
HORACE PIPER, *High School Teacher.*
C. C. MASON, *Pastor M. E. Church, Saco.*

Sergeant Ambler, who, it will be remembered, rendered most efficient service not only during the early days of the late revolution, but through the long years of terrible warfare, drilling thousands of our officers and men in the sabre and bayonet exercise, then eagerly pressing to the front, and who, since the first sound of the bugle note calling patriots to arm themselves for the conflict, devoted the whole of his time to the service of his country, is in this city. It will be remembered this excellent drill-officer was for many years an English soldier. Leaving his native country for an adopted one, he gave his time, money, and health to sustain the principles of our own free government, and in so doing received several terrible wounds, one of which—a musket and bayonet thrust—forever disables the use of his left hand.

Unfortunately Sergeant Ambler has no legal claim upon the government, because he was not mustered into service as a soldier, but he was one who protected our flag through the streets of Baltimore immediately after the brave Sixth Massachusetts had led the way for brave and noble men to follow. Such men should never suffer.

One prominent trait on the part of this unselfish man has been no meanness displayed in asking or receiving remuneration for his teaching. Whole companies have gone into action, every man of which was indebted to our generous friend for months of service on his part.

Sickness, long and painful, is the cause of his present adversity. Expense has caused him to sacrifice everything he had except honor, patriotism, and a devoted Christian character, and hence he appeals to a generous government for that help sufficient only to enable him to obtain the necessities of life.

Sergeant Ambler, it must be remembered, in battle faced the enemy, fighting as bravely as the best and most devoted soldier in our ranks.   Shall not such proof of attachment and such unselfish devotion to our interests be rewarded by a reasonable return on our part.—*Boston Journal.*

CHAPTER XXX.

WITH such a document, backed by governors and generals and other good men, and such testimonials of well-known clergymen, I felt very certain, that with such a formidable battery, I could carry an enemy's works as soon as I unlimbered in Washington for action, and what had I not reason to expect from friends and patriots at the capitol? Representatives and senators, on whose burning words of patriotism and love of country, listening multitudes had often hung in wondrous raptures. If I had been a betting man I should have put ten to one, that I should have succeeded. I went with my head up and should have laughed at the man who should have proposed to charge me one per cent to insure me. Getting into Washington, I put up at the Franklin House, and after getting the dust and dirt out of my throat and eyes, so to get into condition to reconnoiter the ground, I started out, and charged down on some of the clerks at the government buildings, for the purpose of getting an introduction to some of the leading officials, when, to my astonishment, they stared at me, and drew off as if I were a hot potato, or something of the kind, that might burn them if they touched me, or were found in my company. This reception was novel to me; but I got it through my head at last, why it was so; and I rather pitied them, for it seemed to me that they felt compelled to go on the principle of *non commitamus* to save their heads, and so had generally adopted in practice the old proverb, 'every man for himself, and the d—l take the hindmost.' I knew there was one man, at least, from Maine, who cared for the soldier. And I went to him

(Speaker Blaine), and he added his name to my petition, and told me to go to Mr. Lynch, a representative from my district, whose duty it was to attend to the petitions of his constituents, and he had no doubt the Hon. gentleman would lay it before the Military Committee at once, and urge them to report a bill for my relief. I went to Mr. Lynch and stated my case. He told me it would have to go before the Military Committee, and I must be present when it was laid before them, and he told me when he was ready, he would send for me. Well, that looked well, and I waited patiently three weeks for Mr. Lynch to send for me, but he did not do so. I then went to Speaker Blaine and told him how my case was neglected, and Mr. Blaine took me before the committee himself at their next session. I was questioned about my service, etc., and was requested to be present at their next meeting. They were holding their sessions now every two or three days. I went to the next meeting, and the next, and the next, until I had followed them up for three months, and it always happened that something else must be acted upon before my case could be reached. At last Mr. Marcy, one of the committee, told me he had searched all the books to find something to meet my case; but utterly failed to do so. I said to him, 'Sir, I did not come before your honorable body, expecting you to find a law to meet my case, but to set before you the facts, that you might report a bill which, when passed by Congress, would meet it, and give me relief.' And I referred him to my passes, to newspaper reports and my petition, and the signatures of honorable gentlemen recommending me and my claims upon government for compensation in some form. He told me newspaper extracts were not reliable. I told him I did not base my matters on them, they were simply confirmatory of the statements and recommendations of honorable gentlemen, well-known to him and the country, and so far as the newspapers were concerned, I did not know what would have become of the country, if it had not been for them during the war. This ended my meetings with the Military Committee.

About this time, a gentleman came to me—pardon me for using the term—and said he was well-known in Washington, and had done a good deal of business of this kind, and had been very successful in securing pensions, etc., and he would guarantee to get a pension for me, if I would pay him two thousand dollars. I told him I had no funds. He said it was bad for me; but finally offered to get it for one thousand. I told him I could not pay it, for I did not have it, and could not raise it. Then said he, 'you *can't get it*. The Committee won't report a bill in your favor,' which I found to be the case. I don't presume the fellow had any collusion with them however; but he was a regular lobbyist, and knew something of movements generally at head-quarters. My case reminded me of the saying of one of Massachusetts' noted criminal lawyers, the celebrated Rufus Choate, when applied to to defend a man charged with murder. The first question he put to the man soliciting his services was, 'Has he got any money?' When told he was a poor man,—'What,' says Choate, 'a poor man with no money, and charged with murder! There is no hope for him, sir.' Not that I had been charged with crime, and no money; but this lobby member told me that without money, I could not have a bill reported in my favor.

I went to Speaker Blaine and told him the offer that was made me, and asked his advice. He said, 'Mr. Ambler, don't you pay a dollar. If you have not done enough for the country for a little pension, throw your papers to the four winds. You go and tell the Military Committee if they will report a bill in your favor I will pass it through the House without any trouble. You go and see the president of that committee, General Coburn, and also General Slocum, and tell them so.' I went eleven times before I could have an interview with either of them. The servant saying they were not at home. A habit very common, I am told, in this country, when the lady of the house don't want to receive company; and I won't say it is not true of my native land. I made up my mind to try a little

Yankee dodge, and see if that would not bring them *home;* so the servant's usual 'not at home' might be reversed. I went to my good friend Blaine, and got permission to bear his compliments to the gentlemen, and the next day presented myself at the door and handed the servant the following card: 'I. W. Ambler with Speaker Blaine's compliments.' The servant smiled, and bowed, and took the card to the honorable gentleman, who ordered the servant to show me up. So my reader will see how to define the term, 'not at home.' In justice to these gentlemen I will say, that I was received kindly, and informed that at that time they were settling some land matters that would require perhaps a month's time, and could attend to nothing else until that work was concluded, and they advised me to wait in Washington until that was off their hands. Oh, how little do men in easy circumstances realize the sufferings such delays occasion to a poor man! Here I was, in poverty, hanging at the government doors, my bill running up at the hotel, and money all gone, when a simple recommendation to the favorable consideration of Congress, that they could have written out and signed in thirty minutes, would have sent sunshine into my poor heart and home. About this time, my good friend Dr. Kimball, of Saco, sent me fifty dollars, which greatly encouraged me. God bless his big heart, may he never know what it is to want; and he sent me the following kind note:

Saco, April 11, 1872.

Friend Ambler,—I intended to have written before, but lack of time is the reason why I have not. I am sorry you have been so bothered with your business. I truly believed, that your case was so plain that but a very little time would suffice to settle the whole affair; and it is a mystery to me that this should be delayed. The great thing in law is proof, and I think if that is necessary in your case, you have enough to satisfy any reasonable mind upon the subject. I am glad you still persevere, and as you are there, I would stick till the last gun was fired. It does seem to me that you will succeed; that *right will triumph.* There is nothing new here at present. I am obliged to you for your letters and papers. And now hoping and believing in your success, I remain

Truly yours,   J. E. L. KIMBALL.

P. S. Shall be glad to hear from you, and shall hope to hear good news.

Such kind letters were like balm to me in this long struggle. Whether I intended to '*stick*,' as the doctor advised, will be seen by the following letter sent to him.

WASHINGTON, D. C., 1872.

DR. KIMBALL:

My Dear Sir,—I pray that you will excuse me for not writing sooner. I have been waiting on the committee to see what they would do in my case, so that I could write to you and tell you something definite. I have been battling with the Military Committee ever since I wrote you. They have come to the conclusion that I did great service in the late rebellion; but they say if they pass my bill, they are afraid that it will open a door for others. I told them if they could find a man who had gone through as much as I had, having entered the service on the 15th of April, 1861, occupying the position of drill-master, also doing active service in the field, and being crippled for life,—yes, and your government recognized me as a soldier by giving me passes to and fro,—I would not press my claim. I went and told Speaker Blaine what the Military Committee had told me. Speaker Blaine said, 'What do we care about opening doors! *let us have justice.*' And he told me to go and tell them from him, that if they would pass my claim, that he would pass it through the House without any trouble. I went and told them personally what Speaker Blaine had said, and they told me they would let me know in a few days what they would do.

Doctor, if it had not been for your assistance, I could not have battled them up to the present time. A congressman told me the other day, that the committee was going to keep me here till all my money was gone, and then I should be glad to go home. I told him I would have an answer from the committee, yes or no, if I had to stay in Washington till hunger sets upon my cheek, and starvation glared from my eye-balls. I left home with no clothes, only what I had on my back, and now I can see necessity fluttering round my ragged robe.

Adieu,—I am too full to say more.

I. W. Ambler.

It will be seen that my purpose *was* to stick until something was done; but the best of us cannot always bear up into the wind's eye without shaking our sails, and making some lee-way. My anxiety began to wear on me, and while waiting, and backing and filling for months, I was taken sick, and confined to my room at my hotel. For four days, nobody came to my room but the servant, and I could not get even a cup of tea, weak as I was, unless I took it at meal-time.

My friend Shepherd, on whom I had frequently called, missed me and called to see me, and seemed surprised to find me sick. He went and brought me some oranges, and kindly offered me a home with him if I would accept it; but his wife being sick, I could not think of doing so; as like myself, in some measure, he was a soldier and did not revel in wealth, and could ill afford additional expense on my account. He insisted on my taking five dollars to help me along a little, as he expressed it. I did not want him to know how hard up I was, and having used up all my funds, I concluded to send for the president of the Young Men's Christian Association, and let them know how matters stood with me. I had attended some of their meetings, and spoke in several of them, and I thought they might, in a quiet way, render me some service, or help me to some funds until I could repay them. He came to see me, and I told him how I was situated, money all gone, business unfinished, and already in debt to the landlord.

I was coolly advised to leave my valise, etc., in the landlord's possession for my bills, and go to the Providence Hospital. I did not know who were the patrons of this institution at the time. I did not leave my valise with the landlord; but I gave him my watch and chain for my bills. This gentleman got me a permit to go to this hospital, and handed it to me in an envelope, which I did not open until I reached there. Judge ye of my astonishment, when I found my good Protestant brother had got me into a Catholic institution, managed by the sisters of charity. This seemed rather a shrewd operation, for the Young Men's Christian Association, and I concluded if the president managed all their affairs as carefully, to save expense to them, as he did in my case, they might have some funds in their treasury. I handed the envelope containing my permit to one of the sisters in charge. On reading it she remarked, ' Why sir, you are only a pauper; a gentlemanly-looking man like you ought to pay six dollars per week, as some of the others do here, and I could give you a better room, and something better to eat than you can have now.' I told her I had no money, and she would have to put me into the pauper's ward. My first night here satisfied me that this was not my home. I had a consumptive on each side of me, who coughed the live-long night. In a day or two, I took French leave of the good sisters, for I had strong objections to dying a pauper. When a boy, I heard a song called ' the pauper's funeral,' one line of which always grated on my ear, where it spoke about 'rattling his bones over the stones.' When I got out on the sidewalk, I got a man to help me on to the car, and went to General Butler's head-quarters, and got a permit to go to the Freedmen's Hospital, connected with the Howard University, designed for the care mainly of old and decrepid negroes. When I got there, I was very ill with a hemorrhage from the bowels, and I felt gloomy and forsaken. I got some rest, and had the kindest treatment from the physicians in charge when they found out who I was, and I soon felt much better. I was sustained by an abiding faith in the protection of God, who had watched over me thus far in life, and who had stood by me in every trial and adversity, and this led me to hope for better days. I had been trying hard for an education since my conversion, and I made rapid strides in one department of knowledge at the Capital. I learned more of human nature, during my sojourn here, than ever I expected to learn in life, and many things I was sorry to learn.

Solomon had said, 'By long forbearing is a prince persuaded, and a soft tongue breaketh the bone,' and I had been faithfully practicing on this very principle for several months, and wondered why I did not succeed, and I came pretty near falling into a skeptical frame of mind; but I happened to think, that brother Solomon had never been to Washington with a petition, if he had, he would have made an exception to this rule. But Solomon was right when he said, 'Confidence in an unfaithful man in time of trouble is like a broken tooth, and a foot out of joint,' and when I looked on a little further, and read, 'Every man is a friend to him that giveth gifts. All the brethren of the poor do hate him; how much more do his friends go far from him? He pursueth them with words, yet they are wanting to him. The poor useth entreaties; but the rich answereth roughly.' I said, that's true anyhow, for I have learned that lesson from A to Z. It is pretty hard to eat with a broken tooth, or to travel with any comfort on a foot out of joint; yet I had tried to eat and travel too, upheld all through these months of waiting with 'a strange belief, that leaned its idiot back on folly's topmost twig; a lazy, over-credulous faith that leaned on all it met, nor asked if 'twas a reed or oak;' but facts of experience drove this *ignis-fatuus* thoroughly from my mind, and the naked truth burst upon me while lying sick here in this hospital, that I must depend upon God and I. W. Ambler and his wife for our bread; and I decided to go home as soon as I got able.

In some three weeks I got out, and went to the Military Committee for my papers, as I did not want them to remain in their hands. These testimonials of my friends I wanted to preserve, so if I could leave nothing else to my children, I could leave an honorable record of which they might be proud when my poor bones slept in the dust. General C. told me to go to General M., and he said go to Mr. D., and the latter sent me to Mr. L., and L. told me that Mr. B. would get them. Ambler's back was up about this time. It seemed to me that there was a chance about getting even my papers back, and I straightened myself up, and said, 'Mr. L., I'll have those papers before I leave Washington, or I'll be a dead man, and somebody with me,' and, '*mirabile dictu*,' in ten minutes after this brief speech, Mr. L. beckoned to me, and General C. handed him the papers saying, with an upturned nose, 'Brother L., here are those documents,' and L. passed them to me. I confess that I was in a passion when I made that speech, and I beg Mr. L.'s pardon, and I am pretty sure he will grant it, on reflection, for I had been chafing under the delay of months, until it had eaten up all my patience, and substance too; but I meant *all* that I said at the time, and as much more as the reader has a mind to put to it. Therefore this confession. My next thought was how to get home, for I had no money. Some of my friends thought it would be good for my health to take a trip down the Alleghany, as far as Pittsburg. I went to Speaker Blaine again, who always encouraged and comforted me, and told him how things were, and he wrote a letter to ex-secretary Scott, who gave me a pass to Pittsburg. After I got my pass, I read the letter that Mr. B. had written. It so overflowed with sympathy for me, and set forth my condition so truthfully, that it touched me in a tender place, and I lost my mind. What intervened for a day or two I have no knowledge; but when I came to myself, I was back in the Freedmen's Asylum. I soon got out, and thought it unsafe to go down to Pittsburg in my state of health. I decided to get home as soon as I could, and I called on General Butler, who very kindly furnished me the following pass* to Maine; but I had no money to get me anything to eat on the road. It may be asked, why these officials did not furnish it. I wish to say here, that I was not a beggar, and I did not tell them I wanted money for that purpose. They were very kind to me, and if my pride had not kept me from telling them, they would have generously responded. I could ask them for a pass because *that* came out of the government which was my debtor; but I did not want them all to know just how snug on the wind I was running. Some of my friends wanted a speech before I left, and I caught at it as a good way to raise the 'wind,' and notice was given for a meeting in a hall on Pennsylvania avenue. A good number attended. I told them I must speak as I felt. I had just got out of the hospital, and had been reading the following in the *National Republican*, published at Washington, March 28, 1872:

Are Republics Ungrateful? *Ed. Republican,*—The aphorism which gave rise to the above query, and which has been so often asserted, and as frequently denied, seems to have found a practical demonstration in one case, at least, on the negative side; and it would seem that a defender of the nation, who had made almost unparalleled sacrifices, prompted by the inspiration of duty alone, and had left the country's service, after years of most arduous toil, sufferings, and hardships, a maimed, crippled, and helpless man, should, in justice, be entitled to, at least, as great a consideration as the man who served his ninety days and received never a wound, and saw never a battle.

Such is the condition of Sergeant I. W. Ambler, personally and intimately known to the writer while in the army, whose

<hr>

* Washington, April 16, 1872.

Please furnish transportation from Washington to Biddeford, Me., for I. W. Ambler, a Volunteer Soldier, disabled by injuries, en route to the Military Asylum, and render account of the same to General Wm. S. Tilton, Treasurer of the Military Asylum at Augusta. To the agent of the B. & O. R. R. at Washington.

Benj. F. Butler, *Manager N. A. D. V. S.*

long personal service and experience in the English army prepared him for the duties of a drill-officer of very superior ability. At the commencement of the war he was a city missionary
in Biddeford, Maine. Two days after the first firing on Fort
Sumter, he entered upon the work of instructing officers and
soldiers in drill and tactics in Massachusetts, and continued his
labors in Maine—accompanying the Sixth Maine Regiment to
Virginia in July, 1861. When the regiment marched through
Baltimore with bayonets fixed and loaded muskets, in anticipa-
tion of an attack, Sergeant Ambler was requested by Colonel
Burnham to take charge of the colors of the regiment, which
he did, and bore them safely through the city.

During the stay of the regiment at Chain bridge, in whatever active service they were required to go, Sergeant Ambler
was ever among the foremost, and has been seen to snatch a
musket from the hands of an inactive sentry and press to the
front, amid cheers and cries of 'Bully for Ambler!' He remained with the regiment, doing constant and most arduous
duty as drill-master, and instructing the officers in the sword
and the soldiers in bayonet exercise, often volunteering to go
on picket duty, and passing the night on picket line, displaying
on each and every occasion indomitable energy, activity, and
unfaltering courage. In August, 1861, he was prostrated by a
sun-stroke, from which he suffered extremely for many weeks,
but returned to his labors as soon as able to be in the field, returning to Maine to recruit, where he continued with his wonderful energy and activity drilling the Thirteenth, Fifteenth,
Sixteenth, Twenty-first, Twenty-third, and Twenty-fifth Maine
Regiments, and First Maine Cavalry, besides hundreds of officers and soldiers in Massachusetts.

While giving instructions in bayonet exercise he received
a severe and ugly wound, which shattered his left wrist, but
with Spartan-like heroism, he lashed his arm behind his back,
and continued with untiring energy to give instructions in
fencing with his right hand, until an accident disabled that also.

16

And this man, who has testimonials of the highest order from Generals McClellan, Meade, Burnside, Hooker, Chamberlain, Neal Dow, Cogswell, Fessenden, Shepley, Devens, and from Governors Claflin, of Massachusetts; Padelford, of Rhode Island; Stearns, of New Hampshire; ex-Governors Washburn, of Maine; Goodwin, of New Hampshire, and a host of judges, lawyers, doctors, and clergymen, and who has been maimed and permanently disabled in the cause of liberty and right, has never received from the government a single penny of compensation, or other recognition than the granting of railroad passes.

Here we have a man who has given years of the best part of his life with a patriotism almost unequaled in history; has given his arm, which is forever useless, and has rendered services far more valuable to the army and the cause than he could have done as an officer of the line; he has fought and bled for the Union, the country of his adoption; but never having been mustered into the army as a soldier, has not and cannot receive pay for his services without special legislation from Congress; and he now modestly asks that Congress will allow him to be mustered in with the rank only of sergeant, in order that he may receive compensation for his labors and sacrifices. The only objection made by any one to this act of justice, is that it will be made a precedent for others.

The writer was with Sergeant Ambler while in the Sixth Maine Regiment, and can testify from intimate acquaintance, association, and personal practical experience of his uniform energy, activity, and proverbial courage; also of the most excellent moral influence exercised by him over the soldiers in a moral, religious, and temperance point, and of his kind-hearted and generous labors among the sick and suffering, as also will be heartily and gratefully affirmed by every member of the regiment

In Heaven's name, if there are others who have sacrificed and suffered in the cause of freedom and the Union to such a degree as Sergeant Ambler has, let the 'door be opened, and the suffering, starving patriots be allowed to come in and receive relief adequate to their services.' Let it be shown that there is one republic, at least, that can not only feel, but manifest that gratitude to her noble and heroic defenders in a more substantial manner than a mere hollow recognition.   s.

To be true to my promise to speak as I felt, of course I gave them a bad speech. I had not gone far before there was some disturbance, and I had to stop. One gentleman jumped up and handed me fourteen dollars, as a contribution from himself and wife, for telling the truth, as he said. This hushed them a little, and then followed cries of 'go on,' 'go on,' and on I went, telling them some things of which they were cognizant, ugly truths, and the more ugly because true. I told them I had seen men from Washington down in Maine and Massachusetts making speeches, who generally opened with, 'Fellow citizens, soldiers, and comrades,' and who so overflowed with patriotism, and with their deeds of daring on the battle-field, that we almost thought them angels created for the emergency, and who,

'Watchful, unhired, unbribed, and uncorrupt,
And party only to the common weal
In virtue's awful rage, pleaded for right;
With truth so clear, with argument so strong,
With action so sincere, and tone so loud
And deep, as made the despot quake behind
His adamantine gates, and every joint
In terror smite his fellow-joint relaxed;
Or, marching to the field in burnished steel
While, frowning on his brow, tremendous hung
The wrath of the whole people, and led them on
To trample tyrants down, and drive invasion back.
While, still they held inferior place, in *steadfast*
Rectitude of soul. Great their self-denial, and
Great their cares, and great the service done to God
And man.'

And then I asked, what had they done? They had never seen a battlefield, had never toiled for nought, could see the crippled soldier stand upon the corners of the streets with an empty cigar-box receiving the pennies from the passers by, while Priest and Levite like, they would pass them by on the other side, so poor, oh, 'poor as rats,' when calls like these appeared! From such a stench arose that smelled to heaven, so that even the old man in the moon, as he went sailing over the Capital at noon of night, would put his fingers on his nose lest his olfactory organs should be outraged.

At this point, the meeting was disturbed again, and a man arose and asked what I would charge to stop, and it was proposed to give me fifty dollars to cork up my vials of wrath; not that what I had said was untrue, but each wanted some chance to save his life, by escaping out of Sodom before I sank it utterly. Here was a good chance to drive a bargain. Wisdom dictated to me to avail myself of it, and dry up, as I had unlimbered my battery and charged on the enemy's works long enough to feel considerably relieved. The money was handed over, and with many a hearty shake of the hand I left. It was a curious meeting, a curious speech, a curious bargain, a success in raising a little money to pay my scot. Some paid because they valued the truth and the man that dared to speak it, and, I have no doubt, some helped to make up the fifty dollars to prevent my uncovering any more of the skeletons that were rotting about them. It put me in mind of the son of Erin, who was arrested on the charge of having committed a heinous crime, and dragged before the court without any one to plead his case. When he was ordered to stand up, and listen to the charge which had been brought against him, he made a great hulla-balloo, and excited considerable sympathy in the court, when the judge arose, and ordered him to compose himself, and be quiet, assuring him that justice should be done him, which added a *point* to his sorrow, and he burst out, and said, 'If yer honor will allow me to say it, by me soule, its that same that I am afraid of.'

Reader, is it any wonder that I was a little bilious over the way I had been treated by some of the parties at the Capital, enduring months of vexatious delay, and weeks of sickness in a hospital not the best that could be found, my hopes of help all cut off, knowing that this last effort had cost me all the money I had, and all I could raise, and now I must go home and tell my poor wife that we must be turned out of doors, and all would have to go to my creditors. Well, if you cannot excuse me, I can excuse myself, for I could not respect Sergeant Ambler if he had not showed a little spirit then.

I don't mean to be understood to say that many of our public servants at the head of the government are not as noble, generous, self-denying, upright, and sympathetic men as can be found on earth; but these good patriots and statesmen are annoyed to death with a set of toadies, little, mean, bargaining, selfish, unscrupulous scamps, who are often numerous enough, by taking advantage of little technicalities and games of staving off, to clog the wheels of just legislation, an occasion often of painful and ruinous delay, and the course of such is cause often of unjust reflection upon intelligent and patriotic statesmen.

CHAPTER XXXI.

THE next morning, I shook off the dust of my feet as a testimony against the place, for the suffering, anxiety, and poverty that the five months spent in Washington had brought upon me, and bent my weary steps toward the depot, a sadder, but a wiser man than when I left home. On my lonesome way back to Maine, for it is the loneliest place in the world to be surrounded with a crowd of strange faces, either in the cars or on the thronged thoroughfare, I had a great many thoughts arise as to what I was made for, why I lived, what use I could make of all these strange and bitter experiences; and I said, if this is the training and drill that Heaven gives to fit me to battle for spiritual freedom for myself and others, O God, put me through, so I can parry all the longes of Satan, and fit me to teach the heavenly drill to thy disciples, so I can lead them on to victory. I got happy with such meditations on the road, and never felt more like going through the whole war, under the great Captain of our salvation, until the final muster for all hands to receive an honorable discharge, and be welcomed where we shall walk the mount of bliss, that lifts its summit high, sublime in glory; talking with our peers of the incarnate Saviour's love, and past affliction lost in present joy. Oh, wondrous joy! a distant view of which makes pilgrims walk the billows of life's stormy seas, sublimely lifted up above all fear of sinking in their awful depths. How ashamed I felt to think I had ever murmured when thus I rode upon the wings of faith above all earthly things. Yet so it is sometimes. On arriving in Boston, I met my wife, who passed me by, and would not have recognized me if I had not called her by name. I had lost a little less than forty pounds in weight, pale and ragged, and after gazing a moment she rushed into my arms and burst into tears. We journeyed home in company, telling each other on the way our several experiences. She, of the way our creditors had sued and seized our little effects in the shop, in which she was trying to make a living; and I, of what the reader already knows. Yet we were rich in each other's love, and the love of God, for were we not 'persuaded that neither death, nor life, nor angels, nor principalities, nor powers, nor things present, nor things to come, nor height, nor depth, nor any other creature, shall be able to separate us from the love of God, which is in Christ Jesus our Lord.'

My first business was to reconnoitre the ground, and throw up such works as my present weakened condition demanded, to prevent the enemy from carrying everything. I had lost some ground by giving way too much to my poverty. The devil made a terrific charge in this direction, telling me 'what a poor miserable drunkard I had been; how little I had done since my conversion; that I had published my follies in a book; that as an excuse for putting out a book I wanted to get money to educate myself with, and I had left the missionary work for the drill-room and the front; used up my little funds for other purposes; had accomplished nothing; and last, but not least, I had shown a soft spot in my head by presuming on anything in the shape of recognition and remuneration for anything done for the country; and now I had better come over to the old camp, and drink and enjoy myself, and let other folks look out for themselves.' I had a hard tussle with the old fellow, but I resolved 'to fight it out on this line.' I plead guilty to all these charges but the last, which I denied; for the people constitute the country, and when the facts are understood by them they will appreciate them and render a just verdict, and demand of their public servants that justice be done; and so I claimed that my head was level on that point, and what was required now was to 'wait for the wagon,' and Ambler 'would take a ride.' To the others on which I pled guilty, I argued justification. I am a great stickler for that blessing, and envy nobody when I am in possession of that. As to the first charge, of having been a drunkard, and published it also, I admitted it, and from that stand-point I made my strongest appeal; having tasted the woes of the drunkard, I could reach them as no man could who had always lived a temperate life; and so I said, Mr. devil, rum made me what I *was*, religion made me what I *am;* and through this experience I could lift up the poor drunkard. So this was turned into a chapter of power. Then my not having done but little, was a very good reason why I should do more still; I thanked God that I had done a *little*, and I got some justification out of that. The reason also for putting out my first book, to get funds to educate myself with, was all true, and had I not, in the disposal of it, educated myself greatly into the mysteries of human nature, the very field of power and success, of which many theologians are ignorant, and without which no man can be successful. Why, the very greenness of these fledglings that talk so tenderly and reverently of their literary '*Alma-mater*,' makes them a butt of ridicule sometimes when they come in actual contact with live men of business and shrewd good common sense. The thinness of these shadowy men make them targets for many a practical shot. So if I can have only one of two things, viz., a smattering of books, or an actual practical knowledge of men as we meet them, give me the latter, if I want to catch them in the gospel net.

As for leaving the missionary work for the drill-room, I was sure that I could take the missionary or Christian work along with me. I looked upon it as right, yea, as Christian duty, to train men effectually to resist the devil, when he assumed the garb of rebellion, and if a Christian had not a weapon, and was so short as to have to sell his coat to buy one, it was his duty to do it, and route the rebels at any cost; so to save to posterity, to our children, the best government the sun ever shone upon. What was there for them but this, where every man is the peer of his fellow, and even a 'rail-splitter' can become a president, and honored and loved in life, and for whom when he dies, a whole nation mourns. He that for such a heritage, to sustain such a country, would not use his money, spill his blood, go maimed and crippled all his days, live and die in poverty, is unworthy the name of patriot. Now I flattered myself that I had done something for my country personally and by proxy; my pupils were fighting in every battle, among the heroes on every victorious field. Their skill in the use of arms often attested this; and of their bravery, many a rebel had stinging proof, and honorable mention is made of their heroic deeds in the archives of the States. I had drilled thousands of officers, and probably ten thousand men, more or less, for this noble work. Let me give the record of one or two. Here is the adjutant-general's report of the noble Captain Reuel W. Furlong, of Calais, who entered the service July 15, 1861, as lieutenant of company D., Sixth Maine Regiment Infantry, and was afterwards promoted to captain, his rank dating March 17, 1863. He lost his life in the battle of the Rappahannock Station, Nov. 7, 1864, after acquitting himself as a valiant and Christian hero. In this battle, he led one of the most brilliant charges of the war. The regiment at that time was merely deployed as skirmishers, but drove an entire line of battle from their intrenchments, and then held them. Up the ascent, across rifle-pits, and into the intrenchments, where it almost literally rained lead and iron, some portions of the time actually facing ten times its own number, the regiment went alone, and held the position until the Fifth Wisconsin went to its aid. Such was the scene in which the gallant Captain Furlong offered up his life. He had previously signalized himself at Hagerstown, on the 12th of July, where, going beyond the skirmish line, with only twenty-four men, he made a charge on the enemy, killing and wounding twenty-one men and taking thirty-nine prisoners. With such acts, he made a bold, clear record, as a truly brave soldier and efficient officer.' This was the same man that I mentioned before as playing a clever trick on some rebs, when in company with myself we were going down from Chain bridge to Arlington, on the other side of the Potomac. I shall be pardoned by the reader for alluding to a countryman of mine, Captain John H. Ballanger, a brave soldier, who was in my company when we were serving under Wellington.

He entered the army as a private when the rebellion first broke out, in April, 1861, at Machias. He was an ardent lover of his adopted country, and resolved to defend the stars and stripes without bounty or pledges of promotion. As soon as the company was organized he was chosen first lieutenant. The company was assigned to the Sixth Maine Volunteers as company C. I had drilled him in the old country, and had continued to drill him with others of the Sixth Maine Volunteers in camp at Portland, and during my stay with the regiment in Virginia. I knew he was every inch a soldier, and expected a good report from him. The adjutant-general shall tell the story. He writes thus of him, 'Having previously served several years in the English army, he had a most thorough knowledge of all the details of the service, and was therefore well-fitted for the discharge of every duty which devolved upon him.

'In March, 1862, on the very day that the army of the Potomac broke camp to commence active operations against the enemy for the first time, Lieutenant Ballanger was promoted to the command of his company. With it he landed at Old Point Comfort, in the latter part of the month, and marched up the Peninsula. He fought during the siege of Yorktown, and participated in the battle of Lee's Mills and Williamsburg, leading his company with ability and gallantry. He led it up the Peninsula in the advance on Richmond, took part in the principal operations of the army in the vicinity of that city, and, during the "seven days' battles," fought with it at Garnett's Farm, Savage Station, and White Oak Swamp. Naturally of a sanguine and hopeful temperament, he endured hardships cheerfully, displayed marked coolness and bravery in action, almost laughed at disaster, and despaired not in the least degree, even when the army arrived at Harrison's Landing, crippled and worn out.

'When the tide of war surged into Maryland, Captain Ballanger fought at the head of his company at Sugar Loaf Mountain, Crampton's Pass, and Antietam. Late in the autumn, he again marched into Virginia, and fought with his men at the battle of Fredericksburg. During the winter of 1862–3, he visited his home on leave of absence for fifteen days, the only time he was absent from duty during his entire term of service.

'When active operations were resumed in the spring of 1863, Captain B. with his regiment took part in the preliminary operations about Fredericksburg, being on the skirmish line with his company and hotly engaged with the enemy in a skirmish near Franklin's Crossing, May 2. He also led his company in the assault upon the heights of St. Mary, cheering them with unusual gallantry.

'When half-way up the heights, however, and just as he was entering the first rifle-pit, a minie ball crashed through his brain, instantly terminating his patriotic and heroic career. After the enemy was routed and the works captured, his comrades buried him where he had fallen, on the slope made sacred by his blood and that of many of his brave followers. The memory of his heroic deeds will be gratefully cherished by the loyal hearts of a redeemed nation.'

Another pupil of mine was Brigadier-general Hiram Burnham, who entered the Sixth Maine Regiment and was elected lieutenant-colonel. This regiment was mustered in at Portland, July 15, 1861, and was ordered immediately to Washington, where it arrived July 19th, and was stationed at Chain bridge, a few miles above Washington. The command of the regiment devolved upon Lieutenant-colonel Burnham. I gave him a full course of instruction in all the various exercises in drill. The whole regiment was under my instruction at home and at Chain bridge. I predicted brilliant things of Colonel B., on account of his quickness of perception of the different military movements, needed in charging and meeting the charges of the enemy, and I never had a man develop so rapidly in drill, and the skill with which he performed the broadsword and bayonet exercises, and going through the word of command, made him no mean antagonist for an expert to grapple with. The drill of the Sixth Maine Volunteers devolved entirely upon him after I left. It could not have been left in better hands, and the adjutant-general, in his report of General Burnham, writes thus: 'While the army of the Potomac remained in front of Washington, from October, 1861, to March, 1862, Colonel Burnham made good use of the time in drilling and disciplining his regiment, and when, at last, a movement was made by the way of the Peninsula, he had the reputation of commanding *one of the most efficient organizations of the army.'* Here I think the drill-master can be tracked pretty plainly; but I must give you something more, for it is a shame that so little has been said of the glorious Sixth Regiment, and I know the reader will pardon me for bringing out something of the work of the Sixth Maine in its identification with General B.

In the second battle of Fredericksburg, after crossing the Rappahannock, history says: 'Early in the forenoon the Fifth were relieved by the noble Sixth Maine and some other troops, who soon opened a severe and rapid fire upon the enemy. The fire was returned with energy. On the right, "Fighting Joe Hooker" had engaged the enemy, and had met with success.

'Under the fire of the rebel batteries, Newton's and Burnham's regiments lay, some in the outskirts of the town, and some in the cemetery, until General Sedgwick gave the order to advance. When—almost at the same time, both the commands moved up the glacis toward the hights. The Seventh Massachusetts, and Thirty-sixth New York pushed forward up the telegraph road, against the stone-wall bearing to the right of the road. Their haversacks and knapsacks were left behind, that they might be unincumbered with useless burdens. As they approached within about three hundred yards of the wall, a murderous volley checked the advance, and threw the head of the column into disorder. In two minutes the men were rallied, and again they approached the wall, nearer this time than before. A third time they rallied! this time they pushed straight forward to the works.

'Another column under Colonel Spear started briskly forward, divested like the others of knapsacks and haversacks. Marching from the town at double-quick in column of four ranks, they crossed the bridge just outside of the city, when its gallant leader received his mortal wound, and fell at the head of his men. The Sixty-first New York, which led the column, shocked at the death of their beloved leader, broke, and in confusion turned toward the town. This unfortunate confusion spread to the men of the Forty-third New York, who, checked by the disordered mass in their front, and submitted to a galling fire, also commenced falling back; but speedily both commands rallied and bounded forward. They reached the hights soon after the columns on the right, capturing a gun and many prisoners. The Sixth Maine Regiment marched at the head of the columns in line of battle under Colonel Burnham, who advanced on the left of the road. Leaving everything behind them but their guns and ammunition, they continued their advance on the enemy, encountering a shower of bullets, grape, and canister, as soon as they arose above the slight knoll which had partially concealed them.

'The Fifth Maine looked with wondering admiration upon the advancing lines, and when they saw the Sixth Maine with their flag flying at the head of the columns, they cried out, 'Our flag! our flag! 'tis the flag of the glorious Sixth Maine! hurrah! hurrah!"

> " Cheers, cheers for our soldiers,
>   Rough, wrinkled, and brown,
>   The men who make heroes
>   And ask no renown;
>   Unselfish, untired, intrepid, and **true**,
>   The bulwark surrounding the red, white, **and blue.**"

'The Sixth Maine was worthy of the position, its color-guard now bounding forward, now halting a moment for the men to come up, then dashing forward again in the storm of "leaden rain and iron hail," until finally gaining the hights, they planted their flag upon the summit, where the glorious stars and stripes waved in triumph. It was a thrilling spectacle, and filled our hearts with pride. This light division had reason to be proud of its comrades, proud of the Sixth Maine, of its gallant boys. The light division secured, as trophies of this battle, over seven hundred prisoners, and five cannon. It was a glorious day for the Sixth Maine. Never was a charge more gallantly made; but it was, too, a sad day, for many hundreds of our brave comrades lay stretched in death along the glacis, and on the steep ascent, in the ravines, and along the road. More than three thousand wounded men were brought into the city before nightfall.'

It is a very easy thing to talk of war; but it is a very different thing to take part in it, or to view the field after it is all over, to see the mangled bodies lying in all directions, and in all positions as they fell, their bowels torn out with shot and shell, some with headless trunks, limbs torn off and broken, others covered with blood and dirt, their hands sometimes full of dirt, leaves, or twigs, which they had grasped in their dying struggles. Some with upturned faces, bespattered with blood, pale and ghastly, their sightless, but glaring eyes looking up to heaven as if in mute appeal, when the spirit took its flight. And many a moaning, suffering hero, lying terribly wounded on the field for days before he can be properly cared for.

General Burnham gave me a description of the battle personally, only a few days before he went back to the front, where he fell a martyr to the cause of liberty and union. I shall never forget it, as he held me by the hand, when he said with a tremulous voice, showing that he felt the words he uttered in the depths of his soul, 'Sergeant, I thank God Almighty for his safe deliverance from such a horrid scene, for a more terrible fire

was never heard or witnessed than that which was opened upon
us. We were actually under a cross fire; guns in our front and
on each flank firing down upon us from the heights as we
marched along the glacis and up the steep ascent. The rebels
poured down their shot upon us like hailstones. It seemed a
providence of God that any one escaped, and, drill-master, the
instructions you gave me seemed to ring in my ears, so I remembered every step to be taken on a charge, and the word of
command as plain as if it had been given but the day before,
and as we charged up the heights I kept shouting to my men
"steady boys, keep in line," and then ordered the boys to charge
on their batteries. With only one fierce yell they dashed forward up to the muzzles of the rebel guns, and bayoneted them
in their own batteries. I remembered you and your drill when
I saw the boys fighting hand to hand with the rebels in close
quarters, stabbing one another with their bayonets, the blood
spouting over their firelocks until they were so covered and
slippery with blood that they had to grip them hard to keep
their hold, and I frequently gave the word of command,
"Steady, boys, keep cool." And as the rebs thickened on one
side, and then on the other, in their vain attempts at rallying,
I would command, "On the right, shorten!" "On the left,
shorten!" "Thrust!"* "Charge!" "Butt to the front!"
"Strike!"'†

Reader, every officer in this regiment understood the broadsword exercise and the bayonet, and every non-commissioned
officer and private understood thoroughly the bayonet exercise,

---

* *First*—Seize the piece with the right hand in front of the left, let go with the left
hand, and extend the piece quickly to the rear with the right arm; then seize the
piece again with the left hand at the muzzle. *Second*—Thrust the piece quickly forward to the full length of the left arm, the point of the bayonet at the height of the
breast, at the same time straighten the right leg vigorously.

† *First*—Extend the right arm forcibly, and to its full length, to the front, the barrel falling to the rear and resting on the right shoulder; straighten quickly the right
leg, and direct the blow at the height of the belly. *Second*—Follow the blow with
the butt by one over the head with the stock. *Third*—After the blow to the front the
piece should always be brought down forcibly on returning to guard, to represent the
blow with the stock.

and every word of command in all the evolutions and changes
necessary in a hand-to-hand fight; and the boys were thoroughly in hand, and, under the command of their skillful and heroic
leader, they could be hurled against any given point with such
a fearful shock as to compel them to give way before them. No
matter what position they were thrown into, every one had
been taught, and a word brought them into any other position
needed with the ever varying, changing, surging masses. So
they were never lost under the word of command, no matter
what order was given. Such men, so trained, retain their presence of mind, are always cool, and can always be relied upon
in these fearful shocks of hand-to-hand conflicts, and this was
what carried the day, and won for the Union this battle against
fearful odds.

This regiment was assigned to the Fourth Corps, Major-general D. Keyes commanding. With this corps, Colonel Burnham
participated in the siege at Yorktown, and his command received
the thanks of General McClellan for a successful and brilliant
charge on the enemy, in which no other troops were engaged.
The report goes on to say, 'He was in the battle at Lee's Mills.
At Williamsburg, he distinguished himself in Hancock's brilliant charge on the right of the lines, which virtually decided
the battle. So sensible was General McClellan of Colonel
Burnham's services on this occasion, that he personally addressed his regiment, a few days after the battle, thanking them
for their gallantry and good behavior. In front of Richmond,
Colonel Burnham participated in all the operations of the army.
In the "seven days' battles" he again bore a conspicuous part,
his command being engaged with the enemy at Golding's Farm,
Savage's Station, White Oak Swamp, and Malvern Hill (the
reader will please keep in his mind that the Sixth Regiment is
with him right along). His uniform gallantry and efficiency
in all these contests, did not escape the observation of his superior officers, and on arriving at Harrison's Bar, Generals
Hancock, Smith, and Franklin, united in recommending him
for promotion.

In the battle of Antietam, Sept. 17th, Colonel Burnham displayed his usual coolness and bravery.

General Smith organized a light division, composed of the *picked* men of his corps, in which Colonel B. was assigned to duty. The famous charge of the light division, on the 3d of May, 1863, through 'Slaughter-pen,' over the stone-wall, and up the heights of St. Mary, carrying the enemy's strong works, and capturing a battery of seven guns, with many prisoners, again added to the laurels of this officer. General Sedgwick, who witnessed this desperate and successful assault, and the cool valor of Colonel Burnham as he led his men on to victory, rode forward to the captured works, and while the battle yet raged fiercely, thanked him for his glorious achievement, and assured him that his services should be rewarded with promotion at an early day. When General Sedgwick deemed it necessary to withdraw his troops to the left bank of the Rappahannock, to Colonel Burnham was assigned the important duty of covering the withdrawal of the corps; a perilous duty, which he performed to the full satisfaction of the general in command.

The reduced state of the army made it necessary, soon after this, to break up the light division, and General Sedgwick, in general orders, expressed his regret at the necessity which compelled this step, saying, that its services fairly entitled it to a permanent organization, and its gallant leader, Colonel Burnham, to its permanent command.

In the fall of 1863, Colonel Burnham's health being completely shattered by his long, arduous, and exhausting labors, he was detailed to superintend the recruiting service for his regiment in Maine, on which duty he remained until February, 1864. During most of the time, he was also president of a general court-martial convened in Portland. On returning to active service, Colonel Burnham was assigned to the command of the brigade in which his regiment was serving, and so continued until he was promoted to the rank of brigadier-general,

17

April 15, 1864. At the request of General Smith, his old commander,—who was organizing a force at Yorktown, to operate
on the south side of the James river,—he was ordered to report
for service in this force, and assigned to the command of the
Second Brigade, First Division, Thirteenth Army Corps. He
participated with the army of the James in the movement up the
river, and in the subsequent operations at Bermuda Hundred.
His command was constantly engaged with the enemy during
these operations, and his gallantry and efficiency were never
more conspicuous and serviceable.

During the unfortunate battle near Drury's Bluff, May 16th,
he is reported as performing prodigies of valor. Holding his
position for hours after our lines were beaten back at other
points, he repulsed continuous and determined attacks of the
enemy, and captured numerous prisoners. Although two
horses were shot under him during this hotly contested engagement, he miraculously escaped uninjured. In the attack
upon Petersburg, June 15th, he stormed and carried the enemy's works with his skirmishers, capturing five pieces of artil
lery and a considerable number of prisoners. Of this affair an
eye-witness wrote: 'The success which he achieved placed
Petersburg in the grasp of our Union forces, and had there
remained two hours of daylight, the terrible struggle which
was subsequently waged around the "cockade city" would
never have taken place.' His health failing, he proceeded
north, and recruited himself somewhat, with a few weeks' quiet
with his family, when he again returned to his command.
Preparations were being made for an attack upon the enemy's
fortifications at Chapin's Farm.

Within twenty-four hours after his return, he marshaled his
men for a last battle against the enemies of his country. During the night of Sept. 28th, a pontoon bridge was thrown across
the James at Aiken's landing, the 18th corps crossed, and with
the first gleam of morning light commenced an attack upon
the rebels. General Burnham was selected to lead the attack-

ing column. At a short distance from the crossing, he came upon the enemy's skirmishers strongly intrenched. They were speedily routed and pushed back toward their fortifications. A running fire ensued, the rebels being driven rapidly. At a distance of about two miles from the river, General Burnham came upon the enemy's works at Chapin's farm, and commenced the assault. The struggle was desperate and bloody; but the determined resistance of the enemy was in vain. General Burnham carried their works triumphantly, capturing all their artillery, and hundreds of prisoners. Still the enemy clung to a portion of the line, and from the right poured down a destructive fire upon our victorious forces.

General Burnham, who had now dismounted in order to enter the captured fort, now rallied such of his force as he could assemble, and was making a detour to the rear of these troublesome rebels, in order to attack them and secure their capture. As he cheered on his men, a minie ball pierced his abdomen and he fell.

Sorely wounded though he was, and in the agonies of death, he retained all his mental faculties, and saw his approaching death with a composure and resignation which well became so distinguished a soldier, so eminent a patriot, so true a man. With shortening breath, he spoke of his family; and then, as his long and unselfish services for his country seemed to flit through his mind, he said, '*I have tried to do my duty,*' when he died without a struggle, as he was being carried from the field he so nobly won. In honor of his memory, the fort which his stern valor won, was called Fort Burnham. It will be seen by this account, that Colonel Burnham and the Sixth Maine Regiment, so illustrious for capacity, coolness, and bravery and here represented by the adjutant-general as one of the best-drilled organizations in the army, yielded the fruits to be expected, as the result of proper education in all the departments of military drill, a truth which I had labored hard to impress upon all with whom I had anything to do. I had contended earnestly, that many disasters which occurred, in the shape of panics and utter routes and defeat, resulted from want of proper drilling. The officers and men getting confused, by not being perfectly familiar with all the tactics of war, lost confidence in themselves, became panic-stricken, and defeat was often the result, when victory should have been won. General Burnham and his noble regiment had confidence in their *knowledge* of arms, and in themselves *because of it ;* and hence were never flustrated, and in their charges on the enemy, and in their defense when charged, to an observer carried with them an air of sublimity and moral grandeur which could not fail to extort praise from even their enemies. How much more from friends anxiously watching their career, when in the fiercest conflicts with the foe.

I mention only these specimens of good training, to show how far and wide, in a war like ours, may be the influence of even one competent drill-master, who devotes his time as I did from April, 1861, until April, 1865, to educating the officers and privates by thousands, in the drill-room and on the field.

Who can tell how much the little that I had done had to do with saving the lives of our boys, especially when on a charge, or in personal conflicts with the foe; or how much it had to do with the general issue; or with the time when rebellion received its final blow? Again and again I received letters of thanks, from both men and officers, telling me that they were indebted to the instruction I had given them for the preservation of their lives. I will give one which was sent from the front to the *Kennebec Journal* by some officers of the Sixth Maine, when they heard that I had been crippled in the work:

To the Press and the People of Maine.—The undersigned, members of the Sixth Maine Regiment of Volunteers, are desirous of calling the attention of the people of our State to the present position and distress of Sergeant I. W. Ambler, of Biddeford, and of publicly testifying our gratitude to him for the invaluable service he has rendered to us.

Sergeant Ambler was engaged in drilling our regiment, both officers and men, for several months last year in the vicinity of Washington, *and to his instructions, we believe, the regiment owes very much of its efficiency and success. To his teachings some of us owe the preservation of our lives upon the field of battle.*

He has also been engaged in drilling and instructing other of our Maine regiments and many individuals connected with the service, both as officers and privates.

He is now disabled by wounds received while engaged in this noble work, and without the means of earning his support.

Such a man should not suffer while a country remains which we can call our own.

(Signed by) C. EDES,
      L. H. WHITTIER,
      WM. SHERMAN, } *Sixth Maine.*
      SIDNEY W. TUCKER,
      F. G. LEIGHTON,

I, therefore, felt the blessing of justification on this department of my life. Proud of the part I had acted in this drama, proud to be one of the defenders of *National Liberty*, and I came to the conclusion, that 'Uncle Sam' would hardly know the difference between his natural and his adopted children, and would, on the whole, deal as liberally with one as the other.

So, my reader, I found a good deal of comfort in reviewing the whole matter, and I said to myself, my life has not been a blot or a blank, and so giving myself to God and my country, there is no part of my life that I cannot use for the good of my fellow men. And I got a complete victory over the devil in my tussle with him, when he began to throw his fiery darts. Paul had told me how to do it. He said, after I had got the rest of the armor on, 'Above all, taking the shield of faith, wherewith ye shall be able to quench all the fiery darts of the wicked.' So I held up this precious shield, and with it I could parry in prime or tierce, or develop in seconde, all the lunges of the devil. Then I had a little more to comfort me.

I found, on a review, that I had personally got more than a thousand men into the service, of my own countrymen, besides as many more native born Americans, who told on the enemy in the great strife. I had the advantage of most men in being a soldier and a drill-master myself, and I could have put thousands of dollars in my pocket, if I had played the broker in getting them; but all these temptations had no influence with 'me; but with singleness of purpose, aiming to do the most good in every way in my power, to relieve, protect, and defend my adopted country and flag, I worked early and late, and almost day and night, as much as in me lay, as I promised to do when I made my first speech from the balcony of the old Massachusetts State-house, on that memorable Sabbath to which I have referred. So over the whole road, there were flowers strewn for my comfort.

It may be said by some, how is it that Ambler finds flowers in looking over a war record? Strange place for flowers! A strange place among mangled heroes, on bloody battle-fields to find anything like solace! I admit it; but go with me, and you shall see how it is done.

There is a sublimity on a field of battle that is developed nowhere else, as it is there,—an utter self-abnegation, and forgetfulness of everything but one's country, so that even boys, when the death-rattle is in their very throats, cheer their flags and give up the ghost. At the hospitals at Dallis, among the patriot wounded was a boy only nineteen years old. The glorious victory achieved in the battle where he fell, inspired him with enthusiastic joy, notwithstanding the pain from his wounds was intense. The surgeon as he examined the ghastly wound, sadly informed him that he must die, and that his end was very near. Glancing for a moment at his torn and blood-stained limb, a tear glistened in his eye. Drawing from his bosom the picture of his mother, he kissed it, and gave it with a letter to a comrade, and asked him to see that it was sent to her. Then calling a friend to his side, he grasped his hand, saying: '*Matt, they tell me that I am about to die. Before I go, let us give three cheers for the glorious old Union.*' He raised himself up in his bed; but the effort was too much for his exhausted frame, and he sank back upon his pillow, and immediately expired. Look at Thomas Jackson, coxswain of the frigate Wabash. His leg was torn off by a shell, so that it hung by a small portion of the muscle and skin. He deliberately took out his belt-knife, and tried to sever the leg from his body; but the knife was so dull, though he sawed manfully, that he could not separate it. He was taken below, and died in two hours, saying to his comrades that stood about him, '*Boys, I am happy to suffer for the dear old flag.*' What a nobility is this! A country cannot die with such patriots teeming all through her land. See how battles make heroes,— making men utterly careless of death.

Let me give you a letter of a thorough soldier, a captain in the Enniskillen dragoons, under Wellington, during the Crimean war:

November 2.

DEAR JACK,—I am, you see, alive at this date, but God knows for how long after. You have, I presume, devoured all the accounts which have been sent home, as to our glorious charge. Oh, such a charge! Never think of the gallop and trot which you have often witnessed in the Phœnix park when you desire to form a notion of a genuine blood-hot,· all mad charge, such as that I have come out of with a few lance prods, minus some gold lace, a helmet chain, and brown Bill's (the charger's) right ear. From the moment we dashed at the enemy, whose position, and so forth, you doubtless know as much about as I can tell you, I knew nothing, but that I was impelled by some irresistible force onward, and by some invisible and imperceptible influence to crush every obstacle which stumbled before my good sword and brave old charger. I never in my life experienced such a sublime sensation as in the moment of the charge. Some fellows talk of its being 'demoniac.' I know this, that it was such as made me a match for any two ordinary men, and gave me such an amount of glorious indifference as to life, as I thought it impossible to be master of. It would do your Celtic heart good to hear the most magnificent cheers with which we dashed into what P—— W—— calls 'the gully scrimage.' Forward—dash—bang—clank, and there we were in the midst of such smoke, cheer, and clatter as never before stunned a mortal's ear. It was glorious. Down one by one, aye, two by two, fell the thick-skulled and over-numerous Cossasks and other lads of the tribe of Old Nick. Down too, alas, fell many a hero with a warm Celtic heart, and more than one fell screaming loud for victory. I could not pause, I was all push, wheel, frenzy, strike, and down, down, down they went. Twice I was unhorsed, and more than once I had to grip my sword tighter, the blood of foes streaming down over the hilt and running up my very sleeve. Our old Waterloo comrades, the Scott Grays, and ourselves, were the only fellows who flung headlong first into the very heart of the Muscoves. Now we were lost in their ranks—now in little bands battling—now in good order together—now in and now out, until the whole 'levies' on the spot plunged into a forming body of the enemy, and helped us to end the fight by compelling the foe to fly. Never did men run so vehemently but all this you have read in the papers.

I cannot depict my feelings when we returned. I sat down completely exhausted and unable to eat, though deadly hungry. All my uniform, my hands, my very face were bespattered with blood. It was that of the enemy. Grand idea! But my feelings,—they were full of that exultation which it is impossible to describe. At least twelve Russians were sent wholly out of the 'way of the war' by my good steel alone, and at least as many more put on the passage to that peaceful exit by the same excellent weapon. So, also, can others say. What a thing to reflect on! I have almost grown a soldier philosopher, and most probably will one of these days, if the bullets which are flying about so abundantly give me time to brush up.

My dear fellow, our countrymen have not tarnished their fame in this battle. Gallantry and glory will never abandon the march of Celtic bands,—never! Oh, that I could have patience to write you of such deeds of individual heroism as have come within my notice! Fictionists are shabby judges of true bravery. No novel ever had sham hero, who comes up to the realities I have witnessed. One of my troops, for instance, had his horse shot under him in the melee. 'Bloody wars,' he roared, 'this wont do,' and right at a Russian he ran, pulled him from his horse by the sword-hand in the most extraordinary manner; then deliberately cutting off his head as he came down, vaulted into the saddle, and turning the Russian charger against its late friends, fought his way through. This took less time to do than it takes me to tell it.

Dear Jack, there are deeds of daring when you encounter an enemy, as I have done, in a hand to hand fight with the sword. The first sword-cut that I received was two and a half inches long, which I will show you if ever I see you. Good-by, old boy.

From your friend and comrade,

Thomas Nigloon.

I can see in this war, as in the war of the Revolution, the throes of a nobler manhood. The travail of a government, in giving birth to a higher state of liberty and equality, so that when it is delivered of that, of, and for which it has travailed in pain and in blood, it shall rejoice like the mother over her last-born and most perfect child, who shall bear her name and fame down the long years of posterity.

As Tyrrell says, 'Let us pause and reflect upon this history of carnage and horror! We would fain that such gigantic calamities should yield some good to humanity, some lessons to the world. If seas and mountains have their meaning, and with a silent yet sublime eloquence which is felt, not heard, impress on the beholder elevating and gentle thoughts; if the hoarse murmur or shrill scream of the bleak wind through the dense dim forests has a voice to those who listen in the spirit of the seer; if stones, and trees, and running brooks preach mute sermons to the philosophic mind; if the mysterious and silent stars sing in their course like millions of radiant angels, and shed an inspiration on the rapt beholder,—if these things are so (and in a metaphorical sense they are), then surely war, in all its ghastly and fiendish majesty,—war, with its regal preparations, with its pomp, its gold, its scarlet and blue, and its grand swelling strains of music,—war, with its roarings and its thunders, with its terrific lightnings, which more than rival those of heaven, with its cataracts of fire, hurling from ten thousand iron mouths the deadly messengers whose shocks are as if some infernal deity had smote the staggering earth, until the mountains reeled, and the astonished sea stood still,—war, the stupendous destroyer, who sows in wantonness and reaps in blood, whose dreadful harvests are the gory fields, covered with mangled corpses, with blood-bespattered faces, and sightless glaring eyes, fixed on the blue vault of heaven, as if vainly appealing to the merciful God, who seems for a time to have abandoned his creation, and have given it over to be the grim sport of fiends;—surely this dreadful power has its teachings if we could but glean them.' I could not draw much comfort from such scenes as these, did I not have a perfect faith in an overruling providence, who has some plans laid, the foundations of which rest too deep for common fathoming.

There is an awfulness when the tempest rages, that strikes many beholders with terror, from before which the fowls of heaven fly away to the deep, dark forests and hide themselves, and the lowing herds sweep over hill and plain to some sheltered spot; but I see in the sharp lightning's flash, and I hear in the deep-toned thunder, the way God takes to cleanse the air and sweeten it for man. There are very few that look upon the sale of Joseph by his brethren, with any sort of reconciliation; but when the end is seen from the beginning, there is a completeness about it that reflects much of the divine wisdom and power of God, without by any means justifying the motives of Joseph's brethren, or abating a jot from their wickedness; but Joseph saw the divine plan when he said to his brethren, 'Now, therefore, be not grieved nor angry with yourselves, that ye sold me hither, for God did send me before you to preserve life. So now it was not you that sent me hither, but God, and he hath made me a father to Pharaoh, and lord of all his house, and a ruler throughout all the land of Egypt.'

So when the rebels fired on Fort Sumter, and commenced this terrible war for nothing else but to perpetuate slavery, God meant that first gun for the funeral knell of that horrid institution, and so through the long and bloody strife that was meant to rivet the chains forever by wicked men, the great Ruler of nations meant it should strike them off, and make this great people a nation of freemen. And so I gather comfort from the rebellion,—not that men rebelled, not that so many were slain, but that God has overruled this war, and through it, brought us as a country up to a higher patriotism, made us a nobler people, a better model for the nations of the earth to pattern after, and I had helped to accomplish this.

CHAPTER XXXIII.

It now remained for me to lay my plans as best I could for future operations. The war was ended. So there was no more for me to do in that direction; but the great fight was still going on between the kingdom of darkness and the kingdom of light, and I said to myself and to my wife, I must put myself in fighting trim and go at it. I must first settle up all my business affairs. So this being fixed upon, I gave up to my clamoring creditors what I once hoped to hold, my little home, to be divided among them as far as it would go. Some of them did not press me, but others did. They had kept quiet while I was in Washington, expecting I should be successful with my claims; but when they learned of my failure there, their patience ended, and it seems to be a singular business fact, that when everybody thinks a man has money enough, they never feel in haste about their pay; but when they begin to mistrust that you are running a little short, every man wants his money to the last dime. I said to my wife, now we have struck bottom, we will put down a stake, and then take a fair start. I felt now about as poor as Job's turkey, but not quite. It has been said of him that he was so poor that he had to lean up against a tree to gobble. But I did not have to lean against a tree to do that, I could gobble well enough without it generally, and here I must diverge a little, even if I am charged with not exactly sticking to my text, for I just now remember when I was a little tongue-tied in New York when asking for a pass on one of the steamers running to Fall River. I ought to have mentioned

this when speaking of my labors in getting signers to my petition, or rather testimonials to go with my petition to Congress.

My motto has always been to speak well of a bridge that
carries a fellow over well, and I should not do a man justice,
who is now no more, if I did not mention an interview I had
with him, Colonel Fisk, of railroad notoriety.

In the summer of 1871, while I was working up the testimonials to be attached to my petition to Congress for help, I went
to Long Branch to see the President, and not finding him there,
I went to West Point where I learned the President had gone,
and met him there. I showed him the names I had on my list
of testimonials, and asked him for his signature. He told me
it was a big thing, and that I had his sympathy; but it would
not be proper for him to sign it until it passed through Congress. My travels had cost me a good deal of money, and I
found I had not money enough to reach home. When I got
back as far as New York city I had not a dime left. I went to
the telegraph office, and told the officer I wanted to send a
telegram to Mr. Carter, of Saco, to get him to send me some
money to get home with, and asked him how long it would be
before I would get an answer. He said it would probably be
at least four hours. It was then after eight o'clock in the evening. I told him I did not know what I should do, I had no
money to get any supper or a lodging for the night. He said,
'Who are you?' I told him what my name was, and that I
had been getting some testimonials from officers in the army,
to attach to a petition I intended to present to Congress, for
some remuneration for my services in the army, and handed
him the list to look over. After reading it he said, 'Sergeant,
I will let you have five dollars to help you along, and you can
pay me when you get it.' With this I got my supper and
lodging. It was Saturday night when I got this money, and I
paid out of it for two nights' lodging and my board over Sunday. I made up my mind that I would go and see Mr. Fisk,
the owner of the line of boats running to Fall River, and ask

him for a pass. I went to the opera house where he had his office, and saw the major of Fisk's regiment, and told him I wanted to get a pass on Mr. Fisk's boat. He asked me who I was. I told him who I was, and showed him my documents. He then told me he could not give me a pass, but said he wanted me to see the colonel. I told him I did not want to ask him. 'I don't want to go in, because I have been told that he is pretty rough with such fellows as I am, and I feel bad enough without being bluffed.' He said I was mistaken. The colonel was as good-hearted a fellow as ever lived, and I *must* see him and show him the papers I had with me, and he knew Fisk would give me a pass; and, turning to the porter he said, 'when the colonel gets through reading his correspondence, take Sergeant Ambler in to see him first, before anybody else.'

In a little while, I should think there were thirty people in waiting for an interview. I asked him why so many were waiting to see Mr. Fisk? Why, said the major, these are poor people seeking some aid in some way from him.

The porter came out in a little while, and said the colonel was now ready to see me. 'Come right in.' I went in and found him at his desk, and gave him the military salute in the European style. He bowed an acknowledgment, and he said, 'Well, my man, what do you want?' I told him I was a little hard up, and wanted to get a pass on his boat. He said, 'Who are you?' I told him I was Sergeant Ambler, and that I had been down to Long Branch and West Point, to get signers to this petition (holding it in my hand) to present to Congress. He said, 'let me look at it.' I gave it to him and he read it, and then he said, 'Do you want me to sign this?' I said, 'No, sir, I do not.' He then said, 'What do you want?' I told him I just wanted a pass on his boat. 'Well,' said he, 'why did you not ask General Grant for a pass?' I said, 'Because I would not do it, sir.' And he said, 'Will you ask Jim Fisk for a pass, before you would ask General Grant?' I said, 'Yes, sir.' He then turned to his clerk and said to him, 'Here, give this sergeant ten dollars, and a pass on my boat.' He then sai ', 'Sergeant, when you go to Washington to get your pension, come and see me,' and shook me heartily by the hand, and said, 'you are an out-spoken fellow, and frank, and that is what I like,' and bid me good-day. I then waited a while in the outer room, to see how those others fared. Some dozen or more came out, and not one without something. One old lady with two children had received several dollars. Another old man had got five dollars, and several crippled soldiers had each received substantial aid, and came out with a smile on their faces, and a blessing on their lips for the colonel. As I turned away from the door, I thanked God for what I had seen. There was the old, the unfortunate, the lame, the halt, and the blind, all of them receiving aid and sympathy from this man. On the very morning I left Boston for Washington with my petition, intending on my way to call and see the colonel, his dead body was on the way to Vermont, to its narrow home.

God had given me a tongue and a few brains, and with a heart full of love for souls to *propel* things, I made up my mind that *that* was so much stock in trade, and with these I would go to recruiting and drilling men for the kingdom. The same old ghost met me at this point that had often met me before, and would not down at my bidding. I must have more education, for how could an ignorant man expect the people to give him bread, if he was not capable of instructing them to some extent. I meant to preach and study, and so keep both irons in the fire at the same time. And I must have money some way to do it. I thought of the sale of my book that I begun before the war. The first editions had been all sold, and the money had gone to help 'Uncle Sam.'

In the great fire in Portland the stereotype plates and every thing connected with my book were burned up, so I had nothing to start on. I then made up my mind that if I could get out a new edition, correcting the old and adding to it what I had passed through since writing the first, I could sell it to good advantage. I had formed a very extensive acquaintance during the war, and I felt confident that every man who could afford to invest a little in good old Saxon, would buy one. That was all right so far, but up starts the same old ghost, and with a sepulchral tone, inquired, 'Where is your money to do it?' By this time I had become so familiar with this phantom, that I said I'll go and see. I went among my friends and asked their advice about attempting to put out another book, and most of them said, 'Go ahead, it's a good idea. I'll buy one.' So I went to see the printer and talked with him about it, and he approved of it, and I talked around some time before I could get cheek enough to ask him if he would trust me for the work until I could sell books enough to pay him, and here my heart thumped against my ribs pretty hard for fear he would say no.

God and the printer were better than my fears, and he answered, 'Yes, Ambler, I'll trust you, for you can sell it, and I know you will pay me as soon as you realize enough from the sale to do it.' He then put me on the track of a man who was at leisure, and was just the man I needed to help me compile and arrange it for the press. I then went to a publishing house, to see if they would take the responsibility to issue the book, in such numbers as would be necessary for a fair business operation, and God had prepared the way somehow, so that they were ready to issue the work as soon as it could be prepared, and wait for their pay; and so with the engraver. They were all ready, and all willing to trust to my honesty as to their pay. It made me think of the boy whose father called him up one morning very early, and told him to saddle the horse and take a grist to the mill. It was very foggy, and the boy told his father it was so foggy that he was sure he could not find the way. 'Why, father, I can't see down to the gate.' His father said to him, 'Oh, yes, you can my son; get on to the old horse and go as far as you can see, and if you get to a place where you can't see any further, you can stop.' The boy started; but the fog lifted as he proceeded, seeing just about so far all the time, and he found no place to stop until he reached the mill. So in my case. I had a grist to grind, and as I went the fog kept lifting, lifting, and as I stepped along, the way kept clearing for me to go further. Is it not so in following the leadings of Providence most always? Don't we walk by faith, and not by sight?

> ' When the Great Shepherd leads the way,
> Oh, who will fear to go;
> From darkness into realms of day,
> He leads the journey through.'

While going along with my book thus, apparently under easy sail, all at once I was struck aback, by a summons to court by Dresser & Ayer, of Portland, Maine, whom I was owing the small sum of twelve dollars and thirty-three cents, and who had promised to wait until I got eased up in my money matters, so I could conveniently meet the bill. This threw me into Doubting Castle for a night or two, when a good friend advised me to take the poor debtor's oath, and so block all these hungry creatures that eat up the poor as they would eat bread, until such a time as I could pay them.

I hated to do it; but on viewing the whole matter, under all the surrounding circumstances, I made up my mind it was my duty to do so, and that would bring me down on to what the oil men call ' hard pan,' and then I would begin to build without molestation, until I could get my head above water, and then I would pay up all debts, and in the mean time give my Christian friends an opportunity to cultivate one of the graces so necessary in their case,—I mean the grace of patience; for out of it grows experience, and a man is much improved when patience has its perfect work; and the Lord knew there was abundant room for improvement in their case.

Here is the summons. I suppose it is nothing private, at least it was not so marked, and therefore I present it in these columns, and if it is any advantage to my friends to be thus advertised, I will give them the full benefit of it, as freely as I

18

would give them a drink of cold water should they ask it. I am determined to be generous as well as just.

STATE OF MAINE.

York, ss.—To Isaac W. Ambler,　　　　　　　*Greeting.*

We command you to appear before our Judge of our Municipal Court of the city of Saco, in the County of York, to be holden at the Municipal Court room, in said Saco, in .said County, on the fourth Tuesday of November, a. d. 1872, at nine o'clock in the forenoon, then and there to answer unto Aurin L. Dresser and David M. Ayer, both of Portland, County of Cumberland, and State of Maine, doing business under the firm name of Dresser & Ayer, in a plea of the case as set forth in the writ; which plea the said plaintiffs have commenced to be heard and tried at the said Court, and your goods or estate are attached to the value of twenty dollars, for security to satisfy the judgment which the said plaintiffs may recover on the aforesaid trial. Fail not of appearance at your peril. Witness, Samuel F. Chase, Esq., our said Judge, at Saco aforesaid, the fourteenth day of November, in the year of our Lord one thousand eight hundred and seventy-two.

Samuel F. Chase.

Having found out, in the course of my life, that even I might be mistaken, I concluded to call on my good friend Judge Emery, of Saco, and ask his advice, and get a little instruction how to proceed in the matter. I made a full statement to him of my situation, and showed him my summons to court. He advised me in order to save myself from constant annoyance, and from being robbed, to take the poor debtor's oath, and go through the forms necessary, and generously offered to pay the bills.

It is said, 'pride and poverty go together,' and I guess it is true enough, for it was very mortifying to my pride to do this, as I always felt a good deal of pride in paying my bills when they became due, and I could only justify myself on the ground that in this way only could I ever pay my bills. That is, I could say to such as would *not* let me alone, 'Hands off,' gentlemen, until I can get breath, and then if you can observe the common rules of decency, you shall all be paid to the last cent.'

So on the fourth Tuesday of November, 1872, at nine o'clock in the morning, according to orders, I put in my appearance at court, as cited by the summons, Judge Emery appearing for me. E. S. Derby, Esq., of Saco, appeared for Dresser & Ayer. I was put upon the stand and sworn, Judge Chase presiding.

Mr. Derby opened the case and put the following questions:

Ques. Mr. Ambler, what property have you?

Ans. None.

Ques. What have you done with your house?

Ans. My house had two mortgages on it and the parties foreclosed and I could not pay them, and everything went to pay my creditors.

Ques. Have you a watch?

Ans. I had; but when I was in Washington I had to let it go to pay my bills.

Ques. Have you no jewelry, rings, etc.?

Ans. No.

Ques. Have you made way with, or covered anything?

Ans. No.

Ques. What have you got?

Ans. Nothing.

(And here the lawyer, looking at the judge, said, 'Mr. Ambler is a strong man and can earn it in a little while, it is only $14.10.')

I answered if I was able to work I would earn it very quick and pay it.

Ques. Mr. Ambler, you have a trade have you?

Ans. Yes, sir.

Ques. What is your trade?

Ans. I am a soldier.

Ques. When did you enlist?

Ans. Thirty years ago, under the Duke of Wellington; but my business just now is rather dull, and if it was not, I could not do much.

Ques. What is the matter; you look like an able-bodied man?

Ans. I have lost the use of my hand.

Ques. What is the matter with that?

My answer to this was to take off my glove and exhibit my shrunken, crippled wrist and hand. Here the lawyer, advancing, looked at it, and turning to the judge said, ' Your honor, I did not know Mr. Ambler was a cripple.'

Ques. Mr. Ambler, you have a pension?

Ans. No, sir.

Ques. How did you lose the use of your hand?

Ans. Drilling officers of the Union army in the late war.

Ques. And you have no pension?

Ans. No, sir.

This closed the catechising on the complainant's side. Mr. Emery then asked me one question.

Ques. Mr. Ambler, have you not a sword?

Ans. Yes, sir. It is one I had drawn to defend our flag when marching through Baltimore. It was presented to me by the lamented Colonel Ellsworth. I don't know as I can really call it mine, I told my boy if he would commit to memory a piece called 'Bingen on the Rhine,' and repeat it all to me without making any mistakes, I would give him my sword. He learned it and repeated it to me without a mistake, and I gave him the sword.

This ended the examination. The plea of Mr. Derby was very brief. My lawyer did not think it necessary to reply, and the court decided that I was entitled to the benefit of the poor debtor's oath, and I was discharged, and it went upon the record of the court. So here I found myself at the bottom of the ladder, and the thing publicly acknowledged. Mr. Derby, who had been doing the lawyer, in his plea against me, kindly walked over with me to the little shop, where my wife is trying to get bread for us by dressmaking and a little millinery work, and stopped and chatted a while. He told me not to entertain any hard feelings against him, as he was simply doing his duty for his client. I told him I understood perfectly his position, and we could not expect anything better from a lawyer (joking of course), and they needed pardon, and I hoped they would all find it. I showed my good friend some of my papers, the testimonials of Generals Hooker, Burnside, McClellan, Shepley, Dow, and others, in which he was very much interested, and when he left he said, 'Ambler, you are a hero,' and of course he was right. Who would ever think of disputing with a lawyer, especially when there was no chance for a dispute?

Well, here I was down on to 'hard pan,' and I said to myself, Ambler, you are a poor shack now, anyhow, and I guess there will be none to dispute that point, and so I soliloquized a little; not just as the rich man did, who determined to pull down his old barns and build largely, so he could have room where to bestow all his goods; but I said to myself, Ambler, eat, drink (if thou can'st get anything), and take thine ease, for there will be no demands for thee to pay at present. They are all settled *pro tempore.* When, to my astonishment, the evening of the very same day that I went upon the record as a 'flat,' a townsman, knowing it too, came to my place and presented a bill of a small balance which was due him on an account, and said, 'Ambler, I am going to keeping house, and if you have got any plates or crockery of any kind, I will take it at its value toward what you owe me.'

Reader, 'how is that for high?' Well, I said, wife, just give this poor man those half a dozen plates (we had only six in all left), and I will eat off the table like a pig out of his trough. I should have given them to him, for I thought a man that could take the last half dozen plates a poor fellow had to eat off of, should have them for his cheek, if for nothing else. Mrs. Ambler, good wife that she is, begged to differ with me (how presumptuous these women are since woman's rights have been so much discussed), and a protest from her was the end of that man's crockery hopes. I told him I would surely pay him some time. 'No,' he said, 'I know you can never do a day's work with your arm to earn a cent, and I shall have to lose it if you don't let me have those plates.' I have generally entertained strong objections to the developing doctrine, that we sprang from some lower life like the tadpole, and so up through the monkey to the man; but, I said, if that is so, it is pretty hard on the tadpoles and the monkeys that they should have to be linked to such a specimen of littleness. This man had a good business and money at interest. I will not name him. I only hope out of pity for him, that if he ever reads this book, he will put his hand over this page, so not to see it, for if he ever should read this part of *his* history, he will want to get his neighbors to set up nights with him, and help him to hate himself. Well, it seems that I am not out of the woods yet, and I don't know as I ought to expect to be while here in the flesh; but of one thing I am sure, and that is this, if a poor fellow that has met every mishap to which mortal man is subject *can* get out of the woods by persevering, honest effort, I am the man to try. I believe there is in providence something yet in store for me, and if there is anything in the saying, that God helps those that try and help themselves, I shall be helped. It looks to me yet, that God has a work for me to do, especially when I look back to my commencement in life, and trace his watchful hand over all the strange road of life thus far, through all the dangers I have met in various parts of the world, both by sea and land, in civil and in military life. I hope my book which I now present, will find a sale sufficiently ready and extensive to enable me to procure such works as I need, to fit me better to proclaim the glorious gospel of salvation to the poor outcast. Oh, how glad I am, that Jesus came not to call the righteous, but sinners to repentance. My highest ambition is to be unfettered by this cruel poverty, so to preach the unsearchable riches of the kingdom to men, and to do it without fear or favor. This is my faith, that I shall realize a support from this plain, truthful, unvarnished history of my life, so to be independent of a salary, as independent as Paul was. In looking over the field that is all 'white and ready for the harvest,' I am persuaded, that to be successful, much of the modern preaching is fruitless, and that ministers and churches have got to disabuse themselves of the idea, that prosperity consists in getting a splendid church, with a spire that kisses the skies, with rich carpets, expensive pews and altars, and grand organs, and a trained choir to praise God for them, and a congregation numerous and rich enough to run the machine and pay the bills, and then settle down at ease, and when a poor man thinks of joining them, give him to understand that the church is full. In some of our large churches, the poor are barred out as truly as if the sexton stood at the door and told them they were not wanted within, and it is done in this way. The pews in some churches are sold at prices ranging from one hundred to a thousand dollars, and sometimes several thousand dollars, and then to meet the big salaries of ministers, choirs, organists, sextons, and to pay for fuel, lights, repairs, and insurance, the pews are taxed from fifty up to five hundred dollars each. And so heartbroken and discouraged, the poor man, and sometimes the poor members, are driven away, because they can't support their families and pay such bills.

In saying these plain things, and what may appear to some to be hard things, I do it to clear my conscience, and to strike a blow in behalf of the suffering poor whose bitter experience demands it. My own early sufferings are indelibly stamped on every fibre of my being, and my later trials have only confirmed it; so that who suffers '*and I burn not.*' I would be alike untrue to my early experience and my latest knowledge and awfully untrue to God's grandest work, to the travail of

Christ's great soul, if I failed to do this. And while I make these painfully true statements and send them abroad to the world, I make an honest confession, which will be appreciated by a very large class of men, who acknowledge that we are coming at the truth and will hope for a practical application of it, which may prove the salvation of many souls. I would not forget how many noble men whom God has blessed with wealth, are doing as well as they know for the needy, and would do more, much more, if they could have some practical hints thrown out that would open to them deeper and wider fields for effort and Christian usefulness, and when they read this book, and see where the hand can be put to lighten the loads of the distressed, will thank Ambler for pointing out the way, in his homely manner, to do good.

God sometimes takes worms to thresh mountains, and it is written that 'God hath chosen the foolish things of the world to confound the wise, and God hath chosen the weak things of the world to confound the things which are mighty. And base things of the world, and things which are despised, hath God chosen, yea, and things which are not, to bring to nought the things which are; that no flesh should glory in his presence.' The things which secure the blessings of God are so simple, that they are often overlooked. I often think of the terrible efforts a class made once, to spell the name of a river. They seemed to think that the teacher meant to tax their ingenuity to the utmost when he asked them to spell the word Po, and they tried every imaginable hard way to spell it, but failed; and when it come to the lowest one in his class to try it, the poor simple boy spelled it P-o, Po, and went to the head. Sometimes almost every imaginable hard way is tried to love God, and men fail to do so until they begin to love men, and when they find them hungry and give them bread, then they for the first time begin to comprehend the secret of loving God. Now any course that in any way relieves and lightens the loads that human hearts have to bear, is so much done to, and for the Saviour of men.

It is said by some, 'Ambler, you are wrong, in our rich and costly churches we have pews on purpose for the poor, and we *give* them sittings, and surely we are helping them, and they are charitably treated; they can hear the gospel for the coming, if they will only consent to listen to it.' All that is true enough, but here is where the shoe often pinches the poor the hardest. They say it is bad enough to be poor without sitting them apart in a portion of the church assigned for such, so that everybody that comes in shall know that they belong to the poor class. The poor like to be thrown in among the rich sometimes, in such a way that their poverty may not always be known; and it is sometimes very pleasant for them to pass off among the crowd without being noticed *as the poor*, and I have no doubt it is sometimes quite flattering to them to be even mistaken for persons in easy circumstances.

> 'Is there no place on the face of this earth,
>   Where charity dwelleth, where virtue hath birth?
>   Where the bosom in mercy and kindness will heave,
>   And the poor and the wretched may ask and receive?
>   Where quickly a knock from the needy and poor
>   Will bring some kind angel to open the door?
>   Ah, search where you will, wherever you can,
>   There's no open door for a moneyless man.

> 'Go look in yon hall where the chandelier's light
>   Drives off with its splendor the darkness of night;
>   Where the rich hanging velvets in shadowy folds
>   Sweep gracefully down with their trimmings of gold.
>   Aye, look in that hall, and find if you can,
>   A welcoming smile for a moneyless man.

> 'Go look in yon church with its cloud-reaching spire,
>   That throws back to the sun its reflection of fire;
>   Where the arches and columns are gorgeous within,
>   And the walls seem as pure as a soul without sin.
>   Then walk down the aisles, see the rich and the great,
>   In the pomp and the pride of their wordly estate;
>   Then go to their dwellings, and find if you can
>   A welcoming look for a moneyless man.

'Go look at yon judge with his dark flowing gown,
  And the scales of the law weighing equally down,
  Who frowns on the weak and smiles on the strong,
  And punishes right, whilst he justifies wrong;
  Where the jurors their lips on the Bible have laid,
  To render a verdict they've already made.
  Go there in that court-room, and find if you can,
  Any law for the cause of a moneyless man.

'Go look in yon bank where mammon has told
  His hundreds and thousands of silver and gold,
  Where safe from the hands of the starving and poor,
  Lie heaps upon heaps of the glittering ore.
  Walk up to the counter; ah, there you may stay,
  Till your limbs shall grow old and your hairs shall turn gray;
  For you'll find at the bank not one of the clan,
  With a dollar to lend to a moneyless man.

'Then go to your hovel where no raven has fed
  The wife who has suffered so long for her bread,
  Kneel down by her pallet and kiss the death frost
  From the cold icy forehead of her you have lost.
  Then turn to the motherless babes that are left,
  Of money and friends they are wholly bereft;
  Not one in a hundred will lend you a hand,
  But turn, oh how coldly, from a moneyless man.'

A revolution has got to come off in our churches, as radical
as ever took place in the country, to purify them and put them
upon the ground where they can gather in the poor as well as
the rich, and do the work set for them by the Master. We have
no objection to good buildings, rich and comfortable, if the religion of the church and Christianity is not sacrificed thereby, and
worship in these churches made so expensive as to drive the poor
entirely from them. How men can sit and enjoy themselves,
and feel no pricking in their consciences amidst such gorgeous
surroundings, when the very splendor about them bars out God's
poor, and leaves them a prey to any outside influence that corruption can bring to bear upon them, I can't see. Something **must be 'rotten in Denmark.'** Consciences! are there any

among such? It has become really a question with many thoughtful men, and lest my reader shall think it only a little spleen of mine to say such things, I will quote from the *Christian Union*, Vol. VI, No. 23, a brief article headed '*Conscience of Religious Societies*,' and reads thus: 'I make no complaint of religious societies, for I have experience enough among them to know that they are open to the same objections of corporations in general. They are not *responsible*. They have no souls. They will do, in their corporate capacity, what every individual of them would be ashamed to do as a private citizen. Do I not know what small minorities, what little unscrupulous factions, often control them. How many excellent, devoted, long-tried ministers have been sacrificed by nine-tenths of their members, to conciliate and retain less than one-tenth, and those often of the most bigoted and over-bearing character? How often have I seen the best people in those societies, the most liberal and progressive, giving up everything to the worst and most illiberal for the sake of peace and harmony, which they never get? How often have I seen the old national compromises of slavery acted over again here with similar results! *There is and can be no peace with despotism of any kind; but that of death, on one side or the other.*' How true! There are individual consciences working in some of the members; but these are stifled to some extent, lest they shall be called factious, and so, rather than to raise the alarm and take the consequences of a little commotion, they allow themselves to drift along, when to a thoughtful and observing mind the roar of the breakers is already heard, and the seething waters will soon close over them unless they wake to hear the cry of Jesus, in the wants and neglect of the poor. Is it not a fact, that Christ is barred from many a church? It is a painful fact, or God's word is a farce. Oh, with what astonishment neglecters of God's poor will wake up! 'When the Son of Man shall come in his glory and all the holy angels with him,' and shall say to them, 'I was a stranger, and ye took me not in; naked, and ye clothed me not; sick, and in *prison*, and ye visited me not.' Oh, what will it avail them, when they shall answer him, 'saying, Lord, when saw we thee a hungered, or athirst, or a stranger, or naked, or sick, or in prison, and did not minister unto thee? Then shall he answer them, saying, Verily I say unto you, inasmuch as ye did it not to one of the *least* of these, ye did it not to me. And these shall go away into everlasting punishment; but the righteous into life eternal.'

If I know anything of the love of God, it is to love and pity the poor, and to comfort and raise them up. How much comfort and how much encouragement it was to me, when I was a poor drunkard and under conviction for sin, to have Rev. Mr. Pike take me by the hand and say, 'God bless you.' I was like the poor man journeying from Jerusalem to Jericho. I had fallen among thieves. I had been stripped, and wounded, and left half dead. I had seen the priest go by on the other side, and also the Levite, both turning up their noses at poor drunken Ambler; both with flowing robes and lofty mien,— dignity enough to *scare* a man, while over such mockery the enemies of God rejoiced, and loud the unbeliever laughed, boasting a life of fairer character than theirs; but when the good Samaritan took me by the hand, and into my poor bruised and wounded soul poured sympathy, in such golden words, and recognized me as a fellow man, it gave me hope and comfort, and waked in my heart holy purposes of reform, with fullest faith through God I should do valiantly, and come off a conqueror and a man, yea, a *Christian.*

I had seen enough of this hollow-hearted mockery, these whited sepulchres, to make me feel as though a general protest should be entered against it all; and I thought if the devil did not get them,—I mean all those that are like graves which appear not, for the life of me I could not see any use in having any devil. I said, am I alone in this feeling, in this seeing? Am I a misanthrope? When picking up Pollok's Course of Time, I read of Priests and Levites in language that seemed on fire. His indignation burned in looking at those who 'swore away all love of filthy lucre, all desire of earthly pomp, and yet a princely seat they liked, and to the clink of Mammon's box gave most rapacious ear,' until in language of awful meaning he cried of such, 'Most guilty, villainous, dishonest man! Wolf in the clothing of the gentle lamb! Dark traitor in Messiah's holy camp! Leper in saintly garb! Assassin masked in virtue's robe! Vile hypocrite accursed! I strive in vain to set his evil forth. The words that should sufficiently accurse and execrate such reprobate, had need come glowing from the lips of eldest hell. Among the saddest in the den of woe. Thou sawest him the saddest, 'mong the damned *most damned.*' I had seen so much of this *awful separateness*, this 'stand thou yonder, for I am holier than thou,' and I had felt so much of this spirit of 'touch me not lest I be defiled,' that after my conversion, my heart went out so after the lost sheep, that in pity and in tears I sought them, and many a home have I made happy. I was impressed deeply with the fact, that to fill God's house, Christian men and women must go out into the highways and hedges and compel them to come in, with loving hearts, and with the gentleness and charity of Jesus, win them away from death to life, talking with them of our own escape, remembering our own follies and pitying them in theirs, and making always only this difference. That we are all short-comers, and that while one is pardoned and happy in hope, the other *may* be, if he will only repent and believe. Oh, in this way how many, how many might be brought in to the fold who are now lost sheep! Never was I more forcibly struck with what seemed to me to be the real work of Christian men, than in observing the result of the earnest efforts of some Christians in Portland, who go down on the wharves to talk to men, and into an old sail-loft on Sabbath mornings to talk and pray with whoever will come in, and then go over to the jail to weep with the poor unfortunates there, and pray with them and tell them of the Saviour's love, and take them by the hand with a warm grasp that means good-will, and give them good advice and *assure* them if they will only try to do right, they shall have their sympathy, and they will gladly recognize them too on the street, and when they come to the meeting, as brothers for whom a Saviour bled. And many of these unfortunates have got converted and are now living epistles of God's power. It would seem that in this age of light, such a work would be encouraged, especially by every minister. Yet when one minister in Portland, who shall be nameless, was approached concerning this very work of visiting the poor prisoners in the jail, answered with a sneer, that he did not take any stock in that concern. Well, thank God, there are men who are just glad to invest all their powers to do good in that direction, and feel that it *pays*, and *will pay*, especially when it shall be said at last, 'inasmuch as ye have done it unto the least of one of these, ye have done it unto me.' I cannot name the good men who take all the stock they can handle, as God's stewards, in the jails, on the wharves, out in the highways and hedges, beside the sick-bed, in the hovel, among the drunken, and who

**Tell him hope doth yet remain,
If he only will abstain.**

I will not name the men whose goodness is sometimes questioned by those whose very rottenness of heart is the standard by which they judge other and better men, when they see a team hitched by some poor dwelling where people live who are not all angels; but the record of these Christian workers is kept by him who watches with eager eyes the pilgrim who fears not to go where lives a soul for whom the Saviour died, to carry with him, into those abodes of poverty and death the light of God's wondrous love. These men have a bulwark, a tower of strength to keep them from seduction and death, and fear not the reproach of men; but with an inward purpose they go forth to meet the demands of the outcast and despised for whom Christ died. 'How much is this like the work of Christ! But the race of the Pharisees is not all dead. There are lots of these old double and twisted hypocrites, that act just as their old fathers did. How very like! Just go back nearly nineteen hundred years ago, and see Jesus sitting 'at meat in the house, behold many publicans and sinners came and sat down with him and his disciples. And when the Pharisees saw it, they said unto his disciples, Why eateth your Master with publicans and sinners,' which means substantially, we don't take any stock in that company. 'But when Jesus heard that, he said unto them: they that be whole need not a physician, but they 'that are sick.' See how Christ rebuked these ignorant bigots, not that they were not learned in the law, and understood Hebrew, and Greek and Latin; but they were ignorant of the first rudiments of Christianity. Hear the Master put the burning truth, blistering hot, to these old villains. 'But go ye and learn what that meaneth, I will have mercy and not sacrifice; for I am not come to call the righteous, but sinners to repentance.' That's the company I take stock in. That's the company Captain S. takes stock in, and I should not wonder if he should ask some of my readers, when they come to Portland, to go to jail with him. If he does, go right along doubting not, and if he asks you to take a little stock in his enterprise of getting shoes to cover the little bare feet of the children, and good comfortable clothes for them, so they can go to Sunday School and appear respectably on the street, or to get a coffin for some poor soul and pay the funeral charges so they can be decently buried, don't be afraid to go your bottom dollar. It will pay better than any stock on change. It yields a hundred per cent in this life, and in the world to come life everlasting. My reader will see the point I am driving at, and, of course, will allow me to swing round a little, and make my appeal in behalf of God's poor.

CHAPTER XXXIV.

Wᴴɪʟᴇ reading some of these suggestions in my manuscript about the poor, and the way to do them good, the work that had got to be done to get men from the highways and hedges into the house of God, and the revolution that is needed in the churches to get them into working order, to some of my friends before the book was finished, they said to me, 'Ambler, those are God's truths. Oh, how much might be done, if good men would only go among the poor and see them in their homes, so to know how to pity them and help them! Ambler, I want you to preach a sermon in your book right on this very matter, and I want to give you a text. It is this:'

LUKE 15: 3–7.

And he spake this parable unto them, saying, What man of you having a hundred sheep if he lose one of them, doth not leave the ninety and nine in the wilderness, and go after that which is lost until he find it? And when he hath found it he layeth it on his shoulders, rejoicing. And when he cometh home, he calleth together his friends and neighbors, saying unto them, rejoice with me ; for I have found my sheep which was lost. I say unto you, that likewise joy shall be in heaven over one sinner that repenteth, more than over ninety and nine just persons which need no repentance.

Well, I said, I will, and so wherever this book goes, there goes the sermon on the lost sheep. Indeed my narrative is of lost sheep. I knew how to pity them. I was a lost sheep in a howling wilderness, and had been torn by the dogs and wolves in a terrible manner; but the good Shepherd found me, and took me in his arms and brought me back to his fold. I hope my whole book goes to show how much the poor stray lambs suffer, and will lead many to come to the good Shepherd, who giveth his life for the sheep. It won't be expected that a poor man like me, who never attended school a day in my life, will be very scholastic, or very methodical in laying out my subject, and discussing it in all its details. I don't think much of the position which some men take in making a sermon, viz., that it must be clear at all events, even though it be cold enough to freeze the warmest and deepest fountains of the human heart. I go for a warm sermon, if it is not so handsome. I almost offended my printer in the matter of the title-page of this book, on this very point. He has a fine eye for the artistic, and pointed out to me a portion I had prepared for the title-page which he wanted left out, as the page would be so crowded as to mar its beauty, its artistic design; and I had to differ with him, and told him that he made me think of some ministers who thought more of making their sermons clear than of making them effectual, and who were determined that the *sermon-izer* should stand out prominently in the foreground, if the desire to save souls from death did not once appear in the whole effort. It is like playing Hamlet, with Hamlet left out. I said to my printer, don't strike out that portion of my title-page where it says ' *The whole illustrating the fact with which we start, That truth is stranger than fiction, and much more healthy for the morals of the people,*' for that is the *gist* of the whole thing. I want the moral to appear, if the artist is wholly lost sight of, so if the title-page should seem to be a little crowded, the reader will lay it all to Ambler, and not question the taste of the printer. In presenting to my readers the marrow and fatness of this long text, I shall tie myself down upon nobody's iron bedstead, and if I should not be able to make as many heads to my sermon as the beast had which was described in the apocalypse, I shall not be sorry. My object is to make

19

known what the Saviour designed to teach by this beautiful parable. The better it is understood, the more attractive and overpowering appears the loving heart of the good Shepherd. Oh, ye wandering sheep, hear his voice. 'I am the good Shepherd; the good Shepherd giveth his life for the sheep. But he that is a hireling, and not the shepherd, whose own the sheep are not, seeth the wolf coming and leaveth the sheep, and fleeth; and the wolf catcheth them, and scattereth the sheep. The hireling fleeth, because he is a hireling and careth not for the sheep. I am the good Shepherd, and I lay down my life for the sheep, and other sheep I have which are not of this fold. Them also I must bring, and they shall hear my voice; and there shall be one fold and one Shepherd.' He don't go out with dogs and a club to worry and beat them, and drive them back and fill them with terror; but calls after them, 'Come unto me,' ye hungry starving ones. I am the good Shepherd. The wolves will catch and scatter you if you continue to wander, the hireling fleeth, he don't care for you when the wolf comes, when distress comes upon you, because he is a hireling; but I love you, poor, lonely, wandering ones; cold mountains and the midnight air witnesseth it, though it be a bitter cup, I lay down my life for the sheep.

I am not a thief. The thief comes to steal and destroy. Hear the Prophet Ezekiel in the thirty-fourth chapter. 'And the word of the Lord came unto me, saying, Son of man prophesy against the shepherds of Israel, prophesy and say unto them, Thus saith the Lord God unto the shepherds, wo be to the shepherds of Israel that do feed themselves! Should not the shepherds feed the flock? Ye eat the fat and ye clothe yourselves with the wool, ye kill them that are fed, but ye feed not the flock. The diseased have ye not strengthened; neither have ye healed that which was sick; neither have ye bound up that which was broken; neither have ye brought again that which was driven away; neither have ye sought that which was lost; but with *force* and with *cruelty* have ye ruled them, and they were scattered because there is no shepherd (that careth for them), and they became meat to all the beasts of the field when they were scattered. My sheep wandered through all the mountains, and upon every high hill: yea, my flock was scattered upon all the face of the earth, and none did search or seek after them. Therefore, ye shepherds hear the word of the Lord; thus saith the Lord God, Behold, I am against the shepherds (unfaithful ones), and I will require my flock at their hand, and cause them to cease from feeding the flock; neither shall the shepherds feed themselves any more; for I will deliver my flock from *their mouth,* that they may not be meat for them. Behold I, even I, will both search my sheep, and seek them out. As a shepherd seeketh out his flock in the day that he is among his sheep that are scattered; so will I seek out my sheep, and will deliver them out of all places where they have been scattered in the cloudy and dark day. And I will bring them out from the people, and gather them from the countries, and will bring them to their own land and feed them upon the mountains of Israel by the rivers, and in all the inhabited places of the country. I will feed them in a good pasture, and upon the high mountains shall their fold be; there shall they lie in a good field, and in a fat pasture shall they feed. I will feed my flock. I will seek that which was lost, and bring again that which was driven away, and will bind up that which was broken (glory to God), and will strengthen that which was sick; but I will destroy the fat and the strong (hear that ye hirelings). I will feed them with judgment. Seemeth it a small thing unto you that ye have eaten the good pasture; but must ye foul the residue with your feet? Because ye have thrust with side and with shoulder, and pushed all the diseased with your horns until ye have scattered them abroad. Therefore will I save my flock, and I will set up one shepherd over them, and he shall feed them, even my servant David; he shall feed them, and he shall be their shepherd.' Glorious shepherd that! The bleating of the

scattered and lost ones find pity in him. I suppose a great
and grand object is presented in this parable, which constitutes
the text and the substance for discussion. I take it, that the
lost sheep spoken of, means especially the poor sinner totally
gone astray. And as I am not a born theologian, but rather
of a martial turn, and having been trained to a soldier's life,
I shall not divide my subject into firstlies and so on up to the
eighteenthlies; but shall arrange it rather as I would drill a
company. I will put my thoughts into *sections*, and if necessary, into *divisions*, any way that the order of truth may be
preserved in the mind of the reader, and the details followed
out from the *sections*, into what *divisions* may be needful.
Therefore, calling my thoughts *men*, I will put them into four
sections.

*First section, then, to the front. What is meant by the lost
sheep?*

*The second section to be drilled a little in the way to find the
lost sheep.*

*The third section to receive some attention as to the preju-
dices to be met, and what men have to endure in finding the
lost sheep.*

*The fourth section will receive attention as a victor return-
ing home bearing the lost sheep, and the joy of the multitude
over what has been found.*

First section, attention! What is meant by the lost sheep?
There are some men who imagine that the term *lost sheep*
applies to man generally, and the ninety and nine, that the
good shepherd leaves when he goes for the lost one, means the
angels who have not fallen, and that they are in proportion to
men, as ninety and nine to one, and these are the just persons
that needeth no repentance. This opinion is entitled to some
respect. It is at least ingenious, and it may not be untrue;
but to my mind there are some objections to it. It is true that
angels who have kept their first estate need no repentance, and
it is probably true, that there are outbursts of joy when a sin-

ner breaks from the destroyer and is converted, more than over ninety-nine angels who have always been happy in the home and service of God, as we should see, for an illustration, on board a ship, although there may be a thousand souls on board; yet if one of their number falls overboard, the ship is hove to, and boats are lowered and manned while the struggling man is buffeting with the waves; all are watching with painful interest the receding form of the strong swimmer, until the boat reaches him, when, as he is lifted in, the shout goes up, 'a man saved.' There is enthusiasm and wild delight over his rescue, not that he is of more importance than others; but that being lost, he is now saved.

The way some dispose of this view, of who is meant by the ninety-nine sheep, is this. 'The text says *just persons.* Now *angels* are not *persons,* therefore *angels* can't be meant.' A very silly objection this, for there is likely to be personality to an angel, as well as to a man. Clark says the original word simply meant just ones, and the term applies with as much propriety to angels as to men; but there were good men who were not profligate, that may be meant by the *just persons* in opposition to a Gentile, or a heedless, open sinner. The Jews had many distinctions of this kind in their writings. A great many had been brought up to a regular sober course of life, and being true and just in their dealings, they differed materially from the heathen about them (see the first verse of this chapter). As, therefore, these just persons are put over against the extortioners and heathen, *they needed no repentance* in comparison with the others. But let us be *safe* in this matter. I think the Gentiles are particularly referred to. It was thought to be altogether aside from God's plan to save a Gentile, and many very good men thought so. Good old Cornelius and Peter thought so. Let us read Acts 10th, 'There was a certain man in Cesarea called Cornelius, a centurion of the band called the Italian band. A devout man, and one that feared God with all his house, which gave much alms to the people, and prayed to God always. He saw in a vision, evidently, about the ninth hour of the day, an angel of God coming in to him, and saying unto him, Cornelius. And when he looked on him, he was afraid, and said, What is it, Lord? And he said unto him, Thy prayers and thine alms are come up for a memorial before God. And now send men to Joppa, and call for one Simon, whose surname is Peter. He lodgeth with one Simon a tanner, whose house is by the sea-side; he shall tell thee what thou oughtest to do.' This separate feeling was chronic even among these good old souls, and nothing short of God Almighty, with angels, visions, and all manner of four-footed things, could beat it into them, how these lost sheep could be found.

'And when the angel which spake unto Cornelius was departed, he called two of his household servants, and a devout soldier of them that waited on him continually; and when he had declared all these things unto them, he sent them to Joppa. On the morrow, as they went on their journey, and drew nigh unto the city, Peter went up upon the house-top to pray, about the sixth hour. And he became very hungry, and would have eaten; but while they made ready, he fell into a trance, and saw heaven opened, and a certain vessel descending unto him, as it had been a great sheet knit at the four corners, and let down to the earth; wherein were all manner of four-footed beasts of the earth, and wild beasts, and creeping things, and fowls of the air. And there came a voice to him, Rise, Peter; kill, and eat. But Peter said, Not so, Lord; for I have never eaten anything that is common or unclean. And the voice spake unto him again the second time, What God hath cleansed that call not thou common. This was done thrice. Now, while Peter doubted in himself what this vision which he had seen should mean, behold, the men which were sent from Cornelius had made inquiry for Simon's house, and stood before the gate, and called, and asked whether Simon, which was surnamed Peter, were lodged there.

'While Peter thought on the vision, the Spirit said unto him,

Behold, three men seek thee. Arise, therefore, and get thee down, and go with them, doubting nothing; for I have sent them. Then Peter went down to the men which were sent unto him from Cornelius; and said, Behold, I am he whom ye seek; what is the cause wherefore ye are come? And they said, Cornelius, the centurion, a just man, and one that feareth God, and of good report among all the nation of the Jews, was warned from God by a holy angel, to send for thee into his house, and to hear words of thee. Then he called them in and lodged them. And on the morrow Peter went away with them, and certain brethren from Joppa accompanied him. And on the morrow after, they entered into Cesarea. And Cornelius waited for them, and had called together his kinsmen and near friends. And as Peter was coming in, Cornelius met him, and fell down at his feet, and worshipped him. But Peter took him up, saying, Stand up; I myself also am a man. And as he talked with him, he went in, and found many that were come together.' Now Peter begins to preach like a Christian minister, just hear him, 'And he said unto them, Ye know how that it is an unlawful thing for a man that is a Jew to keep company with, or come unto one of another nation; but God hath showed me that I should not call any man common or unclean. Therefore came I unto you without gainsaying, as soon as I was sent for; I ask, therefore, for what intent ye have sent for me?' Then Cornelius told him the whole story about what he experienced when he was praying, the answer God gave him, and how God had sent him to Peter for further instruction.

'Then Peter opened his mouth, and said, of a truth I perceive that God is no respecter of persons; but in every nation, he that feareth him and worketh righteousness, is accepted with him. The word which God sent unto the children of Israel, preaching peace by Jesus Christ (he is Lord of all); that word, I say, ye know, how God anointed Jesus of Nazareth with the Holy Ghost and with power; who went about doing good and healing all that were oppressed of the devil;' and so led out was Peter when he threw off his old Jewish prejudice, and spoke without notes as the Spirit led him, that it is said, 'While Peter yet spake these words, the Holy Ghost fell on all them which heard the word, and they of the circumcision which believed were astonished, as many as came with Peter, because that on the *Gentiles* also was poured out the gift of the Holy Ghost.'

So my readers will see the sheep, the *lost sheep*, has particular reference to the Gentiles, outsiders, the despised and the poor. When Peter got back, after preaching this revival sermon, they that were of the circumcision took a miff at it, and contended with him, saying, 'Thou wentest in to men uncircumcised, and didst eat with them!' But Peter rehearsed the matter from the beginning, telling his experience, and all about the vision, and what a glorious time he had preaching to the Gentiles, and he said, 'As I began to speak, the Holy Ghost fell on them, as on us at the beginning,' and then he said, 'I remembered the word of the Lord, how that he said, John indeed baptized with water; but ye shall be baptized with the Holy Ghost. Forasmuch, then, as God gave them the gift as he did unto us who believed in the Lord Jesus Christ; *what was I* that I could withstand God?' When they heard Peter's explanation, and found that he would not back down from this liberal doctrine, it is said, 'they held their peace, and glorified God, saying, Then hath God also to the Gentiles granted repentance unto life.'

Having handled my *first section* and shown who are the lost sheep, it may go to the rear, until I get ready to bring up my reserves for a final charge. I will now take up the *second section* for a little skirmishing after the lost sheep.

As I understand it, the nature of the sheep should be well studied, especially of a *lost* sheep,—the sinner totally gone astray. A stray sheep is a simple creature in a special sense. When pursued by dogs and wolves, and knowing themselves to be completely separated from the flock, they as readily run in an opposite direction from the fold and right into danger and destruction, as toward home and the flock.

How complete a type is the lost sheep of the poor, heedless, thoughtless sinner. The sheep is the simplest of all animals as to its ability to find its way back to the fold. The swine, without any apparent uneasiness or effort, will root around and at last join the herd; but the sheep that has been separated from the flock, gives by its movements indications of its being astray, and yet apparently without the least judgment which way to go to find the flock, or safety, and in its wildness and fear, will run from a friend as quickly as from a foe. Yet it is often heard bleating for the flock, and uneasy, feeding a few moments apparently careless of its lost condition, yet startled by the falling leaf, and wild with fright at the baying of the dog, or the howling of the wolf. There is no creature that so much needs a good shepherd to go after it, that is so incapable of finding its way back. I have often heard the poor creatures bleating afar off upon the sides of the mountains, after the night had set in, and running in an opposite direction, running right into danger among the very enemies it fears. There is nothing so defenceless, no sight so sad. Even the fowls have been known to pick out the eyes of wandering lambs, and then the poor blind things are destroyed by the birds of prey at their leisure. In this way the devil seeketh whom he may devour. He blinds them with motes and beams with which he fills their eyes, and then worries and destroys them. All ways seem alike to the poor blind wanderer.

There is no creature we seek that requires to be sought after with so much care and caution. A great many times we have to speak, and with a gentle winning voice to these frightened straying ones, to convince them that it is the voice of a friend, and not of an enemy; and it is often necessary to take a little salt along, and let them taste it often, before they will let you take them in your arms and bring them to the fold. In order to handle my second section fully and finish up the instructions which I wish to give on this point, I will put it into *divisions.*

1. *Whatever else you may lack, let there be no lack of pity for the unfortunate.* In affliction, the heart cries out for this. Job, in his distress, cried out, 'Have pity upon me, have pity upon me, O ye my friends, for the hand of God hath touched me." Solomon says, 'He that hath pity on the poor lendeth to the Lord.' This is not a pity in word, but in deed; often a loaf of bread, a pair of shoes, a dress, a warm garment is a regular John to prepare the way of the Lord, and many a heart has been reached through the back, or an empty stomach, that all the fine things a man could say could not reach. 'Like as a father pitieth his children, so the Lord pitieth them that fear him.' If a soul has erred, don't break his teeth with it; but tell him of Jesus and his compassion. Oh, think how weary and foot-sore and hungry the poor sheep may be; see the beautiful fleece torn and hanging in shreds, and as the good shepherd has borne with you, so try to help the poor wanderer over the rough way back to the fold. Lay the bruised and wounded one on your shoulder, and bear it along, carry them in your arms, any way to get them home.

2. *Let your voice be that of the good shepherd.* The wandering sheep know the voice of love, and it wins them. It is hard to fight against it. I will not name the man; but I know a man who once went to visit a sick man to pray with him, and when he got to the house, things looked as though the family were suffering for things to make them comfortable, and the man, before he knelt down to pray, put a few dollars into the hand of the sick man, and then prayed, and that prayer reached the ear of Jehovah, and the heart of the poor unconverted man; like Cornelius, the prayers and alms done the work, and the sick man was made comfortable, and converted too.

Get the dear children of the poor, and put good warm clothes on them, and bring them into Sunday school, and learn them to sing sweet songs, and to speak, and teach them of Christ; tell them all about the good Shepherd, how he carries the lambs in his bosom, and see what it will help you to do. Take the lamb from the wildest mother in your arms, and carry it along, and the old sheep will follow. They won't be separated. How often I have got the little children of the poor and clothed them up nice, and got them into the Sunday school, and got them to singing their little hymns, and pretty soon the mother would come in; and the next I would see would be the father; sly as a wandering sheep, he would just slip inside of the door, and pop right down in the first seat he came to, already to take his hat and leave, if anybody hardly looked that way; and yet, in a little while, by gentle approaches, was reached and saved. Thank God, *the lost may be found* if a man will only lay himself out for the work.

My *third division* under the *second section* is this: *Don't go pell-mell at a poor wandering sheep, and tell him he is the wickedest man in the world, and if he don't make a rush for the fold he will be damned; but use good judgment in your approaches.* There is no work that requires good common sense more than the work of finding the lost sheep and getting them back to the fold. It is said, 'he that winneth souls is wise,' which means that it requires wisdom and prudence. I can't illustrate what I want to make plain better than to tell you a story about the good Shepherd. He traveled a great deal, and often got weary in the work. When traveling on foot from Judea down into Galilee, he got as far as Samaria, and, being wearied with his journey, he sat down on the curb at the well to rest, having traveled several hours in the heat and dust. It was now about noon, and while resting on the well, a woman of Samaria came to the well to draw water. Jesus did not begin to tell her what a sinner she had been, although she was a hard case; but he introduced himself by asking her for a drink of water. I don't suppose a Jew ever thought this lost sheep could be saved, and probably this was the first time that ever one condescended to speak with her, for she was astonished, and said, 'How is it that thou, being a Jew, askest drink of me, which am a woman of Samaria? for the Jews have no dealings with the Samaritans.' This woman, by this wise introduction, became at once, as you see, an inquirer and the good Shepherd said, 'If thou knewest the gift of God, and who it is that saith to thee, Give me to drink, thou would'st have asked of him, and he would have given thee living water.' This opened the way for further conversation; so the woman said, 'Sir, Give me this water, that I thirst not, neither come hither to draw.' She wanted the water of life and asked for it, thank God; but it did not end there. She was bidden to go call her husband. This was a pretty hard thrust; but she could bear it now, as she had got interested in her teacher; but she said, 'I have no husband,' and this was true; but Jesus told her just what she had been, until she cried out, 'Sir, I perceive that thou art a prophet;' and when Jesus explained the whole matter, 'the woman left her water-pot and went her way into the city, and saith to the men : Come, see a man that hath told me all things that ever I did; is not this the Christ? Then they went out of the city and came unto him.' His disciples when they got back marvelled that he talked with the woman, but it was just like him.

Here, then, is the pattern for you and I. Don't be afraid to talk with the most abandoned, and don't feel as though you are not accomplishing anything because the first talk may not be directly on the subject of religion. That poor lost sheep may go away and say, that good man did not feel himself too good to speak to me, and will put himself or herself in the way again, on purpose to be talked with, and to ask questions. That poor lost sheep has been saying, perhaps, in great sadness, 'no man careth for my soul;' but now inwardly they say here is an exception. This man does care for me. And they will tell such their sorrows, and confess to them their need of religion, and then go and tell their friends to come and see a man that is looking after the lost sheep, and he will help them to find the fold. Whole sermons would fail to tell of all the ways to find the lost sheep; but I must leave this to give some attention to my

Third section—viz., *The prejudices to be met, and what one has to endure in going after the lost sheep.*

Let no one think the road he has got to travel, in hunting up the lost sheep, is strewn with flowers. My *first division of this section* is this: *The inward prejudice to be overcome.* It is natural for good men to aspire to higher circles, and it is very pleasant to go with and commune with such as we think better than ourselves, and often there is felt an inward horror of mingling with the multitude that are reeking in filth and moral death; but when the soul is enlarged it will say, 'I will *run* in the way of the commandments,' until with proper views of Christ's mission, its strongest consolation is drawn from its earnest working in the hovels of the poor, and preaching Jesus to the outcasts, the prisoners, and the neglected. When Christ talked with that woman at the well, and the disciples came and prayed him to eat, 'He said, I have meat to eat that ye know not of. Therefore the disciples said one to another, Hath any man brought him aught to eat? Jesus saith unto them, My meat is to do the will of him that sent me,' and he then said to the disciples, just 'lift up your eyes, and look on the fields; for they are white already to harvest.' Oh, the sweetness of that kind of sanctification, that finds its meat in this blessed work.'

Division second of third section. To make a bolt from the ordinary course lays a man liable to be misunderstood, and often to bitter persecution. Jesus was called, in derision, a friend of publicans and sinners, because he did not heartily denounce them, and send down fire from heaven upon them; but hear him defend himself. To the scribes and Pharisees, lawyers and chief priests, he says, 'Go ye and learn what that meaneth, I will have mercy and not sacrifice; for I am not come to call the righteous, but sinners to repentance.' They that be whole need not a physician, but they that are sick.' And for nothing else but this was he finally put to death. See the good old apostle Paul in bonds before Agrippa, telling his experience. He was as much a Pharisee as the fattest of them; but the light from heaven had shown him this wondrous, this glorious truth, that Jesus Christ came into the world to save sinners, of whom he was chief, and now see what he had to meet and endure, in going after the lost sheep. He shall tell his own story, for you would hardly believe it from the lips of any other mortal. It is said in Acts 16th, 'They caught Paul and Silas and drew them into the market-place, unto the rulers, and the magistrates rent off their clothes, and commanded to beat them. And when they had laid many stripes upon them, they cast them into prison.' A great many whippings the old man got, and he says if the Jews are ministers, 'I am more. In labors more abundant, in stripes above measure, in prisons more frequent, in deaths oft. Of the Jews five times received I forty stripes save one. Thrice was I beaten with rods, once was I stoned, thrice I suffered shipwreck, a night and a day I have been in the deep; in journeyings often, in perils of waters, in perils of robbers, in perils by mine own countrymen, in perils by the heathen, in perils in the city, in perils in the wilderness, in perils in the sea, in perils among false brethren, in weariness and painfulness, in watchings often, in hunger and thirst, in fastings often, in cold and nakedness.' No wonder, oh, no wonder the good old man could say, 'Who is weak, and I am not weak? who is offended, and I burn not?' That glorious old soldier knew how to pity his comrades in affliction, because of his own bitter experience. Are the disciples sometimes dodging their pursuers, and taxing their wits, and their friends, to get away from wicked men? So am I, says Paul, 'I had to go through a window in a basket, and be let down by the wall to escape out of their hands.'

Third division of section three. Christian men are not now beaten with stripes, put in prisons, stoned and dragged out of

cities, and left half dead. Thank God that time has gone by;
but they are subject to keener weapons, against which it seems
there is no law of men. The slanderer still lives, and swings
his lip against the disciple with terrible malignity, and it cuts
the sensitive soul deeper than whips. No wonder Pollok, in
his Course of Time, is moved with indignation, and thus draws
his picture in these words:

> 'Slander, the foulest whelp of sin, tho man
> In whom this spirit entered, was undone.
> His pillow was the peace of families destroyed,
> His tongue was set on fire of hell, his heart
> Was black as death, his legs were faint with haste
> To propagate the lie his soul had framed.
> From door to door you might have seen him speed,
> Or placed amid a group of gaping fools,
> And whispering in their ears with his foul lips,
> Devising mischief more, and early rose,
> And made most hellish meals of good men's names,
> Peace fled the neighborhood in which he made
> His haunts, the prudent shunned him and his house
> As one who had a deadly moral plague.'

I have known a good man to go among the base and low
and despised to talk to the lost sheep of the good shepherd,
and how he will take the lame and the sick and carry them in
his arms, and the next day by some of the devil's watch-dogs
it was reported that brother —— was seen to go into a house
of ill-fame and spend a half an hour.

This is a trying position for a sensitive, good man, who
thinks none the less of a good reputation because he has aspired
to be a Christian; and often more than he ever did before, because he had rather die than wound the cause of his Master.
Shall he cease to go on his merciful efforts, because Slander
opens wide his mouth, and breathes over his good name the
mildews of death and hell?

Nay, my good brother. Go wherever lives a soul to be saved,

the chiefest of sinners, Christ died for them; but go clothed
with the panoply of God. With him for your front guard, and
your rear wall, nothing shall harm you. You may tread on
deadly things if God be with you.

Christ talked with the woman at the well, pardoned another
convicted of crime, risking everything, even the cause so dear
to him, stemming the flood that was poured out against him for
his pity for the fallen. The scribes and Pharisees were great
sticklers for outward purity, and wanted to eternally settle a
case against him, so to bring him into disrepute, and blacken this
merciful religion, and they put their heads together and fixed
up a case, and then took their time when he was in the temple
preaching, and brought in a woman whom they said was taken
in adultery, 'and when they had set her in the midst, they said
unto him, Master, this woman was taken in adultery, in the
very act. Now Moses in the law commanded us that such
should be stoned; but what sayest thou? *This they said
tempting him, that they might have to accuse him.*' Jesus
made as though his thoughts were upon something else. 'So
they continued asking him, he lifted up himself and said unto
them, He that is without sin among you, let him first cast a
stone at her. And again he stooped down and wrote on the
ground. And they which heard it, being convicted by their
own consciences, went out one by one, beginning at the eldest
even unto the last.' A pretty sight that, not one of these old
hypocrites could stand the test! All of them had been in the
same boat, with only this difference,—the woman had been
caught, and they had not. How Jesus punctured these old
vacillating theological gas-bags! After they had gone, 'when
Jesus lifted up himself, and saw none but the woman, he said
unto her, Woman, where are those thine accusers? hath no
man condemned thee? She said, No man, Lord. And Jesus
said unto her, Neither do I condemn thee; go, and *sin no more.*'
In the heart of Jesus there was forgiveness for this lost sheep.
She was no doubt penitent, and desired forgiveness, and the

blessed Master dismissed her with this injunction '*sin no more,*' and she went away in peace, no doubt, with a strong purpose to lead a good life. There is often more hope of a genuine reform, a true practical Christianity among such, than of these old unsympathizing, self-conceited bigots, and Jesus said unto them, Matt. 21: 31, 'Verily I say unto you, That the publicans and the harlots go into the kingdom of God before you.'

Then go, Christian comrades, go after the lost sheep. The world can't say worse things of you than they did of the Captain of our salvation. As he went, they said, 'Behold a gluttonous man, and a winebibber, a friend of publicans and sinners.' They cannot say worse things of you. Say, comrade, did you ever notice how grateful these poor lost sheep are to their benefactors? How they thank God for the kind word and look that won them back to the fold!

Let me call your attention to the gratitude of one whom Christ had helped and saved. When Captain Jesus went and sat down to meat in the house of a Pharisee, 'Behold, a woman in the city, which was a sinner, when she knew that Jesus sat at meat in the Pharisee's house, brought an alabaster box of ointment, and stood at his feet behind him weeping, and began to wash his feet with tears, and did wipe them with the hairs of her head, and kissed his feet, and anointed them with the ointment.' Dear thankful soul! but when the Pharisee saw it, he said, 'This man, if he were a prophet, would have known who and what manner of woman this is that toucheth him; for she is a sinner. Jesus, answering, said unto him, Simon, I have somewhat to say unto thee. And he saith, Master, say on. There was a certain creditor which had two debtors, one owed five hundred pence, the other fifty, and when they had nothing to pay, he frankly forgave them both. Tell me, therefore, which of them will love him most? Simon answered, I suppose that he to whom he forgave most. Jesus said, thou hast rightly judged. And he turned to the woman, and said unto Simon, seest thou this woman? I entered into thine house, thou gavest

20

me no water for my feet; but she hath washed my feet with
tears (precious drops) and wiped them with the hairs of her head.
Thou gavest me no kiss; but this woman, since the time I came
in, hath not ceased to kiss my feet. My head with oil thou didst
not anoint; but this woman hath anointed my feet with ointment.
Wherefore, I say unto thee, Her sins, which are many, are forgiven, for she loveth much.'

So down go these old prejudices.   See how these poor
souls, you have thought there was no mercy for, love when the
gospel reaches them.   Some of the disciples were indignant,
and when they could find fault with nothing else they said, 'To
what purpose is this waste? For this ointment might have been
sold for much and given to the poor. When Jesus understood
it, he said, Why trouble ye the woman?   Verily I say unto
you, *Wheresoever this gospel shall be preached in the whole
world, there shall also this, that this woman hath done, be told
as a memorial of her.'*   Oh, this is the way to get at the lost
sheep!   Instead of being ashamed of these trophies of grace,
tell it to the world; yes, tell the vilest, though their sins be as
scarlet, or red like crimson, they shall be as snow and as wool.
Yes, tell them all

> ' There is a fountain filled with blood
>   Drawn from Immanuel's veins,
>   And sinners plunged beneath that flood
>   Lose *all* their guilty stains.
>
> ' The dying thief rejoiced to see
>   That fountain in his day;
>   And *Mary Magdalene* and *me*
>   Do wash our sins away.'

Excuse the paraphrase on the last two lines, it is about as I
feel.

I now hasten to consider briefly the *fourth section,* viz.,
The joy when the lost sheep is found. My *first division* here
shall be *the joy of the lost sheep.* See how the stray sheep

manifests it joy when coming back to the flock. It almost forgets to feed; but goes from one sheep to the other with its quick, short bleat of gladness and affection, rubbing its nose against one, and then another, almost like the kisses between the mother and child, when one has been restored to the bosom of the other. Who can tell the first glowings of joy, when the heart first goes out in sweetly breathing, 'Our Father who art in heaven.' Oh, it is a joy unspeakable and full of glory. The convert calls upon his soul, and all within him, to praise the name of the Lord, and he would wake everything into songs of praise. They felt just so thousands of years ago. Hear one of the ancients: ' Praise ye the Lord from the heavens; praise him in the heights; praise ye him, all his angels; praise him sun and moon; praise him, all ye stars of light; praise him, ye heaven of heavens, and ye waters that be above the heavens. Praise the Lord from the earth, ye dragons and all deeps: fire and hail, snow and vapors, stormy wind fulfilling his word: mountains and all hills; fruitful trees, and all cedars: beasts and all cattle; creeping things and flying fowl: kings of the earth and all people; princes and all judges of the earth: both young men and maidens; old men and children: let them praise the name of the Lord; for his name alone is excellent; his glory is above the earth and heaven.' Oh, if the heart's praise could be embodied in a single sound, no peace jubilee with thousands of voices, its string and wind instruments, its anvil choruses, its thundering cannon, could wake creation with such mighty thundering anthems of glory as would peal on the ears of the slumbering world.

A second division is the joy among good men. The emotions felt in Christian hearts are often unspeakable over the lost that are found. It was meet, said the father, that the best robe be put upon him, that the fatted calf be killed, 'for this my son that was lost is found.' I was once in a meeting where a young man got converted, whose father had felt much anxiety for him; and when he heard his son tell what God had done for him, the old white-headed man was wild with joy, and left the house without hat or overcoat, in a wintry night, and with his bald head exposed and the few silver locks streaming in the wind and snow, run for his home to tell the glad news to his aged wife. He missed neither hat nor coat until, running after him only as a strong young man, full of vigor, can run, I overtook him with both.

One more division of joy under my *fourth section*, and this shall conclude the main drill in the action to recover the lost sheep, viz.:

Heaven is filled with joy when the vilest and the meanest of all the lost sheep is found. How many Bible figures illustrate this fact. Time will only permit one strong statement to support this *division.* As there is joy over the lost sheep that is found, Jesus says, 'I say unto you, that likewise joy shall be in heaven over one sinner that repenteth, more than over ninety and nine just persons, which need no repentance.' 'I say unto you, there is joy in the presence of the angels of God, over one sinner that repenteth.' In contemplating what the Captain of our salvation should work out, how he should save the lost sheep, the heavens rung with songs of joy. When the shepherds watched their flocks by night, two thousand years ago on the plains of Bethlehem, 'The angel of the Lord came upon them, and the glory of the Lord shone round about them. And the angel said unto them, Fear not, for behold I bring you good tidings of great joy, which shall be unto all people. For unto you is born this day, in the city of David, a Saviour which is Christ the Lord. And suddenly there was with the angel a multitude of the heavenly host praising God and saying, Glory to God in the highest, and on earth peace, and good-will toward man.'

Oh yes, over the new creation the morning stars sang together, and all the sons of God shouted for joy; and you and I may touch wires that shall send thrills of joy throughout all the heavenly world. To the work, then, and let the people know, that he that converteth one sinner from the error of his way, shall save a soul from death, and hide a multitude of sins. It will hardly be necessary for me to bring up many *reserves* to the support of my *sections* and *divisions* in my soldier sermon, but it is customary, I believe, for theologians to put in an inference or two in view of the whole subject, and I will bring up a reserve thought or two, in support of what has been said.

1st. '*How much better is a man than a sheep!*' and yet a shepherd is justified in leaving the ninety and nine and going after the one that has wandered, and when he has found it, feels justified not only to be joyful himself, but in calling on his neighbors to join him. Oh the value of a human soul! Oh how grand and glorious the privilege of binding up one broken heart, of finding one bruised and wounded sheep, and presenting it saved to the great Shepherd. Oh how careful that we should not by our coldness, by uncharitableness, drive one of these lambs astray. How many are wandering to-day, who would have been the happiest lambs in the fold had they been dealt kindly with, and encouraged as they should have been. How many old Hebrews must ever accuse themselves for the sufferings of many who have been discouraged and gone away from the fold. To save yourselves from remorse, go after them Take one example: In all the bloom of perfect womanhood, ruined by a villain; and when her father saw her shame, his heart grew stone. He drove her forth to want and wintry winds, and with a horrid curse forbidding her return.

> 'Upon a hoary cliff that watched the sea
> Her babe was found—dead; and on its little cheek
> The tear that nature bade it weep had turned
> An ice-drop, sparkling in the morning sun,
> And to the turf its little helpless hands were frozen,
> For she, the woful mother had gone mad,
> And laid it down, regardless of its fate.
> She never spoke of her deceiver, father, mother, home,
> With woe too wide to see beyond, she died.

Not unatoned for by imputed blood, nor by the
Spirit, that mysterious works.   Aloud her father
Cursed that day, his guilty pride, which would not own
A daughter, whom the God of heaven and earth
Was not ashamed to call his own.'

A second reserve.   In this way only can you show that you
are real Christians and save your own souls. 'By their fruit ye
shall know them.   By this shall all men know that ye are my
disciples if ye have love one for another.' 'Simon, son of Jonas,
lovest thou me? Yea, Lord, thou knowest all things, thou
knowest that I love thee. *Feed my sheep.*' I don't know how
a man can expect to be saved, who does not enter this work.
Finally, I don't believe a man has ever *known* the love of God,
whose heart does not go out after the lost, and feel somewhat
as the Saviour did, when speaking of his work he said, 'How
am I straightened until it be accomplished. Beware, oh beware scribes, Pharisees, hypocrites, hirelings, whose own the
sheep are not, and who seeth the wolf coming, and leaveth the
sheep and fleeth, and the wolf catcheth them, and scattereth
the sheep, for the day of your reckoning is at hand.' 'If the
watchman see the sword come and blow not the trumpet and
the people be not warned, if the sword come and take away
any person from among the people, his blood will I require at
the watchman's hand.'   Comrades, go after the lost sheep.
Comrades, don't offend the little ones, no matter how weak,
the more need of help; no matter how vile they have been, the
more you should encourage and lead them by the hand. Woe
unto that man who puts a straw in the way of the dear lamb,
for it is written, 'Whoso shall offend one of these little ones
which believe in me, it were better for him that a millstone
were hanged about his neck, and that he were drowned in the
depths of the sea.' AMEN.

To this work my soul turns, and that I may be permitted to
enter this field untrammeled is my prayer, that the remnant of

my days may be employed in bringing from the highways and hedges those that are lost, that God's house may be filled. Every one that buys a book of mine helps to strike off my fetters, and though crippled in body, if I can succeed in freeing myself from these bonds of poverty, so to make proclamation of God's love to man without being muzzled, and without charge when the people are poor, the height of my ambition will be reached.

Dear reader, we have gone over the crooked and strange journey of life together, and with many thanks to you for your patience in reading these pages, trusting you will be charitable toward all my errors, there remains for me only to ask you to prepare to meet the Judge of all, if you have not already done so, and to say to you, what has been paining me to think of saying, lest some word I have forgotten to say ought to be said to save some soul from death, that word so often baptized in tears and often repeated from trembling, loving lips, good-by.

Isaac W. Ambler.

MEMOIRS

OF

SERGEANT I. W. AMBLER.

THE PRESS AND PEOPLE'S BOOK.

A wonderful narrative of personal history. Not within the entire range of English or American literature, can there be found, without pay, pension or reward, such a brilliant example of heroic devotion.

His services in behalf of the Union, Generals and Governors of States have been pleased to term herculean, heroic, patriotic and loyal. His trials, sufferings, wounds, sacrifices and privations, entitle him to substantial recognition.

All of which is proved by the unqualified testimony of American heroes and statesmen, who say : " It is the man who deserves, and not only the man who achieves success, that is honored by us."

WM. F. SMITH, late Maj. Gen. U. S. Vols.
GEORGE B. MCCLELLAN, late Maj. Gen. U. S. A.
A. E. BURNSIDE, late Maj. Gen. U. S. A.
J. HOOKER, late Maj. Gen. U. S. A.

C. C. MEADE, late Maj. Gen. U. S. A.
JOSHUA L. CHAMBERLAIN, late Maj. Gen. U. S. Vols.
CHAS. DEVENS, JR., late Brev. Maj. Gen. U. S. Vols.
WM. COGSWELL, late Brig. Gen. U. S. A.
G. F. SHEPLEY, late U. S. Judge, late Brig. Gen. U.S.A.
FRANCIS FESSENDEN, late Brig. Gen. U. S. Vols.
JAMES FESSENDEN, late Brig. Gen. U. S. Vols.
NEAL DOW, late Brig. Gen. U. S. Vols.
WM. DWIGHT, late Col. 70th Regt. N. Y. Vols. and
Brig. Gen. U. S. Vols.
T. W. PORTER, late Col. 14th Maine Regt. U. S. Vols.
ISAAC FRAZIER, late Capt. 6th Me. Regt. U. S. Vols.
J. E. SMITH, late Capt. 38th Regt. Mass. Vols.
JOHN W. TRAFTON, late Capt. 27th Regt. Mass. Vols.
MILTON FRAZIER, late Lieut. 6th Me. Vols.
WM. CLAFLIN, Ex-Gov. of Mass.
ICHABOD GOODWIN, Ex-Gov. of N. H.
ONSLOW STEARNS, Ex-Gov. of N. H.
ISRAEL WASHBURN, JR., Ex-Gov. of Maine.
SETH PADELFORD, Ex-Gov. of R. I.
JOHN D. LONG, Gov. of Mass.
THOMAS TALBOT, Ex-Gov. of Mass.
ALEX. H. RICE, Ex-Gov. of Mass.
GEO. S. BOUTWELL, Ex-Gov. of Mass.
ALEX. H. BULLOCK, Ex-Gov. of Mass.
WM. GASTON, Ex-Gov. of Mass.
J. L. CHAMBERLAIN, Ex-Gov. of Maine.
FREDERICK O. PRINCE, Ex-Mayor of Boston.
HENRY L. PIERCE, Ex-Mayor of Boston.
CHAS. A. SHAW, Ex-Mayor of Biddeford, Me.
HON. D. E. SOMES, late M. Congress.
HON. J. G. BLAINE, Ex-Sec. U. S.
HON. J. G. ABBOTT, Judge, Boston, Mass.
HON. C. LEVI WOODBURY, Judge, Boston, Mass.

Hon. Edw. Avery, Chairman Central Committee.
Fred'k A. Foster, Merchant, of Boston, Mass.
Rob't G. Fitch, Editor Boston Post.
D. A. Goddard, late Editor Boston Advertiser.
E. B. Haskell, Editor Boston Herald.
B. P. Palmer, Editor Boston Globe.
Henry M. Dexter, Editor Congregationalist.
Leverett Saltonstall.
Z. Thompson, Chaplain 6th Me. Regt. 1861 and 1862.
Elbridge G. Stevens, M. D.
J. E. L. Kimball, M. D., late Surgeon 27th Regt. M. Vols.
Wm. J. Dale, Surgeon Gen. Commonwealth of Mass.

EVERYBODY has heard of Sergeant Ambler. Many of our readers know him personally. He was in his youth an English soldier under Wellington. Coming to this country many years ago, he has passed through a varied experience, which he has written in a book and related from many platforms. When Sumter was fired upon he entered into the Union service heart and soul. Not over-prudent in regard to his own interests, as his story shows, he was full of energy, courage and enthusiasm, — honest, loyal and faithful always.

His first service was to form the members of the Young Men's Christian Association, of Boston, into a drill club, and give them their first lesson in war. He had been a drill-master in the English army, and when our need came he volunteered his service where it would do the most good. From that moment he was in great demand, drilling officers and squads of men in the use of the musket, bayonet and broadsword, wherever he could get a room for practice. His overflowing enthusiasm and rough eloquence were also of great use in recruiting the early regiments, to some of whose officers and men he gave their first real instruction, often doing double and treble duty by first coaching the sergeants, who repeated the lesson to their companies. Many of our citizens are familiar with all this. The papers of the time also bear ample testimony to it. There is no doubt of the facts.

In July, 1861, he went to the front with the 6th Maine regiment, which he had been drilling for a few weeks at Camp Preble, the officers assuring him that he would receive the same pay and fare from the government which they received. Unfortunately for him, he was not regularly mustered into the service, but he was the same zealous, self-forgetful soldier as if he had been. When the regiment marched through Baltimore, with bayonets fixed and muskets loaded, expecting attack, Sergeant Ambler took charge of the colors, and bore them safely through. He remained with the regiment during that dreadful summer, performing all soldierly duties, instructing officers in the sword, and men in the bayonet exercise, going out on picket duty, and wherever a strong hand and courageous heart were wanted. He came home in September, prostrated by sunstroke, the War Department passing him as a soldier on government account.

During that and the following year he gave his time and energy to recruiting and drilling for several Maine regiments, and teaching officers and soldiers from other States in New England. From the summer of 1863 to the close of the war he spent much time at Long Island and Gallop's Island drilling officers and men of regiments stationed there before going to the front. In these labors he sustained severe physical injuries which disabled him from ordinary work, and from which he has never fully recovered. The facts are attested by many witnesses whose letters are lying before us. During all this time his services were accepted and made use of by the Government, through its responsible officers; and they were recognized in every way that such services can be recognized, — except one : *He was never paid for them.*

Eight or nine years ago, being brought by ill health into great need, his friends urged him to bring his claim

to the attention of Congress; and, as justice never can be
outlawed, he thought best to undertake it. His petition
was duly presented in person, modestly setting forth the
nature of his services, the fact that he had received no
compensation therefor, either from municipal, state or
national authority, and asking to be mustered into the
service for the period named, with the rank of first sergeant, with pay and pension belonging to that grade, and
such other relief as might be just and proper. To the
truth of his story, and the equity of his claims, everybody
who knew Sergeant Ambler and his history was willing
to testify. The late Hon. John Neal, ex-mayor of Portland, made a statement of his useful services to the several regiments mentioned in his papers,—in the course of
which service he had suffered greatly, and been put to
heavy charges. Mr. Neal earnestly urged the claim to
the favorable consideration of the President, the Secretary of War and of Congress. Generals Chamberlain,
Fessenden and Shepley, and Governors Washburn of
Maine, Padelford and Claflin concurred in the statement
and joined in the recommendation. Many other distinguished officers and civilians who knew the Sergeant personally, or had investigated his case, also joined in it.
We copy from the original papers the cordial indorsements of Generals McClellan, Devens, Hooker, Burnside,
Meade and Cogswell, Ex-Governors Goodwin and Stearns
of New Hampshire, and eighteen or twenty leading citizens of Biddeford, where, at the beginning of the war,
Mr. Ambler was in service as city missionary. With
these papers he went to Washington, but, unfortunately,
he had no influential friends there, and no money to pay
for assistance, and he could not get a hearing. His papers
having been buried in the rooms of the Military Committee for several months, and, being told that nothing

would be done about them, he at last recovered them, and, heart-sick, impoverished, and in despair, he started for home, on a pass issued to him as a volunteer soldier disabled by injuries.

The Franklin-street fire a month ago again swept away the last visible reliance of the old soldier; and, as it is disgraceful that he should be compelled to live by favor while the country is in debt to him, some of those who know the facts propose to ask the attention of Congress to them again, in the hope that justice may be done, even at the eleventh hour. — *Boston Daily Advertiser.*

REPUBLICS may not be ungrateful, but we fear they are sometimes forgetful or neglectful. Valuable services and timely aid do not seem so deserving of reward after the end for which they were sought has been attained as before. Since the close of our civil war many illustrations of this truth have come into notice, but no one has more points of interest than the case of Sergeant I. W. Ambler of our own city. We do not need to go over the points of his eventful life. They have been too often rehearsed to need detailed repetition. When he gallantly offered his services to his adopted country there were enough to proclaim his praises, and dwell with admiration upon his courage, his soldierly qualities, his military experience and the romantic and frequently dangerous adventures of which his life has been so largely made up. He justified all that was said of him and claimed for him. His skill in making soldiers out of civilians was marvellous, and the soldierly training he had himself received in the English army was disseminated among officers and men with the best results. He was at the head of an unorganized department of normal military instruction. He drilled the officers, and imparted his thoroughness and method to them, and they in turn drilled the men. He taught sabre and bayonet practice and sword exercise in both infantry and cavalry, and it is safe to say that he was the hardest worked man in camp. When the Sixth

Maine Regiment went to the front in July, 1861, he joined its fortunes and went to the seat of war.

He was assured by the officers, who certainly could ill have spared him, that he would receive the same pay and fare as themselves. But with native gallantry and soldierly enthusiasm he did not wait to have set down in black and white what he was to receive for his services and his sacrifices. He preferred to leave that to the honor of the Government, and was never regularly mustered in. He remained at the front performing whatever soldierly duty came in his way, until prostrated by sunstroke some months after, when the War Department passed him home as a soldier on Government account. Subsequently he was in the service of the Government till the close of the war, and leading officers of the army, including McClellan, Devens, Hooker, Burnside, Meade. and many others, as well as distinguished civilians in the North, testified to the important and almost invaluable services that he had rendered. But he never technically belonged to the army, and was never paid for what he did. Worn-out, spent and crippled in the service of this country, he asked it to do him justice; to pay him what he could have forced it to pay had he been more calculating in looking out for himself, and less thoughtful for the interests of the country to which he had given his allegiance. The American Congress saw his powerlessness, and virtually snapped its fingers at his petition. This was nine or ten years ago. He went manfully to work to help himself, and those dependent upon him, but adverse fortune followed him, and his losses in the Franklin Street fire added more to his heavy burden. We believe his case will be brought before the present Congress. When this body was Republican it refused this brave and devoted soldier the barest justice. Let a Democratic majority show itself capable of rising above a paltry technicality, and redeem the country from the reproach of deserting a man who contributed his best strength and skill to preserve it. — *Boston Post.*

BOSTON, June 18th, 1878.

Hon. BENJ. F. BUTLER:

My Dear Sir, — I have spent much time this day in a careful examination of documents and certificates in the possession of Sergeant Isaac W. Ambler. You, better than any other person I know, can determine whether such services as Sergeant Ambler rendered in the war of the rebellion, and under such peculiar circumstances, can be adequately, or even at all, compensated by the country under any existing statute. It seems to me that his case is a very remarkable one, or in the unselfish spirit in which they have been given.

Your time, as I tell Sergeant Ambler, is so valuable as to render it impossible for you to examine carefully the many certificates from prominent citizens which he has shown to me. I suppose that only by a special Act of Congress can he be remunerated, and he comes to you to ascertain the best method of bringing his case before that body. His character is vouched for by many persons known to you, and by a very highly esteemed friend of mine, who has long and intimately known him, and his claim seems to me to rest on good foundations.

With the highest personal esteem for yourself,

I am, your obedient servant,

W. B. BROWN,
Secretary of the Boston Water Power Company.

[The original copy of this letter was lost. This is copied from the impression of the original in Mr. Brown's letter-press.]

BOSTON, Mass., 1880.

To the Honorable Senate and House of Representatives of the United States.

The undersigned, I. W. Ambler, respectfully represents that, having had long experience as a soldier and Drill-Master, he devoted himself at the beginning of the late War to the instruction of officers and soldiers for the service of the United States.

He entered upon this work in Boston, Massachusetts, on the 15th of April, 1861, the third day after the attack on Fort Sumter, and continued so engaged in Massachusetts, Maine, and at the front in Virginia, until the 4th of April, 1865, without any compensation therefor, either from Municipal, State or National authorities ; and, moreover, was made a cripple for life by a bayonet wound received while in discharge of his duty.

He further represents that he was recognized as a soldier and Drill-Officer of the Union Army by the Secretary of War, and other officers in authority, who furnished him transportation, as a wounded soldier to the Soldier's Home at Augusta.

In consideration of these facts, proofs of which are given in documents accompanying this, and of his services, shown by commendatory letters herewith, the undersigned, petitioner, humbly begs your Honorable Bodies to grant him such pension or other pecuniary remuneration as to you may seem just and equitable, and as in duty bound will ever pray, etc.

I. W. AMBLER.

PORTLAND, MAINE, March 15, 1871.

This may certify that I have personally known Sergeant I. W. Ambler ever since 1859; that I always found him trustworthy, earnest and laborious, a capital swordsman and drill-master, and gifted with uncommon eloquence.

His services and suffering in the late rebellion, and the injuries he has sustained, whereby he has lost many years of his life, would entitle him to great consideration if they were known to our rulers.

Nevertheless, it would seem that he has claims, which, if not legal and technical, are at least equitable, and ought not to be overlooked in this our day of reckoning and generous acknowledgment of such services he has rendered our country.

Entertaining these views, I do most heartily commend him to the consideration of our national lawgivers, and to the President of the United States and the Secretary of War. All of which is respectfully submitted.

JOHN NEAL.

We, the undersigned, concur in the above representations, and hereby join in the recommendation:

POLICE DEPARTMENT OF THE CITY OF NEW YORK,
300 MULBERRY STREET,

To the Honorable Senate and House of Representatives.

I hereby certify that Sergeant I. W. Ambler served under my command, with the Sixth Regiment Maine Volunteers, and that I find my own signature among his original papers.

W. F. SMITH,

Late Major-General U. S. Volunteers.

NEW YORK, CITY HALL, 1871.

I am satisfied that Sergeant Ambler is fairly entitled to the generous consideration of the authorities for valuable services rendered during the War, and that it is a case wherein technical objections, if such exist, ought not to stand in the way of ample recompense being awarded him.

GEO. B. McCLELLAN,
Late Major-General, U. S. A.

I am glad to concur in the above recommendations favorable to Sergeant Ambler.

A. E. BURNSIDE,
Late Major-General U. S. A.

I concur in the above recommendations.

J. HOOKER,
Late Major-General U. S. A.

I concur in the recommendations of Generals McClellan, Hooker, Burnside and others.

C. C. MEADE,
Late Major-General U. S. A.

NEW YORK.

I have examined the letters and papers in possession of Sergeant Ambler. Captain Bugbee, whose Company Sergeant Ambler instructed, was one of the best and most faithful officers in my regiment, and fell at my side in the battle of Williamsburg, Va., at the opening of the Peninsula Campaign.

I cheerfully concur in the commendations and recommendations of the officers under whom Sergeant Ambler served, and trust that he may receive such pecuniary compensation and relief as his services are entitled to, and his wound demands.

Through Captain Bugbee and Lieutenant Edleison a great many men were furnished to my regiment by Sergeant Ambler of Boston, and I have no reason to doubt that his statement of the number is correct (300).

WILLIAM DWIGHT, Jr.
*Late Col. 70th Regiment, New York Vols.
and Brig.-Gen. U. S. V.*

BOSTON, MASS., 1871.

I know Sergeant Ambler. He drilled many officers under my command. I concur fully in the recommendations above.

CHAS. DEVENS, Jr.,
Late Brev. Maj.-Gen. U. S. V.

BOSTON, MASS., 1871.

From the above endorsements I feel certain that Sergeant Ambler is entitled to great consideration, and if any irregularity exists in regard to his muster in, it would seem to be the duty of our lawgivers to fully reimburse him, and pay for his services.

WM. COGSWELL,
Late Brigadier-General U. S. V.

We, the undersigned, cordially concur in the foregoing petition :

JOHN D. LONG, Governor of Massachusetts.
FREDERICK O. PRINCE, Mayor of Boston, Mass.
J. G. ABBOTT, Judge.
THOMAS TALBOT, Ex-Governor of Massachusetts.
WILLIAM GASTON, Ex-Governor of Massachusetts.

Chas. Levi Woodbury, Judge.
Henry L. Pierce, Ex-Mayor and Congressman.
Frederick A. Foster, Merchant.
Edward Avery, Chairman Central Committee.
Alexander H. Rice, Ex-Governor of Massachusetts.
Robert G. Fitch, Managing Editor of the Post.
Geo. S. Boutwell, Ex-Governor of Massachusetts.
Delano A. Goddard, Editor of the Advertiser.
E. B. Haskell, Editor of the Boston Herald.
B. P. Palmer, Editor of the Boston Globe.
Henry M. Dexter, Editor of the Congregationalist.
Leverett Saltonstall.
Alexander H. Bullock, Ex-Gov. of Massachusetts.
Stephen N. Stockwell, Editor of Boston Journal.

Brunswick, Maine, Nov. 11, 1874.

I am well acquainted with Sergeant Ambler, and know him to be a very deserving man. He rendered essential aid to our army during the war as an instructor, and by his formal participation in some of the battles.

JOSHUA L. CHAMBERLAIN,
Late Major-General U. S. Vols.

State Maine, 1871.

I know Sergeant Ambler as an instructor of troops and a teacher of the sword, and am happy to concur in the above recommendations.

FRANCIS FESSENDEN,
Late Brigadier-General U. S. Army.

I know Sergeant Ambler well, and have done so for many years. Without pay he rendered me important aid in drilling company officers, in my command, as they came into camp from their various localities.

NEAL DOW,
Late Brigadier-General U. S. Vols.

I concur in the above recommendation.

JAMES D. FESSENDEN,

Late Brigadier-General U. S. Vols.

Having long and favorably known Sergeant Ambler, we fully concur in the foregoing commendations :

ICHABOD GOODWIN, Ex-Governor of New Hampshire
JOSHUA L. CHAMBERLAIN, Ex-Governor of Maine.
ISRAEL WASHBURN, Jr., Ex-Governor of Maine.
SETH PADELFORD, Ex-Governor of Rhode Island.
WILLIAM CLAFLIN, Ex-Governor of Massachusetts.
ONSLOW STEARNS, Ex-Governor of New Hampshire,
G. F. SHEPLEY, U. S. Judge, late Brigadier-General United States Volunteers.

WASHINGTON, D. C., Jan. 22, 1872.

I have known Sergeant Ambler personally and by reputation for many years, and I have no doubt that he is eminently deserving the aid and relief he seeks. His services and his sufferings alike entitle him to this recognition.

J. G. BLAINE,

Speaker of the House of Representatives.

STATE MAINE, 1871.

It is with much pleasure, as well as with a deep sense of duty, that I write this commendation of Sergeant I. W. Ambler, drill-master, and fully concur with the accompanying recommendations. I personally and intimately knew Sergeant Ambler in the Army of the Potomac, in the autumn of 1861; how hard and successfully he labored to drill the raw officers in sword, and soldiers in musket and skirmish exercises, particularly in my regiment, the Sixth Maine ; and I remember instances in which his courageous example and soldierly bearing was of great service to our troops which had not been under fire, as, for instance, the affair of Lewinsville, Virginia, under General Smith, Sergeant Ambler was the man selected to bear the colors of the Sixth Maine through Baltimore, when the regiment was on its way to Washington, and when an attack by the mob was expected; he received great injury by poisoned food in Havre-de-Grace, etc., etc.

I remember, also, that for his hard and valuable services in 1861 he received no compensation; and that he was subsequently broken and crippled in body for life in his efforts to aid the Union cause, as his many scars to-day will testify, etc.; I will only say more, that as I know what I above stated is true, I most earnestly hope a just and grateful country will acknowledge and reward his services.

Z. THOMPSON,

Chaplain Sixth Maine Regiment, 1861–62.

LYNN, MASS, July 7, 1877.

The highest praise is due Sergeant I. W. Ambler, who was so well known by the officers and soldiers of the Sixth Maine Regiment.

His services as drill officer were unquestionably of great importance to the regiment, as well as the colonel, who was one of the best regimental commanders in the army.

The Sergeant was ever at his post, ready to impart what knowledge he had of military discipline, and proved himself to be a true and devoted soldier to the Union cause, repeatedly exposing himself to the dangers of the battle-field, both before and after receiving injuries from which he can never recover, and it seems a disgrace to the country and her soldiers to allow a person whom I know, and who has abundant proofs that he performed the duties of a soldier in all its forms, exposing himself to the hardships and dangers of the battle-field, receiving wounds therein, to remain unpaid for the service rendered, and the disabilities he received.

Has our nation got so low that it can afford to stoop to such injustice as to let a man who has been acknowledged by the War Department, as well as some of the commanding generals, as sergeant in the army, suffer for the necessaries of life, while the country is abundantly able to pay for the same. I trust that justice will be done in the matter to the fullest extent.

I write these things from personal knowledge at the time of his service, and supposed that he had been fully paid until within a few days, not having seen him since the close of the war.

ISAAC FRAZIER,
Late Capt. Co. B, 6th Me. Vol. Regt.

I can fully concur in the above statement in regard to Sergeant Ambler, and hope that Congress will, at an early day, consider the claim which the country honestly owes him in my opinion.

Lieut. MILTON FRAZIER,
6th Maine Vol. Regt.

Lynn, Mass., July, 1877.

It gives me great pleasure to recommend Sergeant I. W. Ambler, late of the Sixth Maine Regiment Volunteers, as an accomplished drill-master in the sword and bayonet exercise, having taken lessons from him with some forty other officers during the late war. I can speak from personal experience of his soldierly qualities and gentlemanly deportment.

Sergeant Ambler is certainly deserving of every consideration for his services during the rebellion, in drilling both officers and men, and, after being disabled, while in the service of his adopted country, and in the line of duty, should certainly receive consideration from the government which he so ably helped to sustain. The instruction which I received with other officers from Sergeant Ambler, was while under command of General Charles Devens, Jr.

J. E. SMITH,

Late Capt. 38th Regt. Mass. Vols.

BOSTON, MASS.

I fully concur in what Capt. J. E. Smith writes, in regard to Sergt. Ambler, being one of the officers to whom he refers as taking lessons in the sword exercise while at Long Island, Boston Harbor, then under the command of Gen. Charles Devens.

Sergt. Ambler certainly deserves some recognition from the government for his services during the late war, and it seems a great hardship that so long a time should elapse before some action should be taken in his behalf.

J. W. TRAFTON,

Late Capt. 27th Regt. Infantry, Mass. Vols.

As Ass't Adj't Gen'l at Draft Rendezvous, we became acquainted with Sergt. Ambler, and received instructions from him in the sword exercise, in company with many other officers on duty at that post.

We take great pleasure in endorsing all that Capts. Smith and Trafton have said concerning him, and cheerfully recommend him as a thorough and efficient instructor and soldier, with our associate officers.

W. A. HILL,
Late Capt. 19th Mass. Infantry.
E. A. FISK,
Late Capt. 30th Mass. Infantry.
EZRA FARNSWORTH, Jr.,
Late Capt. 30th Mass. Infantry.
E. G. TUTEIN,
Late Capt. 1st Mass. Regt. Vols.
C. H. HAYWARD,
Late Capt. 23d Mass. Regt. Vols.
C. H. HAMLEN,
Late Capt. 14th Mass. Battery.
B. DAVIS,
Late Capt. 22d Mass. Regt. Vols.
R. B. HENDERSON,
Late Capt. 13th Mass. Regt. Vols.
——BOYD,
Late Capt. 19th Mass. Regt. Vols.

Boston, Mass.

Sergeant I. W. Ambler entered the military service of the United States in the early part of 1861, as an instructor in the Sixth Regiment Maine Infantry Volunteers, where I first made his acquaintance.

He was a proficient, zealous and successful instructor, not only in sword and bayonet exercise, but also in deportment, soldierly bearing, and all the influences which a thoroughly trained soldier exercises upon his less experienced comrades ; his example and teachings were of great value in developing the high military qualities which this gallant regiment so often gave most signal evidence of possessing.

Sergeant Ambler was always to be found at the post of greatest danger—even when by military rule exempt, and on many very trying occasions, by his presence and example, rendered efficient service, not only to his adopted country, but to the establishment of the brilliant military record of troops with which he served.

I most sincerely hope that he may be successful in obtaining a pension, to which, I believe, he is by his military merits and services, fully entitled.

T. W. PORTER,
Late Col. 14th Maine Regt. Vols.

We, the undersigned, members of the Sixth Maine Regiment of Volunteers, are desirous of calling the attention of the people of our State to the present position and distress of Sergeant I. W. Ambler, of Biddeford, and of publicly testifying our gratitude to him for the invaluable service he has rendered to us.

Sergeant Ambler was engaged in drilling our regiment, both officers and men, for several months last year in the vicinity of Washington, *and to his instructions, we believe, the regiment owes very much of its efficiency and success. To his teaching some of us owe the preservation of our lives upon the field of battle.*

He has also been engaged in drilling and instructing other of our Maine regiments, and many individuals connected with the service, both as officers and privates.

He is now disabled by wounds received while engaged in this noble work, and without the means of earning his support.

Such a man should not suffer while a county remains which we can call our own.

(Signed by)

> C. EDES,
> L. H. WHITTIER,
> WM. SHERMAN,
> SIDNEY W. TUCKER,
> F. G. LEIGHTON.

BIDDEFORD, MAINE, 1862.

Sergeant I. W. Ambler proposes to leave us for a season, and we, the undersigned, cannot permit him to go without bearing willing testimony to his Christian character and fidelity, as a good missionary among the poor of this place.

He has been abundant in labors for their good; ministered to their wants; reclaimed many inebriates; kindly expostulated with sellers of liquors, and persuaded them to give up their traffic; visited the sick; consoled the dying; gathered at one time about one hundred and seventy little ones into a most interesting mission school. He has preached the glad tidings frequently, and to many in season and out of season.

Mr. Ambler is an *accomplished military tactician*, having seen long service in foreign lands, and when the news came in 1861 that his adopted flag had been insulted, and that it no longer waved from Sumter, he immediately left the pulpit for the drill-room, giving his whole time, without remuneration, to the instruction of officers and men laboring in Maine, Massachusetts, and Virginia; giving his whole time and energies to aid the cause of freedom, regardless alike of fatigue and personal comfort, and by so doing has been made a cripple for life; thus depriving himself and family of those comforts which otherwise they might have enjoyed.

Mr. Ambler is a reformed man; has gone through all this war and touched not, handled not, tasted not, any intoxicating liquors.

"He that ruleth his spirit is better than he that taketh a city."

(Signed by)

LEONARD ANDREWS, Contractor.
CHARLES HARDY, Inventor.

Rev. John Stevens, Freewill Baptist Minister.
James M. Palmer, Pastor Second Congregational Church.
Charles Tanney, Pastor Pavilion Church.
E. H. Banks, Merchant.
J. Hubbard, Jr., Pastor Baptist Church.
Charles A. Shaw, Mayor.
Alvan Bacon, M. D.
Dryden Smith, M. D.
Wm. Yeoman, Pastor Free Baptist Church.
Wm. Berry, Police Judge.
Abel Jelleson, Judge Municipal Court.
G. N. Weymouth, Attorney-at-Law.
Wm. P. Haines, Treasurer of Pepperell Mills.
R. M. Chapman, Cashier Biddeford Bank.
Horace Piper, High School Teacher.
C. C. Mason, Pastor Methodist Episcopal Church, Saco.

Boston, Mass., March 25, 1880.

This is to certify that I have known Sergeant I. W. Ambler intimately for over twenty years, or ever since he was city missionary at Biddeford, Maine, in 1859–60; that he was engaged in giving military instruction at the breaking out of the war of the rebellion in 1861; that in 1862 he was brought to Biddeford wounded, where he was treated medically by Dr. E. G. Stevens and other physicians; that after partially recovering, he again engaged in military service, giving instructions to both officers and men, in which employment he continued until the close of the war. Mr. Ambler had had nearly ten years' experience in military service before the year 1861, and is considered one of the best swordsmen and teachers of military tactics in the United States. He devoted over four of the best years of his life to the country during the rebellion, was severely wounded, lost his health, and has never received one cent of remuneration; but, on the contrary, has spent a good deal of time and money in vain endeavors to obtain his just dues.

I know Mr. Ambler to be a thoroughly honorable, upright, Christian man, one who has done a great work among his fellow men, as well as for his country; and can bear testimony to the fact, that the impression in the community, especially amongst those most conversant with the subject, is that his claims on the government for remuneration are not only just, but have been, heretofore, very wrongfully ignored.

Dr. E. G. Stevens, whose certificate is given above, is a physician of high standing, in regular practice, and who is thoroughly reliable in every respect.

CHARLES A. SHAW,

Ex-Mayor of Biddeford, Maine.

Co. H, 1st. REG'T.

CAMP SCOTT, June 29th, 1861.

BROTHER AMBLER:

Dear Sir:—I take a spare moment to thank you for your kindness and the services you rendered me. We are here and at home; well received and kindly treated. Colonel Dwight is a fine man, a good officer, and well beloved by all, and we are all happy we are here. My company musters ninety-two men, and I expect to have one hundred inside of the next twenty-four hours.

Edlesson, who was sergeant, but now second lieutenant. wishes you to have those instructions in the sword written off for him.

Capt. W. H. BUGBEE.

Boston, May 2nd, 1861.

To Adjutant-General Schouler,

Dear Sir:—We have known I. W. Ambler for some time, and have all confidence in his integrity. Any arms the department may commit to his care, we have no doubt will be both properly cared for and accounted for.

> Henry Hoyt,
> William R. Stacy,
> Chas. H. Parker,
> Chas. W. Babcock.

Boston, June 11th, 1861

I. W. Ambler, Esq.,

Sir:—The members of the Boston British Drill Club are to meet to-night in Revere Hall, Bowdoin Square, at eight o'clock precisely, your attendance is earnestly requested therefore please fail not.

> By order   HENRY F. MAGEE,
> *Clerk, pro tem.*

Deeming it of the highest importance in these rebellious times to be prepared for any emergency, and to be better qualified to defend our country and uphold the laws of our land, we, young men of Boston not enrolled in any military organization of the city, agree to assemble for instruction and drill for military tactics, under the direction of I. W. Ambler.

Signed by one hundred and four volunteers.

George N. Fuller,	Jacob Cherry,
H. E. Merriau,	J. E. Verrill,
A. Carsley,	E. H. Brazer,
Frank A. Ladd,	C. B. Danforth,
E. M. Wescott,	P. R. Hubbard,

F. A. Sergent,
William A. Lerva,
Thomas Atkinson, Jr.,
S. L. Morison,
Joseph Smith,
W. B. Mayhew,
F. E. Brett,
S. D. Moody,
G. Renton Carter,
J. W. Morrill,
I. I. Kemp,
C. J. Muldor,
Wm. L. Howard,
Alped W. Worthley,
Charles B. Tower,
A. G. Foss,
Oliver L. Briggs,
David Billings,
A. R. Paslin,

Charles H. Dowe,
Edward P. Light,
George E. Pond,
Abram C. Paul,
H. W. Littlefield,
Frank Q. Bundy,
George O. Preston,
Daniel F. Wood,
F. R. Allen,
E. Farnsworth, Jr.,
W. A. Waugh,
E. E. Butterfield,
Robert L. Merrett,
John A. Cole,
Wm. S. Rugg,
E. A. Pearson,
John E. Bailey,
T. E. Bowen,

Post Office, Boston, Mass.

His Excellency the Governor, John A. Andrew:

Sir :—I formed some acquaintance with Mr. Ambler while he was drilling some military officers in our department of this building (the hall in the Post Office building). I understand that he has since *distinguished himself in the field.* He is desirous of being employed in recruiting, in which service I learn that he has been successful; and afterwards to be engaged in instructing his recruits. I ask leave respectfully to recommend him to your Excellency's notice.

I have the honor to be your Excellency's

Most obedient servant,

JOHN G. PALFREY.

HEADQUARTERS 6TH REGT. ME. VOLS.
August 30th, 1861.

Guards will pass Drill-master Ambler to Washington and return on the 31st.

HIRAM BURNHAM, *Lieut. Col.*

Good till Monday.

WM. F. SMITH, *Brig. Gen. Comd'y.*

———

HEADQUARTERS, CAMP LYON.
Sept. 1861.

Pass Drill-officer Ambler, 6th Maine, over Chain Bridge and return.

By order Brig. Gen.

RUFUS KING,
Asst. Adj. Gen.

HEADQUARTERS DEPARTMENT DRAFTED MEN,
LONG ISLAND BOSTON HARBOR.
Oct. 8th, 1863.

Pass Sergeant Ambler to Long Island and return by boat.   Good until further orders,

By order of

Brig. Gen. DEVENS,
W. A. HILL, *Lieut. A. A. A. G.*

This shows the Sergeant's first service here, and the last on the back of this general pass is the following from Captain Rand.

April 4th, 1863.

Corporal of the Guard will consider this good until further orders.

Signed	RAND

WAR DEPARTMENT.

WASHINGTON, Sept. 10th, 1861.

Agent N. H. & N. L. and Stonington Railroad Co., Boston.

Please furnish Sergeant Ambler, Sixth Regiment Maine Volunteers, with passage, free of charge to him, from Boston to New York, on government account.

Relieved from duty upon certificate of Thomas A. Scott. Cause, returning from recruiting.

By order of Secretary of War,

THOMAS A. SCOTT,

General Manager of Government Railways and Telegraphs.

Received Ticket.   1861.

Note.   Please file this order and return it to the department with account stated to the first of each month properly certified for payment.

THE NATIONAL ASYLUM
FOR DISABLED VOLUNTEER SOLDIERS.

WASHINGTON, April 16th, 1872.

Please furnish transportation from Washington to Biddeford, Me., for I. W. Ambler, a Volunteer Soldier disabled by injuries, en route to the Military Asylum, and render account of the same to General W. S. Tilton, Treasurer of the Military Asylum at Augusta.

BENJ. F. BUTLER,
Manager N. A. D. V. S.

To the agent of the B. & O. R. R. at Washington.

WASHINGTON, D.C., 1872.

I have been acquainted with Mr. I. W. Ambler for many years as city missionary, in Biddeford, Me., and while in the service of the United States, as drill-sergeant, during the late war.   Mr. Ambler came to my rooms in this city some time in August, 1861, disabled from sunstroke, and remained with me until he was able to return to the field.   Learning that he is about to apply to Congress for compensation for his services in defence of the Union, I deem it a duty, as well as a pleasure, to earnestly commend him to that honorable body as a gentleman worthy of confidence, and, in my judgment, entitled to relief.

D. E. SOMES,
Late Representative in Congress.

BOSTON, MASS., MARCH, 22, 1880.

I, the undersigned, hereby certify, that I have known Serjeant I. W. Ambler for about twenty years, that after the beginning of the late rebellion of the United States he was employed to give military instruction in drilling the soldiers in the service of the United States, that during the spring of 1862, Sergeant I. W. Ambler made application to me, then in practice of medicine, in the city of Biddeford, Me., for treatment of a hemorrhage of blood from the stomach and bowels, claimed by him to be caused by sudden and severe strain while engaged in giving musket or bayonet exercise in drilling soldiers of the United States Army, and that I did treat him during the time in which he was wearing splints for a fractured arm.

ELBRIDGE G. STEVENS, M.D.

SACO, ME., MARCH 13, 1871.

This may certify that I have known Sergeant I. W. Ambler for a long series of years, both before and since the war of the Rebellion, and on the breaking out of the war he threw all aside and entered heart and hand into the service of the United States.   While thus engaged he received an injury causing the rupture of a blood-vessel, from the effects of which he has never fully recovered, as over-exercise ever since and at the present time, produces a repetition of the trouble. He also received a dislocation of the right wrist and a fracture of the left, and since these injuries, has been unable, and, in my opinion, ever will be, to attend to business of any description to advantage.

J. E. M. KIMBALL, M.D.,
Late Surgeon 27th Regt. Me. Vols.

COMMONWEALTH, MASS.,
SURGEON-GENERAL'S OFFICE,
BOSTON, March 26th, 1880.

I certify that I have this day examined the hand (left) of Sergeant I. W. Ambler, and am of the opinion that the same is useless to him in any occupation, on account of wound of left wrist, incurred in line of duty.

WM. J. DALE,
Surgeon-General.

From the *Boston Daily Advertiser*, January 16, 1880.

The original petition, of which this is an attested copy, together with attested copies of all the papers, letters, passes, etc., referred to in the petition, has been presented to the Senate, and referred to the Committee on Pension Claims. The history on which the petition is based, and of which these letters, papers, etc., have been given in evidence, is briefly set forth in the enclosed printed statement here submitted for information. It was written by myself, and is, to the best of my knowledge and belief, true.

DELANO A. GODDARD,
Editor Boston Daily Advertiser.

Let me add : —

Would such a story be listened to with patience were it a mere invention, or only founded on facts? Would not every American spring to his feet if these charges were made by a sensationist, a book-moter, or by a mere story-teller?

What then shall we say, when assured of their truth— of their unquestionable truth? Shall so great a wrong be passed over unrebuked? Are we not all sharers in the guilt of unthankfulness, and of unqualified injustice? The wonder is why he has not been allowed a pension notwithstanding certain technical objections, alike trivial and worthless. But, enough. Read the book and judge for yourselves, my countrymen.

JOHN NEAL,
Author of " Seventy-Six."

I, Wm. E. Bicknell, Justice of the Peace for the Commonwealth of Massachusetts, do hereby certify that the foregoing are true and correct copies of letters and testimonials in the possession of I. W. Ambler, which he has shown to, and which have been compared by me with the foregoing.

WM. E. BICKNELL,
Justice of the Peace.

SUMMING UP OF EVIDENCE.

BY A FRIEND.

More conclusive evidence of the justice of a claim than is contained in the foregoing chain of testimony, no man could have, and certainly it would be positive and wanton unreason to demand a more complete establishment of case before giving it favorable consideration. This claim has received an indorsement that ought to have over whelming weight. Men of national prominence, in both civil and military affairs, governors of States, literary men, leading newspapers, and leading citizens, after a thorough acquaintance with the merits of this question, declare almost with indignation at the delay, that by every principle and precept of justice Sergeant Ambler is entitled to a pension, to a recognition of his services, and the consideration that has been accorded to others in our late war, whose sacrifices were much less than his, and whose condition is at present much more comfortable. The refusal of the government thus far to recognize his claims has been based on the technical and unmanly plea that there was an irregularity about his mustering in.

Was there ever a more contemptible quibble? Does it not speak the more to his honor that he gave his services to the Union cause through the entire period of the rebellion, without taking precautions looking to personal profit? Does it not show that his only motive in offering his services was the good of his adopted country,—that in her hour of danger and trial he was ready to defend her, that he was above all thought of pecuniary consideration?

If the Sergeant had waited for a large bounty to be offered before offering his services, there would have been no irregularity about his mustering in; no hesitation about giving him his pay, and no refusal to reward his injuries with a pension.

But he was an unselfish soldier, intent only on sustaining the honor of the nation, taking no forethought to secure himself, and for that reason is neglected by the government, which should not only have recognized his services with pecuniary reward, but with the honor of well-deserved promotion.

Can it be, the reader asks, that so brave and unselfish a soldier as Sergeant Ambler has thus been neglected? Can it be that he gave his valuable experience and labor all those years for nothing? Can it be possible that he was made a cripple for life in the army, thus depriving himself and family of those comforts which otherwise they might have enjoyed? Can it be that a great and generous government like that of the United States will allow the charge of leaving one of its bravest soldiers, disabled for life in its service, to fight his way through life unaided because of a flimsy technicality, to be brought against it?

This is the state of the case. Sergeant Ambler has not yet been paid; Sergeant Ambler has not yet been pensioned, because of the irregularity aforesaid. The government did not allow this technicality to stand in the way of accepting his services. It did not say: "Sergeant Ambler,

we can't let you drill and organize our men; we can't let
you make good soldiers of them; we can't let you instruct
them in the use of arms, and in military discipline; we
can't let you accompany them to the front and show them
a brave example under fire, for there is some technical irregularity in your mustering in." O, no, there were no
technicalities standing in the way then; no irregularities
in the way then; no shuffling or cavilling about the way
a good soldier went into the army then; and so the services of Sergeant Ambler, technicality or no technicality,
were gladly received.

But let us consider this alleged irregularity for a moment. The government excuses its action, or inaction, in
regard to Sergeant Ambler's case on the plea that it does
not find his name on the regular muster-roll of the regiment, and for this reason refuses to recognize his services.
But during the war the government recognized Sergeant
Ambler as a soldier in its army. When disabled at the
front he was relieved from duty and furnished passage
home by order of the Secretary of War. What had the
Secretary of War to do with him if he did not belong to
the government service. His pass home and to return de-
scribes him as a volunteer soldier disabled by injuries.
This was surely recognizing him as belonging to the government. Moreover, John Neal, of Portland, writes to
the Secretary of War, informing him that that "brave and
patriotic man, Sergeant Ambler, who was relived from active duty by the government, and sent from the front on
leave of absence to the State of Maine to recruit his
health, is now organizing and drilling regiments with one
arm in splints." In answer to this letter the Secretary of
War sent a dispatch to Mr. Neal, telling him to tell Ser-

geant Ambler to keep on with the noble work till further orders.

John Neal writes to ex-Secretary of State, Hon. J. G. Blaine, saying Sergeant Ambler's sufferings and services make him eminently deserving of reward.

Major General Wm. F. Smith writes to the United States Senate, that Sergeant Ambler served under his command as a volunteer soldier.

Gen. Geo. B. McClellan recognized his services as valuable, and says that technical objections ought not to stand in the way of ample compensation.

Gen. Devens and Gen. Cogswell, of Massachusetts, emphatically assent to the same.

The Generals and Managers of the National Asylum for Disabled Volunteer Soldiers, Washington, D. C., recognized the Sergeant's services and wounds by furnishing him with transportation from Washington to the State of Maine as a volunteer soldier, disabled by injuries, en-route to the Military Asylum at Augusta.

E. G. Stevens, M.D., testified in 1862: Application was made to me to treat Sergeant Ambler for a hemorrhage of blood from the stomach and bowels, and at the same time he received treatment from me he was wearing splints for a fractured arm, received while doing his duty in the Union army.

J. E. S. Kimball, M.D., late Surgeon 27th Regiment M. V., testifies to the nature of the injuries. Surgeon General Dale of Massachusetts testifies to Sergeant Ambler receiving permanent injuries in the line of duty.

The foregoing evidence that Sergeant Ambler was recognized by the government as one of its soldiers is most emphatic and conclusive. Care was taken to make

the pass which procured him the facilities of travel good
for his return. The government not only recognized him
as a soldier, but when he was incapacitated for duty, and
sent home, furnished him with means of getting back
again.

If Sergeant Ambler had deserted at this time the government would have shown him how little it cared for
irregularities of mustering in. But despite irregularity it
was necessary for him to be relieved from duty by order
of the War Department before he could leave his regiment. If he had not been recognized as a Union soldier
no such order would have been necessary.

It follows then that if the government recognized him
as serving in its armies, it is bound by every principle of
justice to allow him the same compensation allowed to
others during the war, and a pension such as others
permanently disabled have received since its close. Until
that is done those who constitute the government have no
right to say that the claims of patriotic soldiers have been
fully recognized. Certainly the pension appropriation is
large enough to cover services like Sergeant Ambler's, and
where is there a claim upon it more thoroughly indorsed
on the score of merit than his?

BATTLE CHARGE,

IN WHICH PRIVATE WM. SCOTT FELL.

Amid all the sad scenes which the soldier is called to witness, a kind Providence has so arranged that there should be mingled with the fearful something of the beautiful as well.

Such was the scene at the battle of Lee's Mills, during the bombardment of the enemy's fort by Capt. Mott's battery, of which I had the honor of drilling some of the men in this country, and in the old country, belonging to that battery. The first impression after coming upon the scene of action was one of wonder and admiration at its brilliancy and sublimity. It was in an open field, surrounded by the grand old pine trees such as you would find in Virginia at that time. In the foreground, beyond some chimneys left standing, was a peach orchard all in bloom, with all the gorgeous hues so well known to those who have seen the sight, and still further on the grand old woods towering towards the heavens in all their majesty. In the distant front was an opening in the woods, in which was seen the Warwick Creek. Across the creek was the enemy's rifle pits, and still further on the fort itself.

In rear of the chimneys mentioned was stationed Capt. Mott's battery, containing six brass field pieces, which were throwing shells into the fort across the creek. Amid the spirited animation of the scene, the officers rode rapidly to and fro, giving in quick tones the words of command; the gunners sprang to their work as if their very life depended upon the energy and activity of their motions; the lightning streaming from the cannon, the howling and hissing of the iron thunderbolts hurled into the distant fort, and the fiend like scream of the whistling demon scoming through the air, as they came nearer and nearer right into their midst, or exploded over their heads, with the fire of fury and death. It is fearfully deafening, and your ears will whistle and sing for days after.

Two hundred brave heroes were picked out for the storming party from the Third Vermont Regiment. They were paraded and marched to the creek, awaiting the signal with almost breathless impatience, with a hope of soon planting their colors on the battered fort. Soon the word of command to advance was given. In a twinkling our men dashed into the creek, and were soon seen breast high in the water, amidst a deadly storm of leaden rain. The ammunition in their pouches was rendered almost useless, and when they reached the opposite side they reformed their ranks.

At the word *forward, march,* they moved with firm and steady step, and the long line of burnished steel, with glittering points sparkling in the glorious light of heaven, seemed pointed with the fire of vengeance. When they dropped into a flashing horizontal as the command charge was given, and the men dashed forward with a wild huzza, and bounded upon the trenches in the face of a constant spitting of rifles from the sharpshooters, and presented them the piercing points of the polished steel in return for their bullets.

It was a sharp and decisive struggle, a fierce encounter

of steel to steel, but the desperate and determined onset of the brave Vermonters bore all before them. The enemy turned tail, and took refuge in their fort, leaving our boys master of their rifle pits. It was then discovered that in fording the stream many of our men had wet their ammunition and could not fire a shot, and were left without supports. The enemy perceiving this soon rallied and charged upon the green mountain boys with overwhelming numbers, and a frightful struggle took place, which ended in driving those heroic men back into the creek, where the dead, wounded and dying layed in mingled masses, totally routed and fearfully defeated.

It can be said in admiration of those heroic men, as Lord St. Vincent said to Lord Nelson after his repulse when he made the attack on Boulogne, " It is not in mortals to command success, but you have done more, you have deserved it."

The first one to fall in this charge was the pardoned soldier William Scott, who was sentenced to be shot for sleeping at his post, and has been immortalized in that beautiful poem by Francis DeHaes Janiver, "The Sleeping Sentinel."

www.ingramcontent.com/pod-product-compliance
Lightning Source LLC
Chambersburg PA
CBHW021712110726
47902CB00005B/1162